ON THE RUN . . . UNDERGROUND.

They looked over the edge.

"Lord," said Kelly. "That's a long way down."

"You and Kelsey won't be going down," Arlo said. "That'll be up to Dallas and me."

Kelsey spoke up. "We've come this far, and we aren't about to be left out at the finish."

"You won't be," Arlo reassured her. "But remember what a hell of a time we had following Death's Head trail to this cave? Well, if that bunch of scoundrels was anywhere in sight, they saw right where we went."

"Then we'd better move out," Dallas said. "If Davis and the rest aren't already searching the tunnels, they soon will be."

"Let's hustle, then," said Arlo. "This may be our last chance to move freely. 'Cause once we find the gold, we're gonna have to fight to keep it."

SKELETON LODE

Ralph Compton

A SIGNET BOOK

SIGNET
Published by New American Library, a division of
Penguin Group (USA) Inc., 375 Hudson Street,
New York, New York 10014, USA
Penguin Group (Canada), 90 Eglinton Avenue East, Suite 700, Toronto,
Ontario M4P 2Y3, Canada (a division of Pearson Penguin Canada Inc.)
Penguin Books Ltd., 80 Strand, London WC2R 0RL, England
Penguin Ireland, 25 St. Stephen's Green, Dublin 2,
Ireland (a division of Penguin Books Ltd.)
Penguin Group (Australia), 250 Camberwell Road, Camberwell, Victoria 3124,
Australia (a division of Pearson Australia Group Pty. Ltd.)
Penguin Books India Pvt. Ltd., 11 Community Centre, Panchsheel Park,
New Delhi - 110 017, India
Penguin Group (NZ), 67 Apollo Drive, Rosedale, Auckland 0632,
New Zealand (a division of Pearson New Zealand Ltd.)
Penguin Books (South Africa) (Pty.) Ltd., 24 Sturdee Avenue,
Rosebank, Johannesburg 2196, South Africa

Penguin Books Ltd., Registered Offices:
80 Strand, London WC2R 0RL, England

First published by Signet, an imprint of New American Library,
a division of Penguin Group (USA) Inc.

First Printing, November 1999
First Printing (Updated Edition), June 2011
10   9   8   7   6   5   4   3   2   1

Author's Foreword

Jacob Waltz, a German immigrant, came to Arizona Territory in the early 1860s as a homesteader. But farming was as unappealing as it was unrewarding, and Waltz was soon stricken by gold fever. He packed his few belongings and headed into the rattlesnake-infested Superstition Mountains. For two decades the old man and his pack mule roamed the mountains east of Phoenix.

Occasionally Waltz would show up in the little towns to trade gold for supplies. He was often followed by men seeking the source of his gold, but they were never successful. By the late 1880s Waltz was back in Phoenix, and there's no evidence that he ever returned to his mine. It is suspected that he drew from several caches of gold ore he had hidden. Waltz was later buried under a cottonwood tree in a cemetery near the state capitol.

Legends about his wealth abound. Some claim that Jacob Waltz had no mine, and that he had found a lost treasure that had once belonged to Jesuits, or that he and another man killed two Mexicans and stole the claim to the mine they were working. Still others believe Waltz's gold came from the Goldfield Mountains, near the Superstitions, or from the Vulture mine, at Wickenburg. A man named Adolph Ruth, in some of his letters, claimed to have found Waltz's mine, but somewhere in the Superstitions Ruth disappeared. Later his bones were found, a bullet hole through the skull.

After Jacob Waltz was dead, a box of high-grade ore was discovered under his bed. Tests at the University of Arizona School of Mines later proved that the ore wasn't from any known mine in Arizona. After more than a century, there is no record that the mine—now called the Lost Dutchman—was ever found.

In the Superstitions there were no trails, little water, and too damned many Apaches. Men rode the rocky slopes and the desolate canyons seeking gold but finding only death, and those who courted Lady Luck discovered she could be—and usually was—a bitch.

After more than a century, the Superstitions remain as secretive, brooding, and mysterious as ever. . . .

Prologue

Los Angeles, California, March 15, 1857

"This could be the easiest haul we've ever made," said Arlo Wells. "Three hundred and forty miles back to Phoenix, with the Colorado the only river we have to cross."

"I wish I was as much of an optimist as you," said his partner, Dallas Holt. "I don't aim to even think about all them miles between here and home. Tonight I'm goin' to sleep in an honest-to-God bed and eat grub we ain't cooked in a skillet over an open fire. Tomorrow, after our wagons is loaded with that barreled whiskey, I'll think about the trail ahead."

Arlo and Dallas had begun punching cows in south Texas while in their teens. Finally, after winning a stake in a poker game, they had ridden west and taken up residence in Tortilla Flat, an undistinguished little town near Phoenix. They had invested their stake in a pair of freight wagons and two teams of mules. For a while, their two-wagon rawhide freight line wasn't much better than punching cows, with unprofitable short hauls to Tombstone, Yuma, or Tucson. But then their luck seemed to take a turn for the better. The owner of Tortilla Flat's Gila Saloon, Joel Hankins, engaged them to haul two wagonloads of scotch whiskey from the docks at Los Angeles. The journey west took them twenty-one days.

Morning came all too quickly, and after a breakfast of fried eggs, ham, coffee, and hot biscuits, the Texans got their teams of mules from the livery and set out for the docks. Each loosed the pucker of his wagon canvas and checked out the load. The whiskey came in fifty-gallon kegs, upright and well loaded. The dock foreman presented Arlo with the bills of lading, which he signed.

"My God," said Dallas, looking at the bill, "Joel paid near a thousand dollars for these two loads of booze."

"Bite your tongue," Arlo replied. "This ain't just booze. It's scotch booze, and it'll go for six bits a shot, even in Tortilla Flat."

Arlo's optimism seemed justified, for the return took only twenty-one days, too, and there was no trouble to speak of. The partners breathed a sigh of relief as they approached Phoenix, but even Arlo's confidence suffered a jolt when they reached Tortilla Flat.

"By God," said Dallas, "if them boards nailed across the windows and the door mean anything, the Gila's closed."

"That can't be!" Arlo exclaimed. "What in tarnation are we goin' to do with all this whiskey?"

"I reckon we can drink it," Dallas said gloomily. "Without the money Joel owes us, we're broke."

"Well, hell," said Arlo, "we might as well find out what's happened."

Jubal Larkin owned the combination livery and blacksmith shop, and having heard the wagons coming, he had stepped out into the dirt street. Arlo and Dallas reined in their teams and it was Arlo who stated the obvious.

"The Gila's boarded up."

"Yep," Jubal said. "You fellers wasn't gone hardly a week. Joel didn't open up, and I went to see about him. Found him dead in his bunk. The doc came, rode out from Phoenix, and said his heart just called it quits. Sheriff Wheaton done some askin' around, and decided old Joel either didn't have no living kin, or they was so far away, he'd never find 'em. So we buried him behind the Gila."

"I don't aim to speak ill of the dead," said Arlo, "but he's left us in one hell of a mess. We hauled these two wagonloads of whiskey all the way from Los Angeles, and now we got nobody to pay us."

"Anything owin' on the whiskey?"

"Not that we know of," Arlo said.

"Then you can claim the whiskey for charges owed," said Jubal.

"That makes sense," Dallas said, "but what are we goin' to do with it? We'll have us a shot on the Fourth of July and at Christmas. This would last us five hundred years."

"Sell it," said Jubal. "Open up the Gila and sell it across the bar."

"It ain't our saloon," Arlo answered.

"It could be," said Jubal. "Joel owned the place and the patch of ground it's on, but Sheriff Wheaton says it goes for taxes at the end of the year if somebody don't pay."

"We can't pay, either," Dallas said.

"It ain't but twenty-five dollars," said Jubal, "and you got seven months to get the money together."

"I don't know, Jubal," Arlo replied. "I reckon we'll have to talk to Sheriff Wheaton, if we got to claim this whiskey. You got a couple of horses and saddles we can borrow? I'm fed up to the eyeballs with jugheaded mules."

"Sure," said Jubal. "I wish you'd consider takin' over the Gila. Hell, all Tortilla Flat's ever had was my livery, Silas Hays's general store, and the Gila. Scratch the Gila, and one third of our town is gone. I bet Silas will grubstake you until you can afford to pay."

"I'm not promisin' anythin' until we talk to Sheriff Wheaton," Arlo said.

Tortilla Flat was twenty miles east of Phoenix and ten miles north of the Superstition Mountains, and the main street was its only street. It had no sheriff, and that accounted for the Gila Saloon's popularity among the cowboys and miners of Gila County. County sheriff Harley Wheaton secretly approved of the arrangement, because it kept most of the hell-raisers out of Phoenix. He never bothered riding to Tortilla Flat for anything less than a killing. Now he listened as Arlo and Dallas explained their circumstances.

"Way I see it," he said, "you're entitled to the whiskey. That's a hell of a lot of firewater. What do you aim to do with it?"

"I reckon we'll sell it," said Arlo.

"By the barrel or by the drink?"

"By the barrel," Arlo said. "Why?"

"You could make ten times as much sellin' by the drink," said Wheaton. "For the tax money you can pick up the Gila. Why don't you do that?"

So the two itinerant cowboys sold their freight wagons and mules, bought a pair of horses and saddles, paid the taxes, and went into the saloon business. They knew nothing about the running of a saloon, but they found it required little skill to slop whiskey from a barrel into a glass. What they *did* understand—and what required considerable skill—was gambling. They put their profits back into the business and added a second floor to the building for living quarters. Soon Tortilla Flat's Gila Saloon became a mecca for gamblers, and Arlo and Dallas seemed set for life—until that fateful night in April 1859.

"You slick-dealin', tinhorn bastard!"

The grizzled miner kicked back his chair and went for his gun, but he didn't have a chance. The gambler in the derby hat palmed a derringer, and it spoke just once. The miner's chair went over backward and the gambler made a break for the door, but a hard-flung chair caught him in the back of the head. He fell facedown on the sawdust floor, and half the miners in the Gila Saloon piled on top of him. The rest began throwing bottles and glasses and shooting out the hanging lamps. The proprietors fought their way out from behind the bar, Arlo with a four-foot-long wooden club and Dallas with a shotgun. They were immediately beaten senseless, and the brawl went on. Some of the struggling men shrieked as flaming coal oil from the shattered lamps set their hair and clothing afire.

The exploding lamps splashed oil on the resinous, pine-paneled walls, and the flames soon took hold.

Dallas sat up, coughing. The place was filled with smoke, but even though he couldn't see the flames, he could feel and hear them. His and Arlo's days in the saloon business were coming to an ignominious end. His head hurt, and when he mopped the sweat from his eyes, he found it was mostly blood. He felt around and got his hands on a full quart bottle of whiskey. It would serve as a club, if he needed one. Then it dawned on him that the fight was over. Not only had the dirty sons of bitches destroyed the saloon, they'd left him and Arlo to the mercy of the flames. Where was Arlo?

"Arlo!" he shouted.

There was no answer. Dallas knew Arlo wouldn't have deserted him. His friend and partner must still be somewhere in the burning saloon. He suddenly remembered that the money—what little they had—was in the upstairs office! Could Arlo be up there, overcome by smoke? On hands and knees, Dallas began crawling toward the stairs, keeping low to the floor, where the smoke wasn't as dense.

"Dallas?"

"Over here, Arlo."

"I ain't run out on you, pard," said Arlo from the stairs. "The Gila's a goner, but I didn't aim for us to lose our last dollar along with it."

Dallas got shakily to his feet, and the two men headed for the back door. Just as they reached it, part of the ceiling caved in. The gaping hole created an updraft and the flames roared to new life. Dallas and Arlo made their way around to the front of the saloon, to what passed for a main street. A crowd—as much of one as Tortilla Flat could muster—had gathered to watch the fire.

"Look at 'em," growled Dallas. "Like a flock of damn buzzards, all waitin' for somethin' to die."

Tortilla Flat couldn't claim more than fifty souls within riding distance, but twice that number now gathered before the burning saloon. In the light from the fire, the partners saw that the now dead gambler and the miner he had shot had been dragged from the burning building.

"Mighty considerate of you folks," said Arlo, "draggin' them dead hombres out, but leavin' me and Dallas in there to roast like Christmas geese."

"Them as lives by the sword dies by it," said Old Lady Snippet, who despised drinking, gambling, fighting, and men in general.

Somebody laughed, and she took that for encouragement.

"The Lord works in mysterious ways," she said, loudly jubilant, as though the Almighty had wrought the very vengeance she had called down.

Arlo and Dallas had kept their horses and saddles at Jubal Larkin's livery during the two years they'd owned the saloon.

"We might as well go out to your spread and settle up," said Arlo to Jubal, who now stood beside the partners, looking at the wreckage sadly. "I reckon we got two hundred dollars."

"Just call it even," Jubal said. "It's my way of helpin' a little. Hell, we might as well fire the rest of old Tortilla Flat too. With the Gila gone, there won't be enough business to sneeze at."

"Jubal," said Dallas, "thanks to them two dead hombres, Sheriff Wheaton will be looking for us to answer some tough questions. We'll be out at Hoss Logan's cabin for a while till we can scratch up some money for wagons and mules."

"Back to the freightin' business, then?" Jubal asked.

"Hell of a lot more secure than runnin' a saloon," replied Arlo. "Nobody's ever burnt our wagons down."

The partners saddled up and rode out, Dallas astride a black stallion and Arlo on a sturdy gray. They had taken their gun rigs out of their saddlebags, and each of them now wore a tied-down Colt on his right hip. Arlo stood six four without hat or boots, and weighed near two hundred pounds, none of it fat. Dallas matched him so nearly the difference wasn't worth arguing. Dallas's broad-brimmed, flat-crowned gray Stetson was tilted low over his smoke-gray eyes. His hair was crow-black, curling down to his ears. Arlo's Stetson was the deep tan of desert sand, its three-cornered brim roll pointed to the front, with a pinch crease in the high crown. His hair was mahogany, and his dark brown eyes were flecked with green. Both men wore brown Levi's, flannel shirts, and scuffed rough-out high-heeled boots. Arlo would be twenty-three his next birthday, while Dallas was a year younger.

Henry Logan, known far and wide as "Hoss," had a cabin near Saguaro Lake, a few miles north of Tortilla Flat. For twenty years Logan, accompanied by a mute Indian called Paiute, had prospected the Superstitions, confident that one day he would find the gold for which the Spanish had searched in vain. He was often away for weeks or months at a time, returning only when starvation nipped at his heels. When Arlo and Dallas had first ridden into the territory, they had stopped at Hoss Logan's cook fire for a meal. A friendship developed, and the old prospector invited Arlo and Dallas to bunk at his cabin whenever their travels took them through his land. Once Arlo and Dallas had begun to earn a little money, they had often grubstaked the old man in his futile search for gold.

"Hoss has been out since before Christmas," said Dallas. "I hope nothing's happened to him."

"He's spent so many years in the Superstitions," Arlo replied, "I don't believe even the Apaches would bother him."

They found the three-room cabin neat and undisturbed. There was wood for a fire and a tin half full of coffee beans, but little else.

"My God, it's quiet out here," said Arlo. "It's somethin' a man don't appreciate until he's killed two years listenin' to drunks cussin' one another, bottles and shot glasses rattlin' and cards slappin' on the table."

"You talk like an hombre whose gamblin' days are behind him," Dallas said.

"We rode out of Texas five years ago," Arlo reminded him, "and we been livin' hand to mouth ever since. Don't you ever hanker for somethin' better?"

"Yeah," Dallas replied, "but what choices have we got? Fence-ridin' cowboys at thirty and found? Our own ten-cow rawhide spread, sixteen-hour days, and not even enough money to buy a sack of Durham? We been starved out of the freight business and burnt out of the saloon business. Pard, there ain't a hell of a lot left."

"Maybe old Hoss has the right idea," said Arlo. "You look for gold, and even if you never find it, there's always that hope. We don't even have that."

Arlo and Dallas rose at dawn, had their coffee, and by midmorning were thoroughly bored. But it didn't last long. Shortly before noon, to the surprise of neither of them, Gila County sheriff Harley Wheaton rode in.

"Step down, Harley," said Dallas, "and come in."

Clearly, Harley Wheaton didn't relish the times when duty demanded he straddle a horse. A big man, he weighed more than he could comfortably carry. He was gruff and outspoken, but friendly enough, for a lawman. He followed Dallas into the cabin, and eased himself down on a three-legged stool with a sigh. Dallas and Arlo sat on the bunks.

"I reckon you gents know why I'm here," said Wheaton. "I got nineteen different versions of what happened last night, and I got to add yours to the pile."

"It ain't complicated," Arlo said. "Gambler shot a man, the dead man's pards bashed in the gambler's head, and then the varmints burnt down our saloon. End of story."

"I don't reckon you knowed the gambler, then?" asked the sheriff.

"If you're suggesting he might have been a house dealer," Arlo said, "the answer is a definite no."

"Me and Arlo dealt for the house," said Dallas, "and in all the months we had the Gila, nobody ever caught us slick-dealing."

Arlo cast him a warning look, and the sheriff laughed.

"I reckon," said Wheaton, with a sigh that might have been regret, "you ain't plannin' to rebuild the Gila."

"With what?" Arlo asked. "We put everything we had back into the place. You ain't aimin' to make it hard on us because of the killings, are you?"

"No," said the sheriff. "I'm takin' your word that you had nothin' to do with the gambler's death. He started it, and far as I'm concerned, he got what was comin' to him. While I'm here, though, there's somethin' else I need to know. When did you last see Hoss Logan?"

"Last fall," Arlo said. "October, I think. Why?"

"He left some ore at the assayer's office," said the sheriff. "Almighty rich ore, too. The California gold rush started over less. The assayer claims this ore sample didn't come from any of the known mines in Arizona Territory."

"Damn considerate of him to get the word out," Dallas said. "Every owl-hoot from New Orleans to San Diego will be lookin' for Hoss, wantin' his claim."

"Don't be so quick to blame the assayer," replied Wheaton. "Peterson only mentioned it to me because Hoss has been gone more'n six months. Why would he leave evidence of a big strike like that and make no move to register the claim? Peterson thinks something may have happened to Hoss, and I think he may be right. You gents are closer to him than anybody else, and that's why I'm tellin' you this. Has he ever said anything to you about a strike, or about leavin' some rich ore with the assayer?"

"No to both questions," Dallas said. "We staked him as usual, and we haven't seen him since."

"You're leadin' up to something, Sheriff," said Arlo. "What?"

"This," Wheaton said. "Sure as hell, something's happened to Henry Logan, and but for you gents, I can't think of a soul who'd ride off into the Superstitions to look for him."

Arlo and Dallas looked at one another. With the saloon

gone, and without the necessary money for wagons and teams, what else did they have to do? Even if old age or Apaches had caught up with Hoss Logan, they could at least find the old man's bones and bury him proper. As friends, they owed him that.

"All right," Arlo said. "We'll have to round up some grub, but come mornin', we'll ride out and look around some."

With the dawn, however, circumstances changed. Arlo and Dallas were awakened by the braying of a mule— Hoss Logan's mule. Astride the gaunt little beast sat Paiute, the mute Indian. Without so much as looking at Arlo and Dallas, Paiute slid off the poor mule. He wore moccasins, out-at-the-knees Levi's, a dirty red flannel shirt, and a black, uncreased high-crowned hat over his gray braids. When Paiute finally did look at them, it was without expression. From the front pocket of his Levi's, he took a soft pouch of leather, closed with a drawstring and presented it to Arlo. The bag was small but heavy, and Arlo removed a chunk of ore the size of his hand.

"My God!" said Dallas. "I've seen gold ore before, but nothin' like that."

"There's something else in here," Arlo said, extracting a paper that had been folded many times to fit into the pouch. It proved to be two sheets of rough tablet paper. The first page was a letter, printed in pencil. Dallas crowded close, and they both began to read.

Arlo and Dallas:
The doc says there's somethin' eatin' away at my insides, an' I got maybe six months. I ain't wantin' to be a bother to nobody. When Paiute brings this to you, the six months will be gone, an' so will I. There's gold in the Superstitions, an' I'm sendin' you this ore as proof. You gents always treated me fair, stakin' me an' standin' by me, and I ain't forgot. Half of the strike is yours, an' all I'm askin' is that you be sure my only blood kin gets the other half. Kelly and Kelsey Logan is my brother Jed's girls, back in Cape Girardeau. Jed was killed a year

*ago, an' the girls ain't of age, so I'm trustin' you to see
they ain't cheated. That fool woman Jed left behind went
an' married a no-account skunk I've knowed all my life,
name of Gary Davis. Me an' him was pards once, until
he took a girl I aimed to marry an' ruint her. I don't like
the way he was so quick to move in after Jed was killed.
He'll try to steal the gold I aim for Jed's girls to have,
and he'll kill you for your share if he can. He'll have the
piece of map I'm sendin' the girls, but he'll never find the
gold without your part of the map an' your help. Look for
the skeletons of the Spaniards who died for the gold, and
when the full moon looks down on the dark slopes of the
Superstitions, remember your old pard,*

Hoss

"Damn!" said Arlo. "He expects us to go lookin' for a
mine littered with bones, takin' with us a pair of underage females and their sidewinder of a stepdaddy."

"Hoss didn't say how his brother died," Dallas said,
"but I get the feelin' this Gary Davis might have had
something to do with it. You reckon Paiute knows where
Hoss is?"

"Hell," said Arlo, "I ain't sure Paiute knows where he
is himself."

The object of their conversation sat with his back
against a pine tree, staring vacantly ahead.

"Well," Dallas finally said, "we're old Hoss's last
hope where those poor girls are concerned. Let's look at
our half of the map."

The map seemed pitifully inadequate. There was a
jagged line with a half circle above it, with an arrow
pointing away from the half circle. At the barb of the arrow there was an inverted V, and above that a crude
death's head. There was nothing more.

"Does that tell you anything?" Arlo asked.

"Yeah," said Dallas. "Hoss is givin' us credit for bein'
a hell of a lot smarter than we are. What do you make
of it?"

"I think this *is* the map. All of it. As Hoss figured, this
scheming Gary Davis will have to work with us."

"Or kill us," Dallas said. "Hoss mentioned that, too. What he didn't say is whether or not he sent an ore sample to Missouri."

"You can be sure he didn't," said Arlo. "That accounts for the ore sample he left with the assayer. Hoss wanted to be dead sure this Gary Davis rides into the Superstitions. By the time he gets to us, he'll have a bur under his tail as big as Texas."

"I reckon we'll end up shootin' the varmint," Dallas said. "Maybe that's the price we're payin' for half a gold mine. Where do we go from here?"

"As much as I hate to," said Arlo, "we'll have to ride to Phoenix and tell the sheriff about this. Otherwise, he'll be expecting us to begin a search for Hoss. If we take this letter from Hoss as gospel—and there's no reason not to—then we've eliminated the need for a search. Instead of lookin' for Hoss, we'll be lookin' for the gold."

"Damn the luck," Dallas spat. "We let the sheriff read this letter, and we're lettin' him in on the gold."

"Forget about the sheriff," replied Arlo. "Even if we *could* keep him in the dark, there's no way we can keep a lid on this. Next thing you know, them underage Logan females and their coyote of a stepdaddy will be here, and God knows what kind of stink they'll stir up."

"Well," Dallas sighed, "long as we got to, let's ride in and talk to the sheriff. We can stock up on grub while we're there."

After ensuring that Paiute had enough sustenance, the pair saddled their horses and rode out, leaving the mute Indian seated with his back to the pine. Reaching Phoenix, Arlo and Dallas went straight to the sheriff's office and found Wheaton alone. Without a word, Arlo handed the sheriff the hand-printed letter from Hoss Logan.

"He mentions gold ore and half a map," said Wheaton, after reading the letter.

"All right," Arlo sighed, producing the leather poke with the ore and the strange map. "I reckon you might as well know as much as we do, because I got a gut feeling this thing may blow up into one hell of a mess."

"I expect you're right," said the sheriff, "and before it's done, you may be almighty glad you leveled with me. From what Hoss has written, this Gary Davis is a lifelong enemy. Why did Hoss send half the map to these Logan girls, knowin' their stepdaddy would get his hands on it? That part don't make sense."

"Neither does leavin' gold-rich ore with the assayer for six months and not registering the claim," Arlo said.

"Old Hoss planned all this," said Dallas. "He must have had some reason."

"There's a wild card somewhere in the deck," agreed the sheriff, "and Hoss is countin' on you boys findin' it. Once this Gary Davis shows up, you'd best not let him shuffle the cards. Stick around the Logan cabin, and I'll send word when your new partner from Missouri arrives. What are you goin' to do with the old Indian?"

"I don't know," Arlo said. "He's no help to us."

"Let's bring him to town," Dallas said with a grin. "He can bunk in the *juzgado*."

"Like hell," said Sheriff Wheaton. "I ain't runnin' a mission."

Arlo and Dallas went to a general store and bought supplies for two weeks.

"We'll have to do some serious buying before we ride into the Superstitions," said Arlo, "but we might as well wait till these folks from Missouri show up with the rest of the map. They may not even want to ride with us."

"I hope they don't show up broke, expectin' us to supply horses and grub," said Dallas.

"I hope they do," Arlo replied. "That will be reason enough to leave them in town and search for the gold on our own."

"You know better than that," said Dallas. "This bunch will already have a good case of gold fever, and if they have to, they'll crawl to the Superstitions on their knees."

Chapter 1

When Arlo and Dallas reached the cabin, they found the mule cropping grass, but the aged Indian was nowhere in sight.

"He couldn't have gone too far on foot," Dallas said.

"Maybe he went down to Saguaro Lake to take a bath," said Arlo. "He sure could use one."

Paiute *had* been to the lake, and when he returned an hour later, he had a dozen big trout strung on a rawhide thong.

"Well," Arlo sighed, "I reckon we got us an Indian. Thank God he's not as worthless as he looks."

Two weeks after Paiute had brought the message from Hoss, Sheriff Wheaton sent a rider to the Logan cabin with a summons for Arlo and Dallas. What remained of Hoss's blood kin had arrived. When Arlo and Dallas reached the sheriff's office, they found the lawman looking grim.

"You're in for it, boys," Wheaton said. "They're at the Frontier Hotel, and there's six of 'em. The Logan girls are beauties, but the rest—my God! This woman, mother to the Logan girls, is gussied up like the Queen of England. Her nose is heisted so high, in a hard rain she'd drown. Gary Davis, her new husband, ain't no Missouri shorthorn. He's a curly wolf if I ever seen one, totin' a tied-down Colt. There's a scrawny little varmint called Barry Rust, who's a friend to Davis, and he's carryin' a hideout gun under his coat. Then there's R. J. Bollinger, a gunslingin' killer of some repute. I've heard of him. Seems the sidewinder was run out of Texas by the Rangers."

"You learned a mighty lot in a hurry," said Dallas.

"Routine," Wheaton said. "I make it a point to meet the stage so's I know who's new in town. When strangers are lookin' for somethin' or somebody, an' they see me standin' there, it ain't unusual for 'em to ask questions of me. Sometimes I am the first in town to know who they are an' why they're here."

"Well, you know why this bunch is here," Arlo said. "You're in this deep enough that you're entitled to set in on whatever happens at the hotel. Come on."

"This varmint Barry Rust done most of the talkin'," said the sheriff. "Talks down to you, like he's just a cut or two below God."

Gary Davis, his wife, and the Logan girls had taken a three-room suite, while Rust and Bollinger were sharing an adjoining room. It was Davis that answered the sheriff's knock. His thick-muscled frame would have made a grizzly envious. He wore an expensive suit, with a gaudy red tie over a ruffled boiled shirt, and polished black boots that shone in the light from the lamp. The Colt at his hip looked well used. His thick black hair and chin whiskers showed some gray, and on his lips was a hint of a smile that failed to reach his dark eyes. He simply nodded when the sheriff introduced Arlo and Dallas.

"We have a sitting room here," Davis said. "We'll talk there." He stepped aside, allowing Arlo and Dallas to enter, but blocked Wheaton's way. "Sorry, Sheriff," he said, "but this is a private meeting."

"Not *that* private," Arlo snapped. "We invited Sheriff Wheaton to sit in. He stays."

"Excuse me, then," said Davis with poor grace, "while I fetch my associates."

Davis left the door open, stepped into the hall, and knocked on the door of another room. Returning with two men, he introduced Barry Rust and R. J. Bollinger. Rust was the shortest man in the room, a startling contrast in stature to Davis and Bollinger. Rust's shoes were low-cut black patent, his suit solid black over a gray shirt and a navy tie. The very top of his head was bald, and his lips turned down at the corners as though he had never smiled in his life. Bollinger had adopted an obnoxious swagger, and his wolf grin seemed calculated to convince Arlo, Dallas, and Sheriff Wheaton that he, R. J. Bollinger, knew something the visiting trio did not. He wore scuffed high-heeled boots, Levi's, and a red flannel shirt open at the throat. His fancy gray Stetson had a thin band of silver, and the polished walnut grips of his Colt gleamed in the lamplight. The six men eyed one another warily, nobody quite sure what the next move should be. Sheriff Wheaton was the first to speak.

"Arlo an' Dallas ain't met the Logan girls an' their mother."

"This is business that don't concern females," replied Davis stiffly.

"I reckon you can speak for Mrs. Davis," Arlo said, "but not for Kelly and Kelsey Logan. Until we meet them, this medicine show stops dead in its tracks."

Bollinger strode across the room until he stood face-to-face with Arlo.

"I don't like you, bucko," snarled the gunman.

"It'd disappoint the hell out of me if you did," Arlo said coldly. His right fist suddenly struck Bollinger on the point of his chin and slammed him against the wall, dropping a framed picture with a tinkling crash. Bollinger staggered but kept his feet, pausing with his hand on the butt of his Colt. Sheriff Wheaton already had him covered.

"You reach for that iron again while you're in this town," said Wheaton, "and I'll take it away from you. We got our own rules here, and you just broke one of 'em."

The tension quickly died as both bedroom doors opened in response to the commotion. Through one door stepped a woman in a long dressing gown, her face painted like a Coahuila *puta*. Arlo and Dallas wouldn't have given her a second look if she'd set herself afire. Their eyes were on the girls who emerged from the other bedroom. They were identical twins, with blue eyes and curly straw-colored hair to their shoulders. First they eyed Bollinger, who stood with his back to the wall, a bruise beginning to purple his chin. Arlo still had his fist clenched, and there was a trace of blood on the knuckles of his right hand. Finally, Gary Davis introduced the Logan girls and their mother. Kelly and Kelsey Logan seemed to have their eyes on Arlo and Dallas, and it infuriated Gary Davis.

"Back to your room," he shouted. "Now!"

Dejectedly the girls returned to the bedroom and closed the door. The man's brutal attitude got the best of Dallas, and he turned on Davis in a fury.

"They're Hoss Logan's kin!" he shouted. "They have a right to know what we're doin', since me and Arlo are involved in this."

"You won't be involved in it much longer," said Davis. He nodded to Rust.

"It is our contention," Rust said, "that this . . . ah . . . claim of Henry Logan's should go, in its entirety, to his blood kin, Kelly and Kelsey Logan. In that light, we are going before the judge at nine o'clock in the morning to contest your right to any portion of Henry Logan's estate and to demand part of a map which is now in your possession. I believe this concludes our business with you. We'll see you in court."

The sheer gall of the ultimatum left Arlo and Dallas speechless, and Sheriff Wheaton was barely able to get them out of the hotel without further violence.

"Now," the sheriff said once they were outside, "I reckon you can see why Hoss needed somebody he could trust to look out for the Logan girls."

"My God, yes," Arlo said angrily. "They're lambs surrounded by lobo wolves."

"I reckon that snake in the grass Rust has a whole deck of cards he can draw from," said Dallas, "but by God, a loaded Colt still beats four of a kind in anybody's game."

"Whoa, boy," Sheriff Wheaton warned. "You heard what I told Bollinger. I don't want Judge Colt handin' down any verdicts while I'm sheriff. I don't want either of you startin' somethin' I might have to finish. You pull iron in Phoenix, then it'd better be in defense of your own hide, an' you'd better have witnesses."

"We don't aim for this slick-tongued coyote to talk us into a corner," Arlo huffed. "How can the court, or anybody else, claim we have no right to this map, when Hoss made it a point of sending it to us?"

"That'll be a good question for you to ask the judge in the morning," replied the sheriff. "It's easy enough to drag somethin' into court, but if it don't belong there, it can just as quick be throwed out. Remember that."

Arlo and Dallas reached the courthouse a few minutes before nine and took seats at the table provided for the defense. The courtroom was packed. While any strangers arriving in Phoenix would have kindled local interest, this bunch from Missouri had fanned the flames by almost immediately revealing the purpose of their presence. Gary Davis and Barry Rust had gone to the assayer's office, showed the letter the Logan girls had received from Hoss Logan, and demanded information about any claim Hoss might have filed. Herk Peterson, the assayer, felt justified in revealing the ore Hoss Logan had left there six months before, and the secret was out.

"This bunch has sure played hell," said Dallas grimly as they waited for the judge to take the bench. "Every sneakin' coyote in Arizona Territory will be on our trail, ready to shoot us in the back for that piece of map."

"For whatever it's worth," Arlo said, "this Gary Davis will be as much a target as we are, since he supposedly has the other half of the map."

"Well, I don't want him gettin' his hands on our half," said Dallas. "Let's hang on to it till hell freezes over, whether we understand it or not."

"Everybody stand," the bailiff suddenly said, as the judge entered.

All conversation ceased and everybody stood.

"Court is now in session," intoned the bailiff, "Judge Tom Grady presiding."

"We will begin," Judge Grady said, "by asking counsel for the plaintiff to explain the nature of his complaint and what he expects of this court."

Rust gave a reasonably close but rambling account of the alleged passing of Hoss Logan and his division of the map.

"To sum it up," said Rust, "we believe Henry Logan has mistakenly given half a gold claim to a pair of common cowboys, a claim that rightfully belongs to Kelly and Kelsey Logan. We are asking the court to seize whatever Henry Logan may have given to Wells and Holt that has led them to believe they are entitled to share in the Logan estate."

"You may be seated, Mr. Rust," Judge Grady said, "and we'll hear from Mr. Wells and Mr. Holt. State your case, gentlemen."

"We'll have our say, Judge," said Arlo, "after you've read this letter from Henry Logan to us."

Judge Grady accepted the letter, read it twice, and then returned it.

"Hoss Logan aimed for us to have an interest, and we have his word as proof. What more do you need?" Arlo asked.

"You have no proof that Henry Logan wrote that letter!" Rust shouted.

"You have no proof that he didn't," Arlo shouted back, "and no way of proving he wrote the letter you have."

"Order in the court!" declared Judge Grady. "Now, Mr. Rust, Mr. Wells voluntarily allowed me to read his letter, while I have yet to see yours. I am no handwriting expert, but I want to compare these two letters."

Again Arlo presented his letter, while Rust seemed reluctant to come forward with his. Finally he took it from an inside coat pocket and passed it to Judge Grady. The judge took only a moment to reach a decision.

"Both letters are printed," said the judge, "so nobody can swear they were written by the same hand, but I am

virtually certain they were. Both these pages were torn
from the same tablet at the same time, and the lettering is
remarkably similar. Clearly, if one of these was written
by Henry Logan, they both were. Now what more do you
people expect of this court?"

"Nothing, sir," said Arlo. "We had no complaint to
start with, and we have none at this time."

"Well, we do," Rust all but screamed, "and the court
has done nothing to resolve it. We maintain that Wells
and Holt have no right to share in the Logan estate, and
we are asking the court to intervene."

"Henry Logan made his wishes clear, insofar as this
court is concerned," said Judge Grady, "and I see no
reason for intervention. If you disagree, state your
grounds."

"Wells and Holt are not Henry Logan's blood kin,"
Rust said angrily, "and Logan did not leave a will. Where
there is no will, the estate goes to the nearest kin. That's
an accepted precedent in all United States courts of law,
as I understand it."

"Mr. Rust," said Judge Grady coldly, "there evidently
is something you *don't* understand. You are not *in* the
United States. This is Arizona Territory, and we are not
bound by precedent. In any court in Arizona these letters
of Henry Logan's will stand as his last will and testament,
and this court accepts them as such. Case dismissed."

There were many smiles and much ill-concealed
laughter as Rust stomped angrily out of the courtroom.
The rest of his party followed, the Logan girls last. As
they turned away, they cast wistful looks at Arlo and Dallas. The cowboy partners had won the first hand, but they
had no time to consider where they stood in the game, for
they found themselves surrounded by insistent, shoving
people who fought for their attention.

"The mine," someone shouted. "Where's the mine?"

"I'm with the *Phoenix Record*," said a fat man, taking
Arlo's arm. "I want your story for my newspaper."

"Damn it," bawled Arlo, "everybody back off! This is
a private matter."

"You can't keep a gold strike private," somebody shouted, a sentiment quickly echoed by a dozen other voices.

"Break it up!" Sheriff Wheaton bawled. "Clear the courtroom."

The sheriff's intervention provided enough of a diversion for Arlo and Dallas to dash through the crowd and get to the door.

"Come on," said Arlo, once they were outside. "We're goin' to offer to work with Davis and Rust, and if they refuse, I have a little surprise for them."

The Missouri party had returned to the hotel, also seeking to avoid the crowd from the courthouse. Reaching the Davis suite, Arlo knocked on the door and Davis opened it. There was no sign of the girls or of Mrs. Davis. Barry Rust and R. J. Bollinger sat next to a folding table on which stood a half-empty whiskey bottle. Arlo and Dallas made no move to enter, nor did Davis invite them in.

"Unless there's some way of us working together," said Arlo, "we aim to start our search tomorrow. Alone."

"Go ahead," sneered Davis. "You don't have the rest of the map."

"We don't need it," Arlo said.

Davis slammed the door, but not before Arlo and Dallas saw his face go white and the shocked expressions on the faces of his companions.

"For whatever it's worth," said Dallas, "you struck pay dirt."

"It's worth plenty," Arlo said, "because they need us, and we *don't* need them. They don't know that both halves of the map are the same, that there is only *one* map."

"You're right," said Dallas, "we're that much ahead. But we don't happen to be all that familiar with the Superstitions. We still have to find the claim."

"If it can be found, we'll find it," Arlo said, "and Hoss was countin' on that. I want the rest of the gold-hungry coyotes that'll be trailin' us to get the same idea. It'll keep us alive until we find the gold."

"We'd best spend the rest of the day gettin' our supplies together," said Dallas. "I'll ride back to the cabin and fetch the mule."

"No," Arlo said, "we'll buy another mule and a pack-saddle here in town. I aim for Paiute to ride that mule that belonged to Hoss."

"Are we takin' him with us for his sake or for ours?"

"Some of both," said Arlo. "He has nowhere to go, and he's spent the last twenty years with Hoss in the Super-stitions. He can't talk, but he knows we're the closest pards Hoss had. I can't shake the feeling that before we reach the end of this trail, we'll be glad that old Indian's with us. I think we'll stay in town tonight and pick him up tomorrow."

"We ain't exactly flush," Dallas noted. "Can we afford a hotel?"

"The best," replied Arlo. "We'll stay right here at the Frontier."

At the desk Arlo requested a first-floor room. Much to his satisfaction, they were given a room right across the hall from the Davis suite.

"I reckon you aim to give them Missouri coyotes a chance to make a move before we ride out in the morn-ing," Dallas said.

"Not so much that," said Arlo, "as the possibility we'll be able to talk to the Logan girls. They haven't been al-lowed to say a word to us. Given a chance, I reckon they could tell us plenty."

"I think you're right about that," Dallas agreed. "I got the feeling they wanted to talk to us but didn't dare. They might risk it if they know we're right across the hall."

"They'll know," said Arlo. Reaching the Davis suite, Arlo nudged the bottom of the door with his boot. When Davis opened the door, Arlo was at his own door, clum-sily trying to insert the key. Davis quickly closed his door, but not before one of the Logan girls had seen Arlo and Dallas preparing to enter their room.

"Now they know we're here," Dallas said when they had entered the room and closed the door. "One of the girls saw us. Whether we ever find the gold or not, I aim to meet those girls. My God, how did they turn out so pretty, their mama bein' the stuck-up old she-buffalo that she is?"

"I don't know," said Arlo, "but she and this Gary Davis strike me as bein' two of a kind. I don't blame Hoss for bein' suspicious, the two of 'em gettin' together so quick after Jed Logan was killed."

"It ain't quite noon," Dallas said. "Why don't we do some lookin' around for a good mule and a packsaddle? We can buy provisions too."

"We might as well," agreed Arlo, "and be done with it. I'd like to get away from here early in the morning, but even then, we won't be alone. Thanks to that fool move Davis and Rust made in court, God knows who we'll have on our back trail."

Gold, even the mention of it, brought out the worst in people. Arlo and Dallas found that men had staked out the hotel, while others watched the livery. Eager eyes observed them as they bought a mule and a packsaddle, and men openly followed them as they made their way to the general store for supplies.

As Gary Davis, Barry Rust, and R. J. Bollinger were about to leave the hotel, Davis turned to his wife, Paulette, and the Logan girls.

"We may be gone a while," Davis said, "and I don't want none of you leavin' this room. Is that clear?"

Paulette nodded. Kelly and Kelsey Logan only looked at him, and he could plainly see the hate in their eyes. The trio stepped into the hall, and Davis had barely closed the door when Kelsey Logan exploded.

"God, how I hate him!" she hissed.

"No more than I," cried Kelly. "He's a brute, the snake that Uncle Henry always said he was."

"That's no way to speak of your father," Paulette shouted angrily. "I won't have it!"

"He's not our father," Kelly cried. "Our daddy's dead, and I believe this . . . this scum, Gary Davis, had more than a little to do with it."

Paulette Davis hit the girl with such force that she stumbled against the wall. Kelly said nothing. She stood there breathing hard, her face white with fury, her eyes a cold blue. Paulette was shocked, for the girl was looking at her in much the same way Jed Logan had the week before he had been killed, the week he had branded Paulette a whore for her relationship with Gary Davis. Jed Logan was gone, but his daughter looked at her with those same accusing eyes. Jed Logan's eyes! In them was a mixture of disgust, pity, and hate that was too much for Paulette Davis.

"Kelly . . . I . . . I'm sorry," she said, backing away.

"Don't be," said Kelly through clenched teeth. "I know what you are, and so did Uncle Henry. Thank God he trusted his gold to those two cowboys."

"Henry Logan was a sentimental old fool," Paulette snapped.

"You never knew or cared about Uncle Henry," said Kelsey quietly, "and he knew it. He saw through you like Daddy never did, until it was too late. Maybe this gold somewhere in the Superstitions is Uncle Henry's way of getting back at you from the grave. You ignored him when he told us of the lonely canyons in the Superstitions, of the crying of the wind among the peaks, of the ghostly shadows in the light of a full moon. Uncle Henry said all who are drawn to the mountains by greed find only death."

Kelsey Logan spoke softly, but her words had a strange effect, as though something—or somebody—spoke through her. Eerie tremors crept up Paulette's spine, and she shuddered.

Leaving the hotel, Gary Davis and his companions got a quick taste of what their foolish day in court had cost them. The men now following them made no attempt to conceal their presence.

"By God, Barry," said Davis sarcastically, "that was smart, showin' our hand to every bastard in town. Now we got to hunt the gold with one eye and watch our backs with the other."

"All right," Rust said curtly, "you've made your point. I'm not perfect like you. I'm new to Western ways, but I'm smart enough to know we're in no danger of being shot in the back until we find the gold. Now that brings us to an important question you haven't answered: What of these troublesome cowboys, who not only have the rest of the map but know what's in our half?"

"There's only one answer," replied Davis. "Henry Logan has made a fool of me. He had no intention of me findin' his claim. Otherwise, why did he trust two fiddle-footed cowboys with the whole map, while sending only half of it to Kelly and Kelsey?"

"That won't make no difference," Bollinger said. "Once we're out of town, away from this hick sheriff, I'll gun those hombres down and we'll take their map."

"Don't be a damn fool," scolded Davis. "We know nothing about the Superstitions. If we *had* the map, what chance would we have of ever finding the mine? Let's allow these friends of Logan to find the gold and *then* gun them down."

"So you have no intention of looking for the gold at all," Rust said. "We'll just be following Wells and Holt."

"Exactly," said Davis. "Can you come up with a better plan?"

"No," Rust admitted, "but I'd be more impressed if we didn't have to share it with the rest of the town, maybe even the territory."

"Well, you know whose fault that is," said Davis roughly.

"So I made a mistake," Rust snapped. "Now get off it. We have to put up a convincing front. What's our first move?"

"We'll hire a guide," answered Davis. "First, so we don't get lost in the mountains, and second, so it will appear that we're searching for the gold in our own right, instead of just following Wells and Holt, like everybody else."

Part of south Phoenix had become so Mexican-dominated, it was referred to as Mex Town. Here in a smoke-filled cantina called the Paisano, sat Yavapai and Sanchez, a pair of ne'er-do-well Mexicans who made a dishonest living by working both sides of the border. Presently down on their luck, they were seeking some means—however devious—of bettering their position.

"I have heard of this Henry Logan," said Sanchez, "and I have long believed there is gold in the Superstitions."

"Ah," Yavapai said, "who but foolish *gringos* would reveal such a secret before seeking to discover the truth of it for themselves?"

"*Por Dios,*" sighed Sanchez, "it is a wretched time for us to be without even a *peso* for food. If we had supplies, it would be so simple to follow these *gringos* until they have found the gold, and then take it from them."

"The Apaches believe their Thunder God lives in the Superstitions," Yavapai said, "and I think before these mountains give up their gold, men will die. Per'ap there's yet a chance for us to share this gold—or take it all."

Assayer Herk Peterson heartily regretted ever having told that bunch from Missouri anything, even if some of them *were* Hoss Logan's blood kin. Gary Davis and Barry Rust talked down to Peterson as though he was beneath them, a *pelado* who hadn't revealed all he knew. Their attitude had rankled Peterson, and he had thoroughly enjoyed seeing them take a beating in court. He now watched with misgivings as the detested pair, accompanied by R. J. Bollinger, approached the assayer's office. Whatever they wanted, Peterson would be courteous, but that was all. When the three men entered, it was Davis who spoke.

"Peterson, I need to hire a guide, a man familiar with the Superstitions. Who can you recommend?"

"Try some of the cantinas in south Phoenix," said Peterson. "Ask for Yavapai and Sanchez. They know most of the mountains in southern Arizona, from the Superstitions to the Maricopas."

Feeling a little guilty, Peterson watched the trio depart. He had told them the truth—most of it, anyway. At present, Yavapai and Sanchez were clean, but in their time they'd hidden from the law in many a mountain stronghold. The infamous duo had been suspected of robbing Butterfield stages, but they'd never been caught. Butterfield had hired more shotgun riders and ordered them to shoot to kill, and that had slowed the stage robberies considerably. Mexico, following its devastating defeat by the United States, had begun cleaning up some of the hellholes on the Mexican side of the border, so there were fewer and fewer havens for misfits like Yavapai and Sanchez. The pair had become as unwelcome south of the border as they were in Texas, New Mexico, and Arizona. They were perilously close to being forced into honest work, if they could find any.

Chapter 2

Davis and his companions had no trouble finding Yavapai and Sanchez. The Mexicans were well dressed in tight-legged black trousers, white ruffled shirts, and waist-length black jackets with fancy red embroidery. Their high-heeled boots were polished black, with big roweled silver spurs. Neither of them spoke, only nodded to confirm their identity after Gary Davis spoke to them.

"I need a guide," said Davis. "One that knows his way around the Superstitions."

"You seek the Logan mine, no?" Sanchez said with a grin.

"Yes," said Davis uncomfortably.

"Fi' dollaire each day," said Yavapai. "For Sanchez and Yavapai, fi' dollaire each."

"Five dollars a day, and that's all," Davis said angrily. "I ain't payin' but one of you."

"Both of us go," said Sanchez, "or neither of us."

The two of them leaned back in their chairs, rested their boots on the table, and tipped their high-crowned hats down over their faces. The *gringos* had been dismissed.

"All right, damn it," Davis growled, "I'll take both of you. I suppose you want some money in advance?"

"No, Señor," said Sanchez. "We trust you." He tilted his hat back on his head and grinned slyly at Davis.

"You will provide the pack mules and provisions," Yavapai said, coming to life. "When and where are we to begin?"

"In the mornin', at daylight," said Davis. "Meet me at the Frontier Hotel."

The Mexicans watched Davis and his companions stalk out the door.

"If there is gold," Sanchez sneered, "so much the better. If there is none, good mules will fetch fifty *pesos* apiece in Tucson or Tombstone."

Arlo and Dallas left their newly acquired mule and packsaddle at the livery and their order for supplies at the general store. The same men who had followed them from the hotel continued to pursue them as they returned to it.

"It's still early in the day," Arlo said. "Maybe we'd better get some sleep. We may be up late tonight."

Unaccustomed to sleeping in the daytime, they dozed fitfully. Early in the evening they went down to the hotel dining room for supper. The only other occupants were Davis, Rust, and Bollinger, who sat drinking coffee and fortifying it with whiskey from a bottle on the table before them. They seemed not to notice Arlo and Dallas as they took a table near the door. They were almost finished eating when Paulette Davis and the Logan twins entered the dining room. As they passed the table where the cowboys were eating, one of the girls dropped a tiny wad of paper at Arlo's feet. He waited until the trio was seated at their table, then purposely let his napkin slip to the floor. As he gathered it up, he concealed the bit of paper in his hand. The two men paid for their meal and returned to their room.

"I was hoping they'd get to us," Arlo said, "because it's damn near impossible for us to get to them."

Arlo smoothed out the wrinkled paper to disclose two printed words: *Late tonight.*

The night wore on, and the cowboys took turns watching, one dozing on the bed while the other waited at the unlocked door. It was well past midnight and Arlo was on guard in the darkened room, when suddenly there was a thin ribbon of light from the hall, and their door moved just a little.

"I'm Kelly," she whispered. "Please let me come in."

Arlo eased the door open enough for her to enter, then silently and swiftly closed it behind her and woke Dallas.

"Here," Arlo said, "you take the chair. Dallas and me can sit on the bed."

"You were Uncle Henry's friends," she said softly, "and the last time we saw him alive, he spoke kindly of you. He knew he could trust the two of you with the gold and that you'd look out for Kelsey and me. Kelsey wanted to come too, but we were afraid for both of us to leave at the same time."

"How old are you and Kelsey?" Arlo asked. "How much longer until both of you are legally free?"

"Practically forever," the girl sighed. "We won't be eighteen until the twenty-third of this December. Seven more months."

"Tell us what we can do to help you," Dallas said.

"Find Uncle Henry's gold," she whispered, "and keep it for Kelsey and me until we're eighteen. Gary Davis is a devil. He'll steal our share and kill you for yours."

"Your Uncle Henry warned us about him," Arlo said. "You'd better tell us the rest of the story."

"Gary Davis was once Uncle Henry's partner," said Kelly, "until he ruined the girl Uncle Henry was to marry. Jed Logan, our daddy and Uncle Henry's only brother, had a freighting business going, and Gary Davis started a competing freight line. Davis cut rates, took Daddy's contracts, and finally forced him to sell out. Daddy took a job with Davis, and . . ."

She paused, gathering her strength, then continued.

"It's so . . . sickening," she said, "there's no decent way to tell it. Our mother had an affair with Gary Davis. He sent Daddy on long hauls, and while he was gone, Davis and our mother . . ."

"That's enough," Arlo said. "We can see how it was. You think Davis had something to do with Jed—your daddy—being killed?"

"Oh, God," the girl cried, "we almost know he did. Kelsey and me heard Daddy confront Mother. He called her a whore and she laughed at him. A week later, Daddy was shot off the wagon box, and two weeks after that, Mother married Gary Davis."

"There was no proof that Davis was behind Jed's killing?" Dallas asked.

"None," said Kelly, "but me and Kelsey knew. Some of the Davis wagons had been attacked before by outlaws and the freight stolen, but when Daddy was killed, nothing was taken. There's been talk, but still no proof, that Davis is the head of a gang, attacking and looting his own wagons and then claiming the insurance. The only way Daddy's killing makes sense is that Gary Davis wanted him dead."

"Has Davis mistreated you and Kelsey?" Arlo asked.

"I have scars all over me," said Kelly, "and so does Kelsey. We ran away right after Mother married him, and when they caught us, Davis beat us half to death."

"Your mother . . ." Dallas began.

"Our mother did nothing," said Kelly bitterly, "except threaten to send us to a house for wayward girls in St. Louis. Please, *please* find the gold, and don't let Gary Davis get his hands on any of it."

"Kelly," Arlo said, "if there's a claim, we'll find it, and we'll live up to your Uncle Henry's trust in us. And we'll go farther than that. We'll help you and Kelsey escape your prison."

"Oh, if you only could!" she sighed. "But what can you do, with us still legally under his and Mother's control?"

"Maybe more than you think," said Arlo. "Does he plan to take you and Kelsey into the Superstitions while he looks for the mine?"

"Yes," Kelly said. "Kelsey and me are his only legal means of going after Uncle Henry's claim. He's afraid we'll run away again if we have the chance."

"Keep him thinking that way," said Arlo. "You won't be too far away from us during the search for the gold. If you need us, we'll help you. He may have a legal hold on you and Kelsey back in Missouri, but in the mountains of Arizona Territory, the only law is the gun."

"When this search for the gold is done," Dallas said, "things may have changed some. I'm givin' you my word—we'll free you from this Gary Davis, if I have to shoot him myself."

"God bless you both," she whispered, "for being Uncle Henry's friends and for being friends to Kelsey and me."

She opened the door just enough to slip through and closed it softly behind her. It was a while before Dallas broke the silence.

"If just half of what she says is true, this Gary Davis ought to be gut-shot and fed to the coyotes."

"I don't doubt a word of it," Arlo said, "and even if we never find the gold, we're going to free Kelly and Kelsey. I think Hoss would approve."

Come first light, Arlo and Dallas loaded their provisions on the pack mule and rode out to the northeast, bound for Hoss Logan's cabin. As expected, they were pursued by more than thirty riders, all would-be gold seekers. Davis and his bunch brought up the rear, led by the newly acquired guides Yavapai and Sanchez. Gary Davis, Bollinger, and the Logan girls seemed comfortable in the saddle, though Paulette Davis and Rust were suffering mightily.

"What a bunch of damn fools," said Dallas in disgust. "They ain't even smart enough to know we're just ridin' out to Hoss Logan's cabin. If we rode into the Superstitions from the north, we could lose these pilgrims so bad they'd never find their way out."

"That's how we're goin' to rid ourselves of most of them," Arlo said. "We'll have Paiute to guide us, and we're going to waste a few days wandering through the roughest damn country we can find. We'll lose some of this bunch so completely that when they get out of the Superstitions, they'll be glad to just ride on home."

They found Paiute with his back to the same pine,

seeming not to have moved. There was ample evidence
to the contrary, however. Not a scrap of food remained in
the cabin, and there was an enormous pile of fish bones
outside the back door.

"Our very own Indian," Dallas sighed. "He smells like
a grizzly that just crawled out of hibernation, he eats like
a starving lobo, and he can't talk."

"The Lord works in mysterious ways," Arlo grinned.
"If I didn't know better, I would suspect that Paiute de-
voured all the grub and Hoss starved to death." He took
from his pocket the leather poke in which Hoss Logan
had sent the letter, the map, and the gold ore. He held up
the poke, getting the Indian's attention. He then pointed
to Paiute, to the mule, and finally to the Superstition
Mountains. Paiute nodded his understanding. The gold
seekers who had followed Arlo and Dallas from town
had halted within sight of the cabin.

"Now," said Arlo, "let's lead this bunch into the Superstitions and burn some of the gold fever out of 'em."

Paiute had rounded up Hoss Logan's mule, and he
mounted with an agility that surprised both cowboys.

"Either he ain't as old as he looks," observed Dallas,
"or he's in mighty good shape."

Paiute rode out, heading south, paralleling the Superstitions. Arlo and Dallas followed, Dallas leading the
pack mule. The horde of gold seekers from town rode in
pursuit. Gary Davis galloped ahead, catching up to
Yavapai and Sanchez.

"What's Wells and Holt doing?" Davis demanded.

"They have returned for the Indian who once rode
with Señor Logan," said Sanchez.

"We're already in the foothills to the north of the Superstitions," Davis growled, "so why are they ridin'
south?"

"Who knows?" said Yavapai, shrugging his shoulders.
"It is you who said we are to follow these hombres. You
do not say we must know what they are about to do and
why they do it."

Davis choked back an angry reply. He was paying this

insolent pair twice what they were worth, and *they* were talking down to *him*. He slowed his horse, allowing the rest of the party to catch up, only to encounter more of Paulette's whining.

"Gary," she groaned, "I haven't ridden in years, and this is killing me. I must stop for a while."

"Go ahead," said Davis brutally. "The Apaches will put you out of your misery."

Davis ignored her unladylike response, and Kelly and Kelsey laughed at her plight. Paulette leaned forward, her arms around the horse's neck, trying to take some of the pressure off her ample backside. Barry Rust wasn't faring any better, but he had just observed Gary Davis's less than understanding reaction to complaints from his own wife, so Rust gritted his teeth and rode on.

"Where you reckon this Indian's takin' us?" Dallas wondered.

"Likely along the trails Hoss always rode," said Arlo. "Canyons and washes slope down from the Superstitions and fan out for miles, every one a wilderness of cactus, thorns, and brambles. I'm countin' on Paiute knowin' the trails and how to find water."

"We should have paid more attention when Hoss rambled on," Dallas said glumly. "But how could we know we'd end up backtrailing him through the Superstitions?"

The Superstitions range extended south to the Salt River, which flowed on to its confluence with the Gila and the San Pedro, just west of Phoenix. They were almost to the Salt before Paiute turned west, entering the Superstitions from the south. In his approach to the mountains, he had chosen the most impenetrable flank possible, but he managed to find a trail where there seemingly was none. He hunched over the neck of his mule, ducking under low-hanging limbs, and pursued a zigzag course westward. They crossed hummocks of solid rock, where nothing grew except cacti, only to plunge immediately into yet another thicket of grease-wood, catclaw, stunted cedar, and a devilish array of thorn-bearing underbrush whose barbs seemed to reach for any living thing that came close. Out of necessity they rode single file, and Arlo and Dallas had to push hard to keep up with the old Indian. So swiftly did they progress, twisting and turning, that it began to seem as though it was the mule who knew the trail and Paiute was just along for the ride. Suddenly from their back trail, there was a shriek, the frightened nicker of a horse, and the thud of hooves.

"Somebody just lost a horse," said Arlo. "I hope it wasn't one of the girls."

"I'm bettin' it was the she-buffalo," Dallas said. "She straddles a horse like an off-balance sack of shelled corn on its way to the mill."

Only Arlo and Dallas were close enough to observe Paiute's devious twists and turns. All those in pursuit knew only the general direction the three lead riders were taking as they rode headlong into impenetrable thickets of thorns and brambles. Paulette Davis, fighting the barbs and brambles clawing at her, had been snatched out of the saddle by a low-hanging limb. Her shriek frightened the horse, and the animal almost trampled her as it lit out down the back trail. Gary Davis ignored the furious Paulette and galloped after her fleeing mount. Thankful for any respite from the brutal journey, Barry Rust reined his horse in, as did Kelly and Kelsey Logan. They all regarded Paulette with amusement, which only added to her fury.

"I declare," said Kelsey in mock horror, "such language! Bull whackers could learn much from her."

While Yavapai continued in pursuit of the rest of the gold seekers, Sanchez rode back to see what had caused the commotion. When he arrived at the small group, he tilted his hat back on his head and grinned at the furious Paulette. That was the scene that greeted Gary Davis when he returned with Paulette's horse, and he vented all his fury on the still grinning Sanchez.

"What'n hell are *you* doin' here?" he snarled. "I'm

payin' you and that *pelado* partner of yours to follow
Wells and Holt. Why ain't you doin' it?"

"We think per'ap you need help until you catch up,"
said Sanchez. "But you are right, Señor. You pay us to
follow those hombres. A thousand pardons, Señor." He
rode away without a backward look and was soon lost in
the thickets ahead.

Davis turned to Paulette, who still sat on the ground.

"Get up," he said angrily, "and from now on, watch
where the hell you're going. Tumble out of that saddle
one more time, and I'll tie you belly down across it."

He helped the unwilling Paulette on to her mount, and
they continued, Davis in the lead. He immediately discovered his folly in berating Sanchez, for the Mexican
had only sought to guide them through this wilderness,
in which they were now lost. He urged his horse ahead,
only to have the animal balk.

Bollinger had kept up with the rest of the gold seekers, but realizing that his own party had fallen behind, he
now rode back to see why. Davis didn't waste any time
explaining to him.

"R. J., can you get us back on the trail?"

"Hell," said Bollinger, "there ain't no trail. We got to
keep the others in sight and foller them. Come on!"

Bollinger managed to guide them until they were
within sight of some stragglers who were following Arlo
and Dallas. Not a breath of air stirred, and the Arizona
sun bore down with a vengeance. Sweat darkened the
flanks of the horses, dripped into the eyes and off the
noses and chins of the riders, and soaked the backs of
their shirts. Some of them, including Paulette Davis,
made a startling discovery—they hadn't brought any
water!

"Gary," Paulette whined, "I'm thirsty. I need water."

"We'll get some somewhere up ahead," said Davis
unsympathetically.

"No," Paulette said, "I need it now. I'm going back to
the river."

"Go ahead," said Davis, ignoring her.

She rode on, cursing him and hating Kelly and Kelsey for their amused grins. It was Bollinger who finally took pity on her.

"When the others stop to water, ma'am, we'll stop too. Not before," he said, though kindly.

The terrain grew rougher. Gary Davis looked back approvingly, for Bollinger now brought up the rear. Except for the gunman and the hired Mexican guides, Davis thought grimly, none of his outfit was suited to the ordeal that lay ahead. But there were Kelly and Kelsey Logan, damn them. The pair rode like they'd been born to the saddle and seemed to delight in every misfortune that befell him.

Up ahead, the two cowboys were growing restless. "This is the longest I ever rode without gettin' *some*where," said Dallas. "I'd swear this mountain ain't changed a bit in two hours, and we don't seem to be a foot higher than when we started."

"I'm startin' to suspect there's some method to Paiute's madness," Arlo said. "I don't know if he understood what I said about losin' this bunch or if he come up with the idea on his own, but I'd bet my last pair of clean socks that's what he's set out to do. I know damn well there's clear ground higher up these mountains. You can see it from Phoenix."

"Well, if Paiute can ride this trail in the dark, he'll lose everybody, includin' us. It's bad enough when you can see where you're going. In the dark, a man could ride into a low-hangin' limb and lose an eye. So could a horse."

"We'll need water," said Arlo, "and before dark, Paiute will lead us to it. Right now, he's makin' it real hard on that bunch that's trailin' us. They're already gettin' dry, but they don't dare look for water, or they risk losin' our trail."

Time after time in this wretched terrain they had crossed canyons where there might have been water, but Paiute did not stop. He paused only occasionally to rest the mule.

"You predicted water by sundown," said Dallas, "but I can do better than that. I can tell you where that water's goin' to be. Friend Arlo, just as sure as God created the heavens and the earth, we're on our way back to good old Saguaro Lake. That crazy Indian is leadin' us in a fifty-mile circle."

At first Arlo laughed, but as they rode on, the truth of it became more and more obvious. The going became easier and the thickets began to thin out, but only because they were nearing the more gentle slopes that marked the end of the Superstitions to the north. Less than an hour before sundown, a westering sun shone on the sparkling waters of Saguaro Lake, half a dozen miles ahead. It was almost within walking distance of old Hoss Logan's cabin, which they had left at daybreak.

"Well, by God!" exclaimed Arlo. "I can't believe it."

"You?" Dallas whooped. "What about that bunch of pilgrims behind us?"

Their thirsty horses broke into a gallop, hot on the heels of Paiute's mule. The weary gold seekers—far behind—reined in and stared in disbelief. Gary Davis galloped his horse ahead until he caught up with Yavapai and Sanchez.

"Damn it," Davis shouted, "they've put us through hell all day, and we're back where we started! Between the two of you, didn't you have brains enough to realize we've been traveling in circles?"

"You pay us to follow these hombres, Señor," said Yavapai, shrugging his shoulders, "and we follow them. *Por Dios,* night comes, and there is much water. One should not be ungrateful, Señor."

Before Davis could respond, his horse joined the others in a mad dash toward the distant lake. To the dismay of the pursuers, Arlo and Dallas didn't unsaddle their mounts or unload their pack mule. Once their horses and mule had watered, and Paiute had watered his mule, the trio rode out, headed for Hoss Logan's cabin.

"Paiute's got the right idea," Arlo laughed. "Why

should we sleep on the ground, when we're this close to the cabin and its bunks?"

At the cabin, they unloaded the pack mule and unsaddled their horses.

Dallas laughed. "I reckon they all hate our guts. This was one hell of a wild goose chase, but it was worth it."

"Damn right it was," said Arlo, "and I'm sorry I ever called Paiute useless. He's worth every bit of the fortune in grub it takes to feed him."

"If I wasn't so god-awful tired," Dallas said, "I'd sneak back after dark and listen in on that bunch at the lake. I'd give a lot to know what they're sayin' about us."

The hangers-on who had camped at Saguaro Lake, including the Davis outfit, were beyond exhaustion. But there was talk, and it was venomous.

"My God," said Rust bitterly, "that was a brilliant plan, following those damn cowboys all day and ending up where we started."

"Yeah," Bollinger agreed, "and the best part of it is, the bastards may pull the same stunt again tomorrow, and the day after that."

"Yes, Gary," said Paulette in a poisonous tone, "tell us what you have planned for tomorrow. When are these damn Mexicans going to start earning their pay?"

"We earn our pay," Sanchez said angrily. "He tell us to follow these hombres, and we follow. If you please, Señor," he said, turning to Davis, "our earnings for this day."

Davis paid them and then stalked off into the darkness to escape the bitter comments of his companions. But there was some laughter, for Kelly and Kelsey Logan were quite satisfied with the day's events. Bollinger took note of their pleasure and turned on them.

"It's time your daddy took a strap to you she-cats," he said angrily. "It's nigh time the pair of you was tamed and made to be civil."

"Gary Davis is not our daddy," said Kelsey coldly, "and anytime you're of a mind to tame me, mister gunslinger, just come on. I'll claw your eyes out."

Yavapai and Sanchez ignored all the hard words being flung about and set to work unloading the Davis pack mule. The pair started a fire, cooked their supper, and sat down to eat.

"What about the rest of us?" Rust asked indignantly. "Where's our supper?"

"Señor Davis pay us to follow this Wells and Holt," said Yavapai, "and this we do. We do not hire on as cooks. You are welcome to use our fire if you wish."

Gary Davis had returned to camp in time to hear Yavapai's response, and he glared at the Mexican guides. They continued eating as though Davis didn't exist, and he turned to Paulette, who lay unmoving, her head on her saddle.

"Why don't you get supper for the rest of us?" said Davis.

"Why don't you go to hell?" Paulette snarled. "I can scarcely move, and I don't care if all of you starve."

Kelly and Kelsey Logan exchanged looks. They were hungry, and whatever were their feelings toward their surly companions, they also needed food.

"Kelsey and me will do the cooking," said Kelly, "until somebody complains. If you don't like our cooking, you can do your own."

"Well, it's about time the two of you contributed *something*," Davis said ungraciously.

"We don't expect any thanks from you," said Kelly defiantly, "but we won't take any abuse either. Remember that."

Supper was a silent meal—nobody was speaking to anybody else. Yavapai and Sanchez got well away from the hostile camp before rolling up in their blankets. Davis sat looking into the fire, conscious that Bollinger and Rust were covertly watching him. If so much as a hint of gold were found, Davis thought, Bollinger would double-cross him. He found himself harboring the same doubts about Rust. While the two of them had been through many shady deals together, he couldn't be sure Rust wouldn't turn on him if there was enough gold and the opportunity presented itself. Reflecting on his circumstances, Davis decided he couldn't return to Missouri. True, he had taken over Jed Logan's freighting business, but he had bankrupted it along with his own, robbing his wagons and collecting the insurance. Not only had he lost all his clients, but the insurance people were investigating him with an eye toward prosecution. Hoss Logan's mine had gotten him out of Missouri just one jump ahead of the law. He had brought Rust and Bollinger with him not so much because he needed them but because they knew too much. He dared not leave them behind. Sooner or later he would have to dispose of the pair, along with Paulette and those troublesome daughters. Finally, he turned his thoughts to Yavapai and Sanchez. Were they what they seemed—a pair of simple Mexicans who would be satisfied with the few dollars they earned as guides—or were they after the gold as well? A thief himself, Gary Davis trusted nobody.

"Tomorrow ought to be interesting," Dallas said, "if Paiute takes us on another dry run through the Superstitions with that bunch of gold hunters following."

"They have no choice," said Arlo. "Once they back off from what looks like another hopeless chase, they don't know that we won't drift up a canyon and lose them."

"We can't go on forever, trying to discourage them," Dallas said. "Sooner or later we're goin' to have to begin our search for the gold, and when we find it, we'll have to settle with whoever's still on our trail."

"We'll give Paiute a couple more days," said Arlo. "I doubt he'll lead us to the mine, but he might get us to some point where the map begins to make sense."

Chapter 3

Arlo and Dallas arose at first light. Paiute was already up and had a fire going—the coffee was ready. Arlo opened the door and looked out toward Saguaro Lake.

"They're waitin' for us, I reckon," said Dallas.

"They sure are," Arlo replied.

When they were ready to move out, they loaded the pack mule, saddled their horses, and pointed to Paiute. Mounting his mule, the Indian led out in the same direction he'd taken the day before.

"Here we go again," said Dallas.

But it soon became apparent that Paiute didn't plan a repeat of the day before. While they took the same torturous trail along the eastern flank of the Superstitions, their pace was almost leisurely. Those who pursued them were more mystified than ever. Again they turned west along the Salt River, reaching a point a little southwest of the Superstitions a good two hours before sundown. Paiute removed the blanket from his mule, turned the animal loose to graze, and stretched out beneath the willows that lined the river.

"Might as well unsaddle the horses and unload the pack mule," Arlo said. "This is where we'll spend the night, I reckon. It ought to further confuse our followers."

"They're not alone," said Dallas. "It's doin' a fair job of confusing me. There's still two hours of daylight."

"Let's get our supper fire going," Arlo said. "It's too early to eat, but I could use some coffee. Something about that map's been bothering me. Come sundown, I aim to check it out."

Paiute filled his tin cup with coffee, cut a slender willow pole, and headed downriver. There would be fish for supper. Arlo and Dallas settled down with their coffee and the map Hoss Logan had sent them.

"Read this map to me," said Arlo. "Tell me what you think it means."

"The jagged line is the horizon," Dallas said. "The half circle is the sun, and the arrow points east or west, depending on whether the sun is rising or setting. The upside-down V is a mountain peak, and I reckon the death's head means the mine with Spanish bones is somewhere in that mountain."

"Pretty good interpretation," said Arlo. "First thing we need to know is whether Hoss is referring to the rising sun or the setting sun. Let's saddle up and ride down the river toward Phoenix far enough that we can see the western rim of the Superstitions."

This activity wasn't lost on Gary Davis and his companions.

"These hombres ride along the river, Señor," said Yavapai. "Do you wish we follow?"

"No," Davis said. "They're not breaking camp, and it'll soon be dark."

Arlo and Dallas rode west of the Superstitions until they could see a good portion of the western rim stretching away to the north, then waited until the sun had slipped beyond the horizon, leaving only a crimson glow.

"I reckon we just ruled out the sunset," said Dallas, "unless we ain't readin' this like Hoss intended. I don't see a single peak along the western rim that stands out enough to be the one the map points to."

"I didn't think there would be," Arlo said, "but I wanted to be sure. Now look at that western rim again. While none of the peaks stand out above the others, it is kind of a jagged line, like the line on the map Hoss drew. Why can't that ragged rim of the Superstitions be the horizon behind the map's setting sun?"

"By God," Dallas shouted, "that's *got* to be it! Once we're up there in the mountains with our backs to the western sun, we'll be facing the peak Hoss drew on the map!"

"Before you get too excited," said Arlo, "remember there are peaks all along the eastern rim. Even if the western rim *is* the horizon on the map, there's miles and miles of mountain. We still won't know at what point we must stand or how we're to recognize the particular peak Hoss refers to."

"We're missing something Hoss is trying to tell us," said Dallas. "I can't believe he'd leave us without some sign to identify the peak."

"Maybe you're right," Arlo replied. "We'll have to wait until we get up there. Maybe Hoss is just gettin' us into position for the mountain to tell us what we need to know."

It was near dark when Arlo and Dallas returned to camp. They found Paiute frying fish. He nodded toward a willow thicket, and there they saw the pack mule, fully loaded. Without a word, Arlo and Dallas led their still-saddled horses into the willows and picketed them with the mule. Once supper was done, they put out the fire, and when a full moon rose over the Superstitions, Paiute mounted his mule. Arlo and Dallas followed suit and, leading the pack mule, trailed Paiute into the forbidding mountains. It was hard going for a while as the three made their way up the southern end of the range. Then the underbrush began to thin out, and they eventually reached a plateau. In the Superstitions, as in most western mountain ranges, a series of saddlebacks connected the different peaks. As they progressed to the higher elevations, Arlo and Dallas made an alarming discovery. There was no graze! The mountain's surface seemed flint-hard—and where there was no vegetation, there certainly would be no water.

Eventually Paiute led them through a gap in the western rim, and they followed a deep gash down the side of the mountain, with stone walls towering above their heads. It was a trail that would be invisible from below, ending on a narrow ledge that became a tunnel angling into the side of the mountain. Paiute slid off the mule and led the animal. Arlo and Dallas dismounted also and followed, with their horses and the mule. They could hear the welcome sound of running water somewhere ahead. Their footsteps and those of the shod horses and mules rang hollow on the solid rock beneath their feet. The passage soon widened into a cavern as large as Hoss Logan's cabin, water splashing down a back wall to form a pool and starlit sky visible through an aperture high above their heads. Clearly, this had long been a haven for Hoss, for there was every evidence of a permanent camp. A good supply of firewood had been laid in, and near the center of the cavern was a stone fire ring. From some concealed nook, Paiute brought out a quart bottle in which a cork stopper protected a supply of sulfur matches. The Indian lit one and used it to fire a pine pitch torch, allowing Dallas and Arlo to better appreciate the sanctuary. At one end of the cavern, a portion of the floor had been covered with straw, obviously as an accommodation for Hoss Logan's mule. There was half a sack of barley and a second unopened hundred-pound sack. Camp utensils consisted of a three-legged iron spider, an iron pot and skillet, and a blackened coffeepot.

"No wonder Hoss could stay out for months at a time," said Dallas. "With enough grub, a man could spend his life here."

"That hole in the roof opens out somewhere on the western rim," Arlo said, "likely up high enough that it's never been discovered."

"Why don't we just unload the pack mule and let this be our permanent camp?" Dallas suggested.

"Good idea," said Arlo, "but we'll have to come and go at night. We also have to find some graze for the horses and mules. They can't survive on just grain, even if we could afford to buy it. Sooner or later, that bunch that's been followin' us will find their way to the top, and I don't want them knowing about this camp. Before we're done, I think we'll need the security we have here."

Dallas and Arlo unsaddled their horses, unloaded the pack mule, and leading their animals, followed Paiute and his mule out of the cavern. The Indian understood the need for graze, and once they again reached a plateau, Paiute mounted his mule. There was nothing for Dallas and Arlo to do but mount their horses bareback, and leading the pack mule, follow the Indian. Paiute took them to yet another exit from the mountain, a dangerously steep one that a rider unfamiliar with the trail wouldn't have dared. They emerged on a grassy plateau that seemed unreachable from the parapets above or from the foothills far below. If the grazing animals strayed, it would have to be back to the hazardous trail down which they'd come.

"Not a lot of graze here," Arlo noted, "but enough for our horses and mules for a few days. If we're here longer than that, one of us will have to slip into town after dark for another sack of barley and some grub for ourselves."

Dallas and Arlo loosed the animals to graze and followed Paiute back up the side of the mountain on foot. Even in the cool of the night, they were sweating by the time they reached the rim.

"By God," Dallas panted, "that Indian's a better man than I am. We'll still have to climb back down here for the horses and mules before dawn."

The trio returned to their hidden camp and slept. Dallas and Arlo awoke long before first light, preparing to go for the horses, but the Indian was gone.

"Well, that beats the goose a-gobblin'," Dallas said. "I doubt we can even *find* that straight-down drop-off in the dark."

But by the time they got their boots on, they could hear the *clop-clop-clop* of hooves, and they soon saw Paiute leading the horses and mules into the cavern. While the old Indian could not or would not help them in their search for the mine, his knowledge of the Superstitions was proving invaluable. Though it was still dark outside, so well were they concealed that Dallas was able to start their breakfast fire.

* * *

Come the dawn, Gary Davis turned his eyes down-river, where Dallas and Arlo had set up their camp the night before. His angry bellow alerted his own camp that something was wrong, and he turned on Yavapai and Sanchez.

"Damn it, get down there and find their trail!"

"We have no breakfast yet, Señor," said Yavapai, unperturbed.

"By God," Davis shouted, "find that trail! *Then* you can eat." Furious, he glared at Kelly and Kelsey just as they were starting the breakfast fire. The look in their eyes warned him to back off.

By the time Yavapai and Sanchez reached the deserted camp, the remaining gold seekers from town—fifteen men in all—were there, cursing, shouting, and destroying what trail there was, even as they sought it. The two Mexicans fought their way into the thickets of the Superstitions and eventually found tracks.

"I think per'ap it is yesterday's trail," Yavapai said.

"*Por Dios,*" said Sanchez in disgust, "it is a trail. He do not say it must be *today's* trail. Let us eat."

Davis ignored breakfast himself and hurried his companions through the meal. By the time they were saddled and ready to ride, the rest of the gold seekers were already well into the thorny thickets of the Superstitions.

"Where the hell *is* that trail?" Davis demanded.

"The others have ridden over it," said Yavapai.

"Well, follow them," Davis snarled.

For three endless hours, Davis and his disgruntled companions struggled to penetrate the undergrowth of the Superstitions, eventually catching up to the frustrated men who had gone before them. The bunch sat in their saddles in silence, wiping sweaty faces on their shirtsleeves.

"If you men can't follow the trail," Davis growled, "get out of the way and let us have it."

"It's all yours," said one of the disgusted men. "It'll take you right to Saguaro Lake."

There was no denying the truth of it. They were

following yesterday's trail. Davis turned angrily to his
Mexican guides. They sat lazily in their saddles, Sanchez
with a leg crooked around the horn, rolling a quirly. At
their seeming indifference, Davis backhanded the Mexican, slapping the unlighted cigarette out of his lips.
Sanchez moved as fast as a striking rattler and smashed
his fist full in Davis's face. His nose spurting blood,
Davis was swept out of his saddle onto his back. He went
for his gun, only to find himself looking into the ugly
muzzle of the Colt that Sanchez held cocked and rock-
steady.

"Lift the *pistola* with the thumb and finger and leave it
on the ground," commanded Sanchez.

Without a word Davis lifted the Colt free of his holster
and dropped it.

"Now, Señor *Gringo,* get to your feet."

Shakily, Davis stood up, his nose dripping crimson,
his eyes killing mean.

"You pay Sanchez and Yavapai," Sanchez said coldly.
"Two days each, you pay. Then we leave you to ride any
trail you wish."

R. J. Bollinger had been in a bad position, at the rear.
All his companions had been between him and the two
Mexicans. He gradually sidestepped his horse, hoping
for a shot at one or both of them. By the time he had a
clear view of Yavapai, he found the Mexican watching
him, expecting just such a move. Bollinger relaxed. It
wasn't his kind of odds. All eyes were on Gary Davis as
he took a pair of gold eagles from his pocket. One he
gave to Sanchez, the other he gave to Yavapai. The pair
backstepped their horses into the brush, keeping their
eyes locked on Davis and his companions, as well as the
bunch of gold seekers from town. Finally hidden from
view, they turned their horses, hit the back trail, and
headed for the Salt River.

It was still dark when Dallas, Arlo, and Paiute finished
breakfast. Paiute lit one of the pine pitch torches from the
fire, walked toward the wall to the left of the cascading

water, and just disappeared. Shocked, Dallas and Arlo were on their feet in an instant. The passage veered away at an angle and couldn't be seen when looking straight at the stone wall. Paiute was waiting for them to follow him. The torch almost went out as cool air sucked at the flame, telling them that somewhere ahead, this tunnel opened to the outside. There were other passages, their dark maws appearing, then vanishing instantly as the flickering light moved beyond them. Finally they reached a ledge that, except for the tunnel they had just exited, was inaccessible. To the west, winking like distant fireflies in the predawn darkness, were the lights of Phoenix. Having no idea why the Indian had brought them here, Dallas and Arlo followed Paiute back to the cavern in which they had made their camp.

"That makes me feel better," Dallas said. "Secure as this seems, I'd hate to be trapped in here, with no means of escape. I wonder if some of those tunnels are somehow connected to the mine?"

"I don't think so," replied Arlo. "Hoss wouldn't risk that, and if Paiute could lead us to the mine, we wouldn't need a map. If anybody even suspected that Paiute knew where the mine is, his life wouldn't be worth a plugged *peso*. From what I've heard, the Spanish used to torture the Apaches, trying to force them to reveal the whereabouts of gold and silver mines. That's why the Apaches, even after two hundred years, don't trust white men who come looking for gold."

"Now that you mention it," Dallas said, "I remember some of the tales Hoss told us. He said the Apaches claim they don't kill the white men who come to the Superstitions. They say that they're killed by the Apache Thunder God and the spirits that live in the mountains. Remember Hoss telling us about the dead men who were found without a mark on them?"

"I remember," said Arlo, "and I think Hoss believed it, but I find it hard to swallow, myself. He never seemed to have trouble with the Apaches."

"I'm startin' to wonder if Paiute hasn't had somethin'

to do with that," Dallas said. "We don't know what Hoss might have told him, or how much he knows, but he's sticking with us. This old boy may be the biggest ace in the hole we've ever had."

When Yavapai and Sanchez reached the Salt River, they rode across it and secreted themselves in some willows on the south bank.

"*Por Dios,*" said Yavapai, "we have lose our job and our food in all the same day."

"Per'ap I will kill the *gringo* dog for his money and his food," Sanchez said angrily, "but I will not have him put his hands on me."

"These other *gringos* are many," said Yavapai. "Per'ap they pay us and feed us while we seek the gold."

"*Si,*" Sanchez said. "We jus' kill three times as many *gringos.*"

When Yavapai and Sanchez had ridden away, Gary Davis took stock of his situation. Besides Barry Rust, R. J. Bollinger, Paulette, and the Logan girls, all of the gold seekers from town had witnessed his falling-out with his Mexican guides. Striving for some dignity, Davis spoke to the men from town.

"We'll have to ride back to the river and start over. Why don't we join forces?"

"You're as lost as we are," answered a surly rider. "What'n hell do we need you for?"

"Maybe because I have half a map," Davis said angrily.

"I wouldn't take orders from you if'n you had a saddlebag full of maps," said another rider. "Now either ride ahead, ride back, or just git the hell out'n the way."

Without a word Davis mounted his horse and rode back toward the Salt River, his companions falling in behind him. It being their only option, the disgruntled bunch from town wheeled their mounts and followed.

In the hidden camp, Dallas punched up the fire, set the iron spider in place, and suspended a pot of water to heat.

When it was ready, Arlo dug out a piece of soap, and
the partners shaved, taking turns with the razor. Paiute
watched in obvious amusement—like most Indians, he
had not a trace of a beard.

"Now," Arlo said, "let's go up on top and look around.
With our horses and mules hidden, maybe we can disappear for a few days. That bunch lookin' for us won't
expect us to be afoot."

When they left the cavern, Paiute made no move to accompany them.

"He's led us to a hidden camp," Dallas said, "and he'll
get the horses and mule to graze at night, but I think
that's as far as he aims to go."

"Maybe as far as he *can* go," said Arlo. "If only for his
own safety, I doubt Hoss ever took him to the mine."

Before leaving the crevice that led to their hidden cavern, Dallas and Arlo looked around carefully. Since they
stood on solid rock, there were no telltale horse or mule
tracks.

"Still too early for them," Dallas said, referring to their
followers. "I'm bettin' they've all lit out along yesterday's trail and they'll end up backtracking."

"Now that they've lost sight of us," said Arlo, "we'll
find out if there's any trackers in the bunch."

"I'd put my money on those shifty-eyed Mex varmints
Davis brought with him," said Dallas. "That pair looks
like the kind who'd know every mountain grizzly hole in
Arizona Territory."

"I won't bet with you," Arlo replied. "Yavapai and
Sanchez have been in trouble with the law before. They
may be taking pay from Davis and eatin' his grub, but before this search is done, those Mex owl-hoots will come
after us in their own right. Secure as our camp seems, I
think we'd better sleep with our Colts in our hands."

Gary Davis was in a foul mood by the time he and his
companions reached the Salt River. They had wasted half
a day and accomplished nothing.

"We'll rest and water the horses," said Davis, "and then we're going up that damned mountain."

"With or without a trail?" Barry Rust asked.

"With, if we can find it, without, if we can't," said Davis shortly. "We know they're up there somewhere, by God, and I'll look behind and under every rock until I find them."

"Gary," Paulette said, "I'm exhausted. Since there's no trail anyway, why can't we wait until morning?"

"Because that bunch from town will get ahead of us," said Davis, "and because I *said* we're going today."

Davis led the party out, forcing his horse through the brush, briars, cactus, and catclaw at the foot of the mountain. They fought their way up the southern flank of the Superstitions, and by the time they reached a plateau where they could rest the horses, even Davis could see this was not a thing to be undertaken when the day was half spent. Horses and riders were drenched with sweat, and the dust stirred by their treacherous ascent coated them with a film of mud. They rested, then moved on, finding each plateau more barren than the last. The uppermost region of the mountain was so desolate that even Davis was speechless. There wasn't a blade of grass, not a drop of water. Depressions in the rock that might have held water now contained only sun-dried mud, spiderwebbed with cracks. Suddenly Paulette laughed at their plight, a shrill sound, touched with madness. Davis cursed long and low.

"My God," said Barry Rust, "a day spent on this damn mountain means a ride up here in the morning and back down at night."

"There has to be an easier way up here," Davis said.

"Then you'd better be finding it," said Paulette ominously.

Davis said nothing, for something much more distressing happened. The remaining gold seekers from town were approaching. Their horses were not spent, nor did the riders seem exhausted. Leading the party were the grinning Yavapai and Sanchez. Turning his horse, Davis rode to meet them, his hand on the butt of his Colt.

"I told you varmints to ride," Davis glowered.

"We ride," said Sanchez coldly, "and that is the last order we take from you. These hombres pay us, and now we ride with them. You make the big mistake, Señor. Do not make another. Do not get in the way."

The Mexicans had fifteen men with them now, and there wasn't a friendly face in the lot, so Davis backed off and the group rode away, Yavapai and Sanchez leading them toward the distant east rim.

"At least our former guides seem to know where they're going," Paulette observed. "If we are to continue this miserable search, let's follow them." It was a point so obvious that even Gary Davis could not deny the wisdom of it.

Bollinger laughed. "The rest of us can, but they told Gary to stay out of the way."

Davis said nothing, but when he looked at Bollinger, the gunman saw in those hard eyes a truth he already suspected. He had outlived his usefulness to Davis, and it hardened his resolve to tolerate the man only until they found the gold. Then he would take the treasure and maybe the women, leaving Davis's bones to rot in some lonesome canyon. The moment passed and Davis led out, the others falling in behind him. Reining their horses in at the rim, they could see the canyon below. Impossible as the passage seemed, Yavapai and Sanchez had led their followers down, slipping and sliding in clouds of dust.

"I will not ride down that wall," Paulette said defiantly.

"Suit yourself," said Davis. "Following them was your idea. See that green along the canyon floor? That means water."

They watched the group of riders reach the canyon floor and disappear.

"There must be a considerable overhang," Davis said. "Maybe even a cave."

"It won't matter to us what's down there," Rust said. "I doubt we'll be welcome."

"If there's water," said Davis angrily, "we have as much right to it as they do. Come on."

Despite Paulette's shrieks, they started down the steep slope. Concealed behind a distant upthrust of rock, Dallas and Arlo watched their descent.

"For the time being," said Arlo, "we're rid of them all. I'd bet a mule those Mexican owl-hoots know some places to hole up where there's water."

"You know," Dallas said, "the more I think about that horizon Hoss drew, the more I doubt the mine is actually in the Superstitions. Look at all the nearby peaks out there to the east. That arrow on the map could be aimed at any one of them."

"It could," replied Arlo, "and probably is. Come sundown I think we'll do some looking toward those other peaks."

"There's Weaver's Needle," Dallas said. "Hoss had names for them all, but that's the only one I remember."

When Arlo and Dallas returned to their hidden camp, Paiute was gone.

"Wherever he is," said Dallas, "he's afoot. His mule's still here."

"The last thing he'd do is give away the location of our camp," Arlo said. "I'd not be surprised if he's down yonder havin' a look at that bunch that went down the mountain. Remember when he took us down that second passage? Must have been half a dozen other tunnels anglin' off. Some of them maybe led to the foot of the mountain."

Barry Rust's prediction proved all too true. When Davis and his companions reached the canyon below, they found an excellent campsite, but it was already taken. Beneath an overhanging shelf of rock, a cavern opened back into the foot of the mountain. The very floor of the passage was a stream of water that trickled for less than a hundred yards before vanishing into the sandy floor of the canyon. Three men, including Yavapai and Sanchez, had been left with the animals, watering them from the runoff. The Mexicans said nothing. The other man carried a Hawken rifle, and it was he who spoke.

"You folks ain't welcome here. This is our camp. Move on."

"You don't own this mountain or this water," said Davis angrily.

"Mister, my name is Edwards, and I'm talkin' for us all. This here's Arizona Territory, and a man can own any damn thing he's got guts and guns enough to hang on to. Now all of you, git!"

Chapter 4

Paiute entered the hidden cavern silently, seeming to step out of the wall where the water cascaded down. He dipped himself a handful of water, slaked his thirst, and sat down with his back to the stone wall.

"It's gettin' late," said Arlo. "Time we went out and had a look at the peaks to the east, now that the sun's behind us."

Dallas and Arlo paused a few yards shy of the mountaintop, listening. Hearing nothing untoward, they climbed out of the crevice and looked around. Far to the west there was a rumble of thunder, and the rising wind was cool to their faces.

"Storm buildin'," remarked Dallas. "Thunderheads could roll in and steal the sunset."

"We'll wait a while," Arlo said. "We have nothing else to do."

They positioned themselves where the western rim rose like a parapet behind them. The westering sun descended until the crimson disk seemed to rest atop the stone rim. It shone on the peaks east of the Superstitions, leaving the lower elevations in the shadow of the coming darkness. Dallas and Arlo watched, uncertain as to what they were seeking. Only seconds away from losing the sun entirely, the cowboys froze, speechless.

"My God," Arlo breathed, "there it is!"

So slowly did the image appear, and so soon did it vanish, it might have been only a shadow, a trick of the imagination. But in the final seconds before the sun slipped away, the image was clear to both of them. Then it darkened, faded, and finally disappeared. Arlo and Dallas looked at one another in awe. For just a few unbelievable seconds, in the dying rays of the setting sun, they had seen the shadowy but unmistakable image from Hoss Logan's map: a grotesque death's head!

For a while, Dallas and Arlo stood there watching the darkening western horizon, as jagged shards of lightning raced ahead of the coming storm.

"Now we know all the map can tell us," Dallas said. "You reckon that peak where the death's head shows in the setting sun is where we'll find the mine?"

"No," said Arlo, "because the other map is just like ours. Knowin' Hoss and how he felt about Gary Davis, I don't think he would have taken any risks."

"Findin' the death's head on the side of that peak ain't been all that easy," Dallas said. "I'm bettin' Davis and his bunch won't ever figure it out."

"Only because Davis thinks he has just half the map," said Arlo. "That may be what Hoss had in mind— discouraging the use of the map by making Davis believe he has only half of it. I don't look to find anything at that death's head peak except some more clues."

"You aim to just ride over there and start pokin' around, with all these other coyotes on our trail?"

"Why not?" Arlo said. "They won't know why we're there, and since the mine likely won't be there, they'll be wasting their time following us. They'll become a problem to us only when we discover where the mine actually is."

"Before we strike off on our own, why don't we see what Paiute thinks about this death's head peak? He can't talk, but we might learn something from his reaction. Let's get him up here tomorrow at sundown and show him the death's head on the side of that mountain."

"That'll mean wasting another day," Arlo said.

"It won't be wasted. It'll give that bunch of claim jumpers time to get nervous, wonderin' what's become of us."

Thankful for shelter from the coming storm, Dallas

and Arlo returned to their camp within the cavern. Thunder boomed, and the very rock beneath their feet trembled. Paiute sat cross-legged, his hat tipped over his face, dozing peacefully. The storm-bred wind flung spray through the aperture in the stone roof high above their heads, a tiny window to a lightning-emblazoned sky.

"I hope Davis found some shelter," said Dallas. "Not for his sake, but because of Kelly and Kelsey Logan. That lightning's dangerous."

"I feel guilty, leaving the girls at the mercy of Gary Davis," Arlo said, "but I still don't know how we're going to help them. After all, their mother *is* Davis's wife, and that puts the law on their side."

"We can see the lights of town at night," said Dallas, "but here in the Superstitions, the law's a mighty long ways off. This is Arizona Territory, and if it comes to a standoff, I don't think Sheriff Wheaton will be much inclined to take sides with Gary Davis. He's a cruel man, from what Kelly told us, and I think we owe it to Hoss to take those girls away from him."

"I don't reckon them bein' the prettiest pair you've ever laid eyes on would have anything to do with your determination," Arlo said dryly.

"Not a damn thing," said Dallas with a straight face. "It's my natural compassion and my regard for the memory of our old pard, Hoss Logan."

They had almost forgotten the sleeping Paiute. In the dimness of the cavern, they were unaware that beneath the old Indian's tilted hat his dark eyes were alert and he was very much awake. Though he was apparently mute, he heard and understood their words. While he had little concern for Hoss Logan's gold, the young squaws were the old man's blood kin. Arlo and Dallas had been Hoss's friends, and while Paiute trusted them, what did they *really* know about these mountains? Paiute's people were long dead, and for twenty summers his only companion had been Hoss Logan. Except for Paiute, no man knew these mountains as intimately as Hoss had. While Paiute didn't understand Logan's reason for this last act—the revelation of gold to draw this *codicioso cua-drilla* into the mountains—he believed the old prospector had conceived some primitive retribution for the *enemigo,* just as he had looked to the *salvaciòn* of his next of kin. The young squaws with fair hair were comely, even in the aged eyes of Paiute, and it came as no surprise to him that the young *vaqueros* Dallas and Arlo were more than a little interested. That was as it should be, for the Logan squaws already had seen too many summers without a man, and what more could Hoss Logan have asked for them than this pair of *duro vaqueros?* Paiute made some decisions, awaiting the sleep of Dallas and Arlo. Far into the night, when the only sound was the sigh of the wind through the lonely reaches of the Superstitions, he arose. Silently, without a light, he crept down the passage behind the cascading water. But he did not follow the passage to the outer rim, the exit he had revealed to Dallas and Arlo. Instead, he took a more obscure route, one that led downward into the very bowels of the mountain. It was a forbidding labyrinth in which a man could become lost forever and perish—and many had. But it was a path that Paiute knew, even in the darkness, and it would lead him to other corridors in the eastern foothills of the Superstitions.

Gary Davis and his companions didn't fare well during the violent storm. Unwelcome in the sanctuary into which Yavapai and Sanchez had led their party, the best Davis could do was seek the shelter of the overhang. There were points along that eastern flank of the mountain where the lip of rock reached out almost a dozen feet, and with the storm roaring out of the west, Davis and his dejected bunch somehow managed to remain dry. At the height of the storm, the lightning was continuous, illuminating the canyon and the peaks beyond like day. Suddenly, a few yards down canyon, lightning struck a paloverde tree, blasting it into oblivion and showering Davis's party with sand and shards of stone.

"My God," Paulette Davis cried, "it's going to hit us!"

But the storm had peaked, and the lightning became less frequent until it died away altogether. When the rain ceased, a chill wind swept away the remaining clouds, leaving a purple sky to the serenity of a quarter moon and the faraway twinkling stars. With the clear skies, the group's flagging spirits rose a little.

"Gary," said Rust, "so far, we've ridden all over hell, with no sense of direction, following others who led us nowhere we couldn't have gone on our own. Ever since we left Missouri, I've had doubts about this expedition. Now it's time for us to make some decisions, or I'm going to make some on my own. Frankly, I'm not convinced there *is* a mine, and if there is, I'm not convinced you can find it. Just two more days, Gary, then I'm leaving. I'm going back to Missouri."

"Count me in," said Bollinger. "I'll be ridin' too."

"I wish you'd all go back to Missouri," Kelly Logan said bitterly. "Whatever Uncle Henry left belongs to Kelsey and me, not to any of you."

"And leave the two of you alone in these mountains?" Paulette cried. "What in the world would you do?"

"Find Dallas Holt and Arlo Wells," said Kelly, "and join them. They were friends to Uncle Henry, and they'd be our friends."

"Wouldn't they, though?" said Davis with a nasty laugh. "Spend their days huntin' gold, with a pair of hot-blooded chippies to warm their blankets at night."

"Gary Davis," Kelly cried, "you're a filthy brute."

"I can testify to that," said Paulette.

"Nobody cares a damn about your testifying, the kind of example you've set," Davis said. "Old Jed had you figured out, and for once in his miserable life, he was right."

R. J. Bollinger laughed. Disgusted, Barry Rust walked away into the night.

Within the cavern at the foot of the mountain, Yavapai and Sanchez soon had a supper fire going. They had used this hideout before, and they'd laid in a good supply of wood. The men from town had brought an ample supply of whiskey, and already some of them were drunk and quarrelsome. Two men had lit a pine pitch torch from the fire and were headed toward the dark corridor that led further into the mountain.

"Do not go into the passage," Sanchez warned. But they ignored him and went on.

"Foolish *gringos*," said Yavapai in disgust.

The curious pair, Ed Carney and Hamp Evers, soon decided they'd had more than enough of the dark passage, which had begun to seem endless. Their torch had begun to burn short, and their whiskey courage was wearing thin.

Soon after they turned back, they reached a point where the passage split. "Didn't seem like we'd come this far," said Ed nervously. "Which one of these forks takes us back the way we come?"

"Left," Hamp said. "I think."

They took the left fork, hoping at any moment to see the welcome glow of fire in the big cavern where their comrades waited. But there was only darkness and a constant dripping of water that seemed ominously loud in the silence.

"Oh, God," Ed groaned, "our light ain't goin' to last but a few more minutes. We got to move faster."

But the stone floor was wet and slippery, and as they tried to hurry, they almost fell. Suddenly, in the darkness ahead, moving toward them, a bobbing light appeared. They froze in their tracks. As the light came nearer, it became a grinning, glowing skull—a death's head! On it came, bodiless, floating hideously down the dark passage. Terrified, they turned to run, stumbling into another passage. Carney dropped what remained of the torch, and they were left in total, terrible darkness. Evers slipped and fell to hands and knees, and Carney fell over him. The pair staggered to their feet and stumbled on. Their screams, magnified by echo, seemed all the more terrible to their own ears. Suddenly the slippery stone

floor vanished and they were falling! Now their cries
were torn from their throats by the rush of wind and lost
in the roar of a turbulent stream far below. But the men
never felt the icy water, for they slammed into jagged
rocks along the way, and their mangled bodies were
claimed by a whirlpool that sucked them into the very
bowels of the earth.

"God Almighty!" shouted one of the comrades of the
doomed men back at the camp. "What was *that*?"

The anguished screams seemed to have come from the
very pit of hell. Instantly thirteen men were on their feet,
looking fearfully toward the pitch-black passage that led
from their cavern into the mountain.

"Ed an' Hamp ain't here," said one of the party.

"Mebbe they went outside," another suggested.

"No, Señor," said Sanchez, pointing toward the dark
passage. "They go into the mountain, and the mountain
take them. They do not return forever."

"Hell," shouted one of the men, "I ain't believin' that.
They're lost in that damned tunnel, and we got to go look
for 'em. Jake, Monk, Shando . . ."

But the men hesitated. Chills crept up their spines and
the hairs on the backs of their necks vibrated like tuning
forks. The horrible screams they had heard had come
from the throats of men who had just been dealt their final hand. Silently the remaining men turned questioning
eyes to Yavapai and Sanchez.

"The Apache say the Thunder God live within the
mountain," said Yavapai. "To tempt him is to die. Yavapai and Sanchez bring you here only to escape the storm.
Do not take the passage into the belly of the mountain, or
you will die, as your *amigos* have."

"I ain't stayin' another minute in this damn mountain,"
said one of the men.

The sentiment was quickly echoed by the rest of them.
Grabbing their saddles, their bedrolls, and their packs,
the thirteen men left the cavern, wading the stream that
ran through the passage to the outside. Beneath the overhang, Gary Davis threw off his blankets and sat up, won-

dering at the exodus after dark. With the storm past, starlight and a quarter moon bathed the canyon in an eerie light. Yavapai and Sanchez were the last to leave the cavern. Davis got to his feet and approached them.

"Since your bunch is movin' out, you got any objection if we move in?"

"None, Señor," said Yavapai.

Uncertainly, Davis watched the two Mexicans follow their companions down the canyon, where the lot of them made camp for the night.

"Come on," Davis told his outfit. "We're gettin' a roof over our heads."

"There must be some reason for that bunch moving out of such a shelter," said Rust. "You think it's wise, us going in without knowing why they didn't stay?"

"Who cares?" Davis said. "Maybe they only wanted shelter from the storm."

Davis went in first and stirred up the fire so they had some light. Once Paulette, Kelly, and Kelsey were inside, Davis turned to Bollinger and Rust.

"Now we'll go get our bedrolls, packs, and saddles."

While the three men were outside, Paulette, Kelly, and Kelsey looked around. Light from the fire barely reached the dark maw of the passage at the back of the cavern.

"It's spooky in here," Kelly said. "I don't blame those men for leaving."

As though in response to her words, there came a moaning from somewhere within the mountain.

"The Thunder God," whispered Kelsey. "Uncle Henry told us about him."

"Nonsense," Paulette said. "Henry Logan was a superstitious old fool. What you're hearing is only the wind blowing through the tunnel."

But from within the dark passage, eyes looked out into the cavern. Eyes that ignored Paulette Davis and focused on Kelly and Kelsey Logan as they moved about in the dim light from the flickering fire.

* * *

Arlo and Dallas arose early, thinking it unusual that
Paiute still slept.

"No graze for the horses and mules last night," Arlo
said, "so we'll for sure have to take them tonight."

"What a shame we can't do that in the daytime," said
Dallas. "We got the whole day ahead of us and not a
blessed thing to do until sundown, when we show Paiute
the death's head on the side of that mountain."

"Until then," Arlo said, "we're going to stay out of
sight. Without knowing where we are, the Davis outfit
and that bunch from town will be on their own. They're
going to be frustrated as hell, not knowing where to even
start looking for the mine."

Just before dawn the Davis contingent was awakened
by gunfire. Davis flung aside his blankets, grabbed his
gun rig, and left the cavern on the run. Bollinger was
right behind him, Rust followed less enthusiastically. As
Davis dashed into the open, arrows began whipping past
him. He turned and ran back to the safety of the cavern,
colliding with Bollinger. The two men stumbled back
along the passage, where they encountered Rust.

"What's going on out there?" Rust asked.

"Indians," Davis gasped. "The whole damn canyon's
full of 'em. There's one bunch comin' up canyon and
more of 'em along the walls. Them claim jumpers from
town is all catchin' hell."

"You ought to be out there helping those men," said
Paulette, "instead of cowering in here. What's going to
stop those savages from coming after us?"

"We don't owe that bunch from town a damn thing,"
Davis said angrily. "By God, it's their fight. We're safe
in here."

"But our horses and pack mules are out there," said
Rust. "You call that safe, being stranded in these mountains on foot?"

"You wanna get yourself shot full of Apache arrows
over some horses and mules," Davis snarled, "go ahead."

On the heels of his words, nine men came splashing

through the stream bed toward their shelter. First into the cavern were the Mexican guides, Yavapai and Sanchez.

"Hold it," said Davis, cocking his Colt. "You ain't welcome in here. Git the hell out!"

"Madre de Dios," cried Sanchez, "the Apaches kill us!"

While Sanchez had Davis's attention, Yavapai drew and fired. Paulette screamed and Davis dropped his Colt. He stared numbly at the blood welling out of his right arm, just above the elbow. Rust had made no move, and Bollinger paused, his hand on the butt of his Colt. Every man who had entered the cavern, except Sanchez, had drawn his gun, lest the Indians attempt to follow. Davis regained his voice, his hate-filled eyes fixed on Yavapai.

"Damn you," he growled. "Damn you!"

"I should have kill you," Yavapai hissed. "Do not tempt me, Señor."

While Paulette was pale and shaken, Kelly and Kelsey stared at the wounded Davis in contempt. Just when it seemed that the commotion outside had ceased, there was a roar of gunfire nearby. With captured weapons, the Apaches began firing through the passage, into the cavern. Slugs slammed into the stone walls, each deadly ricochet screaming across the cavern's stone floor, into the stone overhead, or into another wall.

"Madre de Dios!" Yavapai shouted. "Into the belly of the mountain!"

Followed by Sanchez, Yavapai tumbled into the forbidding passage where Ed and Hamp had so recently vanished forever. Forgetting his dropped Colt and bleeding arm, Davis ran for his life. Kelly and Kelsey followed, while Rust, Bollinger, and the rest of the men from town fought to enter. Paulette Davis was the last to move. Throwing aside her blankets, she got to her hands and knees, only to collapse facedown on the floor. A slug had whanged into a stone wall, and the deadly ricochet had taken off the back of her head. Blood and brains soiled her still-warm blankets.

The thunder of early-morning gunfire wasn't lost on

Arlo and Dallas. Paiute continued to drink his coffee, his expression unchanged.

"Apaches," Dallas said gravely. "I hope we ain't waited too long about helpin' the girls."

"So do I," said Arlo, "but from all the shooting, I'd say the fight is with the bunch from town. I hope Davis had enough savvy to take his people and make a run for it."

"I'm goin' out to look around," Dallas said, getting to his feet. "Don't seem right, us sittin' here doing nothing, when them damn Apaches might be killin' Hoss Logan's only kin."

"I know how you feel," said Arlo, "and I'll go with you, but what can we do? I doubt the Apaches would harm Kelly and Kelsey. At worst, they'd be taken captive."

"But for a woman," Dallas said, "that's a fate worse than death. They'd likely end up bein' Apache wives."

Paiute watched the partners leave the cavern. When he was sure they were gone, he took the cork out of the bottle and removed some matches. Then from the same nook where he kept the bottle, he withdrew a wad of tangled rawhide strips. He looped several of the longer ones to the thong around his lean neck, a thong whose other end was secured to the shaft of a Bowie knife that hung down his back, concealed by his patched flannel shirt. He then entered the passage in the back wall, behind the cascading water. Again he did not follow the narrow corridor to the west rim where he'd once taken Dallas and Arlo. When he came to another passage that forked off, the old Indian felt along the wall until his hand located a single wooden peg driven into a crevice in the rock. He went on, pausing at the next passage long enough to search the wall again. At the third passage, his seeking hand found a pair of wooden pegs in the stone wall. This passage he took, following it as it angled down into the very heart of the Superstitions.

Even after the firing finally ceased, those who had taken refuge in the dark passage remained still, uncertain of their next move.

"Per'ap the Apache be gone," Sanchez said, "Let us go see."

In the dim light of the cavern, Yavapai and Sanchez were the first to view the grisly remains of Paulette Davis. As much death as they had seen, a spark of decency remained in them still, and they felt some pity for the Logan girls. Sanchez returned to the dark passage and spoke to Kelly and Kelsey Logan.

"Per'ap you should remain here," he said, "until we have look outside."

"No," said Kelsey. "It's frightening in here."

She pushed past Sanchez, Kelly following close behind. They were shocked into silence by the awful scene that greeted them. Every man—including Davis—stood there grimly, viewing death in one of its ugliest forms. With choked cries, both girls dropped to their knees on the stone floor. Whatever else she had been, Paulette was their mother.

"Kelly," said Davis lamely. "Kelsey . . ."

When they raised tear-ravaged faces to him, even Davis was moved. While he had seen hate in their eyes before, it had been nothing to equal this.

"Get out!" Kelly screamed. "Get out and leave us alone! I never want to see you again."

Led by Davis, the men of his bunch filed out of the cavern one by one, seeking only to escape the terrible grief inside. But an equally gruesome scene awaited them in the canyon. Six of the gold seekers from town had been scalped and mutilated, and not a horse or a mule remained.

"Damn," one of the remaining men groaned in anguish, "stuck in these god-awful mountains on foot."

"What'n hell are *you* complainin' about?" a comrade growled. "Six of our pards ain't goin' nowhere, 'cept into holes in the ground. Who's goin' to tell their wives an' kids?"

"I will," said another of the bunch. "I'm headin' for town walkin', and thankin' God with every step that I'm alive."

"I'm goin' with you," said yet another. "The sheriff needs to know about this, so's he can send a wagon for the dead. Damn Injuns picked us so clean, we ain't even got anything left to dig a grave with."

Without another word, the seven men turned away, taking to the village yet another story that would add to the bloody history of the Superstitions. The five remaining men eyed one another warily. Davis, his wounded arm giving him hell, was flanked by Bollinger and Rust—a more uncertain alliance he couldn't imagine. Yavapai and Sanchez stood with their thumbs hooked in their pistol belts.

"*Por Dios,*" said Sanchez, "per'ap we should talk."

"By God," Davis said, "I'll give you sidewinders credit for one thing. You got nerve. Shoot a man, and *then* you want to talk."

"Count your blessings, Señor," said Yavapai with a half smile. "I could have kill you. Per'ap I will yet. The day is young."

"The situation have . . . ah . . . change," Sanchez said, ignoring Yavapai's threat. "We all seek the gold, Señor, while the Apaches seek our scalps. We are few. Per'ap we must work together."

"If I get your drift," Davis said, "you want us to throw in with you, and when we find the gold, you'll kill us and take it all."

"Ah, Señor," said Sanchez with a laugh, "we have much the same feeling for you. Now let us return to the safety of the cavern and boil some water. Yavapai, he have a talent for gunshot wounds."

The very last thing Davis wanted was more abuse from Kelly and Kelsey Logan, but something had to be done about the disposition of Paulette's body. Then there was their lack of horses. He sighed, as he, Rust, and Bollinger followed Yavapai and Sanchez back into the silent cavern.

"*Madre de Dios!*" cried Sanchez, "they have disappear!"

Indeed, the body of Paulette Davis was gone, and so

were the bloody blankets. There was no sign of Kelly and Kelsey Logan.

"Kelly! Kelsey!" Davis shouted.

Only an echo answered, and then there was silence.

"Damn it," said Davis, "I ain't believin' this. I can understand somethin' or somebody makin' off with the girls, but where's Paulette?"

"The mountain take them," Sanchez said.

"Like hell it did," Davis scoffed. "They're in that passage somewhere, and they've dragged Paulette with them, just to get back at me. Them Logan girls are my only legal claim to the mine. Come on, let's fire us up some torches and go lookin' for them."

"No, Señor," said Sanchez. "We do not go into the mountain. We leave this place last night because the mountain swallow two men, and the others are afraid to remain."

"So the both of you are afraid," Davis sneered.

"Only of the mountain," said Yavapai. "Not of you."

"Gary," said Rust, "seven men left for town, and there are six dead in the canyon, so that's only thirteen. Yesterday, when they came in here, there were fifteen men."

"Ah," said Yavapai, turning to Rust, "it is well not all *gringos* are fools."

"Your woman's dead, Gary," Bollinger said, "and them Logan girls hate your guts. Back in Missouri, you never cared a damn about what was legal and what wasn't. I say we find the gold if we can, and kill anybody gettin' in the way."

"He's right," said Rust. "Possession is nine-tenths of the law. With those Logan girls alive, you wouldn't get enough gold for a poker stake. They'll see you dead and in hell first."

"Suppose I admit to all that," Davis said. "Legally or illegally, how do we find the gold? Where do we start?"

"You have a map," Yavapai said, "but we do not see it."

"Half a map," corrected Davis.

"Ah," Sanchez said, "how do you know it is but half a map?"

"Because Hoss Logan *said* it's half a map," Davis growled, "and it *looks* like half a map. There's nothin' to it."

"Oh, for God's sake, Gary," said Rust in an exasperated tone, "show them the map. It's not as though we have anything to lose."

Davis took the well-creased sheet of paper from his shirt pocket and passed it to Sanchez. Yavapai moved up beside him, and together, they studied the symbols on the paper.

Chapter 5

"There be a story of long ago," Sanchez said, "of Apache warriors who be pursued by Spanish seekers of gold. There be no escape for the *Indios,* so they leap off the mountain and die."

"That be mountain called Skull Peak," Yavapai added.

"By God," said Davis excitedly, "maybe that's it! But what does the rest of the map mean?"

"Why, hell," said Bollinger, "it's a sunrise or a sunset. Take your pick."

"Maybe," Davis said, "but what does it *mean*?"

"It could designate the east or west rim of the mountain," said Rust, "depending on whether the sun is rising or setting."

"Maybe the mine's on the side where them Injuns jumped off," Bollinger said. "That could explain the skull on the map."

"No," said Davis, "that would make the rising or setting sun unnecessary. I think the skull refers to Skull Peak and the rising or setting sun means either the east or the west side of the mountain."

"Is simple," Yavapai said. "We search both these sides of the mountain."

"We ain't ready for the mountain," said Bollinger. "We got no pack mules and no horses."

"Good point," Davis said. "I want you and Barry to head for town. Get us a pack mule and some horses. Be as quiet about it as you can, and get back here fast. We got to move our saddles, packs, and bedrolls out of this

canyon before the sheriff comes lookin' for these hombres the Apaches scalped."

Rust and Bollinger didn't relish the walk to town, and
they trusted Gary Davis about as far as Davis trusted
them. Still, they needed horses. While Davis might eventually double-cross them, he was in no position to do so
now. So they started out, hoping to avoid some of the
merciless heat the Arizona sun would unleash later in
the day.

By the time Dallas and Arlo reached the upper region
of the mountain, the distant gunfire had ceased.

"It's all over but the burying, I reckon," Arlo said.
"Knowin' Apaches, I'd gamble that whoever's still alive
is also afoot. I think if we keep a sharp watch, we'll see
somebody hoofin' it for town pronto. We might get some
idea as to who survived."

They watched for almost two hours before seeing
seven tiny dots moving westward. Soon they were lost
among the mesquite and paloverde.

"That's got to be what's left of that bunch from town,"
said Dallas, "and that means they've lost eight men since
yesterday."

"We've seen the last of them, I think," Arlo said. "If
they were just interested in more horses, they wouldn't
all be walking to town. I'd say they've pulled out for
good."

"Unless some of that seven is Davis's bunch," said
Dallas.

"Not so," Arlo said. "Look."

A pair of tiny figures plodded slowly westward and
were soon lost in the distance.

"I'd say that's Rust and Bollinger," said Arlo. "They're
probably being sent to town for horses and a pack mule.
That means we're not likely to run into the Davis outfit
anytime soon."

But he was wrong. When Dallas and Arlo returned to
their hidden camp, they stopped dead in their tracks.
Paiute wasn't alone—Kelly and Kelsey Logan were

there. They sprang to their feet with relieved cries at the sight of the two cowboys. Paiute sat with his old hat tipped over his eyes, seeming not to notice.

"Dear God," Kelsey cried, "are we glad to see you!"

"We're just as glad to see you," replied Arlo. "But how do we tell you apart?"

"Kelly has a birthmark just below her belly button. I don't."

The cowboys blushed and the girls laughed. Then the conversation turned serious.

"Who is he?" Kelly asked, pointing to Paiute.

"That's Paiute," said Arlo. "The last twenty years of your uncle's life, Paiute was with him. He's mute, unable to talk."

"He scared us half to death," Kelsey said. "We fought him, but he tied our hands and made us walk for miles through the dark."

"Tell us everything that's happened," said Dallas. "We'll listen while the two of you talk. Then we'll answer your questions and tell you as much as we know about all this."

Kelly and Kelsey talked for more than an hour, taking turns telling of events up to and including the killing of Paulette Davis.

"It was all so strange," said Kelly. "After he—Paiute—forced us back into the dark passage, he tied us so we couldn't get loose. He lit a piece of pine so we wouldn't be alone in the dark, and then he returned to the cavern. When he came back, he had Mother—Mother's body—all wrapped in blankets. We watched him find a place for her in another passage, and . . . and that's where we left her. He untied our feet and led us here."

"I'm glad he took Mother away," Kelsey said. "I want Gary Davis to wonder for the rest of his rotten life what became of her. I want him always to be afraid when he hears a sound in the night."

"I wouldn't be surprised if that's what Paiute had in mind," said Arlo. "He's a sensitive old fellow, and bein' honest, I have to tell you this was entirely his idea."

"We wanted to rescue you," Dallas added hastily, "but we hadn't come up with a plan. Paiute heard us talking, and he knows these mountains well enough that he was able to get to you. God, that was beautiful, the way he slipped both of you away and then took your mother's body."

"Like Kelly told you," said Kelsey, "our mother wasn't true to our daddy, and we hated her for it. Still, she deserved better than Gary Davis. Please, if we never find Uncle Henry's gold, keep us hidden until we're old enough to be on our own."

"There may or may not be a mine," Arlo said. "I believe there is, and I can't escape the feeling that Hoss— your Uncle Henry—is using it to lure Davis to these mountains. Hoss knew or suspected what Davis had done, and somehow Hoss aimed for him to pay. I don't think Gary Davis will leave the Superstitions alive."

"The Superstitions," Kelly shuddered. "Lord, how well the name suits them."

"They have a long and sometimes bloody history," said Arlo. "There's always been an air of mystery surrounding them, and the Apaches have added to it by denying any knowledge of strange deaths and disappearances. To them, the mountains are sacred, the home of their Thunder God."

"It's hard not to believe in the Thunder God," Kelly said. "Uncle Henry told us the legends, and when we first entered the cavern, I felt something I can't really explain. It was like there was some presence we couldn't see, but it made itself felt."

"It touched me the same way," said Kelsey, "but that Indian attack was real, and so was the shot that killed Mother. The Thunder God may get credit, but he had some help."

"With scalped dead men for evidence," Dallas said, "I don't see how the Apaches can lay this on the Thunder God. Those hombres bound for town will have a story to tell."

"He's right," said Arlo, "and that's something we

haven't told you. We spent some time on the rim this morning looking for survivors. First we saw seven men afoot, heading for town, and not too far behind them, two more. We judged the seven to be all that was left of the bunch who followed us from town, while the last two were probably Rust and the gunslinger, Bollinger. We think that means those men who trailed us have given up. We know Davis is still alive and still here, so that tells us he aims to stay. He's sent to town for horses."

"There's Yavapai and Sanchez," Kelsey said. "Davis had a falling-out with them, and they joined the men from town."

"Thieves fall out," said Arlo, "but necessity can unite them again. I won't be too surprised to find Davis trailing with those Mex owl-hoots again. The Apache threat bein' what it is, they'll need one another. Even then, five of them against God knows how many Apaches is poor odds."

"They'll likely hole up in that cavern," Dallas offered.

"I doubt it," said Arlo. "Not after Kelly and Kelsey and their mother's body vanished from there without a trace."

"You don't know Gary Davis," Kelly said. "He's a conceited fool who has no belief in anything or anybody stronger than himself."

"Maybe," replied Arlo, "but he'll have to reckon with Yavapai and Sanchez. They're a pair of no-account owl-hoots, but they'll be superstitious. I don't think they'll be comfortable in a cavern where three people disappeared in a matter of minutes."

"Now that you mention it," Dallas said, "that's all it'll take to drive Davis away from that canyon. Like it or not, when Sheriff Wheaton learns seven people are dead, he'll have to ride out here. I wouldn't want to have to answer the questions the sheriff will be askin' Davis if he's around. Those men on their way to town can verify the Apache killings, but who's going to believe Kelly and Kelsey just vanished into thin air? And what about Mrs. Davis? By God, old Paiute's sharper than any of us."

"He takes some getting used to," said Kelly. "After all his years in these mountains, do you think he has some . . . understanding with the Apaches?"

"We've wondered about that," Arlo said. "I'd have a hard time believin' the Apaches don't know every crack and crevice, and I don't doubt for a minute they know we're here. We don't know, and may never know how Paiute figures into it. Only Hoss could tell us."

"I wish we could have come here while he was alive," said Kelsey. "He told us so much about these mountains, about Arizona, I feel like we've just been away for a while, and that we've come home."

"This *is* home," Kelly said. "There's nothing left for us in Missouri."

"What of your mother's people?" Dallas asked.

"Her parents are dead," said Kelly, "and we've never been close to her brothers and sisters. We don't even know how to reach them, to tell them she's gone."

"One thing you haven't told us," Kelsey said. "How did you know about the symbols on our half of the map?"

Arlo laughed. "Just a lucky guess. Here, take a look at our half."

He handed the folded paper to Kelsey, and Kelly moved over beside her.

"Why, it's the same map Uncle Henry sent us!" Kelly cried.

"Of course it is," said Arlo, "and that's why we think Hoss had a lot more in mind than just seein' that you and Kelsey inherited his claim. We can follow this map as far as it takes us, but it won't take us to the gold, if there is any. Has Davis tried to use his map?"

"I don't think so," Kelsey said. "There's so little of it—just the few symbols—that he thinks it's of no use to him without the part that you have. That's why he tried so hard to follow you, and why he almost killed us all, trying to find you after you got away during the night."

"It *does* seem that Uncle Henry had more on his mind that just leaving Kelsey and me an inheritance," said Kelly. "He sent Gary Davis—through us—enough of a map to lure him to the Superstitions, but left him believing he couldn't find the gold because he had only half the map. That led him to you, and you've stolen us away from him. I just wish Uncle Henry knew how well it's all working out."

"Don't get excited yet," Arlo said. "We still haven't found the gold."

"But we're free of Gary Davis," Kelsey said, "and that's worth more than all the gold in Arizona."

The seven men who had survived the Indian attack and had given up the search for Hoss Logan's mine went immediately to the sheriff's office. Sheriff Wheaton wasted no time in relaying the grim news to the families and friends of the dead men. The bodies, having lain out in the Arizona sun most of the day, would have to be buried on the spot. The sheriff didn't relish the idea of riding into the Superstitions alone, so he decided he must accompany the burial party. He had gone to the livery for his horse, when Barry Rust and R. J. Bollinger arrived. Footsore and weary, they didn't realize the sheriff was there until Wheaton had seen them.

"Well, now," said Sheriff Wheaton, "this is convenient. What can you boys tell me about that Apache attack this morning?"

"Nothing you don't already know," Rust said shortly. "Paulette Davis was killed, and our horses and pack mule were stolen."

"You're needin' horses, then," said the sheriff. "Well, I'm ridin' out there with a burial party. You can travel with us. I'll want to talk to Davis while I'm there."

"Damn it," Bollinger said when the sheriff had ridden away. "Gary's gonna be mad as hell when we show up with the law."

"Gary's always mad as hell about something," said Rust wearily. "It'll be worth all the shouting and hell-raising just to hear him explain what became of Kelly and Kelsey Logan."

"Yeah," Bollinger grinned. "It's gonna seem like,

what with their mama gone, old Gary decided to rid himself of the daughters. Who's goin' to believe they just flat disappeared? There's nobody can tell the truth of it but you, me, Gary, and that pair of Mexicans. You reckon this lawman will believe any of us?"

Rust didn't consider that worthy of a reply.

Two hours shy of sundown, Dallas and Arlo went up on the rim and turned their eyes west, peering through shimmering heat waves.

"It's gettin' late," Dallas said. "They might not make it back today."

"Maybe not the sheriff," said Arlo, "but there'll be somebody comin' to bury those dead men. Nobody could stand getting close to the bodies in this heat, and tonight there'll be coyotes."

"Hey," Dallas exclaimed suddenly, "I thought I saw somethin' out there. It's hard to tell, though, lookin' into the sun, with the heat dancin' a jig."

They soon sighted a series of distant bobbing specks that finally became horsemen, fifteen of them in all.

"I'd bet one of them is Sheriff Wheaton," said Arlo, "and that at least two more will be R. J. Bollinger and Barry Rust. The others will be gravediggers."

"I'm surprised that Bollinger and Rust are ridin' back with the others," Dallas replied.

"I'd say Sheriff Wheaton will have some questions for Gary Davis. Especially when he learns Kelly and Kelsey have disappeared."

"There had to be an uproar in town when those seven men showed up afoot, bringing news of the Apache killings," said Arlo. "It's just a village, not big enough for Bollinger and Rust to slip in, buy horses, and then leave without being seen. I'm surprised they could even *find* any extra horses."

"I hope none of that bunch comes nosin' around up here," Dallas said. "I want Paiute to have a look at that skull that shows up at sunset. Kelly and Kelsey can see it too."

"If there's a chance of any of us being seen, we'll have to skip this sunset," warned Arlo. "Now that we have Kelly and Kelsey with us, it's more important than ever that nobody knows where we are. Without the girls to claim the mine as an inheritance, Davis is just another claim jumper. With Kelly and Kelsey, we have control of the mine."

"Legally," Dallas said, "but out here the law belongs to the hombre with the fastest gun. I think when we're down to the last hand, that hand will be holdin' a Colt."

Arlo and Dallas returned to their camp. It soon would be time to take Paiute, Kelly, and Kelsey up to the mountain rim for a few dramatic moments with the setting sun.

"We were starting to wonder about you," said Kelsey.

"We've been watching for riders from town," Arlo said, "and they're on the way. We counted fifteen. We figure one of them is the sheriff, and another two are probably Barry Rust and R. J. Bollinger. The rest we're thinkin' are gravediggers. We're hoping they'll stay in the canyon and not come near the rim."

"Is there a chance they might find us?" Kelly asked.

"Not unless we're seen," said Arlo. "We just don't want them up here on the rim. Come sundown, we're going to show you as much as your Uncle Henry's map can tell you. We want Paiute there too."

When it was time to go to the rim, Dallas went first to be sure the way was clear. Arlo came last, following Paiute, Kelly, and Kelsey. They all joined Dallas at the place where he and Arlo had seen the death's head in the setting sun.

"There's lots of other peaks out there," Arlo said, "but there's five that seem to stand almost shoulder to shoulder. Keep your eyes on that one in the middle. Once the setting sun dips toward the horizon, we'll have only two or three minutes."

Slowly the sun crept toward the horizon. The shadowy top of the skull appeared first, then the hollow eyes, the gaping mouth, and finally the bony chin.

"Dear God," said Kelsey in awe, "it's the skull from the map!"

Arlo touched Paiute's arm, pointing to the image. The old Indian stumbled back, a look of sheer terror on his wrinkled face. He turned and literally ran to the canyon rim, disappearing into their hidden cavern.

"It's going away!" Kelly cried.

The image vanished as it had appeared, the top of the skull fading first. As the sun dipped out of sight, shadows claimed the land and the distant peak became as barren as those surrounding it.

"We know where the mine is!" Kelsey said excitedly.

"I don't think so," replied Arlo. "There may be clues to the mine, and there may be much more than that. Paiute's no coward, but there's something about that mountain that just scared the hell out of him."

"He can't talk," Dallas said, "but I was hopin' we could learn something from him when he saw that death's head."

"We're learning plenty from him," said Arlo, "but I don't think he knows what Hoss may have planned. Some Indians claim that the spirit voices of the old ones warn them in time of danger. Maybe these spirit voices are sending Paiute messages he can't understand, and somehow this death's head he just saw opened some doors."

"My God!" Kelsey shivered. "Why don't we just forget the gold and go away?"

"We can't," said Arlo. "Not without lettin' Hoss Logan down. He dealt us a hand, and we have to play it out. None of us would ever be satisfied if we just rode away. I reckon we started this for Hoss's sake, but we have to finish it for our own."

"Uncle Henry told us you were cowboys," Kelly said. "Don't you have a ranch somewhere, with horses and cows?"

"No," said Dallas sheepishly, "we . . ."

"The truth is," Arlo interrupted, "we started out as cowboys, and we still know more about cows than we like to admit. We thought we was comin' up in the world when we started us a freight line. We got starved out of that, and ended up with two wagonloads of barrel whiskey. We took over the Gila Saloon, in Tortilla Flat, to sell the whiskey. One night last April somebody shot a slick-dealin' gambler, there was a brawl, and the place burnt to the ground. We come out of it with our horses, saddles, and close to two hundred dollars, and that's all."

Dallas was profoundly embarrassed at Arlo's frankness. The girls' beauty seemed to have disarmed Arlo completely.

"We'd better get back to our camp," Dallas said. "Paiute lit out like his shirttail was afire, and I'd like to see how he faces us."

"I feel sorry for him," said Kelsey. "He can't talk, and so he can't tell us what's bothering him. I can't understand why Uncle Henry never spoke of him to us."

"Hoss never explained Paiute to anybody," Arlo said. "He was always with Hoss, and everybody kind of took him for granted, includin' us. They were like a pair of old lobo wolves, comfortable with one another, not much carin' what anybody thought or said."

"I believe Hoss had some way of talking to that old Indian," said Dallas. "When he brought us the map and the letter from Hoss, Paiute just latched on to us, and he's been around ever since. It's like he's been told to stick with us—and who could have told him that but Hoss?"

"Perhaps he knows more about the gold than you think," Kelly said, "and when the time comes, he'll tell you."

"How?" Dallas asked. "He can't talk."

"Just because he hasn't," said Kelly, "doesn't mean that he can't."

"That's true," Arlo conceded. "Nobody *told* us Paiute couldn't talk. We never heard him speak, and as far as we know, nobody else has either. We just accepted his silence, figurin' he wasn't talking because he couldn't."

The anticipated confrontation with the old Indian never took place, for when they returned to their secluded camp, Paiute was gone. The fire had burned down to a few coals, and in the faint light something glittered on the stone floor. The object proved to be an old watch, enclosed in a silver case.

"That's Uncle Henry's watch!" Kelly cried.

The watch was running, its ticking seeming loud in the silence of the cavern. With trembling hands, Kelsey opened the case. Inside the lid was a faded oval photograph of Kelly and Kelsey Logan.

"We were twelve when that picture was taken," said Kelsey. "Daddy sent it to Uncle Henry at Christmas, and the last time we saw him alive, he let us open the watch and look at the picture."

For a long moment the silence was unbroken except for the ticking of the watch.

"I don't see what this has to do with anything," Dallas said, "unless Paiute's washing his hands of us and this is his way of sayin' *adios*."

"I hope he hasn't left us," Kelly said. "Since he knew Uncle Henry, and he knows these mountains, I felt better with him around."

"I think we all did," said Dallas. "He started out bein' a damn nuisance with a big appetite, but we owe a lot to him, includin' this camp that Hoss must have used."

"We'll all miss him," Arlo added. "Especially when we're wrasslin' these horses and mules to graze through that crack in the rim."

"One look at that death's head mountain scared him off," said Dallas, "so he wouldn't have been any help to us in our search for the mine. I say tomorrow we make tracks to that mountain and begin our search."

"Then let's think of some way to do it without Gary Davis seeing us," Kelly said. "I think we'll be better off if he doesn't know Kelsey and me are alive and in your camp."

"I'd have to agree," said Arlo. "The Superstitions aren't just a single mountain but a group of them. We don't know that it's even possible to reach that one mountain on horseback, especially from here. To begin with, we have to find a way down that eastern rim, without going through the canyon where the Indian attack took place. I doubt Davis will remain there, but we can't count on that. It'll be mighty inconvenient going on foot, but I think that's the best way. On foot we can drop behind rocks, brush, or paloverde if we need to, but the horses and mules wouldn't be that easy to hide."

"We could leave Kelly and Kelsey here," Dallas said. "We may have one hell of a time just gettin' to and from that mountain."

"I don't care how bad it is," declared Kelly. "I'm going with you."

"So am I," Kelsey said. "I love this country, but I'm scared to death of it. I'm glad Uncle Henry won't know what a pair of cowards we are."

"Nothin' cowardly about bein' afraid," Dallas assured her. "Especially when you're up against somethin' you don't understand. We may all be afraid, or even dead, before this is finished."

"Uncle Henry wanted you and Arlo to have half this mine," Kelly said, "with Kelsey and me taking the rest. I think we'd be shaming his memory if we didn't go with you, to fight beside you, to die if we must."

"By God," Dallas shouted, "you got Logan blood all right!" Seizing Kelly, he kissed her full on the mouth. When he came up for air, he grinned at her. "Go on and hit me," he said. "It was worth it."

"Hey," Kelsey cried, "what about *me*?"

Gleefully, Dallas released Kelly and started toward Kelsey, but Arlo got there first. "Get away from her, you hog," he said.

The canyon was already in purple shadow when the fifteen riders from town arrived. Bollinger led three horses, while Rust led the remaining two and a loaded pack mule. The dozen men who had come to dig graves dismounted, picketed their horses, and unlashed picks and shovels. Accompanied by the sheriff, Bollinger and Rust rode toward the head of the canyon. Gary Davis came out through the passage from the mountain, followed by Yavapai and Sanchez. Davis had the right sleeve of his shirt rolled nearly to the shoulder, with a bandage on his upper arm.

"I see you got a taste of Apache," said the sheriff.

"He one brave hombre," Yavapai said with a straight face. "Fight like hell."

Davis said nothing, and Sheriff Wheaton continued, "These gents you sent to town didn't tell me much. Sorry about your missus. I'll have the boys dig another grave, if you want."

"No," started Davis, "I . . ."

"The Señora Davis disappear," Sanchez interrupted helpfully. "The mountain take her and the *hijas*."

Davis threw a murderous look at Sanchez, while receiving an incredulous one from Sheriff Wheaton.

Chapter 6

"I reckon you got some explainin' to do," Sheriff Wheaton said.

"We was in that hole in the mountain," said Davis nervously, "and Paulette was hit by some ricochet lead. The girls just . . . went crazy. We left them alone with her. When we went back, they was all three gone. There's a passage that goes into the mountain . . ."

"I reckon that's the same tunnel that swallowed a couple of men last night," the sheriff said. "The seven that first brought news of the Indian attack had some wild story about Ed Carney and Hamp Evers disappearin' into that hole."

"*Si,*" said Sanchez. "Is true. We hear these screams like *El Diablo* himself have take them, and they no return. Our hombres be afraid to stay, and we leave. Is why the *Indios* find us in the canyon, while the Señor Davis hide in the mountain."

"God Almighty," Wheaton said in disgust, "none of you even made an attempt to find Ed and Hamp or the Logan girls?"

"They be gone," said Yavapai. "If we follow, we be also gone."

"Where's Wells and Holt?" Sheriff Wheaton asked. "Has the mountain swallowed them too?"

"We don't know where they are," said Davis shortly. "They left their camp on the Salt in the middle of the night, and we ain't seen 'em since."

"I'll have to go into that tunnel and at least look

around," Sheriff Wheaton said. "Will some of you go with me?"

"No, Señor." Sanchez blanched as he and Yavapai backed away, shaking their heads. "We see two hombres go in, we hear their screams, and they no come back. Also the mountain take the dead señora and the *hijas.*"

"I wouldn't believe it if I hadn't seen it," Davis said, "but I ain't settin' foot in that tunnel. I'm speakin' for Rust and Bollinger too. We can't afford to lose nobody else."

While the sheriff trusted none of them, he had no proof of any specific crime. Had they fabricated a story, anything would have been more believable than what they'd just told him. Yavapai and Sanchez were a pair of thieves and scoundrels, but Wheaton didn't believe they would lie for Gary Davis, even to save his soul from hell. The sheriff rode back down the canyon and received the response he had expected from the men digging the graves.

"It's already gittin' dark, Sheriff," said one of the men. "I ain't for stayin' here one minute longer'n it takes to plant these poor souls, and I wouldn't go wanderin' through them mountain tunnels if the whole damn United States Army was goin' with me."

The rest of the men, equally afraid, wanted only to be away from these eerie, forbidding mountains. The sheriff sighed. He dared not remain in the Superstitions alone, if for no other reason than that they might be full of Apaches. As he saw it, his duty didn't include getting himself killed in a solitary search that would likely be futile anyhow. When the dead had been buried, the sheriff and the gravediggers rode back to town.

Gary Davis and his four companions watched them go. Davis turned to Rust and Bollinger with the scolding they had expected. "I specifically told you to get into town and out without attracting attention," Davis growled, "and you come ridin' back with the sheriff."

"It's no more than a village," said Rust, "and we were seen. Wheaton was there at the livery, and he made it a point of telling us to ride back with him and the burial party."

"Next time you got business in town," Bollinger said, "go and take care of it yourself. Then if the sheriff gets bothersome, you can just gun him down."

Despite the uncertain days that they knew were ahead, Dallas, Arlo, Kelly, and Kelsey enjoyed their supper that night and the conversation that followed. Whatever ill feelings the girls had harbored toward their mother, her death had been a shock. Arlo and Dallas entertained Kelly and Kelsey with their experiences as cowboys, as teamsters, and as saloon owners, and told them everything they could remember about Hoss Logan. Finally it was late enough that they could risk taking the horses and mules to graze.

"Paiute showed us this plateau," Arlo said, "but we have to wrassle the animals through a gash in the rim, and part of the way down the mountain. Dallas and me can take the horses first, and then come back for the mules, unless you girls can handle 'em. It's a hard way to go."

"Daddy taught us to hitch up, drive, and unhitch a six-mule team," said Kelly. "Just one mule each? Anywhere those mules can go, we can take them there and bring them back."

"We'll pull our own weight," Kelsey affirmed. "Besides, we don't want to be left alone until this is finished and we're far away from Gary Davis. You're stuck with us, and until we're out of these mountains, neither of you can go anywhere without us."

"It won't be proper, us goin' with you to the bushes," said Dallas, in a joking manner.

"It's proper enough," Kelly replied, "when we're afraid to go alone, because we don't know who or what might be hiding in those bushes. Once this is all behind us, we'll go back to whatever you consider proper. Until then, let's do what's practical. Uncle Henry wouldn't argue with that."

"No," said Arlo, "I reckon he wouldn't. For now, let's take all these critters down to graze, then come back and get some sleep. We'll have to be up well before daylight, so we can bring them back in here without being seen."

Arlo and Dallas led the horses over the rim and down the hazardous trail, while Kelly and Kelsey followed with the mules. The descent posed no problem, the girls handling the mules with a skill that delighted Dallas and Arlo. Leaving the animals to graze, the four of them climbed back up the deep gash to the rim and were soon safely in their hidden cavern.

"I wish Paiute had been able to bring our bedrolls," said Kelly.

"Dallas and me can spare each of you a blanket," Arlo said. "One blanket's as good as four or five when all you've got under you is solid rock."

"I don't know if I'll sleep or not," worried Kelsey. "I can't help thinking that Yavapai or Sanchez might know of this place, and I have the awful feeling they might come in while we're asleep. Gary Davis may try to convince them he needs Kelly and me to legalize his claim to the mine."

"After the way you and Kelly disappeared, I don't think those Mex coyotes will go wanderin' through the belly of this mountain," Arlo said. "Even if they were brave enough to try it, they'd never find their way to the passage that comes out in our back wall behind the falling water. The only other way in is the passage we use, where we lead the horses and mules in and out."

"There's a bundle of rawhide strips here," said Dallas. "Why don't we rig a trip wire somewhere along the passage, stretched knee high? There's an old coffee tin we can hang on the line, and it'll make a hell of a racket on the solid rock if somebody tears that rawhide loose."

"Yes, please do it," Kelsey said. "I'd feel so much better. I might even be able to sleep."

"I feel the same way," said Kelly. "I don't think we'll ever feel safe as long as Gary Davis is alive."

"Rig it up, Dallas," Arlo said, "and set it as far out as

you can. If somebody trips it, we'll need time to grab our
Colts. Just remember to take the thing down before we
go after the horses and mules. Drop that tin on solid rock,
and in this mountain air the clatter would be heard all the
way to Tortilla Flat."

When Dallas had completed his task, the four of them
spread their blankets on the stone floor. Kelsey wriggled
over next to Arlo.

"We're dressed, except for our hats and boots," she
said, "and we're all rolled up in our blankets. Is there any
reason I can't sleep next to you?"

"None that I know of," said Arlo. "We'll be warmer,
since we each have but a single blanket."

"Kelsey," Dallas said, "you and Kelly could put your
blankets together and roll up next to one another. You'd
sleep more comfortable, and warmer too."

"Dallas," said Arlo, "will you kindly just shut up?"

Gary Davis and his cohorts spent a restless night beneath the mountain's overhang. By the time Rust and
Bollinger had returned with the horses and the sheriff
had finished questioning them, it was too late to leave the
canyon and seek another camp. Should the Apaches attack, the little group of men would have no protection
whatsoever, but even Davis had no desire to return to the
mysterious cavern where Paulette had died. Sometime
during the night, a small avalanche of gravel had rattled
down the mountainside, and the five of them had shot out
of their blankets, scrambling for their guns. They had
slept little after that, not daring to light a fire for their
breakfast coffee until it was full daylight.

"Before we even think of anything else," Davis said,
"I'm gettin' out of this damn canyon." He turned to
Yavapai and Sanchez. "You hombres know of someplace
we can hole up, maybe with some protection, near this
skull mountain?"

"We know of the mountain, Señor," said Sanchez.
"When we go there, we find camp."

"Then let's get started," Davis said. "If we dally

around till the sun's up, it'll be hot as hell with all the fires lit."

In the cavern, Dallas got up first and awakened the others. First light was little more than an hour away, and it was time to go for the horses and mules. When they returned with the animals, Dallas got their breakfast fire started, crushed the coffee beans with the butt of his Colt, and put the brew on to boil.

"Why don't you let Kelsey and me do the cooking?" Kelly suggested. "We're not bad cooks, for a pair of muleskinners."

"More of Jed Logan's doing, I reckon," said Arlo.

"Yes," Kelly said, laughing. "He wanted sons, but all he ever got was us. He did the best he could with what he had, and that was partly what drove him and Mother apart. She wanted us to be highborn ladies—or at least appear to be—and she was constantly mortified at what Daddy was doing to us. I felt like she was planning to auction us off to the highest bidders as wives to rich doctors or lawyers."

"She gave up on bettering herself through Kelly and me," said Kelsey, "and that's when she turned to Gary Davis."

"We look at women a mite different here in the West," Dallas said. "You don't have to put on airs to be considered a lady, and gettin' your hands dirty don't make you less of one. Here you can ride astraddle, fire a gun, or rope a steer, and still be as much a lady as them highfalutin gals back in St. Louis or New Orleans."

"Then you're not ashamed to be seen with a pair of female muleskinners?" asked Kelsey.

"Ma'am," Arlo said, "once we've found Hoss Logan's mine or give up ever findin' it, we'll back up our brag. You and Kelly can get all dressed up in your finery, and we'll take you to that dance in town. It's held every fourth Saturday night, and I reckon we'll have to fight every cowboy and miner there just to get a dance for ourselves."

By the time it was light enough to see, the four of them were following the eastern rim southward, seeking some point at which they might descend. They had gone well past the canyon in which the Indian attack had taken place so that when they went over the rim they would be less likely to be seen by Davis and his bunch. Being on foot, they used the jagged rent in the side of the mountain, barely wide enough for their bodies, which afforded them purchase for their hands and feet.

"Once we're down this mountain," Dallas said, "I hope we can still find the death's head peak. Damn shame we couldn't go down the rim closer to that canyon where the Davis camp is. We'd be more in a direct line with the peak we're tryin' to reach."

"It won't matter where we go down this mountain," Arlo said. "We still won't be able to travel a straight line. Not unless we come up with some way to fly. While the tops of these peaks are mostly bare rock, the vegetation along their flanks and between them may be hell to get through. We may have to fight our way through three miles of chaparral, cactus, and greasewood just to gain less than a mile as the crow would fly."

"I can believe that," said Kelly. "I'll never forget that first day Gary Davis dragged us around here on your trail. Never have I been scratched and clawed so badly. Whatever other problems we may have, I don't think we'll have to worry about discovery."

"One of the few advantages of leavin' the horses and mules behind," Dallas said. "Anybody looking for us won't expect to find us on foot."

"Even with all the ugliness, there's some beauty," noted Kelsey. "Look at the little plants with the white blossoms and spotted leaves."

"They have a strange name," Arlo said. "Even if I could remember it, I couldn't say it. The Pima Indians use those spotted leaves for a poultice that cures rattlesnake bites."

They eventually found a way down the side of the mountain that would have been totally impossible on horseback. Fortunately, Arlo and Dallas had brought their lariats.

"This is almost straight down," said Arlo, "so steep that even a muleskinner's boot might slip. Kelly, you and Kelsey are going down first, and each of you will have a rope looped around your middle. Dallas and me will follow, takin' up the slack until you reach the bottom."

"Ah don't reckon a *cowboy's* boot ever slips," Kelsey said mischievously, "but if it should, let go of the rope."

They took the descent slowly, and there was no trouble.

"Coming back," said Kelly, "if you want to knot those ropes together and raise me up to the top of the mountain, I won't complain."

"We'd do it in a minute," Dallas said, with a grin, "but they'd never reach that far. Damn it, I *told* Arlo before we started this search for gold, every cow wrassler ought to carry at least three lariats all the time, just in case."

They laughed, relieving the tension of the perilous descent. From there on, however, it proved no laughing matter, as Arlo's prediction of rough terrain became altogether too accurate. They hadn't covered a dozen yards when there was an ominous rattle that froze them all in their tracks.

"All of you stay where you are," Arlo whispered.

The rattle ceased, and so well did the deadly reptile blend into its surroundings, none of them saw it until it slithered away, disappearing into a jumble of broken rock that had at some time in the distant past tumbled down from the mountain rim high above.

"Gary Davis would have shot him," Kelly said, "or tried to."

"Fool thing to do," said Arlo, "for several reasons. If you don't crowd them, they'll go on their way and leave you alone. But you can't say that for the Apaches, and in these mountains, a single shot can draw them from miles away."

They continued on, climbing over huge masses of rock, fighting their way around all those that were impractical or impossible to climb, striving not to frighten a dozing, unseen rattler. There were dense patches of chaparral—thorny thickets—to avoid. Huge upthrusts of lava rock were a deep lavender, with bright green, yellow, and orange patches of lichen.

"Lord," said Kelsey, "I've never seen a land that's so frightening and at the same time so strangely beautiful. The saguaros are so stately . . . so majestic."

Directly ahead of them was a four-armed giant that stood against the blue of the sky like an enormous green candelabrum.

"That one's more than thirty feet high," Arlo pointed out. "I talked to a gent once that spent all his time studying them, and he said one that's topped thirty feet is about a hundred and fifty years old. That means this old boy was just a sprout when George Washington and his army whipped the British."

"My God," said Kelly, "they grow awful slow, don't they?"

"I reckon you'd grow slow, too," Dallas said, "if you just got water maybe once or twice a year."

There was prickly pear, its flat, oval lobes studded with lethal spines. Other cacti littered their path, including fishhook, pincushion, hedgehog, and the most diabolical of them all, the jumping cholla. Among the larger growth they came across sage, chaparral, coffeeberry bush, wait-a-minute bush, and greasewood. An occasional paloverde and some mesquite were also in evidence, and a single tree that Kelly and Kelsey had never seen before.

"Ironwood tree," explained Dallas. "It's so heavy it won't even float and so hard there ain't an ax or saw in the world that'll cut it. So hard, the Indians use it to make arrowheads, and they have to shape it with fire."

"From what Uncle Henry told us," Kelsey said, "we expected the two of you to be just simple cowboys. Now we find that you're . . ."

"Not as dumb as you thought we was," finished Dallas, laughing.

"Are we any closer to the mountain?" Kelly asked.

"We've come less than a mile," said Arlo. "Distances
out here can be deceiving. It's a lot farther than it looked
from our mountaintop, and we're going considerably out
of our way getting to it. Remember, there were five
peaks, and from a distance they all seemed to be in line,
shoulder to shoulder. The one we're looking for, the middle one, is somewhere east of the others."

"We got us a good camp up yonder on the rim," Dallas
said, "and I'd be the last to suggest we give it up. But I
think once we find the death's head mountain, we'd better be looking for a place to spend some nights. I ain't believin' Hoss Logan fought his way through this mess of
thickets, broken rock, and cactus every day."

"Remember," said Arlo, "Hoss wouldn't have been
dodging claim jumpers as we are. He could have traveled
more in a straight line. I wouldn't be surprised if there
are passages beneath these mountains, one connected to
the other. Neither would I be surprised if Paiute knows
most or all of them. We lost our edge when he ran out on
us, and for that reason, I'd have to agree. We do need to
search for a second secluded camp so we don't have to
make this killing hike every day."

Gary Davis and his bunch rode down the canyon, with
Yavapai and Sanchez in the lead. They were bound for
the peak that the Mexicans hoped might be the one referred to in the map. R. J. Bollinger was riding alongside
Davis.

"I don't trust these Mexican varmints," hissed Bollinger.

Davis said nothing. He didn't trust Bollinger *or* the
Mexicans—or for that matter, Barry Rust. Yavapai and
Sanchez were useful for their knowledge of the Superstitions. And for now, he needed all their guns for possible
defense against the Apaches, but once he had the gold,
he'd rid himself of the lot of them.

It was dark when Sheriff Wheaton returned from his
ride into the Superstitions. When he reached the livery,

he dismounted and began unsaddling his horse. That was
where Herk Peterson, the assayer, found him.

"This might be bad news, Sheriff," said Peterson.

"Ain't often I get any other kind," Wheaton sighed.
"I'm listenin'."

"While you was gone," said Peterson, "these jaspers
rode into town from the south. Seven of 'em, and a real
hardcase bunch if I ever saw one. Holed up at the Wagonwheel Saloon. They all got tied-down Colts, and the
leader is a gent name of Cass Bowdre. They hadn't been
here two hours when he come over to the assay office,
askin' questions."

"And I reckon he learned plenty," Wheaton said.

"Not from me," said Peterson. "Hell, Sheriff, after
them seven other gents hiked in from the Superstitions
this mornin', with news of an Injun attack, dead men, a
dead woman, and all them that was swallered by the
mountain, there ain't nothin' else bein' talked about.
Some of them that survived the Injun attack, them that
brought the news, they been over there in the Wagonwheel gettin' drunk. Old Boswell's been down there
with a whole raft of questions, diggin' up a story for his
paper."

Wheaton let out a breath and headed for the Wagonwheel Saloon, forgetting about the supper he had been
anticipating. He had heard of Cass Bowdre. The man was
a stone-cold killer, but he had always gone free on pleas
of self-defense. The men riding with him would be of the
same stripe, or worse. Wheaton hoped this undesirable
lot would just ride on, and he believed he knew what
their destination would be when they did. Peterson had
figured them right. Old Hoss Logan had raised more hell
in death than in all the years he had lived. God only knew
how many more would die in the Superstitions before the
Logan gold was either found or given up for lost.

Arlo, Dallas, Kelly, and Kelsey paused beneath a paloverde, seeking brief respite from the vengeful sun. They

were at last in a position to see the mountain they were trying to reach.

"God," Dallas said, "up close, it looks even worse. There might not *be* a way into it."

"Right now," said Kelsey with a sigh, "I'd trade the gold for a long drink of cold water. Or even warm water."

"We're going to find a source of water," Arlo said, "before we so much as *think* of anything else."

"You and Dallas seem so . . . resourceful," said Kelly. "When you came into the Superstitions, why in the world didn't you bring any canteens?"

"Because Hoss never carried one," Arlo replied. "There's water in the Superstitions, if you know where to look. In this heat water evaporates fast. Even if we could carry it, we'd each need at least a gallon a day just to replace what we lose. And a gallon of water weighs ten pounds."

They trudged on. Then without warning, an arrow ripped into a saguaro a few paces ahead, another snatched off Dallas's hat, and a third tore a gash along Arlo's left sleeve. There was no time for talk. Dallas grabbed Kelly, Arlo got Kelsey, and the four of them went down. The only cover was a dense thicket of chaparral, and they wriggled into it.

"Dear God!" Kelsey whispered. "What now?"

"We wait," said Arlo. "We don't know how many we're up against or where they are."

"What . . . are they going to do?" Kelly stammered fearfully.

"Surround us," said Dallas.

Knowing it for the futile gesture it was, Arlo and Dallas drew their Colts. It would be only a matter of time— a *short* time—until their adversaries crept through the brush and surrounded them.

"Oh, for our packs," Kelly whispered, "where our pistols are."

"If there's enough of them to surround us," said Dallas, "two more guns wouldn't make much difference.

They can fill us full of arrows before we even have anything to shoot at."

"We're in no position to fight," Arlo said grimly. "We might get a couple of them, but they could slaughter all of us. We'll have to put away our guns, try to look peaceful, and talk our way out of this."

"I don't speak a word of Apache," said Dallas, "and unless you been holdin' out on me, neither do you."

"Thanks to the conquistadores," Arlo said, "most Indians know a little Spanish, and I'm countin' on that."

There was no wind, and even in the shade of the chaparral thicket the heat soon became all but unbearable. Cautiously Dallas holstered his Colt and Arlo followed suit. Sudden movement might draw fire. Arlo spoke out.

"Bueno amigos, en paz."

Dallas's prediction proved accurate, for when the Apaches appeared, they seemed to converge from all directions. There were eight of them, every one with a Bowie in his hand, and they had the ominous look of a scalping party. None of them wore more than loincloth and moccasins, and only one had an eagle feather in his hair. It was their move. Dallas and Arlo said nothing, waiting. The eyes of the Apaches were on Kelly and Kelsey. Eagle Feather came close to Kelsey, running his fingers through her fair hair, which sparkled in the sun. The Indian said something, and his comrades responded with what seemed like bawdy remarks. Encouraged, the Apache took a handful of Kelsey's hair, as though he intended to scalp her. Kelsey cried out, swung her small fist, and sent blood spurting from his smashed nose. The Indian stared at her in disbelief while his companions laughed. It was too much. With knives suddenly at their throats, Arlo and Dallas watched the Apache seize the front of Kelsey's shirt and rip it open. The girl was now bare to the waist, but the Indians seemed to have lost interest in her. Their eyes were on Hoss Logan's old silver-encased watch, which Kelsey wore around her neck on a leather thong. They seemed to recognize it.

The Apache who had made the discovery leaned close,

as though listening to Kelsey's heartbeat, but in reality listening to the ticking of the watch. When he backed away, another Indian took his place. Once they had withdrawn enough for her to do so, Kelsey pursued her small advantage. She snapped open the watch case, revealing the face of the instrument along with the old photograph of Kelly and herself. Again the Apaches crowded close. It was almost comical, the way they looked from the photograph to the girls and then back to the photograph. They talked among themselves, and while their captives understood not a word, they began to breathe easier. The Indians had clearly made a connection between the girls and Hoss Logan's watch. Then, without a word or a backward glance, they were gone.

"Well," said Dallas, finally, "now we know why Paiute left us the watch."

"Yes," Arlo said, "and we've learned something more about Hoss. He didn't spend all those years in these mountains without some understanding with the Apaches. Whatever his medicine was, it's strong enough to reach beyond the grave to protect Kelly and Kelsey."

"I don't know whether to be relieved or insulted," said Kelsey, pulling the ruined shirt together. "When he ripped my shirt open, none of them had the slightest interest in anything except Uncle Henry's watch."

"Don't feel too let down," Kelly said. "This pair of cowboys did enough looking for every Indian in Arizona, and they weren't looking at Uncle Henry's watch. You've had your turn. Now let me wear it a while."

"I'll trade it to you for your shirt," said Kelsey. "Mine has no buttons now."

"These thorns are like needles," Arlo said. "Take some of them and fasten your shirt together. They'll hold until we get back to camp, and then I'll let you have an extra shirt of mine. Now let's move on to that mountain and find some water."

Chapter 7

Yavapai and Sanchez led the way, with Davis, Rust, and Bollinger following close behind. The going got so bad at times that the men were forced to dismount and lead their horses and the pack mule.

"Dammit," Bollinger complained, "there oughta be some better way of gettin' there."

"Per'ap there be," said Sanchez cheerfully, "and you be welcome to look for it, Señor Bollinger."

"Is that the one?" Davis asked, pointing toward a peak ahead of them.

"No," said Yavapai. "That be what is call Weaver's Needle. We not go so far."

The mountain they sought, when they reached it, looked far less imposing than the one they'd just left. At its foot were jumbles of rock, a result of avalanches from the rim, and no evidence of any passage that might suggest a mine. They rode on, and when they eventually found water, it was but a shallow seep at the head of a narrow canyon. There was no natural shelter and no protection from attack.

"Damn," said Davis. "We're in the wide open. Injuns can come at us from anywhere, includin' the top of the mountain."

"But there be water, Señor," Sanchez said. "If you wish to hide in the mountain, per'ap you return to him that take the señora and the señoritas."

"Hell, Gary," said Bollinger in disgust, "are you *that* much of a damn greenhorn? The worst place a man can settle for the night is right at some water hole. We can water here and spread our blankets somewhere else."

"I'm fed up with you talkin' down to me like you're my daddy," Davis growled.

"Was I your daddy," said Bollinger with a nasty laugh, "I'd take a switch to you. Reckon it wouldn't be near as hard on you as havin' me gut-shoot you."

"Before I leave these mountains," Davis seethed, "I may do some gut-shootin' of my own."

"When you're ready," Bollinger replied steadily. "Just try to remember my guts is in the front, not the back."

Disgusted at their bickering, Barry Rust wheeled his horse and rode back toward the mountain they'd been seeking. Davis galloped after him.

"Where are you going?" Davis demanded.

Rust reined in and kneed his horse around until he faced Davis.

"By God," said Rust, "I've had enough. How can I trust either of you when you don't trust one another? I'm going back to Missouri."

He paused, expecting some objection, but there was none. Yavapai, Sanchez, and Bollinger had reined in a dozen yards behind Davis.

"Go on," Davis invited. "I'm sick of your whining."

Rust hesitated, uncertain. A bluff was only good until somebody called it. Now he had to fish or cut bait. He turned his horse and rode away. Gary Davis drew his Colt and fired twice. Rust slumped forward, his arms around the neck of the horse. One of the bullets had broken his spine. Spooked by the smell of blood and death, the horse galloped away, spilling the dying Rust from the saddle. Davis turned his horse, his Colt covering the men behind him. When he spoke, his hard eyes were on Bollinger.

"It wasn't to my advantage, havin' him return to Missouri, and I feel the same about you. Keep that in mind."

"You double-crossing son of a bitch," said Bollinger. "When I'm ready to ride, you won't stop me. I aim to kill you before I go."

"What's wrong with right now?" Davis taunted, holstering his Colt. "Are you afraid, mister fast gun?"

But Bollinger made no move for his gun. Instead, he carefully took the makings from his shirt pocket and deftly rolled a quirly. Only then did he speak.

"My time, my place, Gary. I'm like a kid waitin' for Christmas. Just the thinkin' of it, the lookin' forward to it, is as pleasurable as the thing itself. I'm the cat, Gary, and you're the mouse. I'll kill you a thousand times before you finally die."

Yavapai and Sanchez looked at one another. These *gringos* were so *malo loco,* they had forgotten everything but their hatred for one another. Their eyes were alight with madness.

"Madre de Dios," said Sanchez softly, "when the time have come amigo, I think we have just one *gringo* to kill."

When Sheriff Wheaton elbowed his way into the Wagonwheel Saloon, he had no trouble recognizing Cass Bowdre. The man had just ordered drinks for two of those who had left the Superstitions after surviving the Indian attack. When Bowdre's companions saw Sheriff Wheaton enter the saloon, they edged quietly away. Cass Bowdre was a big man, and none of it was fat. He was maybe thirty, black hair curling down over the collar of his denim shirt. A day's growth of whiskers left his face with a blue tint. His nose had once been squashed flat, and it had never recovered. His rough-out boots were worn and run-over, and his Levi's were faded white in places. An old black Stetson, dusty and sweat-stained, was shoved back on his head. The polished walnut butt of his tied-down Colt flashed in the light from an overhead lamp. But the sheriff's eyes dwelt the longest on Bowdre's hands. His nails were manicured, the fingers without callus or rope burn. They were not the hands of a working cowboy but the soft hands of a gambler. Or a killer.

"I reckon you're Bowdre," said the sheriff. "I'm Wheaton, sheriff of Gila County."

"I won't say I'm pleased," Bowdre replied, "because I just ain't that big a liar. So you've heard of me."

"Yes," Wheaton said, "and I hope you're just passing through, because you and your bunch ain't welcome here. Tomorrow I'll expect you to ride on and take your friends with you."

"Well, now," said Bowdre, with a nasty half smile, "you're in luck. We always like to cooperate with the law. Matter of fact, we got business elsewhere, and we do aim to ride out in the morning. Buy you a drink, Sheriff?"

"No," Wheaton said. The rest of Bowdre's bunch eyed him from the corner of the saloon as he turned and left. Walking back to his office, he silently cursed Hoss Logan's mysterious mine, the greed that drew men to gold like flies to honey, and the fact that the Superstition Mountains were within his jurisdiction.

Shaded by a chaparral thicket, the shallow stone basin still held water from the recent storm, but the surface was entirely covered by thick green scum. When Dallas took a stick and swept the muck aside, water bugs skittered away. Arlo laughed as Kelly and Kelsey eyed the water distastefully.

"My God," said Kelly, "do you intend to drink *that*?"

"It's wet," Dallas replied. "Close your eyes. Forget how it looks."

"In this country," said Arlo, "the worse it looks, the safer it is to drink. Find a clear pool, and it may be so loaded with alkali that it's unfit for man or beast. Or it may contain enough arsenic to kill you stone dead. Always look for tadpoles or water bugs, and be thankful when you find them. If they can live in the water, it's safe for you."

"Belly down," Dallas instructed, "close your eyes, and drink. The water bugs will get out of your way."

Thirst overcame their objections, and the girls drank.

Dallas and Arlo took their turns and then the four of them moved on.

"I can stand that once in a while," said Kelsey with a shudder, "but let's find some clean running water for next time. Without the bugs."

"We're lucky we have fresh running water in our camp," Arlo said, "and we have Paiute to thank for leading us to it. When we're away from that, we have to take our chances. As well as Hoss Logan knew these mountains, any sign directing us to the gold may also lead us to a source of fresh water."

Somewhere to the north there were two shots.

"That's got to be one of the Davis bunch. Can't be another Apache attack, or there'd be more shooting," said Dallas.

"They're damn fools to be shooting at anything *less* than Apaches," Arlo said. "Every Indian for miles will have heard those shots."

When they reached the mountain whose western face briefly reflected the death's head at sunset, they got a rude shock, for it appeared unscalable.

"Great God," Dallas groaned, "it's straight up."

"How did Uncle Henry get to that death's head up there?" Kelly wondered.

"He didn't," said Arlo. "He just discovered it. Strange as it seems, it has to be something the elements—wind and rain—have created over the centuries. A hundred years from now, it will likely be changed, becoming just meaningless shadows. I have a feeling that whatever message Hoss left for us won't be on this side of the mountain. Let's work our way around far enough for a look at the rest of it."

The sun was noon-high by the time they were able to see the eastern side of the mountain. There was a scattered mass of rock along the foot of it and, higher up, jutting shelves and ragged holes where the fallen debris had been torn loose.

"Thank God it's got *some* slope to it," Dallas said. "It won't be easy gettin' up to that first ledge, but from there on, we can just about reach the next one by followin' the one below it. It's odd how the rock's been torn away like that, one jagged gash kind of anglin' into the next."

"Some of these rockslides were caused by lightning," said Arlo. "See that white blaze up near the top? I'd bet that's where lightning struck and broke away that big piece of rock."

"The last time we saw Uncle Henry," Kelsey said, "he was having trouble with his knees. Rheumatism, he thought. I don't believe he could have gone up there."

"Smart thinking," said Arlo, "and that tells us there's another way. Maybe a passage, but it's of no help to us, since we don't know where it originates. I'd gamble that somewhere on the face of this mountain, these rockslides have created access to that interior passage. While Hoss was unable to get to it from the outside, he knew we could."

"When we reach the passage," Kelly cried, "we can follow it to the mine!"

"Whoa, little lady," said Arlo. "It may lead us to another of Hoss's hidden camps, or maybe just to some more clues, but not directly to the mine. Remember, Davis has as much map as we do, and sooner or later, he's going to at least try to figure it out. He *could* get this far, and for that reason, I look for things to get damned complicated from here on."

"We have time enough to explore some of those cuts and crevices," Dallas said. "If there is a passage and we can find it, our next trip won't be as tough. By tomorrow, Davis and his bunch may have worked their way this far south. They won't have to be too smart to discover us climbing up this mountain."

"Lord," said Kelly, "that means we have to find that passage today or risk having them follow us."

"Then let's climb that mountain," Kelsey cried, "before they find us."

Again the lariats came into play, for the first break in the side of the mountain was a dozen feet above their heads.

"Sure ain't much up there to dab a loop on," said Dallas doubtfully. "That little stone knob ain't standin' as high as the crown of my hat."

"It's tall enough," Arlo said. "But the way this rock breaks up and falls, it could snap under your weight and drop you headfirst into a pile of jagged stone."

"Kelsey or me can go up first," said Kelly, "and there won't be as much weight on the rope. Once one of us is up there, we can loop the rope around something more solid."

"So one of you could end up with a broken neck, instead of one of us," Dallas said. "It don't seem right, us standin' by, lettin' you take such a risk."

"We're all in this together," said Kelly with fire in her eyes, "and that means we share the risk. I'd rather break my neck than be a helpless female who's afraid to move without some man having a grip on my shirttail."

"That goes for me too," Kelsey assured them. "I can climb that rope as quick as any of you."

Dallas dropped his loop over the nub of rock, but the rope jumped off. He tried again with the same result.

"Let me try," said Arlo.

"No," Dallas said, his pride at stake. "I can do it. Loop's too wide."

He reduced the size of the loop until it seemed barely large enough to drop over the protruding stone. The throw was more difficult, but it was successful, and this time it held. Dallas took a step up the mountain, throwing all his weight on the rope, and it seemed secure.

"Solid enough," said Arlo.

"Even if it is, I still want to go up first," said Kelly.

Dallas stepped back, and without a word, handed her the end of the rope. He looked at Arlo, and his partner winked. They would allow these females to prove themselves and get it over with. Hand over hand, Kelly walked up the side of the mountain to the first jagged break.

"I don't see anything else to fasten the rope to," she called down.

"Then leave it where it is," Arlo said. "How far back into the mountain does that cut go?"

"Not even deep enough to get out of the rain," answered Kelly.

"I'm going up next," Kelsey said.

"Go on," said Arlo. He still had his own lariat coiled over his shoulder. Before they were done, they might need it.

Kelsey reached the first ledge as easily as Kelly had, and Dallas went next. When Arlo made the ascent, Dallas loosened his lariat, and they began looking to the next level in their climb.

"It's gonna be damn funny," Dallas said, "if we fight our way to the top of this thing and don't find a hole big enough for a prairie dog to squeeze through."

"You can do my share of the laughing," said Kelly. "If we're to believe the map with the death's head, there has to be something here."

They reached the next level without using the lariats. Earth and rock had been torn loose in such a way that the second crevice angled downward into one end of the first, like a giant V laid on its side.

"That was too easy," Kelsey said. "We won't find anything here."

She was right. They began looking for some means of climbing higher.

"From here on," said Dallas, "it won't be easy gettin' a loop on anything. Step back far enough for a good throw, and you'll fall off the mountain."

"How disappointing," Kelly mocked. "Uncle Henry was always telling us a cowboy could rope *anything*, even standing on his head."

She tried to keep a straight face, but Dallas looked at her in such a way that she had to laugh. They soon discovered, though, that there was nothing amusing about their situation. The next gap in the side of the mountain was a good twenty feet above their heads, without any apparent abutment they could rope from below.

"One of us is goin' to have to lizard his way up there and find a nub of rock that'll hold a loop," Arlo said.

"Hold it," said Dallas. "There's riders coming."

Four rode in from the north.

"Flatten out along this ledge," Arlo said quickly, "and don't move. Let's just hope they don't ride close and look up."

The four rode on, but came close enough to be spotted. Yavapai and Sanchez were leading, Gary Davis and R. J. Bollinger following.

"Barry Rust is missing," said Kelsey.

"Those pistol shots we heard might explain that," Arlo said. "Might have been a disagreement that ended in a shoot-out."

"Murder, maybe," said Kelly, "but no shoot-out. Barry carried a gun, but he was no gunman. He and Bollinger were always fighting with Davis over something. Or nothing at all."

"If Davis did something as brutal as that," Kelsey said, "I can't believe Bollinger, Yavapai, and Sanchez would still be with him. How could they trust such a cruel devil of a man?"

"Thieves and killers have a tolerance for one another," said Dallas, "until it suits their purpose to split the blanket."

"That's gospel," Arlo said. "Let that bunch come within hollerin' distance of gold, and none of their lives will be worth a plugged *peso*. Those Mex owl-hoots will be out to kill Bollinger and Davis, while Bollinger and Davis will be gunning for the Mexicans, as well as one another."

"Thank God we're away from them," said Kelly. "Mother allowed Davis to slap us around and punish us, but he never tried to . . . take advantage of us. But with Mother gone, he'd have moved in on us. Him and Bollinger both."

"Davis accused us of wanting to become camp whores," Kelsey said. "Once he learns we're alive and sharing your camp, he'll destroy us."

"Not if somebody destroys him first," said Dallas. "In the West, a man that mistreats a woman had better keep him a set of buryin' clothes handy."

"Davis and his pards are gone," Arlo said. "We'd better try to finish our climb before they ride back. They may be looking for a place near water to set up their camp."

"I don't see any holds for hands or feet up there," said Kelly, "but one of us has to reach that ledge and secure a rope. I'm willing to try."

"It's my turn," Arlo said, "and I'm goin' at it the way I used to climb trees when I was a youngun."

He sat down and worked off his boots. His heels and big toes had eaten their way through his socks.

"Careful you don't rip your socks on the way up," said Dallas dryly.

"Shut up," Arlo said, "or I'll let *you* do this, and we'll see what kind of shape *your* socks are in."

Standing on Dallas's shoulders, Arlo explored the mountain's face until he found protruding rock that his hands could grip. He hoisted himself upward, and incredibly, his bare feet sought and found support. Like an enormous spider, he slid to the edge, reaching up when he had a strong enough hold. Below, Dallas and the girls held their breath, releasing a threefold sigh when Arlo got one hand on the ledge he had to reach. He got a leg up, pulled himself over the edge, and lay there fighting for his wind. When he had his strength back, he sleeved the sweat out of his eyes and looked around. Lightning had undoubtedly struck the mountain at this point, for a substantial amount of earth and rock had been torn loose. The gash hadn't been fully visible from below because it was hidden by the protruding lip over which he had climbed. It looked as though the Almighty might have driven a huge shovel into the mountainside from above, tearing into the wall at a downward angle. Quickly Arlo found a jutting finger of rock and secured the end of the rope to it. Then he turned to his anxious companions below and dropped the loose end of the rope to them.

"I think this is it," Arlo said. "Come on up, and don't forget to bring my boots."

Kelsey came first, then Kelly, and finally Dallas. Arlo pulled on his boots, and they turned to the hole that had been torn into the side of the mountain. The aperture didn't open straight out, but veered to the left, and there was barely room for them to move on hands and knees. Arlo went first, followed by Dallas, Kelsey, and Kelly. Strangely, as they progressed, the darkness became less intense. Suddenly Arlo paused, startled by the eerie, macabre item resting directly in their path. It was a human skeleton with the skull missing. Arlo attempted to shove the skeleton aside, but the ghastly thing was unable to survive the movement. It crumbled into an array of individual bones.

"Bones ahead," warned Arlo. "Human bones."

As poised and self-reliant as Kelly and Kelsey seemed, Arlo wasn't willing to risk any shrieks of alarm. If the bloody Superstitions lived up to their reputation, these strange old mountains might prove the last resting place for many human bones. Including their own if something went wrong.

"It's not as dark in here as it oughta be," Dallas said. "Where's the light comin' in?"

"Higher up," said Arlo. "This won't be the only hole to the outside, I'm thinking. I suspect there may be several others."

While entry hadn't been easy, they soon discovered they'd made the right choice. When they finally reached a cavern where they could get to their feet, they discovered the source of the light. The next entry was thirty or more feet above the stone surface on which they stood. Suddenly, far below them, there was a rumble, like distant thunder. The entire mountain trembled, with earth and stone rattling down from above.

"The Thunder God!" Kelly cried.

"Volcano," corrected Arlo. "It's still all growl and no bite, but that may change someday. Hoss always believed these old volcanoes had life left in them."

"I agree with him," Dallas said. "It's easy, blamin' all these rockslides on lightning, and I don't doubt that's caused some of 'em. But a good shaking, like we just felt, could have the same effect. At some weak point, earth and stone could be torn loose by the vibration."

"The western face of the mountain, where the death's head shows up, is unscarred," said Kelly. "Why have all the slides been on the eastern face?"

"This cavity within the mountain is nearer the eastern face," Arlo said, "and being the weaker side, it's taken most of the beating. I don't think we should spend any more time here than we have to. I'm gambling that somewhere in here there'll be a way out, the one Hoss depended on."

"Once we leave this place with its little bit of overhead light," said Kelsey, "it's going to be awful dark."

"I still have a few matches from our camp," Dallas said, "but they won't burn long enough to be of any help to us. Somewhere in here, maybe in the mouth of that tunnel, I'm bettin' Hoss stashed some pine pitch splinters. Let's look for them."

There was no evidence of fire, not a stick of wood, and their search for some of the pine pitch torches proved fruitless.

"There's just nothing here," said Kelly in disappointment, "except that pile of rocks over there."

"Oh, for God's sake," Arlo muttered in disgust, "we're not using our heads. That pile of rocks is against the *west* wall of this hole, and that's the side of the mountain that's strongest. No rock or debris would have fallen there, and look—there's no breaks in the wall."

He hunkered down and began digging into the pile of stone. He quickly uncovered a dozen foot-long slivers of pine, which hid a small hole at the bottom of the wall.

"Lord, I hope it's enough to get us out of here," said Kelsey.

"Hoss wouldn't have shorted us," Arlo said. "There'll be enough to see us back to daylight, unless we take a wrong turn somewhere. Let's go."

Arlo lit one of the pine splinters, and they moved into the darkness of a downward passage. Air sucked at the meager flame, and Arlo shielded it with his hat.

"There's a draft," Dallas said, "and that means that somewhere ahead there's a way out of here."

"Let's just hope it won't be thirty feet over our heads and the size of your hat," said Arlo. "Or through the floor, a hundred feet straight down."

"Oh, Arlo," Kelsey said, "you're *so* encouraging."

They had covered no more than a hundred yards when Arlo stopped. A clammy moisture enveloped them like a fog. Sounding dim and far away, there was a roar, like a mighty wind moving ahead of a storm.

"Underground river," said Arlo. "We'd better take it slow from here on."

Careful as they were, they almost stumbled into the yawning abyss that had swallowed more than a dozen feet of the passage floor. In the flickering light of their torch, they were barely able to see the distant ragged edge of the hole.

"Dear God," said Kelsey, "this accounts for some of those who came to the Superstitions and were never seen again."

"I reckon it does," Arlo said. "Once more, it justifies Hoss Logan cuttin' Dallas and me in for a piece of the mine. We don't know the mountains as well as he did, but we know enough to come in here and stay alive. I think Hoss knew that before we played out the string, you and Kelly would be with us. Now we have to figure some way to get around this death trap."

"It doesn't cover all the floor," Dallas observed. "There's a narrow ledge along each side. Maybe with our backs against the wall, we can inch our way across."

Their torch had burned low, and Dallas lit a second one from the first. Arlo looped one end of the lariat around a boulder that looked solid and tied it securely.

"Now," he told Dallas, "tie this other end under your arms. Kelly, you take the light from him. He'll need both hands free to keep his balance."

"Lord," Kelly said nervously, "I wish there was some other way. I . . . I'm scared, but I'll go with you if it'll help."

"No," said Dallas, touched by her concern. "One slip and we'd both end up dangling from the end of this rope. If anything goes wrong—if that ledge crumbles—I'll need all of you to get me out of that hole."

Chapter 8

His back to the wall, Dallas moved cautiously along the widest ledge, to the right of the gaping hole, while Kelly held the torch, which seemed pitifully inadequate in the blackness of the tunnel. The flame danced in the updraft from the pit. Dallas kept his back flat against the stone wall, his arms spread as though he were walking a tightrope. Cold sweat dripped off his chin, and he could feel it soaking the armpits of his shirt. His progress seemed maddeningly slow. He was halfway across when the worst happened. He had just taken a step, all his weight on his right foot, when the ledge crumbled.

"God Almighty!" he shouted, and then he was gone.

Kelly screamed and dropped the torch, leaving them in total, terrifying darkness. Arlo had hold of the rope as an added precaution, and he felt it snap taut as Dallas hit the end of it.

"Dammit!" Arlo snapped. "Help me pull him up!"

Slowly they hoisted Dallas to safety, and when he was near enough, Kelly seized his sweaty hands and helped him over the edge. When at last he lay gasping on the stone floor, she threw her arms around him, trembling and weeping.

"You all right, pard?" Arlo asked.

"I . . . reckon," Dallas wheezed. "My heart . . . will start beatin' again . . . any day . . . now. Thank God . . . for that rope, but it . . . near 'bout tore me . . . in half, when I . . . hit the end of it. Feel like I been . . . throwed and stomped."

"I have the rest of the pine torches," said Arlo. "I hope you didn't lose the matches."

"Oh, damn the matches *and* the torches *and* the mine!" Kelly cried. "Let's go back the way we came!"

"Can't," said Dallas. "We'd never know where this tunnel comes out. If Hoss Logan got through here, so can we. I just picked the wrong way."

"Dear God," Kelsey cried, "you're not going to try that *again*?"

"Dallas," said Arlo, "when you catch your wind, dig out those matches and let's have some light. I'm going to try to cross on that other ledge."

"Please don't do it," Kelsey begged. "It's not even as wide as the one that just gave way."

Arlo drew her close in the darkness and felt the tears on her cheeks. Dallas sat up, fumbling in his pocket until he found the matches, secured in a little leather pouch. He lit a match and shielded it with his hand so the updraft wouldn't snuff it out. Arlo soon had another of their pine pitch sticks burning, and he passed the rest of them to Dallas.

"Hang on to these," he said, "in case I take a tumble like you did."

"Let me go across first," pleaded Kelsey. "I don't weigh as much as you do."

"Thanks," Arlo said, grinning at her, "but that wouldn't help. Sooner or later, Dallas and me will have to cross, and if that ledge isn't strong enough now, it won't ever be strong enough. Dallas, are you able to haul me up if need be?"

"I reckon," said Dallas. "I ain't sure my back will ever be the same, but if we got it to do, let's get on with it. I'm thirsty, and the sound of that water's drivin' me loco."

Dallas untied the rope that had saved him and passed it to Arlo.

"Oh, please be careful," Kelsey begged.

"I aim to," said Arlo. "This is for luck." He kissed Kelsey long and hard.

"*That's* where I went wrong," Dallas said. "Watch— he'll walk right on across."

They all adopted a confidence they didn't really feel, watching Arlo inch his way across, and everyone breathed a huge sigh of relief when he was safely beyond the chasm.

"Kelsey," said Arlo, "I want you and Kelly to cross next, one at a time. I'm going to tie one end of my lariat over here, and I'll tie the loose end to the rope I used in crossing. Dallas, when you haul your line in, you'll have a rope secured on each side of this hole. When you send Kelly and Kelsey across, use both ropes. Send Kelsey across first, and when she's safe, we'll bring Kelly over the same way. Kelly, when you cross, bring a couple of those matches and a splinter of pine with you. We'll have a light over here in time for Dallas to cross."

With the help of the lariats secured on both sides, Kelsey crossed safely. Arlo freed her from the ropes, and Dallas hauled them in again. He sent Kelly across in the same manner, and then loosed his own lariat from its stone pillar. He would cross with a single line. He tied the end of Arlo's lariat securely under his arms, put his back to the wall, and slowly made his way to the other side. Kelly welcomed him with a kiss and tears of relief.

Nothing had been said, but even in the short time they had been together, an understanding had come about. Their relationship had begun simply because the twins had been genuinely afraid of Gary Davis. At the outset they had felt safe with Arlo and Dallas, because the cowboys had been friends of Hoss Logan. But now it had developed as Dallas and Kelly, Arlo and Kelsey. Each became aware of the mutual attraction that was stronger even than the promise of gold that had brought them together in the beginning.

"Thank God *that's* behind us," Kelsey sighed.

"We still can't afford to get careless," said Arlo. "That death trap's behind us, but there may be others, as bad or worse."

"We've had a hell of a day," Dallas said. "Why don't we follow this passage to some point where we can find it again, without havin' to climb that mountain with the death's head? Since we don't know where this tunnel will end, we could be stranded in the dark, and a long way from our camp. We're needin' food, water, and rest."

"I hear water," said Kelly. "God, I hope it's not another river, with twenty feet of tunnel floor gone."

"The water may be a runoff from the same source," Arlo said, "but that's not loud enough to be a river. It's likely a spring similar to the one in our hidden camp."

The passage widened, and once they reached the cavern, they saw that its stone ceiling was far above their heads. The water flowed out of a split in the rock, a miniature waterfall producing the sound they'd heard. The stream crossed the cavern, taking for its bed the stone floor of the passage, which continued at a gentle slope.

"Clear and cold," Kelsey said, drinking from her cupped hands.

"That place—the cave—where Mother died," said Kelly. "There's just such a stream as this flowing out of the passage where Paiute took us. The water comes right down the passage, runs through the cavern, and on out into the canyon. Could this be the same stream?"

"Maybe," Dallas said. "I don't think there's that many freshwater streams flowing out of the mountains into the open canyons. What do you think, pard?"

"When Paiute took you and Kelsey away and into the tunnel," Arlo asked, "how long were you in the water?"

"Not more than a few minutes," said Kelly. "Paiute pushed us into another passage that led off to our right, and even before that, we were out of the water. It poured into our tunnel from somewhere to the left of us, and when we continued straight ahead we left the water behind."

"The mountain with the death's head image is southeast of the cavern where Paiute found you," Arlo said, "and that's about where we should be now. If this *is* the stream that flows out into the canyon, we can return here by just climbing down the east rim from our camp and following the stream back to where we are right now."

"Lord," said Kelsey, "so much easier than fighting our way through thorns and cactus and then having to climb the death's head mountain."

"It's follow the stream or go back the way we came," Dallas said. "Let's see where this passage takes us. If it leads out of the mountain near our camp, we can come back tomorrow and look for whatever sign Hoss left us."

Cass Bowdre and his bunch had spent most of the day riding around the Superstitions and hadn't seen a soul. Less than an hour before sundown, they rode wearily into the canyon where the Apaches had attacked two days before. Riding with Bowdre was Three-Fingered Joe Dimler, Zondo Carp, Pod Osteen, Os Ellerton, Eldon Sandoval, and a burly Negro—Mose Fowler—who wore a tied-down Colt on each hip.

"Six graves," Bowdre noted. "I reckon this is the canyon where the Injuns raised hell with that bunch from town."

"Ah just don' lak spendin' the night wher' they's dead men," Fowler complained.

"You've accounted for enough of them in your time," said Bowdre, "so don't go gettin' squeamish on us now. Dead men can't hurt you. It's them damn Apaches you ought to be scairt of. We got water and shelter here. Tomorrow we'll flush out them pilgrims that reckon they got an edge on this gold claim, and have a serious talk with 'em. Let's unsaddle our hosses so's they can graze. Then we'll have us a look at that cave. I'll take the first watch over the hosses. Rest of the night, it's two men to a watch."

A little more than a mile east of the mountain that the Mexican guides thought the map had referred to, Yavapai and Sanchez found a secluded canyon that appealed

to Gary Davis. There they made their camp and managed
to avoid being seen by Cass Bowdre's hardcase bunch.

"Who the hell are they?" Davis fumed.

"Scared, Gary?" R. J. Bollinger taunted. "Them coyotes look mean enough to wear out their britches from
the inside."

"Señor Davis shoot his *amigo* beside the very mountain where per'ap we find the gold," said Yavapai with a
sour grin.

"*Si,*" Sanchez replied, "and now these bunch find the
dead hombre and they wonder why. Per'ap they think we
have find the gold for w'ich he die. Señor Davis, the *estupido gringo*, have draw these coyotes to the very
mountain where may'ap the gold be."

The snide bastards, Davis cursed silently. Ostensibly
they spoke to one another, but their words were directed
at him. Davis fixed his malevolent gaze on the two of
them, shifting it occasionally to Bollinger. He trusted
none of them and hated them all. His shaky alliance
had crumbled, and it had all been the result of his back-
shooting Barry Rust. It was a foolish act that Davis now
regretted, not because Rust had once been his friend but
because it left Davis virtually alone in the mountains.
He doubted that Yavapai, Sanchez, or even Bollinger
would side with him now, especially in a fight with the
Apaches. He could see them abandoning him to save
themselves. Davis was faced with a dilemma: Even if he
did get rid of this bothersome trio, how was he to avoid
the new hardcase bunch while he searched for the mine?
But his troubles didn't end there. He hadn't seen Wells
and Holt since they'd slipped away from the Salt River
in the middle of the night, and he agonized over the possibility that the cowboys had found the mine while
he was stumbling through the Superstitions with a murderous trio who waited only for the time and place to
kill him.

* * *

With torch in hand, Dallas led the way, following the stream down the winding passage.

"If this is the stream we think it is," Kelly said, "the water will take a turn to the right, following the other passage to the outside."

"I hope it does take us back to that other cavern," said Kelsey. "Gary Davis would have no use for our belongings. Maybe he left our packs."

Eventually the stream did flow into another tunnel.

"See?" Kelly cried excitedly. "To follow the stream, we must turn back to our right. We're going to come out in the cave where the Indians attacked us."

"No talking from here on," whispered Arlo. "We don't know who might be out there. This is one of the few places with shelter and water."

They could soon see a gray area that was the mouth of the passage. Dallas dropped the torch he carried, and they waded carefully on, trying to avoid splashing the water as they went. Once they were near the mouth of their tunnel, Dallas held up his hand, halting them. He then crept ahead cautiously until he could see into the cavern.

"Nobody out here," he said. "Come on."

"Our packs are here!" Kelly cried when they emerged from the tunnel.

"I'll take a look outside," said Dallas. "If the way's clear, we're only a few minutes from our camp."

But the way was far from clear. A few yards away, Cass Bowdre and his bunch were unsaddling their horses. Dallas quickly ducked back into the safety of the cave.

"Seven riders out there," he said. "They're watering their horses, likely planning to bed down for the night. Real hardcase bunch."

"They'll soon be in here," said Arlo, "so let's go back into the tunnel."

"This means we'll be trapped in here until they leave," Kelsey said. "With shelter and water, suppose they don't? We have no food."

"We'll have water," said Arlo, "and we can survive until morning without food. There will be some shooting, eventually, but this isn't the time or the place. You've seen what a ricochet can do in here."

So they retreated into the blackness of the passage, Dallas and Arlo carrying the girls' packs. Dallas lit a match, and Arlo brought out another of the pine splinters.

"We could just follow this tunnel beyond the point where the water enters it and stay dry," Dallas said, "but let's go back to that big cavern where the stream begins."

"Why so far?" Kelly asked. "My feet are already cold and blistered."

"Because some of that bunch might decide to explore this tunnel," said Arlo, "but it's not likely they'll take any other passage, for fear of getting lost."

"Besides that," Dallas said, "if we're goin' to be trapped in this damn mountain all night, why not use the time to look around? Maybe we'll find whatever message Hoss left for us."

"Good idea," said Arlo, "but only to a point. We only have three of those pine splinters left. We'll have to do some almighty fast looking."

"You underestimate our pard Hoss Logan," Dallas said. "Somewhere in that cavern where the water comes down, Hoss will have stashed more pine sticks. We can use what we have left to look for the others."

Their return journey back along the streambed didn't seem quite as long.

"My God," Kelly groaned, "all I want is to find a dry place, sit down, and take off these wet boots."

"No," said Arlo, "let them dry on your feet."

"That's right," Dallas said. "Take 'em off wet, and once they're dry you'll never get them on again. There's worse things than having wet feet—like bein' barefoot in cactus country."

Both girls stretched out on the stone floor, their heads on their packs while Dallas and Arlo explored the huge cavern. It was circular and at first glance seemed devoid of anything except scattered stone that had fallen from above. It was Arlo who discovered what might have been a clue left by Hoss Logan.

"Look at this," he called to Dallas.

Dallas hunkered down beside him near the wall to see three flat stones arranged in a neat stack, with the largest one on the bottom. Curiosity got the best of Kelly and Kelsey, and they crawled over next to Dallas and Arlo to see what they'd found.

"How do you know they haven't been sitting like that for three hundred years?" Kelsey said.

"We don't know they haven't," answered Arlo, "but common sense tells us it just isn't possible, with these old volcanoes acting up like they do."

"You believe it's a message from Uncle Henry, then," Kelly said.

"Yes," said Arlo. "I don't believe he'd have had us climb that mountain with the image of the death's head and then risk our necks at the underground river for nothing."

"Uncle Henry used to say that three was his lucky number," Kelsey remembered. "But what do these stones tell us, except that maybe he left them like this? What do they mean? Three paces, three miles, three mountains?"

"They're to call our attention to something else," said Dallas. "I believe it's right here within our reach, but we can't find it in the dark. We need more of those pine pitch torches, but where in tarnation could they be?"

The stone ceiling was far above their heads, the walls seemed smooth, and there wasn't enough fallen debris to conceal anything on the stone floor.

"There's not a hole anywhere," Kelsey said, "except where the water flows out of that split in the wall."

"That's it!" exclaimed Arlo.

He took the torch from Dallas and went for a closer look. The stream splashed out of a horizontal split in the rock. It was a yard wide, and there was a gap between the rushing water and the upper lip of the crevice.

"Here, Dallas," Arlo said, "hold the light."

Dallas took the torch, and Arlo reached into the split,

feeling above the fast-flowing water. The bundle of pine
pitch slivers was tied with a single strip of rawhide.

"You found something!" Kelly cried excitedly. "Is that
all there is?"

"That's all," said Arlo. "There's just a narrow shelf.
Centuries ago, the flow of water must have been heavier, but it's slacked off some, leaving that little ledge dry.
Hoss never would have left anything of importance in so
obvious a place. He kept this kindling here for his own
use, concealing it only to avoid leaving sign of his coming and going."

"Well," Dallas said, "we have enough of those splinters for light now, so we can look around. Let's fire up a
second one and go over these walls, from head-high to
the floor."

"Kelsey and me can look too," said Kelly, "but what
are we looking for?"

"Anything that might relate to the number three," Arlo
said. "You'll have to use your own judgment."

The four of them, armed with two torches, began a
careful examination of the cavern's stone walls. Dallas
worked his way to the beginning of the passage down
which the stream flowed, and it was he who made the
discovery.

"I've found something," he cried excitedly. "This has
to be it!"

His three companions were beside him in an instant,
their eyes on the almost imperceptible crevice in the
rock. It was to the right of the tunnel, and just at eye
level. There were three tiny oak pins, their heads flat,
driven flush with the stone. They might have been there
for centuries, but the four pairs of eyes beholding them
knew better. The number matched the strange trio of
stones.

"I think," said Arlo, "when we find the passage where
the gold is, we'll know it by three of these pegs concealed somewhere in the rock."

"Damn it, Hoss," Dallas groaned, "why didn't you tell
us which *mountain*?"

The Logan girls were tired and hungry, and their elation at Dallas's discovery turned swiftly to disappointment. Dallas soon regretted his complaint that Hoss
Logan had not directed them to a specific mountain, and
he tried to undo the damage.

"I reckon I was a mite hasty, growlin' at Hoss," he
said. "It ain't fair to down a man for what he's done, until you know his reasons for it."

"It's kind of you to say that," said Kelly, "but you were
right the first time. We've already been through that
mountain with the death's head, and we're under a different one now. Stand on one of these mountains, and
there are more of them all around, like pigs gathered
around a sow. I swear, if I could get to Uncle Henry right
now, I'd give him a piece of my mind. How long are we
going to keep doing this?"

"Until we find Hoss's mine," Arlo said. "What else is
there to do? You aim to go back to St. Louis and marry
some rich doctor or lawyer?"

Those were the first cross words they'd had, and Dallas was about to say something when Kelsey laughed.

"Before I'd go back to the way things were," she said,
"I'd spend the rest of my life looking for Uncle Henry's
mine, and so would Kelly."

"All right," Kelly sighed, "you've got me. What are
we going to do for the rest of the night?"

"Move over some," said Dallas, "and we'll put our
heads together on that pack of yours. I'm almost bear-
able, once you get to know me."

"Come on," Kelly said. "If I can endure these wet
boots, I reckon I can stand anything."

"Damn," said Dallas, "the way you snatched me out of
that hole a while ago, I reckoned I'd be more welcome. If
the both of us can't share your pack for a pillow, still
wearin' our britches and boots, that don't leave much
hope for later on, does it?"

"The way you ramble," Kelly said, "it won't matter.
You can't get anything done for the talking about it."

"By God," said Arlo, "if you two are goin' to kick and

bite at one another all night like a pair of old mules with burs under your tails, I reckon Kelsey and me will have to find us another mountain."

Kelly laughed. "Stay. If he ever gets over here, I think I can shut him up."

Suddenly there was a rumble like faraway thunder, and the stone floor beneath them trembled.

"We've disturbed the Thunder God," Kelsey lamented, moving closer to Arlo. "I can't get over the feeling that before we leave the Superstitions, one of these strange old mountains is going to fall on us."

"Sounds like a storm buildin'," said Cass Bowdre. The mountain seemed to vibrate around them as they ate supper.

"Ain't been but a few minutes since I was outside," said Three-Fingered Joe Dimler, "and they wasn't a cloud nowhere. That ain't thunder."

"We be too close to them what's buried in the canyon," Mose Fowler said. "I just knows we is."

"Oh, hell," said Bowdre in disgust, "why you reckon they call this bunch of mountains the Superstitions? We're armed, and there ain't a thing that walks, crawls, or flies that can't be stopped with enough lead. I'm goin' out with the hosses. Mose, I'll wake you and Eldon. After that, it'll be Pod and Os, then Zondo and Joe—and see there that don't none of you nod off."

The men in the cavern slept undisturbed, unaware that they were observed from the dark passage from which flowed the stream. It was the last watch, Three-Fingered Joe and Zondo Carp, who sounded the alarm, an hour before dawn.

"The hosses are gone!" Zondo shouted.

"Gone?" Bowdre echoed. "I *told* you jugheads to stay awake!"

"We *been* awake," Three-Fingered Joe howled. "When the moon set, they . . . they just disappeart, an' we didn't see 'em go!"

"I tol' you this be a bad place," said Mose. "De spirits is robbed us!"

"We've been robbed, all right," Bowdre growled, "but not by spirits. I aim to find the thieves, and I promise you, they'll bleed just like anybody else. But we can't move until first light. Get a fire going so we can eat."

By the light of the fire, they made a more alarming discovery: Their packs were also missing! Gone were their food, their spare clothing, and all their extra ammunition.

"Whoever come in here amongst us ain't no ordinary hombre," said Pod Osteen. "Hell, I fought the Mescalero Apaches, and nothin' gits by me, even if I'm asleep. I tell you, there ain't a man alive that could of come in here without wakin' *some* of us. This place is quiet as a tomb."

"Lawd God," Mose Fowler groaned, "this place *be* a tomb! De night won't find me in here a'gin, not for all the gold in Arizony."

"Whoever he is," said Bowdre, "he's some slick coyote. Pod, you and Zondo walk back to town for extra shells and grub. While you're gone, the rest of us will find another camp and trail the hosses."

"Whoa," Zondo said. "I ain't walkin' to town on *nobody*'s orders."

"Me neither," said Pod, and the rest of them quickly agreed with him.

"Damn it," Bowdre said, "we got to have grub."

"We's got to have hosses first," said Mose. "Why don' I walks in to the livery an' buys some?"

"Because the livery in that little one-saloon town ain't goin' to have that many hosses to sell," Bowdre explained. "And if they did, they wouldn't sell to us. Their hard-nosed sheriff would see to that. Hosses leave tracks. We'll trail 'em and *then* worry about the grub."

"Likely the Apaches got our hosses," said Os Ellerton. "An' if they did, you can trail 'em till hell freezes. They'll split up an' go seven different ways."

"I ain't near as ethical as the rest of you jaybirds," Sandoval said. "I aim to find one of them slicks what's lookin' for the gold, shoot the varmint, and take his horse."

"Whatever we do, we'll do it together," Bowdre shouted. "I say we look for our hosses first. When I'm satisfied we can't find 'em, then we'll likely take Sandoval's advice, takin' 'em wherever and however we can find 'em."

They set out down the canyon, seven men accustomed to the saddle, now on foot.

"We could of lit us a pine knot," said Sandoval, "an' searched the tunnel. I can make do without a hoss for a while, but damned if I'm goin' without grub."

"Yeah," Bowdre growled, "and besides our other problems, we'd be lost somewhere in that mountain. For damn sure, our hosses didn't go that way, and if that's the way our packs went, you can be sure the coyote that took 'em knows his way around. We don't, and even if we didn't lose ourselves in the passages, we'd likely walk blind into an ambush or fall down a hole we couldn't climb out of. Anybody hankerin' to explore that tunnel, have at it, but don't look for me to go with you."

"Spirits in de mountain done laid de evil eye on us," said Mose gloomily.

Nobody responded to that, but his companions looked sideways at Mose, wondering if he possessed some spiritual insight they lacked. The sun peeked over the horizon, promising another blistering day. There was nothing more to be said, and for the lack of an alternative, the seven disgruntled men trudged down the canyon, following a doubtful trail.

Chapter 9

Gary Davis had spent a restless, sleepless night, and with the dawn he had reached a decision. It was a solution to the problem he'd wrestled with all night. Not that he was happy with it—under the circumstances it was the best he could do. If his surly companions chose not to go along with him, it could be a painless means of ridding himself of them. If they did accept his proposal—and they would have little choice—they would become less of a danger to him. Davis wasted no time in telling them what he had in mind.

"We're goin' to track down this bunch that rode in yesterday," he said, "and use them to our advantage. They're tougher than those grannies that just got scared off by the Apaches, and I aim to join forces with them."

"Smart move, Gary," Bollinger said. "You goin' to make 'em promise not to gun us down the minute we find the gold?"

"Once we find the gold," said Davis, "I fully expect them to try and take it all. I got about as much confidence in them as I do in you and this pair of Mex coyotes, but if we spent all our time fightin' over who looks for the mine, then none of us is goin' to find it. Me, I'd rather join forces with these pelicans, find the gold, and fight them for it than not find it at all. If we're gunnin' for them, and they're gunnin' for us, with the Apaches out to scalp us all, there'll be no gold for any of us."

"Señor Davis be more *astuto* than he look," said Sanchez admiringly. "We become the *amigos* of these hombres, and per'ap we fight the *Indios* together. Then when we have find the gold, we shoot our new *amigos,* per'ap in the back, no?"

"Per'ap in the back, yes," Bollinger laughed. "Señor Davis treats all his good *amigos* equal."

Davis glared at Bollinger, while the Mexican duo laughed delightedly.

"Per'ap we find these new *amigos* before they find us," Yavapai grinned.

Dallas shared Kelly's pack for a pillow, while Arlo shared Kelsey's, but the stone floor made a poor bed. Kelly's arm was flung across Dallas's chest, and when he sat up, he awakened her.

"God," Dallas said, "I'd swap the mine for a cup of hot coffee."

"You're waking the rest of us to say that?" Kelly asked.

"We're already awake," said Arlo, "and I'd have to agree with him. I feel like we've been in here a week."

"We'll never know when daylight comes," Kelly said. "Let's light a match and see what time it is by Uncle Henry's watch."

Dallas lit a match, and Kelsey opened the front of her shirt enough for Arlo to see the face of the watch, which was on a leather thong around her neck.

"Almost three o'clock," said Arlo. "Another two hours until first light."

"I don't aim to wait that long," Dallas said. "I figure that bunch got their floor shook last night just like we did. I'd bet they'll be out of that hole without takin' time for breakfast."

"Oh, I hope you're right," said Kelsey. "I'm so hungry."

"We're not going to be any less hungry just sittin' here waitin' for daylight," Arlo said, "so why don't we use this time to investigate the new advantage Hoss has given us?"

"How are the three pegs driven into the rock going to help us, unless we're under the mountain where the gold is?" Kelly asked. "There are no passages to consider, except the one the stream runs into. The outside end of it leads to the cavern where Mother was shot, and the other end goes back into the mountain somewhere."

"That's what I aim to investigate," said Arlo. "Once we reach that tunnel, instead of following it and the stream outside, I want to take the other direction, deeper into the mountain. When Paiute stole you and Kelsey away, you said he took a side passage, veering to your right. That means there's a way from where we are right now back to our hidden camp. With what Hoss has just revealed to us, I believe we can find that passage."

"You think the three wooden pegs in the wall serve more than one purpose, then," Dallas said. "Besides marking the location of the gold, they could also tell us which of the passages beneath these mountains are safe."

"I don't just *think* it," Arlo said. "I can prove it. Remember that passage that led us down from the death's head mountain, with its dangerous drop to the underground river? From here, we could follow that same passage back to death's head, but here, where that passage begins, there's nothing along the walls. Doesn't that tell you something? Hoss left no message from *this* end."

"Hoss didn't mark it," said Dallas, "because of the underground river and that god-awful drop-off."

"No," Kelsey said, "but he brought us in from the other direction, and it was just as dangerous, because we had no warning."

"No help for that," said Arlo. "He had to get us in here somehow, and he used the death's head on the side of the mountain to do it. Besides, he knew Dallas and me wouldn't walk into that hole unawares."

"Oh, God," Kelly groaned, "there may be hundreds of passages under these blessed mountains, and that means the gold we're looking for could be somewhere down any tunnel Uncle Henry marked as safe."

"Exactly," said Arlo, "but look at it this way. Not only is Hoss telling us which passages are safe, he's telling us where we *might* find the gold. Suppose we encounter maybe a hundred tunnels? Those without Hoss Logan's

mark are eliminated. True, he may have marked many
passages where there is no gold, but we may need those
passages to find other messages from Hoss, or to take us
nearer to the mine itself."

"If there's a chance we can find the passage that takes
us back to our camp," Kelsey said, "then let's go look for
it. Even if those men are still in the cave at the front of
the passage, they won't know about us because we'll be
going deeper into the mountain."

When they reached the passage down which the stream
flowed to the outside, they listened, but heard nothing.
Turning back to the left, they went on, Dallas in the lead
with a flaming pine torch. He drew up at the yawning
mouth of a tunnel that angled back to their left.

"No," Kelsey whispered. "It was a passage like this,
where Paiute took Mother."

"I'm gambling it won't be a tunnel we'll have to investigate," Arlo said, "but we need to know for sure.
Let's look for Hoss's mark."

Kelly and Kelsey sighed with relief when a careful
search failed to reveal the sign. The four of them continued on, passing two additional tunnels to their left, neither of which Hoss had marked.

"You were right, Arlo," Kelly admitted. "So far we've
found Uncle Henry's mark only once."

"When we find it again," said Arlo, "I expect it'll be
on a passage to our right. That would take us back toward
the western rim, the side of the mountain range facing
town."

"We may be about to prove what we've suspected all
along," Dallas said. "That the mine is nowhere near this
mountain. Hoss was the kind who'd have pitched his
camp as far from the pay dirt as possible."

The fourth passage wandered away to their right. They
passed their poor light over the stone walls as high as
they could reach and found nothing. The floor had a
film of mud, and they could hear dripping water. Dallas thought he saw something, and he knelt and began
sweeping away the mud, revealing an all-but-invisible

crack in the stone. There, side by side, was the trio of wooden pegs!

"This is the way to our camp!" Kelsey cried.

"Not directly," Arlo said. "Our camp's near the rim, and right now we're at the very bottom of the mountain."

Their passage diminished until they were on their hands and knees. When they were able to get to their feet again, they were in a high-ceilinged cavern much like the one where they'd spent the night.

"I remember that narrow place where we had to crawl," said Kelly. "Paiute made us go first, and I was scared to death."

While their original passage ended, two others led out, one to the right and one to the left.

"Paiute led us down the one to the right," Kelsey said.

"That's the way back to our camp, then," said Arlo, "but we're going to have a careful look at them both for any sign Hoss left."

The sign they sought, and soon found, was inside the mouth of the passage to the right, head-high.

"Even if Kelly and Kelsey didn't remember taking the right-hand passage," Dallas said, "common sense says that's the way to our camp. With Hoss tellin' us it's safe, we can come back later and look into this other tunnel."

The passage to the right also angled upward, and by the time it leveled out, they came upon yet another tunnel that dead-ended into their own from the left. It took them only a few moments to find Hoss Logan's familiar mark.

"Unless we've lost all sense of direction," said Arlo, "that one has to lead to the west rim, and fresh air. See how it's drawing our flame?"

"Straight ahead, then," Dallas said, "and we ought to reach our camp."

There were three more passages, all dropping back to the right and all dangerously steep. Hoss Logan's sign marked none of them.

"I'm sorry I was critical of Uncle Henry's markings," said Kelly. "It's kind of spooky, him guiding us through these passages long after he's gone."

Soon there was the familiar sound of splashing water. Dallas dropped the burning pine torch and snuffed it out with his boot. The four of them went on, the sound of water covering their approach. Dallas was the first to reach the end of the passage, coming out behind the miniature waterfall. One of the mules brayed, and all four animals seemed glad to see them.

"Thank God," Kelsey exhaled. "It's like we've been lost for a long time, and suddenly we found our way home."

"Let's get a fire going," said Dallas, "and make some coffee."

"You do that," Arlo said, "and I'll look around. I want to be sure our camp hasn't been disturbed."

"Hell," said Dallas, "I'll save you the trouble. Half our coffee's gone."

"Paiute," Arlo said. "We can't begrudge him that."

"He can't hide from us forever," said Kelsey, "now that we know Uncle Henry's mark. Somewhere in these mountains, there must be another good spot like this, hidden and having water."

"I think you can count on that," Dallas said, "but while Hoss marked some passages for us, he left as many unmarked. It's down one of these unmarked tunnels that he made his final camp. That's where we'll find Paiute, if we find him at all."

"And probably the mine, as well," said Arlo.

"Then why all these markings?" Kelly cried. "I thought we had finally discovered the key to the mine."

"We have," said Arlo, "but that doesn't mean those markings are the only guide. In some passages Hoss has marked, there'll be some final clue that won't mean anything to anybody except maybe you and Kelsey. Something from the past that maybe even Dallas and me won't understand. Anybody might discover his mark—this trio of wooden pegs—and they'll expect that to eventually take them to the mine."

"So Uncle Henry didn't intend for the markers to lead anybody to the mine," Kelsey said, "and they're serving a purpose other than telling us which of the passages are safe. Anybody depending on the markers to lead them to the mine will actually be led away from it."

"Exactly," said Arlo. "Paiute brought Dallas and me to this camp, and he could have shown us the safe passages we followed this morning, but he didn't. Why didn't he?"

"Because Uncle Henry wanted us to discover the mark for ourselves," Kelly said, "and not because it's a trail we can follow to the mine. I think you're right—somewhere in one of these passages he's marked for us, we'll find something—some final lead—that nobody else will understand."

"Be thinking back over the years," said Dallas, "to the times your uncle visited you. The things he said to you, the things he did, just anything that might be important enough for you to remember."

"When we were thirteen," said Kelsey, "the Christmas after Daddy sent Uncle Henry the picture that's in the watch, he bought each of us a spotted pony. He said the Plains Indians favored them. Mother threw a fit. It was the last thing she wanted, us owning horses. After Daddy was . . . killed, we never saw our spotted ponies again. She had Gary Davis sell them."

"We'll eat and rest for a while," Arlo said, "and then I think we ought to explore that other passage Hoss marked."

Gary Davis and his companions had no trouble finding the seven men who were trailing their horses. The animals had been driven down-canyon until it petered out, and there they had scattered.

"They'll all come together somewhere," Bowdre growled, "but when, and how far? By God, we're in big trouble."

"We got company too," said Zondo Carp. "Four hombres."

It was Gary Davis who reined his horse in forty yards away, his three companions fanning out beside him.

Whatever their differences, they managed to present a unified front. Davis spoke.

"I reckon the Apaches paid you a visit last night."

"They did," said Bowdre. "You here to gloat or to help?"

"Depends on you," Davis said. "We've had one run-in with the Apaches, and I doubt the four of us could stand another."

"There were five of you yesterday," said Bowdre, his eyes on the riderless horse that R. J. Bollinger led. "We found the hombre shot in the back. Wasn't much of a testimonial to your friendliness."

"Wasn't intended to be," Davis said coldly. "A man that runs out on me when the going gets tough takes his chances."

"You ain't wantin' to be friends, then," said Bowdre sarcastically, "and that's some relief. So I reckon your interest in us is purely business. For the sake of your hair, you'd like to throw in with us. Then, when we've found the gold, or you reckon we're close to it, you'll pay us off in lead and take it all for yourselves."

"I may have to kill you," said Davis with an evil laugh, "but I won't lie to you. Will you be as honest with me? By God, you're accusing me of plannin' the very thing you'll do, given the chance. Who are you, anyhow?"

"I'm Cass Bowdre. That's Joe Dimler, Zondo Carp, and Pod Osteen to my right. At my left is Os Ellerton, Eldon Sandoval, and Mose Fowler. Now, who the hell are you?"

"Gary Davis. R. J. Bollinger leadin' the hoss. The Mex pair is Yavapai and Sanchez. They claim to be familiar with these mountains."

"You have pick a bad camp, Señor," said Yavapai, looking sadly at Bowdre, "and you be lucky losing only your horses. Already the mountain have take five people, and they no return."

"Hell, we lost more'n our hosses," Pod Osteen said. "Some coyote-footed varmint come in that cave an' took our packs while we was sleepin'. We got no grub. Not even any coffee for breakfast."

"Lawd God," Mose groaned, "I knowed de spirits was in that mountain."

"We got a pack mule and grub at our camp," said Davis affably, "and it ain't too far to walk. I reckon we can talk there. We got one extra hoss, but it'll be tricky as hell comin' up with six more."

"Damn right it will," Bollinger said, "and you won't find 'em in town. Me and Rust only needed five, and a mule. We barely found 'em, and when we did, we paid three prices for 'em."

"You come lookin' for us," said Bowdre, "leavin' your pack mule and grub in camp? That don't strike me as bein' too smart, seein' as how you've been cleaned out by Injuns before."

"The camp be close," Yavapai said, "and it not be dark."

But an unpleasant surprise awaited them. When they reached camp, they found their packs, their food, and the mule gone.

Several of Cass Bowdre's men looked at Gary Davis and his companions in disgust, but they weren't quite in a position to laugh, because at least Davis and his men were mounted. But grub-wise, they were all in the same sorry position.

"By God," said Zondo Carp, "I never seen such . . ."

"Knock it off, Zondo," growled Bowdre. "The truth is, we've all come off like damn fools, allowin' ourselves to be stole from like a bunch of shorthorns. Now we're needin' hosses and grub, and us chawin' on one another ain't goin' to change that. Since there's no hosses to be had in that little town we just come from, that means we got to try another town. Davis, if you'll let me ride that extra hoss, you and me can go hoss hunting."

"It's you that's needin' horses," said Davis. "Sheriff Wheaton's got nothin' on us. We can buy all the grub we need, close by."

"I reckon you can," Bowdre said, turning his hard eyes

on Davis, "and while you're there, buy yourself some help to fight the Apaches."

The implication was clear enough, and Davis shifted his eyes to Bollinger, then to Yavapai and Sanchez. One wrong move, and Gary Davis would become an outcast, scorned by his companions, rejected by these hard-case newcomers. Swallowing hard, he turned to Cass Bowdre.

"Yeah," he said, "you can ride the extra horse. What town you got in mind?"

"Florence," said Bowdre. "It's thirty miles south. We rode through it on our way in. If we can't find six hosses there, we'll ride northeast to Globe. We'll need a pack mule, too."

Davis nodded, holding his temper and biting his tongue. Bowdre had pressed his advantage, making it clear he planned the continued use of the horse that Barry Rust had ridden. Davis consoled himself with the thought that this miserable alliance was, at worst, only temporary. It would end if and when they found the gold, and then he would pay off this hardcase bunch with a different metal—lead.

"Let's ride, then," Bowdre said.

Taking the lead rope from Bollinger, Bowdre mounted the horse and rode out, saying nothing to his men. Gary Davis followed. Bowdre's six men stared at Bollinger and the pair of Mexicans. It was to the latter that Pod Osteen spoke.

"So you *Mejicanos* know these Superstitions."

"Si, Señor," said Sanchez, "and we have learn to respect them."

"We got the whole day, likely, with nothin' to do but wait," Osteen said. "I'm of a mind to light me a pine knot, go back to that cave, and look for our packs. Who's got the sand to go with me?"

"Lawd God," bawled Mose Fowler, "it don't be me!"

"Go," said Yavapai grimly, "and you no come back forever."

"Per'ap you see *El Diablo pronto*," Sanchez said.

"My God," said Osteen, "I never seen so many growed men that was jumpy as old squaws. What about the rest of you? Joe? Zondo? Os? Eldon?"

"We know two men went down that tunnel and never come out," Bollinger said. "I'd say there must be some deep holes and drop-offs in there, deep enough to swallow a man if he don't know his way around. I can match *your* sand any day, bucko, but I ain't a damn fool."

"Well," said Zondo, "that makes sense to me. I ain't a coward, but I've seen stacked decks before. If you know you're goin' to be throwed at the first jump and then stomped, what's the use in mountin' up?"

"If you're of a mind to look around," said Bollinger, "climb up to the top of that mountain, the one with the cave up there at the foot. There's a pair of hombres—Wells and Holt—who's got an edge on all of us. Somewhere on top of that mountain, they're hidin' out, and they got an old Injun with 'em. He used to ride with Logan, the old man who made the gold strike. The three of 'em snuck out at night, rode up there ahead of us, and we ain't seen 'em since."

"They got horses, I reckon," said Osteen.

"Yeah," Bollinger said. "Horses and a pair of mules."

"Stumblin' around in a dark hole is one thing," said Three-Fingered Joe, "but on top of a mountain, and daylight, that's another. I'll go along."

"Me too," Zondo said. "Beats standin' around waitin'."

"Come on, then," said Pod Osteen. "Os, you and Eldon goin'?"

"No point in it," Sandoval said. "There's three of you, and three of them, includin' the old Injun. Hell, I ain't climbin' that mountain on an empty belly."

"That's how I feel about it too," said Ellerton. "Besides, Cass might not like it, us wanderin' around up there. The Apaches done took everything but our scalps, and if we split up, we're even riskin' that."

"Cass ain't my daddy," Osteen spat, "so I don't have to jump ever' time he hollers froggy. Any of you hombres that are afraid to stay here, then come along with Joe, Zondo, and me."

Nobody else chose to go, and the trio set out on foot back toward the fateful canyon where six men had died at the hands of the Apaches. They had no trouble finding the break in the rim where Davis and his companions had descended behind the mob of gold seekers from town.

Breakfast was over, but Dallas had made another pot of coffee.

"There's enough for another week," he said. "Then we either sneak into town for a sack of beans or we give up this search for the mine."

"I reckon Hoss would be almighty put out with you," Arlo said, "if he knew you was ready to give up half a gold mine for a sack of coffee beans. But a lot can happen in a week. After all that time in the dark, I got a hankerin' to see the sun. Kelsey, are you well enough rested to go along? We might follow the east rim a ways and see if we can sight Davis and his men."

"Let me buckle on my pistol," said Kelsey. "I'm going to start wearing it again."

The two left the camp, waiting a while before making their final exit and climbing to the top of the western rim. Seeing nobody, they continued, pausing at the top of the mountain to catch their wind. Suddenly the girl stood on tiptoe, put her arms around Arlo's neck, and kissed him long and hard. When she drew away, he pulled her to him for a repeat performance.

"I just realized I'm happy," she said, "and I used to wonder if I ever would be again, especially after Daddy was gone. When he was alive, and when Uncle Henry would come, those were the best times. First we lost Daddy, and then Uncle Henry. You and Dallas were just his cowboy friends, and I don't know what I expected, but it certainly wasn't this. You're the first man I ever kissed, except for Daddy and Uncle Henry."

"I'm glad," said Arlo, "and I'd like to keep it that way.

At first I couldn't tell you and Kelly apart, but I can now. How am I doing that?"

"I don't know," Kelsey laughed, "unless it's because Kelly's got a little of Mother's perverse nature about her. Mostly we're like our daddy, and as Mother drew away from him, she seemed to care less and less for us. Kelly and me started to feel like . . . like . . . oh, God, like orphans. I'd forgotten what it was like to laugh, to be happy, to . . . to care about someone. I'd live here in these mountains until I'm eighteen, if there's no other way. But what's going to happen to Kelly . . . and me . . . when we leave here?"

"Wal," said Arlo in his best drawl, "Ah cain't speak for Dallas, but Ah aim to take you whar other hombres cain't git to you. That is, 'less you got some objection."

"Looking back," she said, "I can't remember a time when I was so happy. I'd be satisfied to just forget the mine, but I feel like we owe it to Uncle Henry to follow whatever trail he left for us. When we've done that, ask anything of me you want. I promise not to disappoint you."

"Thank you," said Arlo. "Now what do you think about Kelly and Dallas?"

"When she taunts him," she laughed, "I like the way he gives as good as he gets. I think that, before we slip back into camp, we'd better throw a stone in ahead of us to let them know we're coming."

They walked all the way across the east rim, until they could see into the farthest end of the canyon, but not to the very foot of the mountain. When they were close enough to see the three men who were two-thirds of the way up the wall, the strangers had already spotted them!

"Come on," Arlo said. "Run!"

They had a small advantage, for Joe, Pod, and Zondo were winded from their climb and still were some distance from the top.

"We can't get back to our camp without them seeing us!" Kelsey cried.

"We'll have to work our way down the mountain and return through it," Arlo said.

The three men from Cass Bowdre's bunch reached the top of the mountain, and while they were unable to see their quarry, they ran along the mountain rim toward the south. There were few places to hide.

"We get close enough," Pod Osteen grunted, "put a slug in one or both of 'em. That should force 'em back into their camp, and we can see where it is."

Arlo and Kelsey were on their knees behind an upthrust of stone. When they saw the trio coming, Arlo fired twice, kicking up dust at their feet and forcing them to hesitate.

"Come on!" said Arlo. "If we can work our way all the way around the rim without them getting wise, we can slip down the mountain where they came up. That'll put us near the mouth of the cavern. We'll have to make it through the passage without a light, but that's better than a running gunfight in the open."

Chapter 10

Arlo and Kelsey made it as far as the south rim, taking advantage of the little cover there was, before the trio caught sight of them again. There was a rattle of gunfire, and lead sang over their heads like angry bees. Swiftly they made their way to the west rim, finding sanctuary behind an occasional stone abutment. One of the pursuing men tried to cut across the wide-open plateau, but Arlo shot off his hat and burned a second slug along his thigh. He fell, rolling behind a little rise, and his companions paused. Arlo and Kelsey ran on, Arlo reloading his gun as they went.

"Gunfire!" Dallas said. "Somebody's discovered Arlo and Kelsey!"

"Oh, Lord!" said Kelly. "Let's go help them!"

"We can't," Dallas said, "without givin' away our camp. Whoever started this ruckus is tryin' to drive Arlo and Kelsey into a hole, figurin' to find our camp by forcin' them back into it. We go runnin' out there, and we'll only end up with our own tails in a crack, without helpin' them. As well as I know Arlo, he won't lead 'em here. He'll try to work his way down the mountain and come in through the passage, but he won't have a light. Come on—we'll take some pine torches and meet them in the passage."

"How can we know they'll come in that way?"

"They have no choice," Dallas said. "There's not enough cover on the top of this mountain to shelter a toad. They can dodge from stone to stone for temporary cover, but if there's more than one man after them, they'll have to keep moving. Their only chance is to make it down the mountain and then return through the passages."

Kelsey, in the lead, drew her Colt.

"No," said Arlo, "save it. This is no place to make a stand. Let me keep them away from us, if I can. Keep moving."

They paused behind the cover of boulders, breathing hard. The only real cover their pursuers had was what Arlo and Kelsey had already used.

"Sooner or later," Arlo said, "they'll try to rush us as we move out from cover. Once we've gotten far enough along the west rim, we're going to cut across the plateau to that steep trail down the east rim. When I tell you to go, run for it. I'll try to hold them off until you're over the edge. Then I want you to pull that Colt and give 'em hell. Space your shots, and try to lay down enough fire to cover me, so I can join you."

Kelsey moved ahead, and soon they were near enough to cut over the west rim to their hidden camp. But they dared not. Almost straight across the mountaintop was the steep pass that led into the canyon and the safety of the passage within the mountain.

"Now!" Arlo yelled. "Run!"

Kelsey ran, lead kicking up dust all around her. Arlo fired, spacing his six shots, buying Kelsey all the time he could. Then she was over the rim. *With any luck,* he thought, *the murderous coyotes will have to reload.* He wouldn't have a better chance, and without sacrificing the time it would take to reload, he lit out toward the east rim after Kelsey. One of the gunmen cut down on him immediately, and the other two joined in. But Kelsey Logan made her presence felt. She spaced her shots as Arlo had done, and he quickly tumbled over the rim to join her. Kelsey was deftly reloading her Colt.

"Come on," Arlo cried. "They'll be cuttin' down on us again before we reach bottom."

Arlo reloaded as he slid down the steep trail. All too soon, their pursuers were blasting away from the rim. Arlo turned and fired three quick shots over their heads, driving them back for a moment. Then they rushed to the ledge and began the descent, throwing lead as they came. Arlo returned their fire until his Colt clicked on empty. He heard Kelsey shout and turned to face a new danger—three horsemen were galloping up the canyon—Bollinger, Yavapai, and Sanchez. Bollinger was firing not at Kelsey but at Arlo. Kelsey paused, firing twice, and the second shot ripped off Bollinger's hat. The vengeful gunman then turned his fire on the girl.

"No, Kelsey," Arlo shouted. "Run!"

Kelsey turned toward the mouth of the cavern through which the stream ran, Arlo right behind her. Suddenly she seemed to stumble, the force of the lead driving her backward into Arlo. His own Colt empty, Arlo snatched Kelsey's from her limp fingers. His left arm supporting Kelsey Logan's dead weight, Arlo shot Bollinger out of the saddle in his fury. The trio of gunmen coming down the mountain were closer, and Arlo almost fell as a slug tore through the inside of his right thigh. Praying for a miracle, he gathered the unconscious Kelsey in his arms and ran. For a frightening second, he saw that the entire left side of her shirt was soaked with blood.

He slipped in the mud outside the cavern's mouth, and that misstep was what saved him. A slug tore across his scalp just above his left ear, and others slammed into the side of the passage inches from his head. Dizzy, his head pounding, he stumbled into the welcome dark of the mountain. He paused only a moment to catch his breath before pressing on into the blackness of the passage that would take them back to the safety of their camp. He made it past the point in the tunnel where the water cascaded down, then paused, exhausted. Kelsey hadn't made a sound.

"Kelsey," he cried. "Kelsey!"

But in the blackness of the passage there were only the lonely sounds of dripping water and Kelsey's ragged breathing. His right arm was under her arms, and he could feel her blood soaking the sleeve of his shirt.

"You bastards," he sobbed. "You murdering bastards!"

Arlo stumbled on, dizzy from the lead that had creased his skull, feeling the blood from the wound in his thigh squishing in his boot. He could hear shouting somewhere behind him. If they took the time to get a light and had the nerve to follow, all was lost.

Dallas and Kelly hurried down the passage that would eventually take them to the foot of the mountain and to the route they expected Arlo and Kelsey to use. Kelly had brought a couple of blankets, not knowing what difficulty they might encounter. With Dallas in the lead, they reached the point where they had to drop to hands and knees. They were near the end of the cramped passage when Dallas paused.

"Hold it," he whispered. "Somebody's comin'. Here, take the light."

But the light had been seen.

Arlo called, breathing hard. "Dallas? Kelly?"

"Arlo," Dallas cried, "we're here. What's happened?"

"Kelsey's hurt," said Arlo, his voice trembling. "Hit hard, bleedin' bad."

As Kelly spread the blankets on the stone floor, Arlo eased Kelsey down. Kelly cried at the sight of her sister's blood-soaked shirt. Before their eyes, new blood began soaking the blankets. Every minute counted now.

"Kelly," Dallas said, "you take the torch and lead the way. Arlo and me will have to work her through that narrow passage a little at a time."

On hands and knees, Dallas backed into the passage, gripping the foot of Kelsey's blanket bed. Arlo took her head, and they lifted her just enough to clear the stone floor. It was impossible to crawl without using their hands for support, and they were forced to move Kelsey only as far as Arlo could reach. While it took them only a few minutes, it seemed like hours before they were able to stand. Arlo hunkered down to gather up Kelsey, but he was unable to. He went to his knees.

"You'll . . . have to take her, Dallas," he said. "I took a slug . . . in the thigh, and it's . . . givin' me hell."

Kelly took the lead, carrying the torch, while Dallas followed with Kelsey and Arlo limped along behind. When they reached the cavern that was their camp, Kelly stirred up the fire so they had light. She then set the iron spider in place and hung a pot of water to boil. Turning to the wounded Kelsey, she flung the blankets aside and began unbuttoning the girl's shirt.

"We'll go . . . back into the passage," panted Dallas, "while you . . . see to her."

"You'll stay right where you are," Kelly said. "I've never seen a gunshot wound in my life, and I don't know what to do. I'll need you, and I don't intend to swap my sister's modesty for her life. Arlo's been hit too. Get those britches off, cowboy, and try to stop the bleeding. It won't help Kelsey, you standing there bleeding to death."

Arlo stood there in his shirttail, feeling foolish, thankful there were no holes in his drawers. Dallas cut a strip from a blanket and tied the cloth tight around Arlo's thigh, above the wound.

"Didn't hurt the bone," said Dallas, "but you've been bleedin' like a stuck hog. Kelsey is the one we have to worry about."

"My God, yes," Kelly said. "Come look at this wound."

She had stripped away the bloody shirt and pulled Kelsey's Levi's down to her knees. Kelly had washed away the blood, revealing the wound in the girl's left side. It was angry purple, and blood still oozed from it. Arlo limped over to Kelsey and got down beside her.

"One of you take her shoulders and raise her up," he said. "It looks bad, but sometimes where the lead comes out is more important than where it went in. It can hit a rib and be driven away from the vitals, or worse, it can be driven right into them."

Kelly lifted Kelsey enough for Arlo to look for an exit wound. With a sigh of relief, he found it.

"The slug went on through," said Arlo, "but it tore a

mean hole on its way out. We'll have to wrap her in all
the blankets to keep her warm, but the biggest danger
will be infection. I think we can handle that, with the two
quarts of whiskey we have. We'll know by this time tomorrow. If she worsens, we'll either get her to a doc,
or bring one to her. Dallas, bring me a quart of that
red-eye."

At that point, Kelsey opened her eyes. "R. J. Bollinger," she gasped. "He . . . shot me."

"And I shot him," said Arlo. "With your pistol. Mine
was empty."

"How bad . . . am I?"

"You're hurt some," Arlo said, "and you'll be sore as
hell for a while, but the slug went on through. I reckon
you have a loose rib or two, because of the way the lead
angled out. We're going to pour some whiskey into the
wound and then bind it well. Sometime tonight, you'll
have a fever, and you may have to drink half a quart of
the whiskey. It'll sweat the fever and infection out of
you. If that fails—and I don't expect it to—we'll take
you to a doc."

"I'm not much good . . . in a gunfight," she said. "I . . .
I'm sorry."

"The hell you aren't!" said Arlo. "By the time I saw
Bollinger comin', my Colt was empty. If you hadn't
drawn his fire, he'd have shot me dead before I could
have reloaded. He did get one slug in my thigh, though.
That's why my britches are off. I don't usually hunker
down next to a female in my drawers."

She tried to laugh, but it trailed off into a groan of pain.
Dallas handed Arlo the whiskey bottle while Kelly busily
ripped what was once a petticoat into bandages.

"Was that mine or yours?" Kelsey asked.

"I'm not sure," said Kelly, "but in Arizona I reckon
bandages are more useful than fancy female underwear."

"By God," Dallas said, delighted, "she's got the hang
of it!"

"Kelly," said Arlo, "make me a thick pad of . . . whatever it was. I'll soak it with whiskey and place it over the

wound where the slug came out. And then I'll need a second bandage to cover the original wound."

He poured the potent brew into the wound, and Kelsey gasped.

"Now," Arlo said, "raise her up, so I can cover the exit wound."

Arlo soaked the makeshift pad with whiskey, and when Kelly lifted Kelsey high enough, he placed the pad over the wound where the lead had torn its way out.

"Bring me the second pad," said Arlo.

He placed the second pad over the entry wound and soaked the cloth with whiskey. He then returned the two-thirds empty bottle to Dallas.

"Now, Kelly," he said, "bring me some long strips that'll reach all the way around here, so I can bind these pads in place."

Kelly brought the strips, then lifted Kelsey again, allowing Arlo to pass the strips around her middle, securing the pads. Kelly then brought all the blankets they had, tugged off Kelsey's boots, removed her Levi's, and rolled her naked into the mass of heavy wool blankets. Arlo leaned forward and kissed Kelsey on her pale cheek. Already her skin felt dry and feverish.

"Thank you," said Kelsey, "but you've been shot too. You should have let Dallas and Kelly do for me."

"Couldn't do that," Arlo said. "I have a personal interest in you, and I want you around to live up to that promise."

"Kelly," said Dallas, "there's things we ain't bein' told."

"There's things you never *will* be told," Arlo said. "Now bring me that bottle of whiskey, else I'll have some infection of my own. I could live with the pain, but not without the leg."

"I'll see to your wound," said Kelly, "unless you'd rather do it yourself or have Dallas do it."

"You do it," Arlo said. "Dallas is likely to get nervous, me and him havin' been pards for so long. I just ain't comfortable, standin' around nine-tenths naked."

"Be thankful you weren't hit higher up," said Kelly. "You might have lost more than blood, and you wouldn't even be wearing your drawers. Hand me the rest of that whiskey, put your head on your saddle, and stretch out that leg. Dallas, make yourself useful. Bring me the pot with the rest of the hot water."

Dallas and Arlo watched admiringly as Kelly cleaned Arlo's wound, applied the whiskey, and tied the pads in place. She had cleaned and bandaged Arlo's wound as efficiently as he had seen to Kelsey's.

"Kelly," Dallas said, "you've just learned half of everything a Western woman needs to know."

"Oh?" said Kelly, suspiciously, "what's the other half?"

"Removin' Injun arrows," Dallas said.

"Save the rest of the lesson for the next Indian attack," said Kelly. "I've learned enough for today."

Pod Osteen, Joe Dimler, and Zondo Carp stood looking at the lifeless body of R. J. Bollinger. Yavapai and Sanchez had reined in their horses a few yards away. Yavapai had caught Bollinger's horse before it could run. Osteen spoke to the Mexican riders.

"I reckon you *Mejicanos* know that pair we chased off the mountain. Who are they?"

"Señor Wells," said Sanchez, "and one of the *señoritas* that be lost in the mountain after the fight with the *Indios*."

"There ain't nobody been swallowed by that damn mountain," Osteen said. "Can't you see that? This Wells and Holt grabbed the Logan women while the rest of you were being attacked by the Apaches."

"This pair we was shootin' at sure wasn't afraid of that mountain and its tunnels," insisted Zondo. "They got Logan's old Injun with 'em, and they're holed up in the belly of one of these mountains."

"That makes more sense than anything I've heard since we rode into this place," said Three-Fingered Joe, "but I still ain't wantin' to go wanderin' through the guts of these mountains in the dark. I say we wait for Cass and tell him what we stumbled onto."

"I'll drink to that," Zondo answered. "Whatever we do, let's do it together. If we got to search these tunnels, then let it be all of us, with loaded guns and plenty of light."

"By God," said Osteen, "it's about *time* you gents seen what's got to be done. We ain't goin' to find rich claims layin' out in some open canyon. So what if this Wells and Holt are guided by some old Injun? Ain't we got a pair of Mex guides that knows these mountains?"

"We know the outside of these mountains, Señor," said Sanchez, "but not their bellies, where the Thunder God lives."

"So you ain't goin' in the tunnels with us," Osteen mocked. "Why'n hell do we need you *pelados*? That's a question I aim to put to Bowdre when he gets back."

"Señor Bowdre be gone for horses," said Sanchez, with his infuriating grin. "When each of you are in the belly of the mountain, per'ap you take your horse with you. *Indios* have take them before, no?"

Bowdre's men looked at one another. They were going to have to split their forces or again risk losing their horses to the Apaches.

"Cass will decide who stays with the horses," Osteen said grudgingly. "The rest of us will go look for the gold, wherever the search takes us. But if I got any say, them that ain't got the sand to take a turn in the tunnel, they don't share the gold."

Yavapai and Sanchez said nothing, but their easygoing grins vanished. New battle lines were being drawn.

All Gary Davis and Cass Bowdre had in common was mutual distrust, so they rode south to Florence in virtual silence. Davis had made up his mind he would share only the cost of grub. The horses—or lack of them—were Bowdre's problem. They were nearing the town when Bowdre finally spoke.

"I can inquire about the hosses, if you want to see to the grub."

"No," said Davis, "I'll go with you to see about the horses, and then we'll both go for the grub. What's the use of buyin' anything until we have a pack mule? I'll split the cost with you, if we can find one." He wanted to make it clear he wouldn't share the cost of the horses Bowdre needed and that he had no intention of paying for supplies for Bowdre's outfit.

The livery owner was a thin old man named Boggs. He had watery blue eyes and an outward meekness that belied his inner strength.

"Sorry," he said, in response to Bowdre's inquiry. "No mules. I reckon I can spare you three horses. They ain't prime, but they're all I got, an' they're forty dollars apiece."

"God Almighty!" Bowdre exploded, "That's robbery. I didn't come here to buy the damn livery."

"You need horses, and I got horses to sell," said Boggs, unperturbed. "Take 'em or leave 'em."

"I'll take 'em," Bowdre huffed and followed Boggs to the barn.

Davis grinned at the sour expression on Bowdre's face when he led the three animals out. There was a roan, a black, and a bay, and they all had some years on them. Having been a freighter, Davis was familiar with horses and mules used as pack animals, and he guessed these horses had been used to pack ore. Now they had been retired to whatever use could be made of them.

"Let's ride on to Globe," said Bowdre, stuffing the bills of sale into his pocket. "We can get grub there and we won't have to pack it as far."

Arlo and Kelsey spent the day in pain, for they had nothing to lessen it.

"I could slip into town after dark," said Dallas, "and get some laudanum."

"If we can make it till after dark," Arlo said, "we can down that other quart of whiskey. It should make us sleep the night, rid us of fever, and by tomorrow, have us on the mend."

"It's only midday," said Kelly, "and Kelsey's already feverish."

"So am I," Arlo said, "but let's hold off on the whiskey. Since we have nothing for pain, it'll be easier on us if we can sleep the night through."

"I reckon we'd better stay in hiding," said Dallas, "until you and Kelsey are well enough to continue the hunt for the mine. This is a hardcase bunch that took after you two, and by now they know we have a hidden camp. They'll be back."

"When they do return," Arlo said, "I just hope they don't come in through the passage from the bottom of the mountain."

"Oh, Lord," said Kelly, "they *could*."

"They could," Arlo said, "and eventually they will. They saw Kelsey and me run for the cavern, and from there we had nowhere else to go but back into the passage. They'll know we have some knowledge of these tunnels beneath the mountains, and while they'll have to move slowly, they'll be coming after us."

"I'm going to slow us down," said Kelsey, awake now. "The rest of you should go on and look for the mine. Leave me here. I'll have my pistol."

"Let's do this," Dallas suggested. "Once the both of you are free of fever, Kelly and me can travel back down this passage to the foot of the mountain. From there, we can look into that other passage that angles off to the left, the one Hoss marked as safe. Since there's a chance they'll find this camp, we ought to be finding ourselves another."

"Easier said than done," Arlo said. "Even if you find an ideal camp down some other tunnel, we'll have a pair of problems. We can't take our horses and mules, and if we could, there'd be no graze. We need the little bit of grass we're able to reach from here, but this bunch that's after us will soon get wise to how we're grazing our stock. All they'll have to do is stake out the top of the mountain until they see us taking our stock to and from grass."

"Now that they have some idea where we are," said Kelly, "they'll just forget the map and spend their time looking for us."

"That's what I expect," Arlo said. "I figure Davis has thrown in with this new bunch of coyotes, since Bollinger rode in shooting. I doubt that Davis has even told them he has a map, or what he thinks is half a map. I look for the whole bunch to come after us, because we're able to find our way around in these tunnels. Davis may have convinced them we've already found the mine, or at least know where it is."

"We have to buy ourselves a little time," Dallas said. "At least until it's safe for Kelsey to be up and around."

By early afternoon the blue of the far western horizon had changed to a dirty gray, and the west wind had freshened. The sun set crimson behind a cloud bank, sending heavenward an aura that began as fuchsia, faded to pink, and finally became dusky rose. Far to the west, lightning did a brief dance and was gone. A roiling mass of thunderheads soon swallowed the sun, sweeping eastward before a rising wind.

Cass Bowdre and Gary Davis didn't fare much better in Globe than in Florence. The town was smaller, and Bowdre had to do some searching to find even three horses. Again, prices were outrageously high—it rubbed him the wrong way to *buy* horses, anyhow. Cass Bowdre was accustomed to taking what he needed, when he needed it, but that nosy county sheriff knew Bowdre and his men were in the area. Being hanged for horse stealing would be a disgrace, since they were wanted for far more heinous crimes. Bowdre had found no mules for sale at any price, nor had he located a packsaddle. Their provisions had been gunnysacked and the necks of two sacks tied together, then roped to the backs of two horses.

"Storm comin'," Bowdre observed as they rode west.

"You know of a camp with any shelter where we can watch the hosses?"

"No," said Davis truthfully. "Yavapai and Sanchez knew the place where you stayed last night, but if they know of anything better, they've kept it from me."

"I'll have some words with that pair of varmints," Bowdre said.

Davis said nothing, but he'd had his fill of Cass Bowdre. The man's arrogance exceeded even Davis's own, and Davis decided their alliance would be brief and volatile. While he doubted his own influence with Yavapai and Sanchez, it irked him to have Bowdre step in and start giving orders. Davis clenched and unclenched his big fists as he rode. *Somebody* had to lead this gold-hunting expedition. Perhaps it was time he, Gary Davis, challenged Cass Bowdre. However, Davis admitted, one wrong move on his part could turn every man against him. He would hold his peace until the odds favored him.

"Hell's fire," Pod Osteen observed, when Bowdre and Davis rode in, "I never seen a more scrubby-lookin' bunch of cayuse. They look like they pulled a stage from Saint Loo to San Diego without a rest."

"Well, by God," Bowdre snarled, "you don't like 'em, leave 'em alone."

"Let's pitch camp and eat," Zondo said. "After that, you jaybirds can cut each other's throats with dull knives for all I care. I'm half starved, and I ain't waitin' no longer."

"Hey," said Davis, "I got a man missing. Where's Bollinger?"

"He be dead," said Sanchez.

"Onliest one of your bunch with any sand," said Pod Osteen, his eyes on Davis.

"Damn it!" Davis shouted. "I didn't ask for a character reference. Can't somebody just tell me what the hell happened to Bollinger?"

"What difference does it make?" Bowdre asked sarcastically. "It won't make him any less dead."

Gary Davis saw red. He brought his big right fist

around all the way from his boot tops. Bowdre was totally unprepared, and the blow caught him on the point of his chin. He went down on his back in a cloud of dust. Slowly he struggled to hands and knees, blood dripping from the corners of his mouth. Davis had backed away so that he faced them all, his right hand only inches from the butt of his Colt.

"I ain't fist-fightin' all of you at once," Davis said, "and I ain't riskin' bein' back-shot while me and this coyote are settlin' our differences. Anybody else wants to buy in, do it now or stay out of it."

Nobody made a move. Their eyes were on Cass Bowdre. Unsteadily he got to his feet, spitting blood. "Stay out of this," he told them when he finally could speak. "I stomp my own snakes, and it'll go hard on any one of you gettin' between me and this damn fool."

Chapter 11

A cool wind swept through the canyon, and thunder rumbled closer. Davis waited, more sure of himself now that the threat of gunplay was past. Now, but for the questionable loyalty of Yavapai and Sanchez, he was alone. He must win acceptance if not respect, at least until they found the mine. The blow to the chin had temporarily stunned Bowdre, but by the time Davis had flung down the challenge to the rest of the men, Bowdre was ready. He came after Davis, his bloody lips making his wolfish grin all the more hideous.

Davis back-stepped to avoid Bowdre's vicious right, moving under it with one of his own. But Bowdre was expecting that, and he countered the blow by seizing the arm and dragging Davis toward him. Bowdre brought up a hard-driving left knee, and Davis twisted away just enough to avoid taking it in his groin. Instead, it smashed into his thigh, numbing the leg and leaving him off balance. Bowdre's left came streaking in, smashing Davis full on his right ear, driving him to his knees. Davis recovered barely in time to seize the booted foot aimed at his head. He twisted the foot savagely, and Bowdre cried out. Davis flung Bowdre away from him, and at that point the storm broke. The first wind-blown sheet of rain drenched them all. The rest of the men moved back into what shelter the mountain's overhang afforded, leaving Bowdre and Davis in the driving rain and the mud. Bowdre was on hands and knees, Davis aiming a murderous kick at his head, when lightning struck a few yards away. A pinnacle of stone exploded and fragments were flung

everywhere. Some of the horses were pelted, screaming
in pain as the men fought to hold them. Davis took a blast
of the stone shrapnel in the seat of his pants. With a howl,
he ran for the meager protection of the mountain's overhang, where the rest of the men had taken refuge.

"Help me!" Bowdre cried. "Somebody help me!" He
stood precariously on his left foot, eerily outlined as
tongues of blue and green lightning licked down into the
canyon. Night had come right on the heels of the storm,
causing the darkness to seem all the more intense. Only
Zondo Carp responded to Bowdre's frantic plea, allowing the injured man to lean on him as they made their
way out of the rain.

Thunder boomed, and as usual the mountains seemed
to vibrate violently. Cool air swept into the cavern where
Kelsey Logan slept while her companions listened to the
storm.

"With the storm," said Kelly, "maybe they'll leave us
alone tonight. Kelsey's feverish and it's getting worse."

"I doubt we'll be bothered tonight," Arlo said. "The
meaner the storm gets, the better it is for us. With this
lightning, nothing but a damn fool would be out there on
the top of a mountain. Dallas, get that second bottle of
whiskey. I reckon it's time for Kelsey and me to take our
medicine."

"God," said Kelly, "just the smell of whiskey makes
me sick. How can anybody drink it?"

"Aw," Dallas joked, "this is some of the better stuff.
Come out of a run that was aged nearly fifteen minutes."

Arlo downed a slug of the whiskey. When his coughing and choking had subsided, he swallowed as much
cold water as he could take. He had passed the bottle to
Kelly, who was pouring some of the potent brew into a
tin cup when Kelsey awakened. "I'm thirsty," she said,
"and it's so hot in here, I feel like I'm being burned
alive."

"You have fever," said Arlo. "Kelly's fixing you some

whiskey. After you drink that, you can have all the water you want."

"Maybe I ought to weaken it with water," Kelly said. "It's awful strong."

"No," said Kelsey. "Mix it with water, and there'll just be more of it. Let me swallow it quick as I can and be done with it."

"I'll raise you up some," Dallas said, "and Kelly will hold the cup. Try to keep it down. This is our last bottle of whiskey."

"My God," Kelsey sputtered, after the first sip, "it tastes like poison. I can't do it."

"It *is* poison," said Arlo, "and you have to do it. It takes poison to kill poison, and that's what infection is. Before the night's done, you'll be out of your head with fever. If you don't take enough now to sweat out the fever, you'll just have to take more later. Kelly, mix it half and half with water. It's hell takin' it straight."

"All right," Kelsey said, "I'll do it. Somehow." Little by little she swallowed the vile stuff, and since she wasn't used to it, it quickly had the desired effect. She slept soundly. Despite his concern for Kelsey, Arlo slept too. Awakening much later, he found his face was sweaty. Dallas dozed, but Kelly was awake.

"Kelsey's burning up with fever," said Kelly. "She keeps throwing off her blankets. I'm afraid for her."

"If we don't see a change soon," Arlo said, "we'll have to force some more whiskey down her. She should have had a third cup earlier. Our sparing her, not giving her enough to break that fever, will only make it worse for her now."

"She's already in a stupor," said Kelly, "and I'm afraid if we try to get more whiskey down her, she'll strangle. Let's wait a little longer. Maybe her fever will break."

Kelsey mumbled in fitful sleep as Arlo silently cursed himself for not having taken her to town to a doctor. He feared her fever wasn't going to break, and it was too late for a hard ride to town. The whiskey remedy was all they had. Kelly had folded the remnant of the petticoat into a pad, and after soaking it in cold water, laid the cloth over Kelsey's feverish face. Time after time she repeated the process, until Arlo could stand it no longer.

"No more cold water," he said. "She ought to be sweating by now."

Kelly stirred up the fire so they might see a little better. Arlo was on his knees beside Kelsey, silently begging for some evidence that the crisis was past. Finally, in the flickering light from the fire, he saw the shine of moisture on Kelsey's cheeks and forehead. He could have shouted with relief, but instead, he grabbed Kelly in a jubilant bear hug.

"I saw that," said Kelsey weakly. "How long has this been going on?"

"Since we knocked you out with whiskey," Kelly teased. "How do you feel?"

"Awful," said Kelsey. "There's a big thumping ache in my head, and I'm thirsty. I want cold water, and lots of it."

The storm continued into the small hours of the morning. Dallas dozed, his hat tipped over his eyes, until Kelly lifted the hat and dropped it on his face.

"Damn it," Dallas growled, "ain't you got some better way of wakin' a man?"

"Lots of them," said Kelly, "but for another time and another place. It's time we were taking the horses and mules to graze."

Thunder rumbled down the canyons, so frequent that one drumming seemed an echo of the last. Lightning—blue, green, and gold—leaped from one mountain to another and drove deep into the gullies. Bowdre, Davis, and their companions huddled against the east wall of the mountain, with only a slight overhang to keep them dry. Bowdre's right foot and ankle had begun to swell, and he removed his boot while he could still get it off. Amid the continued fury of the storm, the men fought to control the horses. Lightning flared almost continuously, and it was in this eerie light that they first saw the grisly apparition.

"Madre de Dios!" Yavapai shouted. "The bones walk."

The macabre thing—a skeleton, bleached white— emerged from the brush to the south of the canyon and proceeded to cross it. The skeleton's feet, moving in an erratic, shambling gait, never touched the ground. Occasionally it paused, seeming to frolic in a strange dance all its own. Just before the bony spectacle reached the brush along the south wall of the canyon, the lightning began to diminish. After a few seconds of utter darkness the lightning flared again, but the ghastly specter was gone.

"God Almighty," said Three-Fingered Joe in awe, "I ain't *never* seen nothin' like that. Not even halfway through a three-day drunk."

"Lawd God," Mose Fowler groaned, "if daylight ever come, I be gone."

"Sangre de Christo," said Sanchez, *"El Diablo* make the bones to walk."

"El Diablo, hell," scoffed Gary Davis. "A cheap trick. Somebody's tryin' to spook us. Come daylight, I'll prove it."

"Why you not prove it now?" Sanchez asked, his voice heavy with sarcasm.

"Everybody just shut the hell up," Bowdre bawled. "Nobody leaves without I say so. Now scare up some wood, get a fire goin', and boil some water. I'm hurtin'."

"Per'ap there be *Indios,"* Sanchez said. "They see fire, they come."

"By God, let the varmints come," said Bowdre savagely.

The storm had passed, but the sky remained cloudy, allowing Dallas and Kelly to take the horses and mules from the concealed camp with little risk of being seen.

"Grass is gettin' mighty thin," Dallas said.

"I know," said Kelly, "and with Arlo and Kelsey laid up, we'll lose some time. All those hours I kept trying to get Kelsey to sweat, I've been sweating too. Let's sit on the grass a little while before we go back."

"The grass is wet," Dallas said.

"I don't care. Stand if you want, but I'm sitting."

"I just said the grass is wet," he laughed, sitting beside her. "I didn't say I wasn't goin' to join you."

"It's like another world out here," she said, as they watched the few twinkling lights of town. "It must be three in the morning. Whose lights burn this late?"

"Saloons, I reckon," said Dallas.

"Did you like running a saloon?"

"It was easy work," Dallas said. "We just poured the drinks, collected the money, and watched a bunch of damn fools set there gettin' owl-eyed. No, I didn't much like bein' a saloonkeeper, but there was parts of it that wasn't bad—like havin' a regular place to sleep, a roof over my head. It's the longest I ever stayed in one place."

"I know Arlo was teasing you about rebuilding the saloon, but what *do* you plan to do once we've found the gold?"

"Depends," he said.

"On what?" Kelly asked.

"On you, I reckon. I know we've been here just a little while, without much time together, but it's plumb ruint me for the old fiddle-foot days on the long trail."

"I'll tell you a secret," said Kelly, moving closer. "Arlo has the same problem. While we were waiting for Kelsey's fever to break, he was more afraid than I was."

"Arlo and Kelsey—have an understanding," Dallas said. "I can tell they're both thinkin' beyond this search for the mine, and that's why I . . . why I . . ."

"You want to think beyond it too," said Kelly.

"Yes," Dallas said. "When we find the gold, I don't want to go my way, while you go yours. I don't want it to be the end . . . for us."

"It won't be the end for us," said Kelly, "nor for Arlo and Kelsey. There's nothing for Kelsey and me in Missouri, so we have no place to go. Unless . . ."

He removed all doubt, pulling her to him in the wet grass, and for a long moment they clung together. At last he helped her to her feet, and they climbed to their camp near the rim.

With the addition of Yavapai, Sanchez, and Gary Davis, Cass Bowdre's outfit totaled ten men, including Bowdre himself. He split the outfit into teams of three men, assigning them to watches for the rest of the night.

"Just be damn sure them hosses are there at the beginnin' and end of each watch," Bowdre said. "If them Apaches rob us again, then I aim to raise nine kinds of hell with whoever's responsible."

"Davis knows what he's talkin' about," said Pod Osteen. "We got more agin us than just Injuns. Come daylight, I'm goin' down to where that bunch of bones waltzed across the canyon and look for sign."

"Davis ain't bossin' this outfit," Bowdre said angrily, "and this ain't no damn spook hunt. We're here for gold, and we ain't wastin' time lookin' for anything else."

"*Si,*" Sanchez agreed. "We not look for the walking bones, and per'ap they not look for us."

"Lawd, no," said Mose Fowler. "Let 'em rest in pieces."

Pod Osteen turned on Bowdre. "You aim to set here with a sore hind leg, I reckon, while the rest of us scat around, follerin' your orders."

Bowdre sat with his back against a stone, his thumb hooked in his belt, inches above the butt of his Colt. In a cold, flint-hard voice he spoke.

"Yeah, that's what I aim to do, until I can do better."

While it was a statement, it was also a challenge, and every man knew it. A line had been drawn, and Cass Bowdre was prepared to kill the man who crossed it. Pod Osteen said nothing, and with nobody else taking up the argument, the moment passed.

Gary Davis, although he found himself without authority and taking orders from Cass Bowdre, was secretly pleased. There was animosity within the ranks of Bowdre's outfit, and Davis set his devious mind to the task of finding a means by which he might harness the gathering storm, and direct it to his own advantage.

Dawn came and Kelsey Logan slept soundly. When Kelly changed her dressing, the wound didn't seem inflamed. Though Arlo could scarcely stand because of the soreness, his leg wound also showed no sign of infection. It was to him that Dallas spoke.

"Kelly and me ought to take some torches and explore that other passage that angles off the main tunnel. The one Hoss calls safe. I don't think we ought to lose any time. This new bunch of gold-hungry coyotes that's moved in will either start lookin' for us or they'll begin searchin' these passages. Maybe both."

"Go ahead," said Arlo, "but don't be surprised if that passage runs into another. If you take a second or third, be sure to find some way to mark your path. There may be miles of these tunnels, and you could become so lost we'd never find you. Be sure you stay out of any passage where Hoss didn't leave a sign."

Hoss Logan had brought in several sections of resinous pine logs, and from one of these, Dallas cut a large supply of long slivers. He separated the pine pitch torches into two bundles, binding them with rawhide, one for Kelly and one for himself. Finally, they set out to explore yet another tunnel Hoss had marked as safe.

"One thing bothers me," said Kelly, as she and Dallas made their way down the long tunnel to the bottom of the mountain. "Suppose that bunch that went after Arlo and Kelsey should return to the top of the mountain to look for our camp? And suppose they find it, with Arlo and Kelsey there wounded?"

"It's a chance we'll have to take," Dallas said. "Even if they caught all of us in camp, it's no place to put up a fight. With stone all around, a ricochet could be deadly. The most important thing is that they don't grab all of us. Don't worry, Arlo won't take any chances on gettin' himself and Kelsey shot. Even if they're discovered, we'll still be free, and Arlo would buy some time, lookin' to us for help."

Dallas and Kelly followed their downward path until it ended in the high-domed cavern from which two other passages led. One ran to the outside at the eastern foot of the mountain, where Cass Bowdre and his men had lost their horses the night before. The second angled deeper into the mountain, Hoss Logan's trio of wooden pegs attesting to its safety.

"Perhaps this one will take us to the mine," Kelly said.

"I doubt it," said Dallas. "Arlo and me don't believe Hoss would have set up his camp so near the gold. Over the centuries, with volcanoes shiftin' the innards of these mountains around, there may be caves and tunnels under them all. A man like Hoss, who spent all of twenty years in the Superstitions and managed to stay alive, might have discovered his gold beneath one of the mountains."

"Going to and from it by way of these passages that connect to each other," said Kelly.

"That's what I think," Dallas said. "Some of the movement must have unearthed the gold Hoss found. That would also explain why it hadn't been found sooner."

"That's scary," said Kelly. "The earth could shift again, burying the gold all over again, and us with it."

"It might," Dallas agreed. "What I don't understand is why Hoss never mentioned the tunnels and caves to Arlo and me. We spent most of two weeks with him right here in these mountains, and not once did he mention going underground."

"That would have been before he found the gold," said Kelly. "It was the last time we saw him."

"It fits what I remember," Dallas said. "He had just come back from Missouri when he asked Arlo and me to ride into the Superstitions with him. It was almost . . . well, like he had something on his mind, something he wanted to tell us or show us. But then he seemed to have decided against it."

"He knew there was big trouble between Mother and

Daddy," said Kelly. "They had a terrible fight, and Uncle Henry left sooner than he planned to."

"From what you've just told me," Dallas replied, "I'd have to disagree with you as to the time Hoss found the gold. I think he'd already found it the last time you and Kelsey saw him. Was that when he learned about Gary Davis and your mother?"

"Yes. That's what Mother and Daddy were fighting about."

"That would account for Hoss not saying anything about the gold," said Dallas. "He wanted to see how Gary Davis was going to fit into things. He must have felt the need to talk, to confide in somebody, but he couldn't quite get up the nerve to talk to Arlo and me about somethin' so touchy. Then when his health went bad, he had to turn to somebody, and we were his friends."

"It breaks my heart," said Kelly, "thinking of him alone in his last days, not knowing if his wishes would be attended to. But when Daddy was killed, Uncle Henry would have known he'd done the right thing, wouldn't he?"

"I'm sure he felt that way," Dallas said, "or he wouldn't have drawn Arlo and me into this. He knew we'd play fair with you and Kelsey, and I just wish he'd had the nerve to talk to us while he could. It would have made everything so much simpler, and we might never have gotten Gary Davis out here, alerting the whole country to the gold."

"I think Uncle Henry *wanted* Gary Davis here," said Kelly. "Why else would he have sent us the map, knowing Davis would get his hands on it?"

"Strange logic," Dallas said, "but it seems to fit. Davis is the kind that will likely have to be shot before this is done. If not by Arlo or me, then by one of that bunch of sidewinders he's ridin' with. However he gets it, I reckon Hoss was countin' on that. Let's fire up some pine and see what this new passage can tell us."

* * *

Cass Bowdre and his men sat around their breakfast fire drinking coffee. Gary Davis, Yavapai, and Sanchez, while part of the group, had separated themselves from the others.

"Startin' today," said Bowdre, "we're goin' into the caves and tunnels. Any man that don't agree with that can saddle up and ride."

His hard eyes were on Yavapai, Sanchez, and the nervous Mose Fowler. The superstitious trio looked at him and swallowed hard but said nothing.

"Somewhere beneath the rim of that first mountain," Pod Osteen said, "the one facin' town—this Wells and Holt has got a camp. We proved that yesterday. Why ain't we goin' back up there and lookin' around?"

"Because Wells and Holt ain't holed up in camp," said Bowdre, "and us findin' them won't tell us a damn thing. They're searchin' the tunnels under these mountains, and that's exactly what we're goin' to do."

"Sounds like a standoff," Three-Fingered Joe said. "They'll have a light and we'll have a light. Can't be no gunplay. With solid rock all around us, ricochet lead would cut us all to ribbons."

"No call for gunplay till somebody finds the gold," said Bowdre. "But you're right. Them tunnels ain't no place for a gunfight. When it's time to burn powder, it'll have to be an almighty short ruckus. Whoever has the advantage will win the fight and the gold. Keep that in mind when the showdown comes."

"I'm promisin' you one damn thing," said Zondo Carp. "When some coyote cuts down on me, I'm shootin' back, ricochet or not."

There was a chorus of agreement from the others.

"All right," Bowdre growled, "but them other jaspers will likely feel the same way, and somebody's gonna git shot to doll rags."

"Won't be you, though," said Pod Osteen maliciously. "You got a swole-up foot and can't go."

"No," Gary Davis cut in, "but I can, and I will. Has anybody got guts enough to go with me? Bowdre, pick two or three men to stay with you to see to the horses and grub. The rest—them with sand enough, that is—will go with me into those tunnels."

Bowdre grinned in spite of himself. While he hated Davis, he had to admire the way the man flung down a challenge. Bowdre chose Yavapai, Sanchez, and Mose Fowler to remain with the horses. Maybe the superstitious Mexicans and the spirit-conscious Negro would be less afraid once the rest of the men returned from their quest unharmed.

"Who's ramroddin' this party?" Pod Osteen demanded, his eyes on Gary Davis.

"You are," said Davis, "for all I care. I'll side you, as long as you don't pull some fool stunt that'll get us all killed."

"By God, I'll ride with that," Eldon Sandoval said.

The others agreed, for the first time looking upon Davis with some approval. He noted the obvious friction between Bowdre and Osteen. He was satisfied that a carefully fanned spark might produce a useful flame.

"We'll leave the camp where it is," said Bowdre. "Keep track of the time, and pull out of that mountain before dark. Don't leave just the four of us to face the Apaches come night."

Pod Osteen looked at Bowdre with some amusement, but resisted the obvious temptation to speak. Instead, he went to the resinous pine log he'd found and began peeling off long slivers with his Bowie. He aimed to have enough pine torches to last the day. At last they were ready, and the six of them—Three-Fingered Joe, Zondo Carp, Os Ellerton, Eldon Sandoval, Gary Davis, and Pod Osteen—set out for the mysterious passage at the foot of the mountain.

Dallas and Kelly proceeded along the new passage, which gradually grew steeper as it began to curve.

"I have the feeling we're on our way to another mountain," Dallas said. "This passage angles away from the others, and now it's turning even more, and in the same direction."

"Steep as it is," said Kelly, "we must be headed for the top of the mountain. Maybe we'll come out at some point where we can see well enough to get our bearings. I'd like to know where we are in relation to the other mountains."

The first break in the wall was no more than a crevice, narrow and not even head-high. Dallas and Kelly carefully examined the wall on each side of the split but found nothing.

"Thank God Uncle Henry didn't mark that one," Kelly said. "I'd hate to try and get into it or out of it."

Their passage continued, the way growing steeper, with no alternate tunnels. Much of the stone walls were encrusted with gray-green lichen, so they almost overlooked the crude drawings.

"Look," Kelly cried.

Barely visible in the pale light from their torch was a "stick" man, and the head of another. Dallas brushed away the lichen, revealing the crude likeness of a horse.

"Old Indian drawings," said Kelly.

"Maybe," Dallas said. He continued to brush the surface of the stone, revealing two more horses in a line behind the first. But that was all.

"They're no help to us," Kelly said. "They've been here hundreds of years."

"The man and the first horse, maybe," said Dallas, "but the second and third horses are different from the first. They're fatter, and they've been here just long enough for the stone to moss over. Look at the outline of the old Indian horse. It's almost faded out, while the outlines of the other two are still plain."

Excited now, Kelly took her bandanna and began to rub the stone flanks of the second and third horses. Slowly a series of tiny dots that had been chiseled into the stone emerged.

"Dear God," Kelly cried, "it's the spotted ponies! He remembered them!"

"Yes," said Dallas, "and he counted on you and Kelsey remembering, too."

"Then this is the passage to the mine!"

"Maybe," Dallas said, "but I doubt it. Hoss just wanted us to know we're goin' the right way. Now you'd better take some dirt and hide the spotted horses again. Gary Davis might remember them too, especially if it's obvious we've cleaned that part of the wall."

"Perhaps they won't get this far."

"They will," said Dallas. "They know we're in the tunnels, and by now they've decided if there's any gold, it'll be down one of these passages."

"Then let's go on as far as we can. At least to the end of this one."

When it seemed they must be nearing the very top of the mountain, the passage suddenly turned to a steep descent.

"Here," Dallas said, "take my hand. We may be headed for another of those drop-offs where a stretch of the floor's gone."

When they eventually reached the chasm it was more formidable than anything their wildest imagination might have conceived. First there was a faraway sound of rushing water, and as they drew closer, they heard an eerie echo.

"There's our underground river again," said Dallas, "and I'd say we're in for a damn unpleasant surprise. Hoss tried to ease the blow with the spotted horses. I reckon he must have thought we'd need some encouragement, because there may be somethin' ahead that'll scare the hell out of us."

Chapter 12

The furious voice of the river grew louder, yet still seemed distant. Their way grew less steep, leveling out until they stood on a ledge. In the poor light of the torch, they could see a ragged edge, and beyond that, nothing. But for the sound of the water far below, they would have thought the void bottomless.

"My God," Kelly shuddered, "it must be a mile deep."

"A good four or five hundred feet," said Dallas. "We're gettin' no spray, so that tells us we're a long ways above the water. Let's go a little closer, so I can get some idea how far down it is."

"No!" Kelly cried. "Remember how the ledge broke off when you tried to cross that hole in the other passage?"

"I don't aim to get that close," said Dallas. "I want to drop a lighted piece of pine and see how long it takes to reach the water."

From the torch he carried, Dallas lit another. When the flame had caught enough that the downdraft wouldn't suck it out, he dropped the torch over the edge. The flame grew smaller and smaller, and by the time it was swallowed by the swirling water, they could barely see the tiny point of light.

"My God," said Kelly in awe.

"While we're here," Dallas said, "we might as well look around and see if Hoss left us some sign."

Dallas began searching the stone walls of the passage that led to the ledge, but found nothing. A dozen feet from the edge of the drop-off, he got on his knees and ran his hands over the cracked and broken stone.

"I know what you're looking for," said Kelly, "and I hope you don't find it."

But he did find it. Near the edge of the precipice, driven into a crevice in the rock, were three little oak pins.

Pod Osteen led the way down the dark passage Paiute had followed after stealing Kelly and Kelsey Logan away. Osteen hesitated when he reached the point where the stream flowed in from a second passage. Should he continue straight ahead or turn and follow the stream?

"We'll follow the water," said Osteen. "Might lead us to somebody's camp. If it comes to nothin', or plays out, we can always backtrack."

They reached the cavern where Dallas, Arlo, Kelly, and Kelsey had spent a restless night. There they found nothing to interest them, for Arlo had scattered Hoss Logan's trio of stones.

"Come on," said Osteen. "There's another tunnel leadin' out."

The next passage they took—the only one—led into the mountain whose western flank bore the shadowy likeness of a death's head at sunset. Osteen and his followers were halted abruptly at the abyss above the underground river.

"Maybe we can put our backs to the wall," Osteen said, "and ease across the ledge to the other side."

"Go on," Sandoval said, "if you're that big a fool. I ain't."

"Me neither," said Three-Fingered Joe. Os Ellerton and Zondo Carp quickly agreed with Joe and Sandoval.

"We'll need a rope to cross that," said Gary Davis. "Maybe a pair of them. That way, if a man slips, the rest of us can haul him back up."

"Good thinkin'," Osteen said. "Who'll go back for a pair of catch ropes?"

"I'll go," said Davis. He followed the stream until it joined the main passage, where it flowed out of the mountain. But as he stepped into the main passage, a shadow moved behind him. Then a strong, bony arm circled his throat, and a powerful blow to the head silenced him without a whimper.

"I don't feel safe here anymore," worried Kelsey Logan, awake now. "After they ran us into the tunnel, they'll know it leads to our camp."

"I'm afraid you're right," Arlo said. "Even though they may not be looking for us, they'll have to take to the passages looking for the gold, so they could just stumble onto us without even trying. Soon as you're able to be up and around, we'll have to get out of here."

"Let's start by getting me some clothes on—but not until I've had a bath. I've sweated so much I stink. Please stir up the fire, heat some water, and help me wash myself."

"Wouldn't you rather Kelly did that?"

"Of course not," she said. "Why are you suddenly so modest?"

"I'm not," he laughed, "but I thought you might be."

"How could I be," Kelsey said, "after the three of you took off all my clothes, got me drunk, and let me spend most of a day and a night without even a blanket?"

"Hell," Arlo said, "you had *all* the blankets, and you kept fighting your way out of them. You even embarrassed Dallas, which ain't easy."

"Then let's spare the poor boy any more embarrassment," she said. "Let's get me all cleaned up and dressed before he gets back."

Dallas and Kelly returned to find Kelsey dressed and—despite Arlo's protests—up and about. Arlo and Kelsey listened as Dallas explained what they had discovered.

"Now that's a real break," said Arlo, "and it's going to determine where we go from here. For the drop-off you've discovered, we're going to need longer, stronger ropes and coal oil lanterns. That means a trip to town. Dallas, it'll be up to you and Kelly."

"Then we'd better get started," Dallas said. "We can be back before dark, and in the morning we'll be ready to go over the edge and down to that crazy river."

"Lord," said Kelly, "it's an awful long way down. It scares me just thinking of it."

"You and Kelsey won't be going down," Arlo said. "Dallas and I will."

"I'm scared," said Kelly, "but I'm going, however far down it is."

"So am I," Kelsey said. "I've come this far, and I don't want to be left out at the finish."

"You won't be," Arlo assured her. "Remember what a hell of a time we had, just getting into that mountain that had the death's head at sundown, only to find that a passage led into it from the other end? We had to take the hard way in, because we knew of no other. Well, it's going to be the same with the underground river. Only a fool would believe Hoss Logan hauled gold ore up over a bluff as high and as dangerous as that. So again, there has to be a better way in and out, but to find it we must first get in, and that means goin' down the bluff. The underground stream has to go somewhere, and I believe at some point it'll empty into the Salt River. Once we learn where it goes—and maybe where it originates—we'll find a better way in and out."

"Much as I hate to give up this camp," Dallas said, "when Kelly and me return from town, I think we'd better move out. Maybe off the mountain. If this bunch Davis is tied in with ain't searchin' the tunnels, they soon will be. Besides, we're plumb out of graze for our horses and mules."

"Hustle, then," said Arlo, "and if there's anything else you can think of that we might need, bring it. This may be our last chance for supplies. Once we find the gold, we'll have to fight to keep it."

Gary Davis had been gone for an hour, and Pod Osteen was fuming.

"Eldon, you and Zondo go and bring some rope. By God, this Davis had better have a good excuse. Like two busted legs."

Sandoval and Carp returned to camp and told Cass Bowdre of the missing Davis.

"Hell, I ain't seen him since he left with you," said Bowdre, mystified. "His hoss, his pack, and his grub's still here. Maybe he took a wrong turn."

"All he had to do was foller that stream of water," said Sandoval. "A blind mule could of done that."

"Ah knowed it," Mose Fowler groaned. "He done been took by the spirits."

"Damn it," Bowdre growled, "it don't make sense. If he was wadin' water, soon as he left it, there'd have been tracks. Some mud, anyhow."

"No tracks, no mud, no sign," said Carp.

"Is simple," Sanchez said. "Señor Davis no leave mountain."

"Per'ap he never will," Yavapai added. "It have take others, and now it take him."

"Damn fool superstitions," Bowdre scoffed. "For whatever reason, Davis went down the wrong end of that shaft, and he's lost in there. Let him find his way out, or stay lost. Now you hombres take a pair of ropes and get back to Osteen and the others."

Sandoval and Carp took the lariats and started back, while Cass Bowdre eyed his three companions in disgust. While Fowler and the *Mejicanos* might pull their weight in a fight with Apaches, they wouldn't be worth a damn in a search of the dark passages beneath the Superstitions. Silently Bowdre cursed Gary Davis for a swollen foot and ankle that still refused to support his weight.

From the east rim, Dallas and Kelly delayed their descent until Sandoval and Carp had disappeared into the mountain.

"Like we figured," said Dallas. "They're into the tunnels, and I reckon they've reached that hole I fell into, so they went back for ropes."

"I just hope they don't find their way to our camp," Kelly replied, "with only Arlo and Kelsey there."

"They'll be a while gettin' across that hole," Dallas said, "and when they do, all they'll get is a trip back the way they come. But it's the only passage they know of, where the stream flows out and into the canyon. Once they cross that hole, find nothing, and have to cross it again, the day will be mostly spent."

"So they won't have time to find their way into our camp before tomorrow, even if they choose the right passages?" asked Kelly.

"No," Dallas said, "because they'll waste today findin' out they're barkin' up the wrong tree. By then we'll be back and will have moved our camp."

"Where are we going?"

"Out of these mountains, for sure," said Dallas. "We could camp in the brakes along the Salt River, but I'm favorin' a move back to Hoss's cabin, near Saguaro Lake. It's not far when you ain't dodgin' a bunch of gold-crazy hombres."

"But you can see for miles up here," Kelly said. "When we ride back to search for the mine, they'll see us coming."

"They ain't gonna be watchin' from the rim if they're in the passages and caves under the Superstitions," said Dallas. "When they find the way to our deserted camp, they'll have an idea we're off the mountain. But I'm inclined to agree with Arlo. I think once we make it over the edge and down to that river, we'll find a way to the outside, probably where the underground stream joins the Salt River. If that's how it is, it'll mean we can reach that underground canyon at some point distant from the mountains. Even if Gary Davis and that bunch do find the drop-off, they'll have no reason to believe it's the way to the mine. They'll need a strong reason to climb down into that chasm, and they won't have one. Would *you* climb down that way without a sign from Hoss?"

"My God, no!" she cried. "And you're right—they won't have a sign to guide them."

"Right," said Dallas. "Arlo and me will have to go one

more time, to descend that bluff and find a way out. The in and out that Hoss used."

"I just wish there was some other way," Kelly said, "so you and Arlo didn't have to go down into that terrible void. I wouldn't have either of you hurt or killed for all the gold in Arizona. Or the world, for that matter."

Dallas laughed. "Thanks, but I reckon it's not as dangerous as it looks. Hoss wouldn't have brought us this far just to get us killed. I think that's why he didn't hesitate to send you and Kelsey the same map he sent Arlo and me. He planned this so nobody—Gary Davis included—could figure it out without you and Kelsey."

"Uncle Henry was awful sure we'd get together. Suppose we hadn't?"

"Hoss knew Arlo and me pretty damn well, I reckon. Well enough that he had some idea which way we'd jump, once you and Kelsey showed up. As pretty a pair as two fiddle-footed cowboys ever laid eyes on. Of course," he added gleefully, "we've laid eyes on considerably more of Kelsey than of you."

"Once we find the gold," she said, "that could change."

"I aim for it to," said Dallas, "but I'd like to manage it without you bein' stripped by Apaches and shot by Davis and that bunch of outlaws."

"So would I," she said, "and I'd like to leave Arlo and Kelsey out of it."

They slid their horses down the steep trail into the canyon where Kelsey had been shot. Dallas was in the lead, and he reined up, waiting for Kelly.

"What is it?" Kelly asked.

"Bad luck canyon," said Dallas. "We almost lost Kelsey here, and I ain't riskin' you. Let's ride."

By the time Carp and Sandoval returned with the rope, Pod Osteen was in a vile mood.

"That damn Davis," he snarled. "He sneaked off on his own. When he shows up again, he'll claim he's been lost."

Osteen snubbed one end of a rope to a boulder and tied the other end under his arms. Three-Fingered Joe held the flaming pine torch.

"I'll work my way across," said Osteen. "If I should slip, or if that ledge won't hold, haul me in, and do it quick."

From the opposite side of the abyss, he began inching his way along the broadest of the two ledges, the same one that had crumbled beneath Arlo's feet. He had taken only a few steps when the ledge gave way and he was falling. His terrified shriek was cut short when he hit the end of the rope and the wind was knocked out of him. When his companions had dragged him to safety, Osteen lay there sweating and gasping for breath.

"Maybe we oughta just go back the way we come," said Three-Fingered Joe.

"Like hell," Osteen grunted. "This may be the very shaft we need to search, and we're gonna do it. Soon as I get my wind, I'll try the other ledge."

"By God," said Os Ellerton, "either you got sand in your craw or you're a damn fool. If that ledge won't hold, what makes you think the other one will?"

"Because the other ledge is narrower and should be stronger," Osteen said. "Besides, we got to get across that hole. I'm heavier than any of you, and if I can cross, the rest of you will be able to."

Osteen got to his feet, and with his back to the wall, began inching his way across the other side of the gaping hole. This time he was successful.

"All right," he said, loosening his end of the rope, "haul in the rope and the rest of you come on over. Whoever comes next, bring a piece of that pine and some matches, so's we got light from this side."

Osteen waited impatiently while his companions worked their way along the narrow ledge, one at a time. The abyss behind them, the five followed the passage to a cavern from which the only exit was straight down the side of the mountain. They were now within the mountain where the shadowy death's head appeared at sundown.

"Not a damn thing here," said Sandoval, "except some old bones without a head. We risked our necks crossin' that black hole, and now we got to do it again, all for nothin'."

"Maybe not," Osteen said. "There's breaks in these walls, and there's some light. Maybe we can get back to the outside from here."

Three-Fingered Joe had already found the hole where Arlo, Dallas, and the Logan girls had come in from the outside. He crept back into the cavern on hands and knees, a frown on his face.

"Well?" Osteen inquired impatiently.

"Yeah, you can get out that way," said Joe, "if you're a bird. It's a good two hundred feet, straight down."

"Damn," Zondo Carp said, "most of a day shot, nothin' to show for it, and we *still* got to cross that ledge again."

"We'll follow that stream back to the main passage," said Osteen. "Then we'll take that main passage on into the mountain."

"Maybe you will," Sandoval said, "but I'm callin' it a day and havin' some grub."

"Same here," said Three-Fingered Joe. "We'll be a while just gettin' out of here, and Cass wants us back before dark. God knows how many of these tunnels we'll have to search. We can't do it all in one day."

Wearily, one at a time, they inched their way across the narrow ledge in the opposite direction. Reaching the point where the stream flowed into the main passage, they paused.

"That's got to be the way Davis went," Osteen said. "Before we leave, let's go back there a ways and look around."

Carrying the torch, he led out. They had gone only a few steps when he drew up. On the stone floor at his feet was a hat. Osteen picked it up and for a moment nobody said anything. Os Ellerton was the first to speak.

"I never knowed a man to lose his hat an' leave it,

unless he was dead or dyin'. I'm wonderin' if Davis ain't met somethin' bigger an' meaner than he was."

It was a disturbing possibility that no man could ignore.

"These damn mountains are startin' to spook me," said Three-Fingered Joe. "As for Davis, I don't even like the varmint, but I flat don't believe he's run out on us. Somethin' or somebody grabbed him."

"I ain't a superstitious Mex, myself," Zondo Carp said, "but I'm ready to agree that somethin' ain't natural about these mountains."

His words suddenly seemed all the more sinister, for deep within the mountain sounded a rumbling that shook the stone on which they stood. Zondo Carp had lit a pine torch of his own, and when he set out down the passage that led to the outside, the others followed. Pod Osteen was the last to leave, and for once he had nothing to say. In his hands was the hat Gary Davis had left, and on his mind were troublesome questions to which he had no answers.

Dallas reined in his horse and waited until Kelly was beside him. "There's just been a change in plans," he said. "There ain't a thing we need that can't be had at Silas Hays's general store in Tortilla Flat."

"So we're going there, avoiding the sheriff?"

"Right," Dallas said. "While we haven't broken any laws, I can't see spending a couple of hours bringin' Sheriff Wheaton up to date on what's happened. I reckon I should have thought of that in time to discuss it with Arlo, but there's no help for it now. I think you and Kelsey should remain among the missing, as far as the sheriff and everybody else is concerned. At least until we've either found the gold or given up on it."

"You don't think the people in Tortilla Flat will talk?"

"Sure," Dallas said, "but it's unlikely we'll see anybody except old Silas at the store. While he ain't above telling anything he knows, he won't go out of his way to get word to the sheriff."

Dallas and Kelly soon reached Tortilla Flat and rode past the blackened ruins of the Gila Saloon, to the general store without seeing anyone. With luck, nobody had seen them either. Silas Hays, the store's bespectacled owner, was alone. Of course he had seen them ride up, but when Dallas and Kelly entered the store, Silas was busy trying to look busy.

"Howdy, Dallas," said Silas, his eyes on Kelly.

"Silas," Dallas said recklessly, "this is Kelly Logan. We're gettin' hitched, and we're needin' some stuff to set up housekeeping."

This direct, unexpected turn was calculated to throw the nosy old fellow's inquisitive nature off the track, and to the amusement of Dallas and Kelly, it had considerably more than the desired effect.

"Uh . . . . congratulations," Silas stammered. "Arlo . . . what about . . ."

"Arlo's goin' with us on the honeymoon," Dallas cut in, trying not to look at Silas. "We look to save all kinds of money takin' just one hotel room. We'll need some half-inch rope. Make it eight hundred feet, and cut it into four lengths of two hundred feet each. Besides that, we want five gallons of coal oil, two lanterns, ten pounds of coffee beans, and four quarts of whiskey."

"A gallon of whiskey, then," said Silas.

"A gallon," Dallas said, "but in four one-quart bottles."

Silas looked doubtfully at Dallas, wondering if all this was some kind of joke at his expense. But Dallas never changed expression, and Kelly forced herself to look equally serious. Silas began gathering their order. When it was ready, Dallas paid, and they departed without a word or a backward look.

"You ought to be ashamed of yourself," Kelly laughed, once they were outside. "You shocked the poor old fellow so badly, he couldn't think of anything to say."

"Only enough that he forgot to question us," said Dallas, "and that was the idea. The very last thing we needed was questions about the mine. If I'd *really* wanted to shock him, I'd have told him that Arlo and me was rebuildin' the Gila Saloon and you was one of the whores who'd be workin' upstairs."

"Don't push your luck, cowboy."

Dallas divided the load between his horse and Kelly's. They rode out as they had come in, until they were out of sight of Tortilla Flat. It was Kelly who finally spoke.

"We should have brought one of the mules."

"Won't need one," said Dallas. "We ain't goin' that far."

"We're not taking this back to the mountains?"

"No use packin' it up the mountain only to haul it down again," Dallas said. "Since we plan to move the camp, I think we'll take this on to Hoss's cabin and leave it there. It'll be safe enough until we return."

"Do you think Arlo will agree to us leaving the mountains and moving back to Uncle Henry's cabin?"

"Yes," Dallas said, "for several reasons. Mostly because our camp won't be safe when the others who are searching for the mine take to the underground. Besides that, we're going to need some time for Arlo and Kelsey to heal, and that means some protection from the elements. See that mass of clouds to the west? There's another storm buildin', if not today, then tomorrow. With any luck, we can find the mine before Davis and that bunch of coyotes he's throwed in with discover we've moved back to the cabin."

Cass Bowdre was worried. Despite his callous declaration that he didn't care if Gary Davis was lost somewhere beneath the Superstitions, he was shaken when Pod Osteen handed him the hat Davis had been wearing. It was a bad omen. While Osteen's arrogance hadn't diminished in the slightest, the men who had accompanied him were subdued. When they spoke, it was with doubt and some fear.

"I ain't sure Davis is lost in that mountain," said Sandoval. "I'll never get so damn lost I can't pick up my hat."

"Me neither," said Three-Fingered Joe. "Suppose we

foller the rest of them tunnels and don't find hide nor hair of Davis?"

"You will find no sign of the Señor Davis," Sanchez said. "Per'ap then you believe the Thunder God lives."

"I've had a bellyful of the Thunder God," Osteen snorted, "and I'm layin' down a new rule. Once we find the gold, I ain't sharin' it with them that's too damn cowardly to help search for it. Now if there's any man that don't like that, let him speak his piece an' do it now."

Nobody spoke. Every man's eyes were on Cass Bowdre. It was a hard decision and a direct challenge to Bowdre's leadership. It was going to cost Osteen. But the Apache threat to them all was very real, and he relied on that. But Cass Bowdre couldn't allow them to see even a hint of intimidation, and he turned hard eyes on Osteen.

"As I recall, Pod," said Bowdre, "when the Apaches grabbed our hosses, you done your share of hell-raisin'. Now, if I understand your gripe, you want every man looking for gold, again leavin' our horses to the mercy of the Injuns. Is that what you're sayin', Pod?"

"By God," Osteen shouted, "I'm sayin' the same hombres don't set on their hunkers ever' day, while the rest of us search them passages under the mountains."

"What the hell difference does it make who watches the hosses?" Bowdre demanded. "Since you don't believe in the Thunder God, how can searching under the mountains be as risky as gettin' your gut shot full of Apache arrows? You're up against just one Thunder God, while the three men left with the hosses might have to face God knows how many Apaches."

"Damn good point," said Three-Fingered Joe. "I ain't sure about this old Thunder God, but them Apaches is real enough to suit me."

There was nervous laughter, but surprisingly the men stood by Cass Bowdre, leaving Pod Osteen furious. He glared at them all in surly silence, aware that Bowdre had once again bested him and unsure what he might do in retaliation.

Chapter 13

Two hours before sundown, Dallas and Kelly returned to their camp below the rim, and Dallas explained to Arlo his reasons for leaving their new purchases at Hoss's cabin.

"Good thinking," Arlo said. "We should have discussed that before you rode out. If they're goin' into the passages with ropes, it means they've reached that big hole above the underground river. Once they've crossed that, found nothing, and crossed it again, they'll be ready to follow the main tunnel into the mountain. As soon as tomorrow, they could be in the shaft that'll bring them to where we are right now. We don't have any time to spare in getting out of here."

"We'd better move on out and head for the cabin right now," Dallas said. "The storm that's on the way ought to be here sometime tonight, and it'll eliminate our tracks."

While the ride wasn't a long one, Kelsey was gritting her teeth before they reached the cabin. Arlo helped the girl to dismount and got her inside.

"There's only three bunks," said Dallas, "but it's not likely we'll be here long enough for that to be a problem. The important thing is, we'll have a roof over our heads. We're goin' to need it."

Sundown was still an hour away, but the sun had slipped behind a growing mass of gray thunderheads and a cool west wind brought the feel of rain.

"Now that we're out of the Superstitions," Kelly said, "I feel kind of . . . well, free. I didn't notice it too much while we were there, but it was like the mountains had some kind of control over us, some hold that was broken only by our leaving."

"There is somethin' about the Superstitions that draws you to them," said Arlo. "Dallas and me never understood why Hoss went back again and again when he never found even a trace of color. I remember him sayin' that you're always a little uneasy, there in the Superstitions, but when you're away from them, you miss them. Then, when you return, you're never exactly sure as to why."

"I believe our coming to these mountains brought us closer to Uncle Henry," said Kelsey, "and even if we never find the gold, I'm glad we came. With or without the gold, I'd like to spend the rest of my life in the shadow of the Superstitions. I want to see them at sunset, ever changing, and then by starlight, or beneath a full moon. I just feel like I've been away for a long time, and now I . . . I've come home."

"I reckon Hoss would be pleased," Dallas said, "but not surprised."

Not daring to leave their horses to the mercy of the elements and the Apaches, Cass Bowdre and his men had again made their camp against the east wall of the mountain where they'd weathered the previous night's storm. Everybody—even Pod Osteen—was silent. They couldn't afford the luxury of bickering now, for the impending storm was spooking the horses, and holding them had become increasingly difficult. The thunder rumbled closer, and while the lightning hadn't yet become a danger, its eerie dance across the horizon was a harbinger of the fury to come. Bowdre and his companions, the violence of the last storm strong in their minds, eyed the darkening sky with growing apprehension.

"We're in for a hell of a blow," said Sandoval. "This would be a good time for the Apaches to come after us."

Nobody bothered with a response, but it was a sobering thought. Once the lightning became continuous— and there was every evidence it would—they would all be outlined against the side of the mountain—perfect targets. It could become a perilous situation, where a man might lose his horse, his hair, or both. The lightning, Bowdre noticed, was building up to truly terrifying proportions. That, he hoped, might be the thing that would intimidate the Apaches.

"She's gonna throw some mean lightning at us," he voiced, "and that might work for us. If the Injuns do come after us, forget the hosses and fight like hell. There's worse things than losin' a hoss. Like gainin' an arrow in your belly."

Soon the entire canyon before them was bathed in an almost continuous eerie light. Without warning, the macabre skeleton appeared, shambling across the canyon, as it had before.

"*Madre de Dios,*" Yavapai shouted. "Again the bones walk!"

Pod Osteen foolishly drew his Colt and began firing at the apparition, sending the already skittish horses into a new frenzy of rearing and nickering.

"Damn it," Bowdre roared, "hold your fire!"

By the time they had calmed the horses, the lightning had begun to subside, and the bony apparition had again crossed the rain-swept canyon and disappeared. Ignoring his still painful foot, Bowdre snatched a fistful of Osteen's shirt as his right hand drew and cocked his Colt. Brutally he rammed the cold muzzle of the weapon into Osteen's nose, and a shower of blood mingled with the driving rain streaming down Pod's face.

"By God," Bowdre snarled, "I ought to kill you."

Osteen's life hung in the balance, and nobody was more aware of it than he, for the fear in his eyes was genuine. Disgusted, Bowdre flung the man away, and he fell on his back in the mud. The wind was dying now, and the rain was settling into a steady downpour. The mountain's rim had enough overhang so that their packs and bedrolls had been protected, and there was enough room for them to sleep dry.

"Two watches," Bowdre ordered. "I'll take the first, along with Os and Eldon. You're part of it too, Osteen."

The insult was obvious. Bowdre distrusted Osteen to the extent that he refused to sleep with the man on watch. The rest of them—those who would take the second watch—turned to their bedrolls to get what sleep they could.

The cabin Hoss Logan had built was sturdy and dry. An occasional gust down the chimney blew smoke into the room, as the storm-bred wind rattled sheets of rain against the log walls and the shake roof.

Dallas laughed. "I'd bet my saddle that bunch up yonder in the Superstitions is havin' one hell of a night."

"Plenty of shelter," Arlo said, "and they don't dare take advantage of it, lest Apaches grab their horses."

"I'm almost afraid to ask," said Kelly, "but when will you and Dallas go into the chasm to the underground river?"

"I'd like to go tomorrow," Arlo said, "but I reckon I'd better give this wound another day. This would be a poor time to have a leg give out on me. I feel a mite uneasy, both of us goin' and leaving you and Kelsey here alone. But a man's got no business going into the Superstitions by himself. I'm counting on us finding our way into and out of that river before Davis and that bunch in the mountains figure out what's goin' on. They eventually will, when they find nothing in the tunnels beneath the mountains."

"We'll feel better taking our chances here alone," said Kelsey, "than in having just one of you go back into those mountains. With Gary Davis in the mountains, what could happen to us here?"

"I don't know," Arlo said. "Nothing, I hope. Anyway, we won't be leaving you alone at night. I just don't believe Hoss would send us down that bluff unless there's some better way in and out. If we start early, we may find it in a day. Then we can be done with this."

"Oh, and I do want us to be done with this!" Kelly

cried. "But what happens if . . . when . . . we find the gold?"

"We'll file a claim," said Arlo, "and leave that greedy bunch of coyotes up there in the mountains wondering what happened."

"I'm afraid that won't stop them from coming after us," Kelsey said.

"Maybe not," said Dallas, "but we'll have a legal claim, and that has us within the law. We can hire us some pistoleros and gun the varmints down if they won't have it any other way."

"Dear God," Kelly said, "that would be barbaric, us killing people just to hold on to a gold claim."

"We don't know it will come to that," Arlo said, "but would it be any less terrible if we allowed them to kill us and take a claim that in no way belongs to them? Hell, these varmints will steal us blind if they can. What kind of justice is that?"

"You're right," Kelly sighed. "This is the West, the frontier. I suppose it will never become civilized in our lifetimes."

"Too damn much civilization will be the ruination of the world," said Dallas. "I hope the frontier, just the way it is, outlives me. It's the last even break a man will ever get. I reckon the time will come when some slicked-up varmint tells us we can't carry our guns, when crooked politicians, judges, and lawyers can rob us all legal and proper, in the courts. Like they done old Jed Logan, back in Missouri."

"That's exactly what was done to him," Kelsey said bitterly. "So let's hold on to the frontier as long as we can. Even with its faults, I love it. We're going to find that mine of Uncle Henry's, and if we have to fight to hold it, I'm ready."

Cass Bowdre's men kept an uneasy vigil for the rest of the night. The second watch—Three-Fingered Joe, Zondo Carp, Yavapai, Sanchez, and Mose Fowler—had little to say among themselves. The ghastly skeleton had further unnerved them, as had Pod Osteen's foolish stunt. Not one of the men faulted Cass Bowdre for his brutal treatment of Osteen. The two were obviously headed for a showdown that might destroy the gang's already shaky alliance, dooming their chances of ever finding the gold. But that was the way of the frontier, and they all understood that.

"Come on," Bowdre growled, "roll out."

Having been part of the second watch, Mose Fowler already had a breakfast fire going and the coffee boiling.

"I'm goin' out there where that rack of bones drifted across the canyon," said Zondo Carp, "and see if there's any sign."

"I'll go with you," Sandoval said, grinning derisively at Osteen. "Maybe the varmint's layin' out yonder shot dead, and we just can't see him from here."

While it was an obvious dig at Pod Osteen, it struck the rest of the gang as hilariously funny. Mose Fowler slapped his hat against his thigh, and even the superstitious Yavapai and Sanchez joined in the laughter. Bowdre grinned, and the furious Pod Osteen turned away, his face flaming with embarrassment. He distanced himself from the rest of the men, sat down on a stone pillar, and ignored them. Carp and Sandoval soon returned, having found nothing.

"I never seen a man empty a Colt," said Os Ellerton, "and not make at least one hit. If the Apaches attack, he might as well throw rocks."

There was more laughter, and they finished breakfast without Osteen. But the laughter soon ceased, for the power struggle between Osteen and Bowdre was yet to be resolved. As long as the two men were at odds, the search for the mine would suffer. Would Osteen continue to take orders from Bowdre? They would soon know. Bowdre still limped, but he could walk, and he began the day by addressing the sulking Osteen.

"Are you goin' to join us, Pod, or do you just aim to perch on that rock for the rest of the day?"

His back to them, Osteen said nothing, and Bowdre

began walking slowly toward him. Halting a few steps away, Bowdre spoke, his voice cold.

"Pod, I ain't one to leave loose ends danglin' that might trip me up somewhere down the trail, when I ain't expectin' it. There's more'n one way we can settle this, but I reckon the best way is for you to saddle up and ride. And keep ridin'."

Slowly Osteen got to his feet, and when he faced Bowdre, the hate in his eyes said he had an alternative in mind. He hooked his thumb over his pistol belt, just inches above the butt of his Colt. Slowly he backed away until he and Bowdre were a dozen yards apart. Sidewinder quick, Osteen had his Colt out and spitting lead before Bowdre drew, but Osteen's first shot went wide. Bowdre fired once, and Osteen's Colt began to sag. His second shot drove a slug into the ground at his feet, and he stared at Bowdre with venom in his eyes, as his own blood soaked the front of his denim shirt. He stumbled backward, his knees buckling, and fell on his back. Bowdre waited a moment before reloading his Colt, but Osteen didn't move. Bowdre holstered the Colt and turned to face the rest of the men.

"That leaves us a man short," said Bowdre, "but he wouldn't have it any other way. The bone orchard's full of damn fools with more pride than horse sense. I'll be taking Osteen's place in the tunnels. Mose, I want you, Yavapai, and Sanchez to watch the hosses. We'll be back here before dark. Any questions?"

There were none. Bowdre and his companions set out for the mountain and its tunnels while Mose, Yavapai, and Sanchez watched them until they were out of sight. Sanchez stood slightly behind Mose, so the Negro couldn't see the look Sanchez passed to Yavapai. It was time.

There was no talk until Bowdre and his men entered the mountain and reached the point where the passage divided.

"So you follered the stream to the end," said Bowdre, "and took the only other passage until it ran out."

"We did," Carp said. "When we got back to here, we took just a few steps on into the mountain, and that's where we found the hat."

"We'll foller the other leg of this passage, then," said Bowdre, "and go as far as it'll take us."

They passed other tunnels, but Bowdre kept straight ahead. He paused only when the passage narrowed down until they could no longer stand.

"Git on yer hands and knees," Bowdre said. "We'll foller it a ways. Maybe it'll widen some, and if it don't, we'll turn back."

"Waste of time," answered Sandoval. "It'll likely pinch down to nothin'. We might as well backtrack and try another tunnel."

"Only if this one plays out," Bowdre said. "Let's go."

Bowdre took the lead, laughing exultantly as the passage expanded. They soon found themselves in a huge cavern, and although their original passage had ended, there were two others leading out in different directions.

"Let's try the one on the right," said Carp. "I'm bettin' it'll take us to Wells and Holt. Or at least to the camp they've been usin'."

The rest of the men enthusiastically agreed, and Bowdre went along with it. The way grew steeper, and there were other passages leading off, but they kept to their original course. From somewhere ahead, they could hear falling water.

"Hold it," Bowdre said. "They would have needed fresh water. This *could* be Wells and Holt's hideout."

They moved cautiously ahead until Bowdre could see into the cavern that had so recently been occupied by Arlo, Dallas, and the Logan girls.

"Nobody here," he said.

His companions followed, and immediately they took the second passage that opened beneath the mountain's west rim, where the horses and mules had been taken in and out.

"By God," Os Ellerton said, "this is some dandy camp. We been rained on, dodged Apaches and lightnin' bolts, an' hunted water, while these hombres and their horses was kept safe an' dry, with fresh water a-plenty."

"Yeah," said Three-Fingered Joe, "and it's damn strange. Don't make sense, runnin' out on a camp like this."

"The hell it don't," Zondo Carp responded. "We run a pair of 'em into the tunnel, didn't we? They was smart enough to know we'd foller 'em into the tunnels and end up here. So they skedaddled."

"That's it," Bowdre agreed.

"Since they knew of this passage," said Sandoval, "maybe they have another one, down another tunnel."

"I doubt it," Bowdre said. "They'd expect us to find any other such camp the same way we found this one."

"This is one damn fine camp," said Ellerton. "Since they pulled out, why don't we take this place for ourselves?"

"Because we got eight hosses that have to eat," Bowdre said, "and even if they could live on nothin' but grain, we can't afford it."

"Could get damn unhealthy in here, anyhow," said Sandoval. "If this Wells and Holt took to throwin' lead in here agin these stone walls an' ceilin', the ricochets would be hell. I reckon we'd all end up as coyote bait."

"There must be some kind of trail down this side of the mountain," Three-Fingered Joe offered. "Why don't we take this other passage to the outside and find out?"

"Because we don't need it," replied Bowdre. "Not unless we decided to make this our camp. We're goin' back the way we come, and when we get to the bottom of this mountain, we'll try that other passage."

They hadn't traveled far on their return journey when they reached a side passage that angled off to their right. They paused when their torch flickered, a draft sucking at the flame.

"That's bound to lead to the outside," said Three-Fingered Joe. "Let's see where it comes out."

It was the passage Paiute had once shown Dallas and

Arlo. It led to a point well below the western rim, without access to the top or to the foot of the mountain. But it afforded a view for miles, and after dark the lights of the distant town would be visible. Once Cass Bowdre and his companions discovered it was a dead end with only hundreds of feet of empty space below, they lost interest. All but Sandoval, for he had seen something the others had missed.

"Horses and men," Sandoval called out. "Over yonder to the northwest."

The midmorning sun bore down with a vengeance, and heat waves danced across the distant plain, making visibility difficult. The tiny figures appeared, vanished, and appeared again.

"Two riders," said Bowdre, "and eight riderless horses, trailin' northwest. Who are they, and where . . ."

"By God," Sandoval roared, "them's got to be our horses, and I'd bet a pair of Texas boots the coyotes drivin' 'em ain't Apaches."

The terrible truth hit them with the force of a buffalo stampede. Bowdre, cursing under his breath, lit out down the passage, the others following. They ran through the cavern and fought their way up the crevice to the mountaintop. They paused, breathing hard, and then set out for the east rim. They slipped and slid down the precipitous trail, crossing the canyon where the Apache attack had taken place, then entering the adjoining canyon where they had made their camp. They saw and heard nothing. Not a horse was in sight. Mose Fowler lay facedown, his hands bound behind his back, his feet rawhided together. There was a nasty gash across the back of his head, still oozing blood. Bowdre cut the man loose and he sat up, blinking in confusion.

"What the hell happened?" Bowdre demanded.

"Them no-account Mexes," said Mose bitterly. "The rest of you not be more'n out of sight, when the varmints wallops me on the head and takes the hosses. I be 'shamed, bein' took so easy. I git the hosses back."

"Wasn't your fault, Mose," Bowdre said in a rare

moment of compassion. "Them two played us all for suckers, and I oughta be hung upside down over a slow fire for believin' they was anything more than thievin' *pelados*. They ain't been interested in lookin' for gold. The coyotes just hung around until the time was right to steal our hosses."

"They ain't got that much of a start on us," said Sandoval. "They jumped Mose early, figurin' to have a whole day before we come out of the passages and found they'd robbed us. They wasn't expectin' us to see 'em from the mountaintop."

"But we're afoot," Three-Fingered Joe pointed out. "There's no way in hell we'll ever catch up to 'em before they sell the horses."

"Maybe not," said Bowdre, "but we're gonna give it one hell of a good try. While they got our hosses, they got no bills of sale. They'll have to ride long and hard, and sell where nobody knows 'em. Let's get on their trail."

Yavapai and Sanchez took their time, secure in their belief that Bowdre and his men would spend most of the day in the passages beneath the Superstitions before learning that their horses were gone. Including the mounts Gary Davis and Pod Osteen had ridden, the Mexicans had eight horses besides their own mounts. Good horses weren't that plentiful in the territory, and these animals might bring as much as four hundred dollars. It would be more money than the ne'er-do-well pair had seen in a while.

"Por Dios," Yavapai sighed, "Señor Wheaton's town be so close, but this *diablo* of a *gringo* sheriff do not trust us."

"Si," Sanchez laughed. "He see us, he say there be that damn Yavapai and Sanchez. When they speak they be lying. When they have somethings—especially horses—they have steal them."

Yavapai and Sanchez had chosen a course that took them between the Gila County seat and Tortilla Flat, then to the west of Saguaro Lake. There they would rest and water the horses before traveling north, perhaps to Flagstaff or Prescott. They dared not ride south, where one *gringo* sheriff after another stood ready to accuse them of any crime that had taken place while they were within a hundred miles of the area. Yavapai reined in, sniffing the air.

"Smoke," said Yavapai.

"Per'ap you ride ahead," Sanchez said.

He gathered their small herd, holding them while Yavapai investigated the smoke.

"Smoke be from Señor Logan's cabin," said Yavapai when he returned. "There be two horses and two mules. Horses look ver' much like those w'ich the Señors Wells and Holt be riding."

"Ah," Sanchez laughed. "*Comico, comico.* Señor Bowdre seeks gold w'ich these Wells and Holt hombres already find. Why else would they have go from the mountains?"

"*Si,*" agreed Yavapai. "Per'ap we sell these horses, buy ourselfs the food, and return. Once we have follow them to the gold, how could they refuse to share it with us?"

"I think they do not object if we take it all for ourselfs," Sanchez grinned, "since they all be dead."

The pair rode on. They were unknown in northern Arizona Territory, but so was the territory unknown to them. It was a wild land where Apaches reigned supreme, from the Mazatzal Mountains north to Tonto Basin.

The day following the arrival of the four young folks at Hoss Logan's cabin was a day of rest for Arlo and Kelsey. Since they were less than a mile from Saguaro Lake, that's where Dallas and Kelly headed when boredom got the best of them. They had gone to the western edge of the lake and were resting beneath some willows when they first saw the driven horses and the two riders. The pair had circled the lake from the south and would pass well to the west of it without coming within sight of the cabin.

"Yavapai and Sanchez," Kelly said. "What are they up to? Where are they going? I can't figure them out."

"I can," said Dallas, laughing. "They're horse thieves, and now that bunch up there in the Superstitions lookin' for Hoss's gold ain't got a horse to their name. That Mex pair was just waitin' for the right time and place, and I reckon they found both."

"They must have been left to watch the horses while the rest of the men started searching the passages," Kelly said.

"That's how I figure it," said Dallas. "Gary Davis played hell, leavin' that pair on watch. Now they're ridin' north, hopin' to find a town where the sheriff won't recognize them."

"This will bring the rest of those men out of the tunnels and out of the mountains," Kelly said, "and when they trail Yavapai and Sanchez, they'll pass close to our cabin. Hadn't we better hide the horses and the mules?"

"Only the mules," said Dallas. "By the time they get this far on foot, Arlo and me will be gone. If that bunch learns we've moved to the cabin, they may decide we've already found the mine, and begin hunting us instead. We don't want them knowin' we've pulled out from the Superstitions until we've had a chance to explore that underground canyon where the river runs. I believe that's where we're going to find either the mine itself or the secret to it. Before these other hombres discover the dropoff and the river, it's damned important that Arlo and me climb down there and find some better way in and out. The very last thing we want is to be discovered and to have to fight with them in one of the passages. With what we're expecting to discover somewhere along that underground river, we may eliminate that very possibility."

"Perhaps we owe Yavapai and Sanchez a debt of gratitude, then," Kelly said. "Those men are going to be angry when they discover their horses are gone. Won't this slow them down in their search for the gold?"

"I'd say so," said Dallas. "Even if they've got food,

they'll be on edge, uneasy, being without horses. A Western man just ain't comfortable without his horse, even if he's got a pair of broke legs and can't ride."

Dallas and Kelly returned to the cabin, reported what they had seen, and Dallas added his own conclusions.

"In the morning before first light," said Arlo, "I aim for us to ride out for the Superstitions. Before we go, we'll picket the mules a considerable distance away from here. This bunch would walk in here and steal them in a minute."

"That ain't the biggest problem," Dallas said. "Kelly and Kelsey will be here alone."

"I'm thinking of that," said Arlo, "but there's no help for it. We'll leave them well armed, and I don't aim for them coyotes to have a reason for nosin' around here. We'll have our breakfast before daylight. Kelly, you and Kelsey will have to stay inside and don't show any smoke at any time during the day."

Chapter 14

Darkness caught Yavapai and Sanchez in the foothills of the Mazatzal Mountains. Thinking they were a day ahead of Cass Bowdre and his vengeful bunch, they made camp beside a fast-running creek. They cooked their supper, and with the horses safely picketed, shucked their dusty, sweaty clothes and waded into the water. It was already dusk and they had seen nobody. But suddenly that changed.

"*Madre de Dios!*" Yavapai shouted. "*Indios* come!"

They came riding in from the north, a dozen strong. Arrows thudded into the farthest bank of the creek, while others zipped over the heads of the terrified Mexicans. Fear set their feet in motion and they scrambled out on the farther bank. Yavapai screeched as an Apache arrow tore a gash along his naked flank, and without regard for the possible consequences, they leaped headlong into a thicket. There they lay, scratched and bleeding, hardly daring even to breathe. They could hear splashing as some of the Indians rode across the creek. But it was dark, and the searchers soon turned away, lured by the delighted shouts of their comrades as they tore into the bountiful supplies Yavapai and Sanchez had taken from Bowdre's camp. To the horror of the miserable Mexicans, the Indians built up a fire, made camp, and prepared to remain there for the night. Yavapai and Sanchez had to stay in the thicket, naked and sleepless, until dawn streaked the eastern sky. Only then did the Indians mount up and ride back the way they had come, driving the ten horses before them. Yavapai and Sanchez waited until they were certain the Indians had gone before they got wearily to their feet and stumbled out into the open. They were half frozen, a mass of cuts and scratches, full of thorns in their feet and other tender parts.

"*Por Dios,*" Yavapai sighed. "The world have gone to hell when a man's stolen horses are taken from him by *bastardo Indios.*"

"*Si,*" Sanchez agreed, "but may'ap they leave our clothes and our boots."

They splashed across the creek, the cold water reviving the many hurts they had suffered, and found nothing but a smoldering fire. They quickly discovered their already miserable situation had only become worse, for among the ashes were the blackened remains of the boots and clothes they so desperately needed.

"They be welcome to the horses," Yavapai shouted, "but I kill the *bastardos* for burning my boots and clothes."

"The *Indios* have leave us with our lives," said Sanchez. "I be wondering if may'ap the Señor Bowdre not be so generous."

"Señor Bowdre cannot accuse us of stealing horses," Yavapai said, "when we have not even a horse to ride. Per'ap we have misjudge the *gringo* sheriff Wheaton. He be less a *diablo* than the Señor Bowdre."

"He not be 'appy to see us," said Sanchez, "naked and in the daylight."

"It be long walk," Yavapai said. "It be dark before we get there."

The dejected pair set out, heading southwest, carefully avoiding their back trail, which they fully expected Cass Bowdre to follow.

Coming within sight of Hoss Logan's cabin, Bowdre and his weary followers paused. When they saw no sign of life, they trudged on, following a trail made easy by the abundant rain of the night before.

"Damn a yellow coyote that takes a man's horse," Sandoval growled. "Why ain't there some way a horse-stealin' Mex can be killed more'n once?"

"I'd settle for once," said Three-Fingered Joe, "if I just knowed we'd get 'em, and get our horses back."

"We will," Bowdre said, "because we ain't stoppin' for the night. We'll make up the time they lose and catch up sometime in the morning."

Bowdre and his comrades passed to the west of Saguaro Lake and went on, following the trail.

"The varmints must know this country," said Zondo Carp. "Elsewise, they wouldn't be headed this way. Them mountains ain't too far ahead, and to me that means Injuns. Damn Apaches, likely."

"I doubt that pair of thieving coyotes know this north country any better than we do," Bowdre said. "They're just trying to get to someplace where nobody knows 'em."

"Well, by God, that's encouragin'," huffed Os Ellerton. "We could run headlong into Apaches and lose our hair as well as our horses."

"We got that pair of varmints ridin' ahead of us," Bowdre said, "and if they can make it, so can we."

"We might find 'em with their bellies shot full of Apache arrows," said Sandoval. "If that happens, where do we go from there?"

"Back the way we come," Bowdre said, "just as fast as we can hoof it."

"It hurt us, losin' Osteen," Zondo said. "I know he was *El Diablo* to get along with, but he was another gun."

"He made his choice," Bowdre said, turning hard eyes on Zondo. "Osteen proved two important things a man on the frontier can't afford to forget. First, you gotta have good judgment, and second, a fast draw can be the death of you if you can't hit what you're shootin' at."

Bowdre called a halt when they reached a spring half a dozen miles north of Saguaro Lake. When they eventually resumed their journey, the sun was less than an hour above the western horizon.

"Won't be much moon tonight," Sandoval said. "Somebody with better eyes than me will have to pick out the trail."

"They're travelin' almost due north," said Bowdre, "and you don't need a full moon to tell you which way that is. We'll just keep headin' north, and come first light, we'll circle until we cross the trail. No way in hell we'll ever catch 'em if we dawdle around and wait for daylight."

Wearily they stumbled on, resting only when Bowdre permitted it. An hour before dawn, Bowdre called a halt until first light. They found the trail without difficulty and followed it to its end at the deserted Indian camp beside the creek. None of them liked the way the story seemed to have ended, but the sign was there plain enough. The tracks of their shod horses led north, overlaid with the tracks of half a dozen unshod ponies.

"Damn it," growled Three-Fingered Joe, "we walk halfway across Arizona Territory and what's our gain? We got to walk all the way back."

"I reckon it'd be worth the walk," Bowdre said, "if the Injuns had roasted that pair of coyotes over a slow fire."

"Could be they did," said Carp, kicking at charred objects in the ashes of the dead fire. "If I'm any judge, there's what's left of a couple pairs of boots and a considerable pile of buttons."

"Burnt their clothes and boots," Bowdre said, "but that don't mean they was in 'em at the time. Injuns might have stripped 'em, took 'em back to camp, an' forced 'em to run the gauntlet. Just to be sure, let's look around a mite, on the chance the varmints might of made a run for it."

"Injuns rode in from the north," said Sandoval, "and looks like a couple of 'em run their horses across the creek. Why would they of done that, stoppin' there?"

"Might have been close to dark when the Injuns showed up," Ellerton said. "The Mex varmints saw 'em comin' and made a break into the brush."

"Leavin' their clothes and boots behind," said Bowdre.

"Wouldn't you," Sandoval asked, "if you was in the creek washin' yourself and a passel of Injuns come gallopin' at you?"

"I reckon I would," Bowdre grinned. "If it happened close to dark, them Mex coyotes likely got away. Let's all drop back to the south and circle. I want to know if the varmints are alive. Just because I can't gut-shoot the pair of 'em today don't mean I can't do it some other time."

Three-Fingered Joe found the first bare footprint in a patch of sand.

"They lit out for town," Bowdre said.

"Where we ain't welcome," said Os Ellerton. "You aim to buck that hardheaded Sheriff Wheaton just to get at them Mexes?"

"They can wait," Bowdre said. "I just wanted to know they're alive, that they'll be around when I'm ready for 'em. We got to have hosses, and right now that comes ahead of ever'thing else."

"I'll amen that," said Sandoval, "but we got a pair of problems. They likely ain't no horses to be had, and if they was, we ain't got the money to buy."

"No matter," Bowdre said, "because we ain't buyin'. We'll pick some of these minin' towns, such as Globe, and take the hosses we need. Before this sheriff can tie it back to us, we'll be out of the territory."

Sheriff Wheaton took pride in the fact that his town, except for occasional uproar in the Mexican quarter, had become a peaceful village. There were still killings in distant towns within Gila County, but fortunately most of the voters lived near the county seat. At first the sheriff thought the pounding on his door was part of a bad dream, but when he sat up in bed, wide awake, the noise continued. At the door he found a young Mexican boy, barefoot and clad only in his nightshirt.

"What is it, Pablo? Somebody dead or dying?"

"Per'ap *muy pronto,* Señor Sheriff," said Pablo. "It be Yavapai and Sanchez. They be stealing, *desnudo.*"

"I reckon Yavapai and Sanchez showin' up possum naked at three in the mornin' ain't a pretty sight, Pablo, but that ain't reason enough for shootin' the varmints. Not even in Arizona Territory. What else they done?"

"They steal," said Pablo. "They rob our clothesline. You no come, Mama kill."

"All right," Wheaton sighed. "Give me time to get my britches and boots on."

The sheriff closed the door and stood there knuckling the sleep from his eyes. He was sorely tempted to go back to bed and let Pablo's mama shoot the troublesome Mexicans, but curiosity got the best of him. Their need for clothing was obvious, but how had the fool Mexicans ended up stark naked and trying to rob a clothesline? By the time Wheaton reached Pablo's backyard, a crowd had gathered, some of them with lanterns. Women and young girls giggled, men laughed, but Pablo's mama was all business, holding a shotgun on the hapless Yavapai and Sanchez. Disturbed by the commotion, chickens wandered about, clucking in sleepy confusion. When Sheriff Wheaton appeared, everybody began shouting at once.

"Quiet!" the sheriff bawled. The uproar trailed off into silence.

"Señor Sheriff . . ." Sanchez began.

"Save it," Wheaton growled. "I'll hear your story in the morning, and it'd better be damn good. Now the rest of you get back to bed. The show's over."

As Yavapai and Sanchez trudged ahead of him toward the jail, Sheriff Wheaton grinned at their scratched and bloody backsides. *For once,* he thought, *these slippery coyotes won't have to lie. The truth will be spectacular enough.* For the first time in their lives Yavapai and Sanchez welcomed a jail cell.

"The leg still pains me some," Arlo said, "but it'll support me. Anyway, I can't stand another day of loafing. Kelsey, how are you feeling?"

"Still sore," said Kelsey, "but I need to be doing something. I just wish Kelly and me were going with you."

"I'm still not sure we shouldn't," Kelly said. "If something happened, and you didn't come back, we'd go crazy worrying."

"We'll keep that in mind," said Dallas, "and we'll be

back before dark. I can't imagine anything going wrong, unless we've miscalculated somehow. But if there's no way in or out except the way we're goin' in, we'll have us a time of it, climbin' them ropes back up that drop-off."

"I hate to mention this," Kelsey said, "but once you're at the bottom, your ropes will still be secured at the top. Won't that be a dead giveaway once Davis and his bunch reach that drop-off overlooking the river?"

"It would be if we left them there," said Arlo, "but once we've found another way out, we'll have to go back through the passage and get the ropes. We may need them again, anyway. This is another step in our search for the mine, but we don't know that it's the last one."

Dallas and Arlo picketed the mules in a thicket far enough from the cabin to prevent discovery. Finally they were ready. When they rode out with their ropes and coal oil lanterns, it was a sad parting. For the first time since Kelly and Kelsey had joined them in the search for Hoss Logan's mine, they were leaving the girls behind. For some troublesome reason they didn't understand, Kelly and Kelsey were afraid. After Arlo and Dallas had ridden away, it was Kelsey who spoke of it.

"I know it's foolish to think this way, but every time we have a chance to be happy, it seems like something always happens and takes it away from us. Daddy got into the freighting business and Gary Davis ruined him. Then Mother got involved with Davis and Daddy was killed. Because Uncle Henry hated Davis, we never saw Uncle Henry again, and now he's gone. Am I being silly, worrying about Arlo and Dallas?"

"No," said Kelly. She sat down on the bunk next to her sister. "If you're being silly, then so am I. We've known these cowboys for just a few days, but even in that short a time, I can't imagine what our lives would be like without them. They're strong men, good men, just like Uncle Henry told us. But I'm afraid of . . . of those mountains. I'm somehow drawn to them, but I'm scared to death of them."

"We're drawn to them the way Uncle Henry must have

been," Kelsey said, "but I don't think he feared them. Perhaps we won't either . . . after today."

Arlo and Dallas rode west of Saguaro Lake and then south. That way, if they were observed from the mountain, it wouldn't be so obvious they had come from the Logan cabin. Just as they were about to turn south, they crossed the northbound trail of the horses Yavapai and Sanchez had taken.

"Ten horses," said Dallas, reading sign. "That pair of Mex thieves must have taken every last one of them."

"Let's follow that trail a ways," Arlo said. "There's plenty of boot tracks, and maybe we can get some idea as to how many men are in that bunch that's trailin' the horses."

Without difficulty they found the tracks of six men.

"Ten horses," Dallas said. "But includin' Yavapai and Sanchez, there's only eight riders. They're missing two men."

"They might have left them behind," said Arlo, "but with the Apache threat, that wouldn't make any sense, and neither does this trail. Yavapai and Sanchez are headed straight for the Mazatzals, and that's Apache stompin' grounds."

"The whole bunch may lose more than their horses," Dallas said. "These six hombres on foot may not be familiar with the Mazatzals, but Yavapai and Sanchez have been around these parts long enough that they should know the risk."

As Arlo and Dallas approached the Superstitions, they rode southwest. They would depend on the hidden trail getting them to their old camp.

"We may have the mountain to ourselves for a while," said Arlo, "but we can't afford to take any chances with our horses. I reckon we'd better leave them where they used to graze when we camped below the west rim. We can enter the passage from our old camp, follow it to the foot of the mountain, and take the second passage to the drop-off overlooking the river."

Leaving the horses to the scant graze, they cautiously approached the hidden cavern that had so recently been their camp. Before they entered it, Dallas lit one of the lanterns.

"They've been here," Arlo said.

There were many boot tracks in the dust, and they led out the way Arlo and Dallas had come in.

"They got here through the passage from the foot of the mountain," said Dallas, "but when they left, they followed that crevice that goes up to the mountaintop. Now why didn't they go back the way they came, along the same passage we're about to go into?"

"Something more important must have come up," Arlo said. "Look at the length of their strides. I'd say they left here on the run."

"Maybe this was as far as they got before they learned Yavapai and Sanchez had taken their horses and headed for the Mazatzals," said Dallas. "It's a definite edge for us. Now we can get down to that river without wonderin' if they're right behind us."

"They may have gone into the other passage before they did this one," Arlo said, "but it won't matter. Without the signs Hoss left, they'd have no reason to fight their way down to the river."

"On our way to Tortilla Flat," said Dallas, "Kelly and me saw a pair of them goin' into that passage that opens into the canyon on the east side of the mountain. I reckoned the lariats they had was for crossin' that big hole in the passage that leads to the skull peak. That should have kept them busy for most of a day, since they'd have to come out the same way they went in. We still have an edge."

The two cowboys continued along the downward path leading to the cavern at the bottom of the mountain. From there, one passage opened into the canyon at the eastern foot, while a second angled away farther into the mountain. It was this passage that led to the precipitous drop-off and the underground canyon through which the river flowed. As they went, Dallas scanned the stone

walls, seeking some evidence that Davis and his followers had been in the passage. He paused when they
reached the drawings he and Kelly had discovered.

"Brush off the flanks of those last two horse drawings," Dallas said.

Once again the spots Hoss had cut into the stone were
revealed.

"Hoss Logan was one shrewd old devil," said Arlo.
"Who else would have thought to add a pair of spotted
ponies to an old Indian drawing in such a way that they'd
be meaningless to anyone except Kelly and Kelsey?
Hoss wanted to be damn sure we wouldn't give up when
we got to the drop-off and the river."

"That's why I think we'll have this river to ourselves
for a while," Dallas said. "These other hombres, unless
they're sharper than I think they are, won't have the as-
surance that Hoss left to us. But just the thought of
swingin' off down that drop-off is enough to scare the
hell out of a man."

"It may not be all that scary," said Arlo. "It has to be
forbidding when you're at the brink with only a lighted
splinter, but what seems like the pits of hell may change
when you add some decent light. We'll let one of these
lanterns down the side on a rope, and maybe we can get
some idea as to what we're up against."

As they neared the precipice, Arlo lit the second
lantern and knotted one end of a length of rope to the
lantern's bail.

"It's got to be more than two hundred feet down," Dallas said. "Want more rope?"

"Not for the lantern. Its light won't be good for more
than a few feet at a time. Rope your lantern and we'll
ease 'em both over the edge at the same time. Maybe
then we can light the way down far enough to see if
there's any slope to this wall."

Slowly they played out the rope, taking care to avoid
creating a pendulum motion that might smash a lantern
globe against the stone wall. The dim glow from the
lanterns proved effective for maybe a dozen feet.

"At least it ain't straight down," Dallas said. "It slopes some along the upper part."

"That's good, but not good enough," said Arlo. "We'll have to go at this like the calf ate the grindstone—a little at a time. That means we'll have to go down far enough to find a place to rest, lower the lantern some more, and then take a new start from there.

Dallas raised the lantern back to the rim, and by its light Arlo tied the end of his rope to a boulder that seemed firmly anchored, holding the other lantern in place below the rim. Then he took another two hundred feet of rope and began tying knots in it spaced two feet apart. Next he tied one end of the rope to an abutment and the other end firmly under his arms. He grasped the rope and tested it. Pulled tight, it held, supporting his weight.

"While I'm working my way down," said Arlo, "take another length of rope and start tying knots for handholds."

Arlo bellied down near the edge of the precipice, his feet toward the drop-off, the rope taut in his hands. Once he was over and swinging free, the wall sloped outward to the extent that he was able to get his feet against the face of it. Handhold by handhold, keeping the rope taut, he inched down the wall.

"All right?" Dallas inquired anxiously.

"So far," said Arlo. "Let the lantern down until I stop you."

Arlo clung to the rope, watching the lantern descend, its feeble light penetrating the blackness below.

"Hold it," Arlo shouted. "I'm goin' on down as far as the lantern."

The hole in the face of the bluff hadn't been visible until the lantern had been lowered past it. At some point in distant time, an enormous boulder had been torn loose, leaving an oval recess half a dozen feet deep. Once Arlo was even with the depression, he kicked away from the wall, and on an inward swing gained the ledge. He sank down on his knees, breathing hard, hands and arms numb with strain.

"Arlo?" Dallas shouted.

"Here," said Arlo. "There's a hole in the wall, maybe twenty-five feet down. I have the lantern. Turn the rope loose, then lower the other lantern. When I loosen this line, haul it up, loop it under your arms, and come on down like I did. You'll be in the dark for the first few feet, but there'll be light by the time you need it. Don't forget that last piece of rope."

Dallas lowered the second lantern and Arlo hauled it in, rope and all. Arlo then freed himself from the rope he had used to descend, and Dallas pulled it back up. He then secured the line to himself and went over the edge, walking down the wall to the shelf where Arlo waited.

"When I've rested some," Dallas said, "I'll take the next turn. Kind of bare in here—nothin' to tie a rope to."

"I know," said Arlo. "I've made allowance for that. We can always tie another two hundred feet of rope to that one, if we have to. All we need is a few more resting places like this to get us the rest of the way down."

Dallas took the next turn, following the lantern until he found another break in the wall where they could rest. When he found it—another twenty-five feet down—it was adequate—just barely. Arlo followed, and they stood with their backs to the wall, for that was all the space they had.

"My God," said Dallas, "what's that awful smell? Somethin' must be dead."

"Something or somebody," Arlo replied. "From what Kelsey's told me, before that first Apache attack two of those men from town disappeared in the mountain. They could easily have taken a turn toward the death's head mountain and fallen into that hole we crossed in the passage floor."

"God," said Dallas, shuddering, "what a way to die. We ought to call this river the Death's Head. How many of those who never returned from the Superstitions do you reckon have left their bones here in this tomb?"

"Some," Arlo said, "but by no means all. There are some whose bones were found, except for the head.

Remember, we found some of them ourselves when we first climbed the mountain with the death's head at sundown. But who or what would kill a man and take only the head?"

"I don't know, and I ain't sure I *want* to know," said Dallas. "It gives me the whim-whams just thinkin' about it. I just want to get to the bottom of this and find some better way in and out."

"So do I," Arlo said, "and we'll be a week gettin' down this bluff, doin' it this way. There has to be a faster way. I aim to run my belt through that lantern's bail and take the light with me. With my feet against the wall and the lantern hanging behind me, I believe I can go down far enough to find another resting place before I give out."

"Suppose you don't find one? No way I can haul you back up here. You'll be dangling from the end of the rope, not able to go up or down."

"This wall's sloping more and more," Arlo said. "Before we reach the bottom, I think we may be able to work our way down without ropes."

The lantern hung behind Arlo as he began his descent. Suddenly the wall seemed to vanish and his feet dangled in the air, throwing all his weight on his arms and shoulders. Desperately he hand-walked down the rope until the light revealed his predicament. He had gone over a hump, like a huge stone chin, and the wall beneath it was recessed far beyond his groping feet. Dimly he could see sanctuary—a shelf beneath the overhang—but he couldn't reach it. There was no feeling in his hands as they clung frantically to the rope, and his body broke out in a cold sweat. He began kicking, forcing himself to become a pendulum. Desperately he swung to and fro, toward the stone wall, which seemed farther and farther away. Sweat blinded his eyes until he couldn't see. On his final forward swing, which might have taken him to safety, he was unable to clear the stone abutment that had been his undoing. His head smashed into the stone, his numb hands lost their grip, and the rope went slack.

"Arlo!" Dallas cried. "Arlo, are you all right?"

But there was no answer. Dallas heard only the pounding of his heart and the rushing of the underground river he himself had called the Death's Head.

Chapter 15

Sunset was less than two hours away when Cass Bowdre and his angry companions reached the west bank of Saguaro Lake on their return journey. Their feet were blistered almost beyond endurance, and they hadn't eaten since breakfast of the day before.

"We got to have grub," Bowdre said. "Must be a ranch or some miner's shack where we can get a feed."

Nobody said anything. They stumbled on, following the southern perimeter of the lake until they came within sight of Hoss Logan's cabin.

"Place looks deserted," said Three-Fingered Joe.

"All the better," Zondo Carp said. "Still might be grub there. We can break in and help ourselves."

Quietly they made their way to the cabin and Bowdre tried the door.

"Damn," he growled, "it's barred from the inside. Zondo, see if there's a back door, and if there is, try it."

"The back door's barred too," reported Zondo when he returned. "That means somebody's in there."

"We'll find out," Bowdre said. "If nobody answers, we'll bust in." He pounded on the door with the butt of his Colt.

Kelly Logan, looking out a slit in one of the shuttered windows did not like the looks of the six men at the door.

"Who are you?" she demanded. "And what do you want?"

"Who we are don't concern you," said Bowdre. "Injuns took our hosses. We're afoot and hungry."

"Sorry," Kelly said. "We don't know you. My sister's

sick, and we don't have more than enough food for ourselves."

Angrily Zondo Carp kicked the door as hard as he could. There was a roar from within the cabin and two slugs ripped through the door. One of them snatched off Bowdre's hat and the other nicked Carp's left ear. The men scattered to either side of the door, out of the line of fire.

"Break that door in," Kelly shouted angrily, "and I'll kill the first man through it. Leave us alone!"

Bowdre backed away and the others followed.

"Damn them," growled Zondo, nursing his bleeding ear. "I'll gather some dead leaves and brush, and burn the place down on top of 'em."

"Just what we need," Sandoval said sarcastically. "A big smoke to draw attention to us, when we ain't got a horse to our name. Damn good thinkin', Zondo."

"Come on," said Bowdre. "Botherin' a woman could get us all strung up quicker than hoss stealin'. We'll find us one of them little minin' settlements and get us some grub at their general store."

Kelsey Logan watched them leave, still gripping the Colt with both hands.

"Who could they have been?" Kelsey asked.

"I believe it's that bunch from the Superstitions," said Kelly. "They're on foot, so that means they didn't recover the horses Yavapai and Sanchez took. But there's something I don't understand. There were only six men, but Yavapai and Sanchez had eight extra horses. What's become of Gary Davis?"

"Perhaps he got on the bad side of this bunch and they killed him," Kelsey suggested. "Davis was mean and cruel, but he was no gunman."

Bowdre and his weary companions finally reached what remained of a little town after its silver strike had played out. Nothing was left but a few die-hard residents and a not-too-well-provisioned general store.

"Know of anybody with some hosses to sell?" Bowdre inquired. "We lost ours to the Injuns."

"Nope," said the store owner, "but if you'd been here a mite sooner, you might have dickered for some big mules. Not more'n two hours ago, six gents was through here with twenty-one mules. Big brutes, ever' one of 'em, brung in from Missouri through Santa Fe. On their way south fer work in the mines, I reckon."

When Bowdre and his men left the store it was almost dark, but they could still see to pick up the trail of the drovers and their mules.

"Be a sight easier to wait for these hombres to bed down, and us just kill the lot of 'em," Os Ellerton said. "Then we don't have to worry about 'em follerin' us with fire in their eyes an' guns in their hands."

"Don't be a damn fool," Bowdre growled. "Kill 'em and we'd have the law on our tail. You think that old gent back there at the store ain't gonna remember the six of us on foot and askin' for hosses? No, we find these mules, and slick as we can, stampede 'em to hell and gone. With nobody seein' us, we grab six of the brutes and ride 'em into the Superstitions. For a while we can leave 'em at that hidden camp where Wells and Holt was hidin' out."

Following Bowdre's orders, they found and staked out the drovers' camp until moonset. Soon after, the mules stampeded.

Deep in the shadow of the overhang, his back against the wall, Paiute watched as Arlo tried desperately to swing himself in close enough to gain the safety of the ledge. On the last forward swing, just as Arlo smashed his head against the stone, Paiute seized the young cowboy's belt. Though Arlo was a dead weight and almost dragged the old Indian over the edge, Paiute held fast. Stretching Arlo out belly down on the stone ledge, he felt for a pulse and found it strong. He then disappeared into the shadows.

"Arlo!" Dallas shouted.

There was no response. Dallas attached the other

lantern to his belt, looped the extra rope over his shoulder, and began hand-walking down the same rope that was still tied under Arlo's arms. Finally, just as Arlo had been, Dallas was suspended in space, unable to reach the ledge on which Arlo now lay. Arlo stirred, finally able to sit up, and was shocked into action by the predicament in which he found Dallas. He pulled on the rope, bringing Dallas close enough that he was able to get his feet on the ledge. Dallas fell to his knees, gasping for breath.

"That was a damn fool move," Arlo said, "comin' down after me without knowin' what the trouble was. It was very nearly the death of me. I wasn't far enough down for my head to clear that stone, and I swung right into it. I was knocked plumb blind and crazy for a minute or two."

"I don't see how you made it," said Dallas. "You was all sprawled out, the lantern still burnin', when I first saw you."

"When it hit my head," Arlo said, "just a second before I blacked out, I'd swear somethin' grabbed me. I still don't know how I made that ledge. I just don't remember it. I thought I was a goner."

"This ledge narrows down some," said Dallas, "but it runs along the face of the rock for a ways. Since you come near to gettin' your brains bashed out, you just lay back and rest. I'm gonna take a lantern and look around some. I want to see how far I can go before the ledge plays out."

The ledge soon became so narrow that Dallas had to walk sideways, his back flat against the wall. This was not a passage, but a mere crack in the sheer stone, and kneeling was impossible. He held the lantern in his right hand, raising it, then lowering it as far down as he could. He had progressed only a few feet when he came upon a thin, head-high crevice, into which were driven three oak pins.

"Arlo!" Dallas shouted. "I've found a way down to the river!"

Arlo brought the other lantern, and they crept slowly

through the split in the stone. The split slanted downward toward the rushing river, which now grew louder. When they finally stepped out of the confining rock, water sloshed around their boots and spray wet their faces, dampening their clothes and hissing against the hot lantern globes. Even shouting, they were barely able to hear one another above the river's mighty roar as it dashed over the huge upthrusts. Slowly, carefully, they worked their way past the rapids and the river quieted.

"It's time for the crucial test," proclaimed Arlo. "Let's see if we can get out of here without going back the way we came in."

"It's hard to get any sense of direction," Dallas said, looking around, "but we'll have to turn back to the south-west if this flows into the Salt."

As they progressed, the voice of the river again became a roar, and it seemed they were approaching another rapids. But it was more than that. They soon saw that the river churned over a precipice and dropped fifty feet in a spectacular waterfall. They climbed down one side of it, over volcanic rock slippery with spray, as the cavern through which the river flowed began to narrow drastically.

"This is gettin' a little scary," shouted Dallas. "By the time this thing gets to the Salt, it may be pinched down so thin that we can't get out."

"I don't think we'll have to follow it all the way to the Salt," Arlo replied. "I'm looking for a break somewhere in this wall while we're still under the Superstitions."

The split, when they found it, wasn't in the cavern wall but in the river itself. At some point in time the earth had shifted, and the underground stream had taken a new, lower channel, while the original veered away to their left. Its stone bed was dry, as it might have been for many years. A draft sucked at the flames of their lanterns, and the way out—when they finally found it—was even more deceptive than they had expected. Before them was what had once been the mouth of a tunnel. Now it was closed off by a mass of debris that had slid down the side of the mountain. But just as Arlo and Dallas reached what had seemed a dead end, they found that though the fallen stone blocked the original mouth, it had left an invisible gap at one side through which they could pass. It was a tight squeeze, and they again had to struggle sideways, but once through it they stepped out into a forest of chaparral and greasewood.

"Thank God!" Dallas sighed. "I never thought I'd welcome being up to my ears in a thorny thicket."

"Less than two hours of daylight," noted Arlo. "We have to figure out where we are and get back to the girls before dark."

They found that they were on the western flank of the Superstitions, two miles south of the perilous trail that had led up to their old camp. They began working their way out of the thicket, and a dozen feet from where they had come out, they looked back. The fallen mass of stone and debris solid against the mountain's base looked truly impenetrable.

"Nobody will ever find that," Dallas said, "unless they come at it from the other side, like we did, or follow us back to it."

"We'd better be damn sure we can find it ourselves," said Arlo. "One chaparral patch looks just like another."

When Arlo and Dallas reached the plateau where they had left the horses, they found the animals grazing undisturbed.

"We ought to go back through the passage and remove that rope," Arlo said. "When those other hombres reach the drop-off, they won't have any trouble figurin' what we've been up to."

"The hell with it," said Dallas. "Let's leave it there. I don't figure they'll find their way down that bluff any quicker or easier than we did. Besides, if we take the time to go back in there after the rope, we'll be after dark gettin' back to the cabin. We promised we wouldn't leave Kelly and Kelsey alone after dark, and if we're not back they'll be scared to death somethin' happened to us."

"You're right," Arlo said. "Let's ride."

Sheriff Wheaton had decided Yavapai and Sanchez were actually telling the truth for a change. He was skeptical only about how the pair had managed to escape with their lives. Wheaton was well aware that the Apaches weren't known for their compassion or their carelessness. He had appealed to the Mexican quarter of town, and clothes had readily been donated to the hapless Yavapai and Sanchez. The pair left the jail barefooted and clad in ill-fitting garb that would have shamed a peon. But that wasn't the worst of it. Men who had witnessed their disgrace the night before now grinned at them, while the women giggled and gossiped among themselves.

"This be hell," said Yavapai. "Per'ap we go back to Tucson and again we rob the mule trains of the silver ore."

"*Por Dios,*" Sanchez said bitterly. "I am not finish here, and I am not leave. *El Diablo* himself cannot drive me away. Those who laugh, I do not forget forever."

"We have no food, no boots, no horse," said Yavapai. "We have not among us even one *peso* for which to buy *barato* mescal."

"*Si,*" said Sanchez, "but we have one ace in the hole. Señor Domingo Vasquez make us offer once, and per'ap now be the time to say we be ready for whatever he have in mind. Per'ap he pay us well for this gold the Señors Wells and Holt have find."

"*Por Dios,*" Yavapai replied. "We do not know they have find this gold, or if they do, where it be."

"*Por El Diablo's cuernos,*" Sanchez chuckled. "You know this and I know this, but the Señor Domingo Vasquez, he not know."

"*Madre de Dios,*" said Yavapai in awe. "We double-cross the Señor Vasquez, we meet *El Diablo muy pronto.*"

"Only if he find us, *amigo,*" Sanchez said.

* * *

Cass Bowdre and his men rode through the night, and having been afoot already for two days, nobody complained about the lack of saddles. Or even about the mules, to which none of them were accustomed. Lightning flared in the west and there was a distant rumbling of thunder.

"Storm on the way," said Bowdre. "I never seen this much rain in this part of the country, but it'll save our hides. Come mornin' there won't be a mule track nowhere."

"I reckon you've noticed that all these big brutes is trail-branded," Sandoval said, "and we got no bills of sale."

"No help for that," said Bowdre, "unless you're satisfied to stay afoot."

"Hell," Carp said, "the drovers will round up the mules they can find, and just move on. Who's goin' to accuse us? So what if these big varmints is branded? We found 'em all runnin' loose. Besides, soon as I can get me an honest-to-God horse, they can have this Missouri jack. He beats walkin', but not by much."

"It be better when we gits our saddles," said Mose Fowler.

"If they're still there," Os Ellerton said.

"They'll be there," said Bowdre sourly. "What use would Injuns have for saddles?"

"But we're still needin' grub," said Three-Fingered Joe. "Why don't we hole up close to Tortilla Flat, and load up with grub in the mornin'?"

"Because the last damn thing we need is to have somebody remember us and the brands on these mules," Bowdre said. "We'll ride back to the Superstitions, let the rain hide our trail, and later on, one of us can ride out for grub. One man and one mule won't be as obvious as six of each."

Darkness was only minutes away when Arlo and Dallas arrived at Hoss Logan's cabin.

"My God, are we glad to see you!" Kelly cried, swinging wide the door.

"No gladder than we are to be here," said Dallas, his eyes fixing on the bullet holes in the door. "What happened?"

Quickly Kelly told him of the arrival of Cass Bowdre and his men.

"They didn't catch up to Yavapai and Sanchez, then," said Arlo.

"Come mornin'," Dallas added, "it means somebody's likely to be missin' some horses. That bunch has had a hell of a hike."

"There's one thing I don't understand," said Kelly. "Yavapai and Sanchez had eight horses, but only six men showed up here, and Gary Davis wasn't one of them. What happened to the other man and to Davis?"

"That's something we may never know," answered Arlo. "Dallas and me didn't accomplish a thing today except to find a way in and out. Now that we can reach that underground river without going through the mountain and down the bluff, I want to spend every day looking for the gold."

"The two of you have accomplished more today than any day since we started out," said Kelsey. "I don't see that as a day wasted."

"Neither do I," Kelly added, "and I'm just so glad we may be reaching the end of this ordeal."

It was dark in the cabin, and not until Kelsey lit a lamp did she see the livid bruise on Arlo's temple.

"I was afraid without knowing why," said Kelsey, "and I still have a bad feeling about all this."

"Whatever final message Hoss left us," Arlo said, "I believe we'll find it somewhere along this wild river. Tomorrow I want us to go in there and begin looking for that sign."

Far in the night they were awakened by the crash of thunder and the sound of hard rain slashing the cabin.

*　*　*

"Lawd," said Mose, "I hopes them bones don't be walkin' again."

Lightning sliced through the darkness and the driving rain, and suddenly they saw an apparition stumbling down the canyon toward them that was far more unnerving than the skeletons had been. Gary Davis shambled along as though his feet had a mind of their own, while his mind knew nothing of the ultimate destination. Mose Fowler buried his face in his hat, refusing to look.

"Davis!" Bowdre shouted.

It had no effect. Davis kept coming, seeming not to even notice the six mounted men. Bowdre dismounted and caught him by the arm, and then the man just seemed to explode. With a single wild punch, he felled Bowdre, then threw himself at the still-mounted Zondo Carp. Zondo came off the mule and the two of them went down in a tangle, Davis screeching like a madman. Bowdre recovered and joined the fray, along with Three-Fingered Joe and Os Ellerton, but it was Sandoval who ended it. Drawing his Colt and taking advantage of the next flare of lightning, he slugged Davis unconscious.

"My God," Carp gasped, "he's plumb crazy and stronger than a bull."

"A couple of you tote him up under the overhang," said Bowdre. "If this madness ain't permanent, I'd like to know where he's been."

"We gonna risk a fire?" Three-Fingered Joe asked.

"No," said Bowdre. "With no coffee and no grub, why should we?"

Carp and Sandoval carried the unconscious Davis to the protection of the mountain's overhang.

"Our saddles still be here," Mose Fowler observed.

But nobody seemed to hear him, for they had gathered around Gary Davis, prepared to resume the battle if they had to.

"Hey," said Sandoval, "he's got somethin' in his hand."

Bowdre took Davis's big right fist and forced the clenched fingers apart. Zondo Carp turned his back to the wind, lit a match, and cupped it in his hands. The

crumbled object in Bowdre's hand gleamed dull yellow
in the feeble light of the match. As small a sample as it
was, every man knew what he was seeing, yet not one of
them could believe his eyes. It was gold ore. Fabulously
rich gold ore!

"By God," Sandoval breathed, "he's found the gold!"

"Looks like it," said Bowdre. "Let's hope he don't go
loon crazy again when he comes out of it."

But the blow to his head seemed to have brought Davis
to his senses. He groaned and tried to sit up.

"Stay where you are, Davis," Bowdre said. "Can you
tell us what happened to you?"

"No," Davis mumbled, and they waited impatiently for him to speak again. "Somethin' hit me," he finally said.

"You didn't see anything? Anybody?" Bowdre asked.

"No," said Davis. "I woke up . . . in the dark. There
was a . . . a canteen, and I . . . drank. Water tasted . . .
funny . . ."

"Hell's fire," Sandoval shouted, "you been gone three
damn days. You must of seen somethin' or somebody!"

"No," said Davis weakly. "Nothing . . . nobody . . ."

"We come up on you in the canyon," Bowdre said,
"and you was wild as a cougar. Like to of busted my jaw.
And this is what we found clenched in your fist. Now
where did you get it?"

Bowdre held out his hand with the gold ore, and again
Davis went crazy. It took four of them to subdue him, and
even when they finally had him flat on his back and helpless, he snarled at them like a cornered lobo wolf.

"It's mine," he howled. "Mine!"

"It's just a handful of ore," said Bowdre, "worthless
unless you know where it came from. Where? Where did
you get it?"

"I don't know," Davis bawled, his mood changing. "I
swear I don't know!"

"Lawd God," breathed Mose Fowler in awe. "He find
the gold, but lose his soul to the spirits in the mountain."

Nobody disagreed, or even laughed. They were seeing

frightful evidence of a thing they didn't understand, and it had a sobering effect. Had Gary Davis swapped his very sanity for a fistful of gold ore?

"I ain't a superstitious man," said Zondo Carp, "but there's somethin' purely unnatural about this. Where'n hell do we go from here?"

"We wait for mornin'," Bowdre said. "Two things we're sure of. We know there's gold, and we know Davis has been near enough to grab a handful of ore. In the daylight maybe he'll come to his senses and remember where he got it."

"If he comes to his senses and remembers anything," said Os Ellerton, "he ain't gonna cut us in. Not the way he fought over that handful of ore he brung out. You're all fools if you expect him to share with us."

"Oh, he'll share with us," Bowdre said, "alive or dead. The choice will be his."

Domingo Vasquez was a fat cigar-smoking little man who dressed like a beggar. For all practical purposes, his only interest was his little cantina in the Mexican quarter. But things were not always as they seemed, for Vasquez was the silent partner in every successful saloon and whorehouse in the quarter. All these questionable enterprises lived or died by his favor. When there was a crime serious enough to involve the law, Sheriff Wheaton never bothered to search for the culprit. Instead, the sheriff went to Domingo Vasquez, and the problem was resolved quietly. The troublemaker was never seen or heard from again, having disappeared voluntarily or otherwise. While some of the "citizens" of the quarter were of questionable reputation, they were all in the employ of Domingo Vasquez and so enjoyed a measure of protection. It was just such a status that Yavapai and Sanchez sought. But in his dingy office behind the cantina, Vasquez eyed the pair skeptically.

"So the hombres who seek the gold drive you away," said Domingo, "and while you are running for your lives, *Indios* take your horses and your clothes."

"Si," said Yavapai and Sanchez in a single voice.

"So the pair of you sneak into town like coyotes and rob a poor *señora's* clothesline. You have vexed my friend the sheriff, made *asnos* of yourselves, and now you are expecting me to take you in."

"Si," said the humble duo, "but we do much in return."

"Let us see if what you do includes the telling of the truth!" Domingo roared. Leaning across the desk, he reached one big hand for Yavapai and the other for Sanchez. Taking a fistful of each man's shirt, he dragged them halfway across the desk. "Coyotes," he growled. *"Desnudo bastardos!* I believe the *Indios* take your clothes and your horses, but I also believe there is more. Why do these hombres chase you away from the mountains? The truth, *cucaraches,* the truth!"

"Si," said Sanchez unhappily, "the truth." He wiped sweat from his face on the sleeve of his borrowed shirt.

"We steal all the horses," Yavapai said fearfully, "and these hombres follow. We do not run to the south, for there the sheriffs misunderstand us. We must ride to the north, and there be *Indios.*"

Domingo Vasquez flung the cowering pair back into their chairs with a crash. He then flattened his big hands on the desk and roared with laughter. Yavapai and Sanchez had finally begun to breathe again when he spoke.

"You will take the room at the head of the stairs." On a sheet of paper he wrote rapidly in Spanish, signed his name, and passed the message to Sanchez. "Take that to the general store and buy for yourselves clothing, boots, guns, and ammunition. When you have done these things, we will talk again."

"Horses," Yavapai began. "We be without . . ."

"Por Dios," Domingo roared. "They will be at the livery when you have need of them."

"The *señor* sheriff," said Sanchez. "Per'ap he wonder . . ."

"I talk to the sheriff," Domingo said impatiently.

"Now vamoose, and from this very *momento,* the pair of you will do nothing until I have ordered it. *Comprender?*" He passed the flat of his hand across his throat like the blade of a knife.

Yavapai and Sanchez swallowed hard. *"Si,"* they said in a single voice. *"Comprender."*

Chapter 16

Arlo, Dallas, Kelly, and Kelsey rode out at first light, bound for the newly discovered entrance to the Superstitions.

"Because of last night's rain, we're leavin' tracks," said Arlo, "but there shouldn't be anybody to follow us."

"Let's not count on that," Dallas warned. "Since we're not going in through the mountain, why don't we leave our horses a good distance away? It'll mean some walkin', just gettin' to the mountain, but it's better than givin' away all that we've worked so hard to find."

"I'm glad we have the lanterns," said Kelly. "We'll need the extra light."

"That could become a problem," Arlo observed, "if those other hombres follow the passage to that drop-off overlooking the river. It's so dark in there, even the flames from these lanterns can be seen from a long way off."

"As of yesterday morning," said Kelsey, "six of them were on foot. It's hard to believe they'd go back to the Superstitions without horses, even to look for gold."

"They'll need grub, too," Dallas said. "I can't see Yavapai and Sanchez taking all the horses and leaving the provisions behind."

"Since Yavapai and Sanchez know of the mine, what's to stop them from coming back and looking for it on their own?" said Kelly.

"Six good reasons," Arlo said, "and every one of them with blistered feet. Horse thieves just about have to quit the territory, but the smart ones generally don't drive their horses through Apache country. I'll be surprised if Yavapai and Sanchez made it even as far as the Mazatzals with their hair and their horses."

Bowdre and his men slept little, kept awake by the fitful mumbling of Gary Davis. He seemed plagued with devils and demons, and his unsavory companions welcomed the first gray light of dawn.

"We got to rid ourselves of this spooky varmint," Zondo Carp muttered about Davis. "He's playin' hell with my nerves."

"He's seen the gold," said Bowdre, "and until he convinces me he can't find it again, I'll put up with him."

"I'll go along with that," Os Ellerton said. "Now who's gonna ride back to Tortilla Flat for grub? I ain't liftin' a hand to do nothin' until I eat."

But the lack of food soon became the least of their problems. The Apaches hit them swiftly and without warning. Mose Fowler grunted, his horrified eyes on the arrow buried deep in his belly.

"Lawd . . . God!" he cried. "I . . . be . . . dead."

Suddenly, Apaches burst out of the brush on both sides of the canyon at a zigzag run, loosing more arrows as they came. Bowdre and his men pulled their Colts and returned the fire belly down.

"Damn it, Davis!" Bowdre shouted. "Get down!"

But Gary Davis seemed not to hear. Unarmed, he struck off toward the advancing Apaches at an erratic lope, screaming like a cougar. Arrows whipped past all around him, and it seemed a miracle that not one of them touched him. It all seemed eerie, unnatural. Again Davis squalled like a gut-shot mountain lion, and the sound halted the Indians in their tracks. They ran for the brush, vanishing as quickly as they had appeared. Davis seemed confused. With only the empty canyon before him, he turned and walked slowly back the way he had come.

"My God," said Zondo Carp, "look at them eyes!"

Davis seemed not to see them, or anything else. In his eyes was a look that defied description. His arms hung loose at his sides, and he kept clenching and unclenching his fists. Mose Fowler lay on his back dead, his hands gripping the shaft of the arrow in a final, futile attempt to withdraw it. Davis paused, looked at the dead man, and let loose a blood-chilling scream that seemed anything but human.

"He purely scared hell out of that bunch of Apaches," said Bowdre. "They think he's crazy as a loon."

"I can't fault 'em for that," Sandoval said. "I think he is too."

"By God, I ain't spendin' another night in camp with the loco varmint," said Three-Fingered Joe. "He's got the strength of a bull buffalo, and he could kill us all. Way he was clenchin' them fists, he's just waitin' to get 'em on somebody's throat, and I don't aim for it to be mine."

"He still may come out of it and lead us to the gold," Bowdre said. "He's the best lead we got, and with them Apaches thinkin' he's crazy, he's worth more to us than a company of soldiers."

"If he's all that valuable," said Zondo Carp, "you'd best figure on keepin' him away from me. If he comes at me twitchin' them big hands, I'll shoot him dead."

"Somethin' about the Injun attack set him off," Bowdre said. "Take four of the mules around to the west side of that mountain and find the trail up to the rim. Take the mules to that hidden camp Wells and Holt was usin', and take Davis with you. I'll take an extra mule with me, and ride to Tortilla Flat to get us some grub. We'll be needin' grain for the mules, too."

"Some risky," Sandoval said, "them mules runnin' off, and you showin' up with two of 'em trail-branded."

"A risk I'll have to take," said Bowdre.

"You want we should do somethin' with Mose?" Os Ellerton asked.

"Yeah," said Bowdre. "Take his Colt, holster, and belt, and go through his pockets."

Domingo Vasquez wasted no time in getting Yavapai and Sanchez involved in the search for Hoss Logan's mine. Vasquez had done some investigating on his own, and like everyone else in town, he was very much aware of the rich ore sample Hoss Logan had left at the assayer's office. While Vasquez hadn't all that much confidence in Yavapai and Sanchez, they *had* been involved in the search for the mine almost since the beginning. The search for gold would enable Vasquez to utilize certain of his men who were ill-suited for any activity subject to the ever-watchful eyes of Sheriff Wheaton. But men often died in the Superstitions, and when they did, it became difficult—if not impossible—to affix the blame. So, much to their dismay and contrary to their expectations, Yavapai and Sanchez now found themselves part of a gang, taking orders from a leader appointed by Domingo Vasquez, a big, ugly Spaniard known only as Juarez. He carried two tied-down Colts and secreted a Bowie down his back on a leather thong, like an Indian. He was a killer, and south of the border there was more than one price on his head.

"All of you will answer to Juarez," said Domingo, his eyes on Yavapai and Sanchez, "and Juarez will answer to me."

The rest of the unsavory outfit consisted of Pepino Frio, Garcia Ruiz, and the Ortega brothers, Juan and Juno. Pepino was a skinny youth with a nervous twitch. Before he was out of his teens, five notches decorated the butt of his Colt. Ruiz was a brute with bad teeth who was constantly fiddling with a deck of cards. Like Juarez, he concealed his razor-keen Bowie Indian fashion. The Ortegas were so much alike that it was difficult to tell them apart. Both were thin and wiry, and their flat-crowned hats were banded with silver conchos. The pair had ambushed a government wagon train, gunned down its military escort, and fled Mexico to escape a firing squad. The lot of them now sat around a table at the rear of Domingo Vasquez's cantina. Domingo's instructions to them were brief.

"Yavapai and Sanchez know these mountains," he said, "and they be familiar also with this Wells and Holt.

Follow them. When you are sure we have found the gold, take it."

He didn't elaborate, nor did he need to. They had all stolen before, and always without complaint, for the dead did not speak.

Cass Bowdre paused within sight of the general store at Tortilla Flat. A single horse was tied at the hitch rail, and Bowdre cursed under his breath. He had come early, hoping he might find the place deserted. Now it seemed there would be at least one person other than the storekeeper who might later identify him. He quickly decided against concealing the mules and walking to the store, for such a furtive move would only attract attention. Besides, he had to buy several hundred pounds of grain. He waited a while, hoping the lone horseman would mount up and ride away, but it didn't happen. Perhaps the horse belonged to the storekeeper. Pinning his hopes on that possibility and impatient to make his purchases and be gone, Bowdre rode in. He tethered the mules to the rail on the side of the store away from the horse. Just as he entered, the other rider left. Unless he had come for tobacco, the man had bought nothing, and that troubled Bowdre. The rider was looking for something. Or somebody. Bowdre resisted a powerful temptation to turn and watch the other man ride away. Instead, he went on into the store and quickly made his purchases.

"Need help totin' it out?" the storekeeper asked.

"No, thanks," said Bowdre. "I can manage it." He didn't want the man seeing and maybe remembering the mules.

Bowdre soon rode out, watchful but seeing nobody. Once he was on the plain, among the chaparral and greasewood, he began to breathe easier. But he had been too hasty, letting down his guard. From somewhere behind him, a man spoke.

"Hold it, mister." There was the ominous *snick* of a pistol being cocked, and the icy voice spoke again.

"Turn around, and make it slow. Then you can tell me

where you got them mules, and it'd better be a good story."

Arlo, Dallas, Kelly, and Kelsey approached the Superstitions from the west, leaving their mounts far from the newly discovered entrance to the river that ran beneath the mountains. If they were being followed, it would seem that they were approaching the concealed trail that led to their old camp beneath the rim. Instead, they would follow the base of the mountain until they reached the entrance to the hidden riverbed. Their approach put them in a good position to view Cass Bowdre's outfit laboring up the precipitous trail toward the mountain rim.

"They're on their way to our old camp," Dallas said.

"Five of them," said Arlo, "but just four mules."

"If that's the men who tried to break in on us," Kelly said, "they got some mules in a hurry. But where is the sixth man?"

"No way for us to know," said Arlo, "but we do know that they haven't given up, and that they're likely movin' in to our old camp. That means by tomorrow they'll be lookin' for the gold again."

"Then we'd better explore the upper end of that river today," Dallas said. "We need to be as far downriver from that drop-off as we can before they get back into those tunnels."

They watched the five men and the mules disappear into the split in the mountain, on their way to the western rim.

"If we really wanted to deal 'em some grief," said Arlo, "we could wait until they're in the passages beneath the mountain and then take their mules."

"It would serve them right," Kelsey said. "Why don't we?"

"It would just take time that we really can't spare," said Dallas. "Besides, that won't stop them from finding this drop-off leading to the underground river."

* * *

Only once before had Cass Bowdre been in so perilous a position, and he still bore a pair of mean scars to remind him of it. When a man had the drop from behind, only a fool bucked the odds, but Bowdre had no choice. His only ace was the mules, for they would be between himself and the man with the gun. Bowdre rolled out of his saddle on the off side, pulling and cocking his Colt as he fell. The stranger's gun roared once, twice, three times, one of the slugs nicking the Bowdre's mule. The animal reared, braying in fear and pain, and galloped away. The stranger's fourth shot was high, as Bowdre's slug tore through his middle. He slid out of his saddle, losing the gun as he hit the ground.

The dying man looked at Bowdre through squinted, pain-wracked eyes and spoke. "You'd kill a man . . . fer . . . a pair . . . of mules?"

"I done no more than you aimed to do," said Bowdre callously, "and you had the drop. You're a fool."

Bowdre turned away, hating the man for forcing him into a shoot-out. The man's frightened horse had lit out for God knew where, and the empty saddle would tell his companions all they needed to know. The pack mule had galloped after the one Bowdre had been riding, and eventually he found them. His mount had a nasty gash along its left flank. He led the mules back near where the dead man lay, but not close enough for the smell of death to spook them. Before he could go on, he had to dispose of the body. If he left it, buzzards would be circling before he could get back to the Superstitions. Even worse, he thought gloomily, was the possibility that the shots had been heard in the early-morning stillness. He quickly searched the area and eventually found an arroyo that disappeared into a chaparral thicket. He went through the dead man's pockets and took a wallet that contained a little more than a hundred dollars. Finally he rolled the body into the deepest part of the arroyo and caved in the sides. He smoothed over the damp earth, eliminating his tracks, and then returned to the scene of the shooting. Fortunately the area was overrun with buffalo grass, and

there was virtually no evidence of what had transpired.
But there were the tracks of the dead man's horse after he
had left the store and the tracks of Bowdre's mules.
Worse, the runaway horse could have backtracked, and it
would be just a matter of time until the dead man would
be discovered. There had been six drovers with the mule
herd, and that meant the hombre Bowdre had gunned
down would have five friends looking for him. More
than enough for a necktie party.

Arlo and Dallas had no trouble finding the rockslide
that hid the passage to the underground river.

"I see only one thing wrong with this," said Kelly,
viewing the narrow aperture that they would have to enter. "There's no way Uncle Henry could have gotten his
mule in here, so he'd have been limited as to how much
gold he could carry to the outside. We'll have the same
problem."

"Well, hell's bells," Dallas said, "that still beats
haulin' it up that god-awful bluff with ropes. Besides, we
ain't found any gold yet."

"If the ore's as rich as what I've seen," said Arlo,
"even a man on foot could carry out a fortune in just a little while."

Dallas lit one lantern and Arlo the other, and the four
of them stepped into the intense darkness beneath the
mountain. In the distance, like a mighty wind, they could
hear the roar of the river.

"The river doesn't seem as frightening now that we're
down here close to it," said Kelsey. "When we were
crossing that hole in the passage floor, it was like if we
lost our footing, we might just . . . fall forever."

"That's close to how I felt when that ledge broke under
my feet," said Dallas. "Those rocks, like big fingers, are
pokin' up out of that river, and my God, what a mess
they'd make of a man who fell three or four hundred feet
onto them."

"Hush," Kelly said. "It makes me sick, just thinking
of it."

"You may get sicker yet," said Arlo. "When Dallas and me was climbin' down that drop-off, there was an awful stink somewhere below us. We figure those two gents that disappeared in the mountain actually fell through that hole in the passage floor. So it wasn't the Thunder God that claimed them. They took a nasty fall and died on those rocks in the river below."

"That's why I'm callin' this river the Death's Head," Dallas said. "I wouldn't be a bit surprised if it's full of bones."

"That's a terrible name for it," shivered Kelsey, "but it fits."

At the waterfall, they found it hard going, for they were climbing slippery, moss-covered rocks. Arlo and Dallas kept their bodies between the lanterns and the river, lest the turbulent spray crack the glass globes. The water was surprisingly cold, and the mist that swept over them numbed their faces, ears, and hands.

"Oh, I'm freezing," Kelly cried.

"You'll be all right," said Arlo, "once we're past this waterfall. The drop-off is just a little ways ahead, on our right. I reckon we forgot to tell you that we had to use the ropes maybe a third of the way down. We found a narrow cut in the wall that took us the rest of the way, and right at the mouth of the split Dallas found the sign Hoss left for us."

"I'm glad for your sakes," Kelsey said, "but can't those other men come down here the same way?"

"Not unless they come a third of the way down on ropes," said Dallas, "and it was damn near the death of us. Even then, they'll have to find that split in the wall, without havin' any idea where it leads."

Soon they became aware of the stench Arlo and Dallas had noticed the day before, and as they progressed, it became worse and worse.

"Look," Kelly said. "A hat!"

Trapped in an eddy, the hat bobbed in a shallow pool of backwater. It removed any doubt as to the origin of the putrid smell that assaulted them. Arlo set the lantern down and tied his bandanna over his nose and mouth.

"Use your bandannas," Arlo said. "They're down here, and we can't avoid the odor, but we can stand it."

"Dear God," said Kelsey, "I hope we don't find the gold anywhere close to that smell. I'd be tempted to give up the mine just to escape that awful odor. I realize death claims us all, but don't we deserve a decent burial, a chance to be returned to the earth from which we came?"

"It's pretty gruesome," Dallas said, "knowin' they're rotting here in this hole, and not a thing we can do about it. But I agree with you. If we found the mine right now, amid all this stink, I'd not be in any hurry to claim it."

They followed the underground river a few hundred yards, eventually reaching a point where it was impossible for them to go farther. The water rushed out from beneath a great cleft of rock, and the cavern ended against a stone wall.

"Well," Kelly said with a sigh, "I really don't know what I expected, but certainly not this. Now what do we do?"

"I think we'll take a closer look at the walls along this side of the river," said Arlo. "If we don't come up with anything here, then we'll try the other side. We need a hole, a crevice, something we can get into. Wherever this gold is, it won't be easy to find, and for certain, it won't be in plain sight."

"We're lookin' at it like this mine has to be somewhere beneath this particular mountain," Dallas said, "but that may not be the case. Remember, when we discovered a way to the outside, we could still have followed the river a ways? Instead, we went on out. The mine could be somewhere beyond where we left the river, but before it reaches the Salt."

"Maybe," Arlo said, "but somehow I doubt it. I think when we finally find the mine, it'll be right here under the Superstitions. We're going to take a closer look at the upper reaches of this river first. After that, if we come up empty-handed, we'll be forced to get into that stretch you're thinking about. But I'm hoping it don't come to that, because at the lower end it all narrows down to the extent that if there's any gold, it'll almost have to be in the riverbed itself."

"It won't be in the riverbed," said Dallas. "That ore sample Hoss sent us had been dug out of a lode. Riverbed gold is nearly always dust or nuggets, washed down from some higher elevation. It's got to be somewhere under this mountain."

Cass Bowdre now cursed the very rain he had blessed the night before. While it had wiped out the tracks of the stampeded mules, the soft earth now made it virtually impossible for Bowdre to hide his trail back to the Superstitions. In a vain attempt to confuse pursuers, he rode out of his way and, when he reached the mountains, avoided the most direct way to the camp beneath the west rim. Instead, he rode up the canyon where they had first been attacked by Apaches and followed the tortuous trail up the eastern flank of the mountain. From there he crossed to the west side and led his mules through the break in the rim.

"Well, by God," Zondo Carp growled, when Bowdre entered the cavern, "it sure took you long enough. It ain't more'n spittin' distance from here to Tortilla Flat. I could of walked there and back in less time than it took you."

"You may damn well wish you had," said Bowdre angrily. "Some hombre recognized the mules and braced me. I had to kill him, and then I rode halfway to Mexico tryin' to hide my trail. I'd like to see you do any better."

"So now the rest of them mule drovers will come after us with a pistol in one hand and a noose in the other," Sandoval said.

"That's about the straight of it," said Bowdre. "Or if the law gets into it, a posse from town. This is Gila County, and old Wheaton might be forced to make a show of doin' his job."

"Ever since we got into this search for gold," Os Ellerton complained, "there ain't nothin' went right. Why'n hell don't we just fold and git out of this game? We could ride to Santa Fe, work up a deal there. Anything would be better than this."

"Damn smart," mocked Bowdre. "I hear there's all manner of honest work there, such as milkin' cows and tendin' sheep."

"If I got me a choice," Ellerton said, "I'd ruther be a live sheepman than a dead prospector. I ain't about to git my neck stretched for stealin' no damn mule."

"Me neither," said Three-Fingered Joe.

"This ain't the time to cut and run," Bowdre said in a soothing voice. "If they're already after us, we got to stay put. Otherwise, they'll dog us until we have to fight, likely out in the open. We got us a pretty good hideout here, and we already know enough about these passages to lose ourselves if we have to. These mule drovers lost a man, but they can't afford to hunker here forever, tryin' to even the score. I'd say we hang on here and ride this out, even if we don't find any gold. Hell's fire, let's don't tuck our tails and run like a bunch of yellow coyotes."

"I reckon I'll buy that," said Sandoval. "If we got to face a damn bunch of vigilantes with hangin' on their minds, then let's do it on our terms, not theirs. If we got to fort up and fight, I favor doin' it here."

"Damn right," Bowdre said, pressing his small advantage. "While three of us search for the mine, two will always be on watch. One of us will watch from the east rim, while the other watches from the west. We can see for miles, and at first sight of any riders, one of the hombres on watch can light a shuck down the passage and warn the rest of us. We got control of the high ground, and with time to lay an ambush, we can gun the varmints down before they can get at us."

It was a logical assessment, one that satisfied them for the time being, and Bowdre sighed in relief. He had little doubt that the family or friends of the man he had killed would be coming, and he knew that his own men would not fight to the death over half a dozen mules. If and when the riders came, Bowdre would have to make the first move.

"Now," he said when they had settled into their camp, "I'm goin' down to that passage that opens out below the rim. It's a damn good lookout position."

"Yeah," Zondo said, "but only toward Phoenix. You come in from Tortilla Flat, which is the other direction."

"Damn it," spat Bowdre, "I *told* you I circled thirty miles out of my way just to come in from the west. Don't you reckon if anybody's trailin' me, they'll ride in from the same direction?"

The others laughed and Carp said nothing. When Bowdre entered the passage, Sandoval went with him to the shelf where they could see far to the west. They stood there for a while, allowing their eyes to become accustomed to the light and to the heat waves that shimmered across the plain. The tiny horsemen were moving dots, appearing, disappearing, then appearing again.

"Seven of 'em," Sandoval said. "Wasn't but six of them mule drovers, and you cashed one. Who are the others?"

"One of the extra men could be the sheriff," said Bowdre. "I reckon one of us ought to keep watch until they're close enough for us to identify 'em. I need to know if Sheriff Wheaton is or ain't in the bunch. Since it's me they're likely lookin' for, I reckon I'll stay out here until I know who they are."

"I ain't sure about the others," Ellerton said peering into the distance, "but by God, two of 'em is that pair of *Mejicano* coyotes, Yavapai and Sanchez."

"You're right," said Bowdre, "and that tells us this bunch ain't got the backin' of the law. Not with them thievin' Mexes along."

"Wisht I had me a Sharps buffalo gun," Ellerton said. "I'd cut 'em right down. But we'll lose them in the brush before they're in range."

"Let 'em go for now," said Bowdre. "They've been to Mex town and rounded up some coyotes to throw in with 'em. Now they're after the gold, and even if we don't find the mine, I'll get my enjoys out of gut-shootin' that pair."

"They're headed right at us," Ellerton said. "You reckon they know of that trail up to the rim and the cavern where we're holed up?"

"We won't know that," Bowdre said, "unless they show on that plateau just before they begin the last climb. One of us will have to stay out here and maybe get some idea as to what that bunch has in mind."

"Can't even see 'em now," said Ellerton. "They can't ride through them chaparral and greasewood thickets at the foot of the mountain, so that means they'll have to dismount. We oughta sneak down there, grab them horses, and leave the mules."

"Kind of what I got in mind," Bowdre grinned. "What hombre wouldn't jump at the chance to swap his hoss for a big Missouri jack?"

Chapter 17

Long before Yavapai, Sanchez, and their companions reached the foot of the mountains, other eyes had seen them as well. He wore a used-up old black hat with a hole in the dented crown, moccasins, and buckskins. Swiftly he moved through the chaparral to the horses and mules Arlo and Dallas had picketed. Riding one mule, leading the second and two horses, he was soon lost in the thickets to the north.

Cass Bowdre gave the seven riders almost an hour before he crept along the steep, precarious trail that led down from the west rim. Reaching the brush-shrouded foothills, he paused, listening. He pushed on toward the place where they had last seen the seven riders, pausing at intervals to listen. Suddenly a horse snorted, and Bowdre knew where the animals were. He found a clearing where he could see the west rim and be seen by his men. He waved his hat toward the rim, stepped back into the brush, and waited. Finally his four companions emerged from the brush. Each man led a mule, except Sandoval, who led two.

"You should have rousted Davis out," said Bowdre. "He could have led one of the mules."

"Hell," Carp said, "he ain't got enough savvy to lead a mule. You want that varmint, trot up there and lead him down."

The others laughed and Bowdre choked back an angry response. Sandoval cut in with a question.

"You aim to take these horses up the same trail them mules come down and then brush out the tracks?"

"No," Bowdre said, forcing himself to speak calmly, "you and Ellerton brush out the tracks back to the foot of the mountain. I aim to leave a trail plain enough for that bunch to foller in the dark. It's got to be a trail so plain they won't bother lookin' back any farther."

Sandoval and Ellerton went to the foot of the mountain trail, and with brushy tops cut from young cedars, they wiped out all mule and boot tracks back to the place where the horses and mules were.

"Now," Bowdre said, "we're goin' to take all these hosses and, leadin' the mules, head for Phoenix. I want mule tracks plain as day. Once we hit the creek this side of town, we'll swat them mules and two extra hosses, runnin' 'em on across. Then we light out up the creek and don't leave it until we're all the way past the eastern flank of the mountains."

"Then we circle back and climb up that trail to the east rim," finished Three-Fingered Joe.

"Exactly," Bowdre laughed. "And when we've done that, we'll cover our back trail. When them mule drovers come lookin' for tracks, they'll sure find 'em. Now if the rest of that *Mejicano* bunch just happens to catch up with them mules, you reckon they ain't gonna round up them jacks, take a load off their feet and ride?"

Sandoval laughed. "I reckon they will, and it'll likely be their last ride. Like you said, them five hombres will be lookin' for mule tracks, and when they catch up, I wouldn't be settin' a-straddle of one of them jacks for all the gold in these danged mountains."

Juarez had no trouble following the tracks from Hoss Logan's cabin to where Arlo and Dallas had picketed the horses and mules, but beyond that he found no trail. Angrily, he turned on Yavapai and Sanchez.

"Where they go?" he demanded.

Sanchez shrugged, pointing to the western flank of the Superstitions. Yavapai looked at Sanchez, and the two suppressed grins. Domingo Vasquez had appointed this *bastardo* Juarez the *comandante,* so let Juarez decide what had become of their quarry and what he should do next.

"We look," said Juarez, dismounting.

The rest of them dismounted, left their horses, and followed Juarez as he approached the foot of the mountain. They fought their way through catclaw, chaparral, and greasewood, only to find the mountain devoid of any crevice. They stumbled through one thorny thicket after another, carefully avoiding the jumping cactus that seemed eager to snag them. Juarez led them south along the foot of the mountain all the way to the Gila River, yet they found nothing. While Yavapai and Sanchez were amused, their grim-faced companions were not. They were openly hostile, and big Garcia Ruiz turned angrily on Juarez.

"We follow you for hours," said Ruiz. "Where in hell you be going?"

"He look for stair steps up the mountain," Pepino Frio said with a giggle.

Pepino had a nauseating high-pitched voice. Juan and Juno Ortega laughed, and Juarez thought better of the nasty response that was on the tip of his tongue. Finally he spoke, and his voice was deceptively mild.

"We go back to the horses."

Juarez had no idea what he was looking for, beyond some kind of entry into what he believed was an impenetrable mountain. He dared not admit defeat, however, for he must somehow continue to pursue the riders they had been trailing. When Juarez and his weary comrades neared the area where they had left their horses, the day was already two-thirds spent. To a man, they were in a vile mood, casting killing looks at Juarez for having led them on such a wild goose chase. But the worst was yet to come.

"Oil in the lanterns is gettin' low," Arlo said, "and we'd best begin makin' our way back to the outside."

"Yeah," said Dallas. "I reckon that wall along the other side of the river will still be there tomorrow."

"Lord," Kelly said, "I just want all this to be over and done. I can't help believing we'll spend another day searching that other wall, only to find that we're still no closer to finding the gold."

"I think this is the last stage of the search," said Arlo. "If we come up dry after we've searched both sides of this river, it means we've overlooked something. We'll have to backtrack."

They retraced their steps, finding the cavern walls less and less promising as they neared the point where they would leave the river. Dallas was first through the aperture, and seeing nobody, he bid the others follow. They crept through the chaparral, trying not to leave tracks as they made their way to where they had left their horses and mules.

"Let's ride back toward Phoenix a ways," said Arlo, "before we return to the cabin. I reckon we can't avoid leavin' a trail back to it, but we won't make it easy for anybody to learn who and where we are."

It was their caution that led them to cross the tracks of the seven horses and five mules as they galloped toward town. Overlying the horse and mule tracks were many boot prints.

"Folks in the Superstitions have one hell of a time keepin' track of their horses and mules," Dallas observed.

"Whoever they are," said Kelly, "I'm surprised they didn't take ours."

"They would have," Arlo said, "if they'd been aware of them. This makes no sense at all. Not unless they lost their horses before they got close enough to discover ours. Since they didn't take ours, that tells us something. They wouldn't have seen us enter the mountain because we got here ahead of them, and they couldn't have seen us leave, since they were after their horses before we came out."

"They're afoot," noted Dallas. "Why don't we catch up and see who they are?"

"Good thinking," Arlo replied. "but we don't know how long they've been gone or how near they are to town. Still, we'll trail them for a while."

"Madre de Dios!" Ruiz shouted. "The horses be gone!"

His words froze the rest of them in their tracks, but only for a moment. They turned on the hapless Juarez, cursing him and his ancestors back three generations. Rarely did Juarez fear anything or anybody, but he was afraid now. His cutthroat companions were the kind who would not only blame him for their being afoot but exact cruel revenge. They would fight among themselves for the privilege of shooting him dead. But desperation overcame his fear, and he thought fast.

"The horses do not wander!" Juarez shouted. "Some *bastardos* have drive them away. See? There be tracks of *mulos*!"

Overlying the tracks of their horses were five sets of mule tracks, every horse galloping hard toward town. Their horses had been deliberately stolen, and that threw a different light on the situation. It was the only advantage Juarez had, and he seized it.

"We have our guns," he shouted. "Let us find the *bastardos* that take our horses! Let us kill them!"

It was just the kind of brutal, bloody logic that appealed to them, and when Juarez took the trail on foot, the others eagerly followed, cursing loudly as they went. Once they were well out of sight, a horseman rode out of the chaparral a few hundred yards to the north. He rode a mule, leading a second mule and two horses. He dismounted, picketing the animals where Arlo and Dallas had previously left them. This done, he looked toward the west, where the disgruntled men had gone, and while he didn't quite smile, there was a mischievous twinkle in his old eyes. And then he was gone, vanishing into a chaparral thicket toward the western foot of the forbidding Superstitions.

Juarez trudged on, oblivious to the cursing and the threats of his trailing companions. They were insignificant as buffalo gnats compared to the probable wrath of old Domingo Vasquez. If seven horses showed up in town, saddled and riderless, the sheriff would be forced to investigate, and since the men left afoot were under the protective wing of Domingo Vasquez, it would undoubtedly raise questions that Señor Vasquez might find very difficult to answer. Besides, the town would laugh at these foolish *Mejicanos* who obviously couldn't prevent their own horses from running away. But Sheriff Wheaton and Domingo Vasquez, they would not laugh. Juarez could see himself shamed and sent back across the border, where, by rope or by gun, he would die before sundown. He swallowed hard and walked faster.

Arlo led out, with Dallas, Kelly, and Kelsey following. Rather than keeping to the trail, they rode half a mile north, then west.

"Not much cover from here to town," said Dallas. "If they're watching their back trail they'll know we're after them. They could fan out and pick us off with rifles before we could get a shot away."

"They could, but I don't think so," Arlo said. "I'd gamble that every man left his long gun in his saddle boot. Besides, bein' afoot, all they'll have on their minds is catchin' their horses. I reckon they'll try to do that before they get close to town. I figure there'll be a hell of a fight, and I doubt that either side will want the sheriff involved. I'd like to know who all these hombres are, those who grabbed the horses, and the bunch left afoot. I'd say somethin' downright weird is goin' on."

"I'd have to agree," Dallas said, leaning down from his saddle for a closer look at the mule tracks. "Look at the stride of them mules and how shallow the tracks are. Those horses are being ridden, but I'd say the mules are all on lead ropes. I'm almighty curious as to what took place, and why."

"I'm curious, myself," said Arlo. "I think we'll stay on the trail of this bunch that's afoot until we know who they are. I have a feeling that will answer some of our questions."

Reaching the creek, Bowdre and his men dropped back, allowing the two extra horses and the mules to surge ahead. The pair of horses and the five mules hit the creek at a fast gallop, took the farthest bank, and continued on toward town. Bowdre and his companions kept their horses in the creek, following it northeast. Once they were well beyond the eastern rim of the Superstitions, they found a place where thick buffalo grass would hide their tracks, and there they left the creek.

"We'll approach the mountains from the northeast," said Bowdre. "We'll keep to the grass and thickets until we reach the head of that canyon where the trail leads up to the east rim."

They reached the trail without incident, and leading the reluctant horses, made their way up the hazardous cleft to the rim.

"Carp," said Bowdre, "you and Ellerton go back down that canyon a ways, take some brush and drag out our tracks leadin' up to that split in the wall. The rest of us will take the hosses on to our camp and get 'em out of sight."

Once the horses had been taken to the new camp, Bowdre waited for Carp and Ellerton to return before assigning the next duty.

"We're keepin' a man on watch out here on the rim," Bowdre said, "and Ellerton, we might as well start with you."

"We got rid of that Mex bunch and throwed the mule drovers off our trail," protested Ellerton, "so why in tarnation we got to stand out yonder on that damn rim and look at all the greasewood and chaparral thickets between here an' Phoenix?"

"By God," Bowdre glowered, "because I said so!"

Sullenly, Os Ellerton started down the passage toward the lookout point below the west rim. Zondo Carp turned on Bowdre.

"You're about as sociable as a grizzly that's been woke up in the dead of winter," said Carp. "I don't see nothin' wrong with Ellerton's question."

"You wouldn't," Bowdre said. "You're follerin' Ellerton's lead like a blind mule, with neither of you lookin' or thinkin' beyond the obvious. You *think* Wells and Holt are still holed up somewhere in the Superstitions."

"Oh," said Carp sarcastically, "and I reckon you don't?"

"No," Bowdre said, "I don't. Remember that cabin near Saguaro Lake where we was refused grub and you tried to kick in the door? And that woman with her sick sister who told us to vamoose? I'm figurin' them Logan women—old Logan's kin—have throwed in with Wells and Holt, and they're the ones holed up in that cabin. That day we was at the cabin, I'm figurin', Wells and Holt was right here in these mountains, lookin' for the Logan mine."

"Kelly and Kelsey," Gary Davis mumbled. He got to his feet, seizing Bowdre by his shirt front. "Kelly and Kelsey Logan," Davis bawled.

"I'm gettin' a mite tired of this," said Sandoval, as he slugged Davis in the back of the head with the muzzle of his Colt.

"I reckon I see what you got in mind," Zondo said. "If Wells and Holt ain't camped here in the mountains, they'll be ridin' back to the cabin before sundown, and back here to the mountains in the morning."

"That's the idea," said Bowdre, "but *where* they're holed up ain't really important. What *is* important is that if they've left the mountains, they ain't searchin' the passages. That means they know somethin' we don't. It also means they got to ride in every day to continue their search, and if we keep our eyes on them, they'll lead us right to the gold. I'd bet my last *peso* them ugly *Mejicanos* that Yavapai and Sanchez has throwed in with has got the same idea."

Two hours later, Os Ellerton entered the cavern and confirmed Bowdre's suspicions.

"Four riders just loped out of the chaparral near the

foot of the mountain," he reported. "I watched 'em until they come across the trail of our horses and them mules. They reined up, studyin' them tracks, and then, by God, the four of 'em struck off, follerin' that trail."

"*That's* what Yavapai, Sanchez, and that Mex bunch was doin' out here," figured Sandoval. "They trailed Wells and Holt."

"I reckon they've narrowed down the search," Carp said, "so's they don't have to stumble through every hole under these mountains. So why don't we watch for 'em to ride in, and then follow 'em?"

"Oh, hell, Zondo," Bowdre sighed, "use your head. They'll get here long before first light, picket their hosses out in the brush, and give us the slip like they done that bunch Yavapai and Sanchez is with."

"So Yavapai and Sanchez was followin' tracks," said Sandoval, "and after Wells and Holt left their horses at the foot of the mountain, they just disappeared."

"That's what I reckon," Bowdre said. "I think them hombres was searchin' along the foot of the mountain, and I don't think they found anything. But there's somethin' that don't fit. Once that bunch found their hosses gone, why didn't they take the four mounts that Wells, Holt, and the Logan women must have picketed down there? For sure, the four hosses wasn't enough, but better than none."

"Maybe Wells and Holt found a passage that's big enough to take their horses in with 'em," Three-Fingered Joe suggested.

"No way," said Bowdre. "A hole that big, in the side of a mountain, and you think seven men could waste half a day and not find it?"

"This Wells and Holt are always three jumps ahead of us," Sandoval cursed. "What are you aimin' to do?"

"Startin' tomorrow," said Bowdre, "we leave one man in camp, and two of us will explore another passage. The other two of us will be at the foot of the mountain before first light. We goin' to do our damnedest to foller this Wells and Holt wherever they go."

"You just raked me over for suggestin' that very thing," grumbled Carp. "I reckon you think it makes more sense, comin' from you?"

"All right, Zondo," Bowdre said, "back off. It was your idea, and while I still don't think it'll work, we ain't losin' nothin' but time, givin' it a try. There, now, does that satisfy you?"

"It makes more sense than anything you've said so far," said Sandoval. "I never been one to lay all my *pesos* down on a single hand. You just hit on somethin' that'll keep all of us busy. What are you aimin' to do with Davis, besides crackin' his skull every time he throws a fit?"

"On our own, or by follerin' Wells and Holt, I aim to narrow down this search for gold," said Bowdre. "When we finally settle on a certain area, I'm hopin' something will break loose in his memory, and Davis will lead us straight to the gold. Damn it, there has to be *something* that stuck in his mind. What kind of man could get his hands into ore as rich as that and not remember a blasted thing about where or how he found it?"

"Ah, hell," Carp said, "he's got just enough brains left to know he found the gold but not enough to remember where. You'd better hope the loco varmint don't get crazy and jump me when it's my day in camp. I'll drill some holes in his gizzard and put him out of his misery."

"Carp," said Bowdre with a glare, "I ain't wantin' trouble, but I'm always willin' to make exceptions for them that won't have it any other way. Remember that. Osteen didn't."

Arlo reined in his horse behind a patch of greasewood and the others stopped next to him.

"We're catchin' up to them," said Arlo. "If all of us ride in, it would raise a dust and give away our hands. Wait for me here. I'll circle around and get ahead of them."

Arlo rode ahead, far enough northeast that he wouldn't be seen. Once he was sure the plodding men were well behind him, he rode south until they would pass close enough for him to see their faces. Hiding himself and his horse in the chaparral, he waited. He could see the patches of sweat that darkened their shirts. He recognized none of the men except the two that limped along well behind the others. He waited until they had all passed from his view and then rode back to his companions.

"Five of them I've never seen before," he reported, "but six and seven are none other than our old friends Yavapai and Sanchez. Whoever they've throwed in with, they're an ugly-lookin' bunch."

"They must have followed our tracks from the cabin," said Dallas, "and the seven of them have been beatin' the bushes around the foot of the Superstitions, tryin' to discover where we went."

"I reckon that's a good guess," Arlo said, "but we still don't know how those mules figure into all this."

"No," said Kelly, "but with with Yavapai and Sanchez involved, don't you suppose there's something crooked going on?"

"I'd bet a pile on it, myself," Dallas said. "They've followed us once, and they'll do it again. By leavin' for the Superstitions before first light, we can lose 'em, but we'll be leavin' our horses and mules at their mercy. They could leave us on foot any time, just for the hell of it."

"That's a chance we'll have to take," said Arlo. "Hard as it is to spot that break in the wall, it's not impossible. Somebody's goin' to find it if they look long enough and hard enough. I reckon we'll have two or three days to find Hoss Logan's mine before somebody learns the way into that river cavern."

"I just have the awful feeling we won't find any sign tomorrow when we spend the day on that canyon wall across the river. Where do we go from there?" Kelsey said.

"I don't have the faintest idea," said Arlo. "Hoss must have known we'd go over those walls an inch at a time, and it would be a hell of a lot of effort for nothing. I just can't believe we won't find a message of some kind."

"Riders comin'," Dallas warned, "and they've seen us."

"I'd bet they're followin' the same trail we did," Arlo said. "I expect we're about to learn a little more about these strange goings-on. Keep your pistols handy until we know their intentions."

The five strangers stopped thirty yards away. Each man was armed with a Colt and carried a rifle in his saddle boot. They were a hard lot, one and all, with raven-black hair, cold blue eyes, and thin, unsmiling lips. After several moments of uncomfortable silence, the leader spoke.

"We're the Vonnegals. We brung a herd of mules down the Santa Fe from St. Joe. Last night they scattered all to hell an' gone."

"That's not surprising," Arlo said. "Bad storm."

"We been through worse, an' they didn't run," the man said sourly. "Truth is, some thievin' varmints took advantage of the storm, stampeded the herd, an' helped theirselves to six of our Missouri jacks."

"Got any proof it was thieves, and not the storm?" Dallas asked.

"Proof enough fer us," said the stranger. "Storm wipeᵈ out all the tracks, so we took to ridin' to ranches an' towns, askin' questions. Our brother Tad rode to Tortilla Flat this mornin', an' was at the store when a gent showed up with two of our mules. When Tad's hoss come in riderless, we back-trailed him and found Tad shot dead. We don't care a damn about the mules, but Tad was kin—blood kin—and them what kilt him is goin' to pay. You folks has been follerin' that trail. What's your stake in this?"

"None," Arlo said, meeting their hard stares with one of his own.

On the Western frontier, a man who asked too many questions found himself not liking the answers. Without another word the five wheeled their horses and rode off to the southwest, returning to the trail they'd been following.

"Well," said Dallas, "that explains where the mules came from."

"Six men afoot, six stolen mules," Kelly said. "It fits."

"In spades," Arlo said. "That hardcase bunch from the Superstitions saw a chance to swap stolen mules for horses, and took it."

"When them five hombres from St. Joe catches up, whoever is closest to them mules is in for one hell of a fight," said Dallas. "I reckon Yavapai and Sanchez is about to get throwed and stomped. When they come out of this—if they do—their coyote hides won't hold shucks."

Chapter 18

Big Juarez splashed across the creek and paused on the farthest bank. The mule tracks and those of two horses continued, but that was all.

"What you be waiting for?" Garcia Ruiz shouted.

Juarez said nothing, waiting until Ruiz, Pepino Frio, and the Ortega brothers had all crossed the creek.

"Something's not right," said Juarez. "All *mulos* come out of the water, but only two of the horses."

"Estupido," said Ruiz. "The others follow the creek."

"Madre de Dios," Juarez snarled, "you t'ink I not know that? There be two ways, *tonto pelado. Dos.* Which one?"

They might follow the stream for hours, only to discover the horsemen had gone the other way. Then, from somewhere ahead, came the braying of a mule. It offered a way out of the dilemma, and Juarez seized it.

"Mulos!" Juarez shouted. "Let us take them."

He set out after the beasts, and for lack of an alternative the others followed. Yavapai and Sanchez, however, paused, looking uncertainly up and down the creek. Suppose they showed up in town mounted on mules, instead of the horses Señor Domingo Vasquez had provided? It was more of a risk than they cared to take, and with a sigh, the perplexed pair limped off up the creek seeking the place the horses had left the stream.

"We find them!" Juarez shouted when he sighted the grazing mules.

"Silencio," snarled Ruiz. "You frighten them away and I kill you."

But weariness and desperation lent caution to their footsteps, and they were successful in catching the five mules. Only when they were mounted did it occur to Juarez that the bothersome Yavapai and Sanchez were nowhere in sight.

"El Diablo's hijos," Juarez bawled, "where be Yavapai and Sanchez? The *Señor* Vasquez say we must watch them, and now they be gone. We must find them."

"Si," Ruiz agreed. "The *señor* say we must watch them, but he do not say while we watch them, we cannot shoot them dead." Drawing his pistol, Ruiz fell in behind Juarez and the five of them galloped their mules back toward the creek.

Meanwhile, Yavapai and Sanchez had made a shocking discovery.

"Sangre de Christo," Yavapai gasped, pointing. "Hombres come, and they be tracking us."

The five Vonnegals were nearing the creek. Two hundred yards upstream, Yavapai and Sanchez went belly down in the tall grass. They dared not move until the Vonnegals had crossed the creek and were well out of sight. Two miles west of the creek, Juarez and his four companions topped a rise and came face-to-face with the five men coming up the other side. Recognizing their mules, the Vonnegals had an edge. Juarez, in the lead, bore the brunt of their fury. Four slugs ripped into him, flinging him to the ground, his pistol unfired. The remaining four men dropped into the knee-high grass, pulling their pistols as they went. A mule screamed as a slug grazed its flank, and all the animals lit out back the way they'd come. The Vonnegals had dismounted, and for the moment there was silence, as both factions considered their situation and sought some advantage. "Drop them guns an' come out with your hands in the air," one of the Vonnegals shouted, "or you git no mercy!"

"We ask none and we give none, *gringo bastardo*," Ruiz responded.

It was a foolish taunt, and Ruiz soon discovered his folly. While the high grass was good cover, much of it had seeded, and was dry enough to burn. Soon enough, the Vonnegals set the ground on fire. As the flames swept up the rise, there was enough smoke to cover the Vonnegals advance. The youthful braggart Pepino Frio was the first to make a break for it. In a zigzag run, Pepino almost reached the crest of the ridge before lead cut him down. Though the Vonnegals had little to shoot at, they simply poured lead into the tall grass, and one of the slugs caught Garcia Ruiz in the face. Juan and Juno Ortega were on their knees, Colts blazing, and in the few seconds before they died, they downed two of the Vonnegals. Finally, but for the distant cawing of a crow and the sigh of the wind, there was silence. While flames swept over the dead bodies of their recent companions, Yavapai and Sanchez got to their knees and peered cautiously down the creek, unsure as to their next move.

"There be some hell of a fight," said Yavapai. "Why it be?"

"Who know?" Sanchez replied. "Per'ap Juarez and his *companeros* be dead. Per'ap it be us who must explain to the Señor Vasquez."

"*Si,*" said Yavapai gloomily. "Then *we* be dead."

While the wait was long and their patience worn thin, Yavapai and Sanchez held their position until they knew who had won the fight and how many were yet alive. Finally they saw three riders—strangers—approach the creek from the west, riding back the way they had come. The trio of *gringos* led two riderless horses and drove the five mules.

"The *gringos* kill for *mulos,*" said Yavapai.

"Is not concern us," Sanchez replied. "*Bastardos* who steal our horses take only five. There be two yet loose. Per'ap we catch them before they be reaching the town."

"For why?" Yavapai asked. "These horses belong to Señor Vasquez, an' when he learn of this, I not wish to be where he get his hands on me."

"Nor I," said Sanchez. "I think per'ap when we find these horses we ride south, where there be silver to steal and the stagecoach to rob. Per'ap the sheriff in Tucson have been shot dead. A new one cannot know of us so good."

Again Yavapai and Sanchez headed for town, carefully avoiding the rise where the grass still smoldered where lay the riddled, blackened bodies of all their former companions.

The wind was out of the southwest. Arlo slowed his horse and the rest of them drew up beside him. Though the ominous popping came from miles away, Arlo and Dallas recognized it for what it was.

"Hell's busted loose," said Dallas. "I reckon them Missouri hombres found their mules."

"I just hope we find some sign tomorrow," Kelsey said. "I'm so tired."

"After dark, why don't we all walk to Saguaro Lake and have us a bath and a swim? It's plenty warm enough," said Arlo.

"Good idea," Dallas agreed. "All of us together, huh?"

"Why, hell no," said Arlo. "You find a place for you and Kelly, and I'll find one for Kelsey and me."

"I thought we was pards," Dallas said mournfully. "We always shared."

"We share grub, money, and horses," said Arlo, "and you're welcome to my last clean shirt and my last pair of socks. But Kelsey and me have our own plans, and they don't include you. I reckoned you and Kelly would have plans of your own by now. What'n hell's come over you?"

"We do have plans," Kelly said in disgust. "It's that damn cowboy humor again. Can't you tell he's ragging you?"

"I'm not sure he is," said Kelsey. "After I'd been shot, out of my head and stark naked, every time I'd kick off my blankets, the first person I'd see would be Dallas."

"I'm not that sure you were out of your head every time you kicked off the blankets," Kelly suggested. "You hogged all the attention."

"Oh, I had a wonderful time," said Kelsey, "and I had half a quart of whiskey all to myself. Don't forget that."

Their laughter rang out in the twilight, and the first twinkling stars looked down from a purpling sky, as they rode on toward Hoss Logan's cabin.

Cass Bowdre and his companions watched the five riders take the trail toward town in pursuit of the horses, mules, and the men afoot.

"They been follerin' two mules all the way from Tortilla Flat," Sandoval said, "and now there's tracks of five. They ain't thinkin' straight."

"I'm countin' on that," said Bowdre. "Once they find them mules, whoever's closest to 'em is in for one hell of a fight, and we win two pots with a single draw. We settle the score with Yavapai and Sanchez, and we get them mule drovers off our trail. By God, it ain't often things work out like this."

"Tomorrow before first light," Ellerton said, "you aim to have two of us watchin' for this Wells and Holt. Who you got in mind?"

"Myself, for one," said Bowdre. "Are you volunteerin' to side me?"

"Yeah," Ellerton said. "I've had a bellyful of stumblin' around under these mountains. I think this Wells and Holt knows somethin' we don't, and if we're there when they ride in, there ain't no reason we can't foller 'em to whatever they've found."

"Why you?" Zondo Carp demanded. "You reckon the rest of us can't see good enough to trail 'em?"

"Think what you want," said Ellerton. "It don't make a damn to me what you think. I've had more'n enough of these mountains, and I'm ready to move on. By my lonesome, if that's what it takes."

"Nobody leaves till I say this is done," Bowdre said.

An hour before first light, Arlo, Dallas, Kelly, and Kelsey walked out.

"I don't feel comfortable, leaving our horses and

mules," said Kelly. "Why can't we leave them farther away, so they'll be more difficult to find?"

"We can," Arlo said, "but it'll mean a longer walk."

"I don't care," said Kelly. "Even if those men don't bother our mounts, they can still hear us coming if we ride in too close."

"We can't be *that* quiet on foot," Kelsey said, "in the dark, through all the cactus and underbrush."

"No," said Dallas, "but I think Kelly's right. In the quiet just before first light sound carries far. A hoof against a stone can sound like a smithy's hammer. Since we know they're likely up there in our old camp, why don't we ride a mile or two south of that trail that leads up to the rim?"

"You got no argument from me," Arlo said. "Even if they suspect we're coming, they won't know where to watch for us. They'll be depending on us to make some noise they can follow. It'll be to our advantage to ride in somewhere south of the trail we took yesterday and to dismount as far from them as we can."

"We'll have lots farther to travel," said Kelly, "but at least when we pass that trail that leads up to the rim, we'll be on foot."

"Yes," Dallas said, "and the more I think about it, the more I believe it'll be worth the walk. When we come out, it'll be daylight. Even if they do find our mounts, we'll be far enough to the north that they still won't know where we're going to come away from the mountain."

They circled toward the south, leaving their animals beyond the trail that led up to the western rim of the mountain.

"Kelsey, you and Kelly bring the lanterns," Arlo said, "and stay well behind us. Dallas and me may have to pull our guns in a hurry. If there's a sound—or the slightest possibility that they're waiting for us—go back the way we came and wait for us. We may have to circle wide, go farther north, and then work our way back to you."

They made their way carefully along the base of the

mountain. Kelly and Kelsey, at Arlo's insistence, kept back. The moon was down, and the stars seemed to draw away, cloaking the earth in blackness. A sudden sound, slight like the rolling of a stone under a man's booted foot, broke the silence. More ominous was the sound that followed—the *snick* of a pistol being cocked! Shooting by sound was difficult, and a man who fired first in the dark risked targeting himself by his muzzle flash. The only advantage was that if he drew return fire, he then had the other man's muzzle flash to work with. Dallas and Arlo fired so close together, it sounded like a single shot. Before the echo died, they had thrown themselves to the ground and rolled away from their original positions. The return fire came, two slugs whistling through the empty air where they had been standing. Arlo and Dallas fired again, this time at the muzzle flashes. There was a grunt of pain, and then only silence. Arlo and Dallas lay unmoving for at least a quarter of an hour. Dallas felt around until he found a stone at least the size of his fist, and flung it away, well off to one side. It drew no response.

"They've shucked out," Arlo said.

"Kelly, Kelsey," Dallas called softly, "are you all right?"

"Yes," said Kelly. "It's so dark, why did you shoot?"

"To get them off our tail," Dallas said. "It ain't easy for a man to resist shootin' back when he's got a muzzle flash to shoot at, so we gave him one. I think we nicked him. If he's hit, they won't be so quick to follow us again. Come on, let's find our passage and disappear."

Cass Bowdre and Os Ellerton made their way up the trail to their camp below the west rim. They were silent, Ellerton pressing a bandanna to the bloody wound in his left arm, just above the elbow. Neither man spoke until they had reached their camp. Their comrades sat around a small fire, drinking coffee.

"We heard shootin'," said Carp. "What'd you do, Ellerton, light a smoke?"

"He might as well have," Bowdre said in disgust. "He cocked his pistol and them two pistoleros cut down on us, shootin' at the sound. They come damn close, and Ellerton, he shoots back, givin' 'em the target they was askin' for."

"Looks like you was right the first time, Bowdre," said Sandoval. "Ain't much use trailin' that pair in the dark."

"No," Bowdre said. "They shoot quick and straight. One of you put on some water to boil, so's we can patch up Ellerton's arm. Three-Fingered Joe, you'll keep watch today from the east rim. Carp, you'll take the west rim. Sandoval and me will search that next passage. Ellerton, you'll stay here in camp, and stay out of trouble with Davis. One more fool move out of you, and I'll shoot you myself, and it won't be in the arm."

Ellerton's face went white with anger, but he said nothing. He sat on his saddle, looking into the fire. He expected no sympathy and got none—his was a deserved reprimand. When the water was hot, Three-Fingered Joe cleansed Ellerton's wound. It was clean, for the slug had missed the bone.

The men had their bacon and coffee in silence, and when they had finished, Bowdre spoke. "Joe, I want you and Zondo on watch as soon as it's light enough to see."

With Arlo and Dallas leading the way, Kelly and Kelsey following, they reached their concealed passage without further difficulty. The men lit the lanterns, and the four of them found a shallow stretch where they could cross the river. The far bank was wider, and they were able to get past the waterfall without being drenched with violent spray. But a hundred yards above the waterfall, they found a mass of volcanic rock blocking their way, extending into the water on the river side and almost to the wall of the cavern on the other. There was barely room for them to squeeze between the stone wall and the mossy volcanic upthrust that towered over their heads.

"These walls on this side of the river are awful

smooth," Kelly said. "We haven't seen a hole or a split wide enough to get a hand into."

"No matter," replied Arlo. "We'll go back to the head of this cavern, to the start of the river, and work our way back."

"Remember the spotted ponies," Dallas said. "The sign on the wall or floor may not have anything to do with that particular spot, but it may tell us where we must go from there."

Bowdre and Sandoval had taken the passage from their camp to the bottom of the mountain, to what seemed the most promising of the passages yet to be explored.

"Injuns have been here," said Sandoval when they reached the place where the crude horse figures had been cut into the wall.

"Yeah," Bowdre replied. "I reckon there's some that ain't all that scared of the Thunder God."

"Listen," said Sandoval, once they were deep into the passage. "It's that damn river again. God, I hope this ain't another of them tunnels with a long stretch of the floor gone."

"May be worse than that," Bowdre said. "I reckon we'd better take it slow and be almighty careful."

The drop-off, when they reached it, all but took their breath away, and the updraft sucked out their pine torch, leaving them momentarily in the dark. Sandoval turned his back on the abyss and lit another match. Then Bowdre spoke.

"Put it out and stand quiet. Somebody's down there."

In the darkness far below them were two bobbing orbs of light. Both the lights were moving away from them and growing dim with distance, soon lost to view.

"Wells and Holt," said Sandoval, "and they got lanterns."

"Now," Bowdre said, "shield that match with your hat, light that torch, and let's see what's between us and the river."

Sandoval lit the pine torch and when he neared the drop-off, the updraft again sucked out the light.

"Back off," said Bowdre. "Wells and Holt have the right idea. We can't tackle this damn cliff with lighted pine splinters. We need lanterns and plenty of rope. Let's go get some and come back."

"My God," Sandoval said, "it must be a good five-hundred-foot drop to that river. You reckon Wells and Holt went down that wall?"

"I figure they done it once," said Bowdre. "Then they follered the river and found some better way. If they done it, so can we. But we'll wait for them to pull out before we make our try."

"Smart thinkin'," Sandoval said. "We'd make mighty good targets, workin' our way down that wall with lighted lanterns."

Yavapai and Sanchez stumbled on, and to their joy, they caught up to the pair of saddled horses Bowdre had stampeded with the mules. Tired from their run, the animals had stopped to graze.

"These horse belong to Señor Domingo Vasquez," said Yavapai. "We take them, and he kill us dead."

"Madre de Dios," Sanchez said, "you already be dead in the *cabeza*. We ride these horse back to town, and what do you t'ink happen to us? The Señor Vasquez, he say 'Where my other horse? Where Juarez and these other hombres I send with you?' We say other horse be gone. We say Juarez and all his *companeros* be dead. What you t'ink the Señor Vasquez do? He tell the sheriff, 'These no-good Yavapai and Sanchez kill my men and steal my horse.' Do we become the thieving *bastardos* the Señor Vasquez call us, take these horse and ride like hell for Tucson? Or do we tell the *señor* the truth, which he do not believe, and die like dogs for having kill Juarez and his *companeros* and steal their horse?"

"I t'ink," said Yavapai, "I be ready to become *muy bueno amigos* with the *malo gringo* sheriff in Tucson."

They looked to the sky above the distant ridge where

already buzzards were circling. Without another word they mounted, and kicking their horses into a fast gallop, headed south.

Kelly and Kelsey held the lanterns while Arlo and Dallas began the painstaking investigation of the walls along the other side of the river. For the rest of the day they searched, without finding any sign. Slowly they worked their way back down the river toward the exit from the underground cavern. It was Arlo who eventually broke the silence.

"All of you stay where you are while I go out and look around. After the gunplay this morning, I don't look for them to try again, but we can't risk it."

"I thought the world of Uncle Henry," Kelsey said, "but I'm so tired of this. Why don't we just give it up?"

"We've been over this before," said Dallas. "We can't give it up. Hoss wouldn't like that. We're overlooking something that's so obvious we can't see it. I reckon Arlo and me will stay with it. You and Kelly can go back to the cabin if you like."

"I'm going to be right here until the end," Kelly said. "I say either we all go on together or we all quit together. Me, I'm for going on."

"Then so will I," said Kelsey, "and I won't complain anymore."

"Come on," Arlo said. "I don't see anybody outside."

"Now," said Dallas, "the big question is, have they taken our horses and mules, leavin' us on foot?"

The animals were still there. But from his post on the west rim of the Superstitions, Zondo Carp watched the four ride out.

"We're ready, then," said Bowdre, when Carp took him the news. "Just as soon as Joe gets here with the lanterns and the rope."

"Hope he ain't run into trouble," Carp said. "He's been gone a while."

"Ain't likely," said Bowdre. "That's why I sent him to

Globe instead of Tortilla Flat. It's a mite farther, but less of a risk."

"It's one hell of a drop to that river," Sandoval said. "Might take us all night just to get down."

"That's what I expect," said Bowdre. "I just want to get down that bluff and follow the river to a place where we can get out into the open without goin' back through that tunnel. Once we've done that, we can follow Wells and Holt, or we can search on our own durin' the night."

"When we find a way in and out without goin' down that drop-off," Sandoval said, "let's take Davis down along that river. Might be close enough to the gold to bust through that fog in his head."

"Exactly what I aim to do," said Bowdre.

"Joe's comin'," Carp called.

"Good," said Bowdre. "We'll eat, and then we'll head for the river. From now on, we got us a double shot at that gold. When Wells and Holt ain't there, we can do our own searching. But if they should find it first, we can always take it off their hands."

Supper was eaten in glum silence.

"Kelly, let's walk over to Saguaro Lake," Dallas finally said. "This is gettin' on my nerves, us all sittin' here lookin' at one another like somebody just died."

When Dallas and Kelly had gone, Kelsey turned to Arlo.

"He's right," she said. "I shouldn't have said what I did about us quitting, just because we'd had a bad day."

"I understand your feelings," said Arlo. "We've been together a while, and we're kind of at loose ends. We can't make any plans, because we're committed to this search for the gold."

"It's not just that. It's . . . well . . . Dallas and Kelly. Kelly's my sister, and I think the world of Dallas, but damn it, they're *always* around. Am I being terribly selfish when I wish we had some time away from them, some time to ourselves?"

"No," Arlo said, and he sat down on the bunk beside

her. "After you'd been shot and Kelly stripped you, I felt like tellin' Dallas to get the hell out, to go sit on a rock and look at the prairie. Somehow I felt cheated, and I was jealous as hell. We've been pards for ten years. Am I normal, or just a selfish damn fool cowboy that don't know straight from crooked?"

"You're a normal damn fool cowboy," she whispered in his ear, "and I'm flattered that you think so highly of me. Sorry I kept kicking off all the blankets, but I was so hot, I felt like I was on fire."

"That was the whiskey," said Arlo. "I wonder about Kelly, how she feels about Dallas. While she was doctorin' you, it didn't seem to bother her that Dallas was there, takin' you in."

"That's Kelly," she laughed. "In some ways, she's stronger than I am, and she never feels threatened. Once when we were about fifteen, while we were out riding, we stripped for a swim in a creek. When we came out, there was that skunk Gary Davis, grinning at us. I was just mortified, and grabbed my clothes, but not Kelly. She stood face-to-face with Davis and cussed him until his face went red and he turned away. So if you're looking for the strongest of us, you've made a bad choice."

"You're strong when you need to be," Arlo assured her. "After them foolish words with Dallas when we was ridin' in, I just wanted you to know I didn't like sharin' you with him, even when we had no privacy and no choice."

"Let's put that behind us," Kelsey said, "and enjoy this time alone."

Arlo moved closer and for a while they forgot everything, including the elusive mine Hoss Logan had left to them.

Chapter 19

Dallas and Kelly walked all the way to Saguaro Lake in total silence. For a while they sat beneath the willows, not touching. The stars and a pale quarter moon were reflected in the dark waters, as though there were heavens above them and heavens below. Dallas finally spoke.

"Kelly, you ain't . . . souring on me, are you?"

"Should I be?" The tone of her voice told him nothing.

"When I was bullyraggin' Arlo about him and me always sharin', it . . . that . . . wasn't meant to include you and Kelsey," he stammered.

"My stars," Kelly laughed, "Dallas Holt, this gun-throwin' Arizona cowboy, is finally embarrassed. You mean Kelsey got your goat with that bit about you always being close by when she kicked off the blankets?"

Dallas laughed uneasily. "Yeah, I reckon she did. She . . . well . . . made it seem like I . . . I was . . . damn it, like I was more interested in her than I was . . . am . . . in you."

"And you aren't?"

He grabbed her in a bear hug, while she giggled and fought him just for the hell of it. In the struggle, she almost bloodied his nose and blacked his left eye with her elbow before he finally subdued her. There followed several prolonged kisses, and when they came up for air, their feet were in the water.

"Damn," he said, "how are we gonna explain why we went wadin' with our boots on?"

Kelly laughed. "We'll lie. I fell in the lake and you rescued me."

"Not a very convincin' lie," Dallas said, "with just our boots wet. We got to do better than that."

He seized her, and despite her shrieks, pitched her into the lake.

"Damn you," she howled, "this water's cold! I'm freezing!"

"Fear not, fair lady," he bawled, "I'll save you." Shucking only his hat, he leaped in after her.

"I reckon I can save myself," she said. "It's only knee deep."

Getting to his feet, he gallantly extended his hand. She ignored it, knuckling the water out of her eyes. She then stumbled out, he followed, and they stood there dripping wet, shivering in the night wind. He got in front of her and put his hands on her sodden shoulders.

"I reckon now you *are* put out with me," he said.

"Whatever gave you that idea?" she asked softly. Throwing her arms around him, she kissed him with gusto.

Bowdre and Sandoval reached the drop-off with their lanterns, and the first thing they discovered with the improved light was the rope Arlo and Dallas had left looped over a boulder.

"Backs up what we figured," Bowdre said. "Let's haul that rope up and see how far down it goes."

The length of rope fell far short of their expectations.

"Not even a hundred feet," said Sandoval. "That means when they got to the end of this one, they found somethin' else to tie to. This rope ain't even close to bein' long enough to reach bottom."

"This is some hell of a drop," Bowdre said. "I reckon the length of this rope is proof they found somethin' down there to rest on, but I ain't one to lean on somebody else's luck. We'll lower one of these lanterns over the edge and maybe get some idea as to what's down there."

Using the hundred-foot length of rope, they lowered a lighted lantern. By its dim glow they could barely see the first ledge Arlo and Dallas had discovered. Beyond that, the poor light from the lantern couldn't compete with the intense darkness.

Bowdre looped his belt through the bail of the lantern, and then tied the loose end of the rope securely under his arms. He then eased himself over the edge, using knots in the rope to hand-walk his way down. He was within a few feet of the ledge when there was no longer a reassuring pull on the rope. There was only a terrifying slackness. The rope had broken, and he was falling!

Cass Bowdre hit the narrow ledge with his left foot and, off balance, dug his fingers into the rough stone of the wall down which he had rapidly descended. Dripping cold sweat, he got his other foot on the ledge and managed to regain his balance. He stood there shaking, weak in the knees.

"Bowdre," Sandoval shouted, "you all right?"

"Yeah," Bowdre panted. "I was close enough that I was able to hang on when the rope broke."

"Broke, hell," said Sandoval. "It was cut halfway through, near where it was looped around this rock. That damned Wells and Holt cut it just enough so's it'd break when we put some weight on it."

"We're a prime pair of fools for not thinkin' of that," Bowdre replied. "I'll use this rope to let the lantern on down. Tie one of our ropes around that boulder, bring the other lantern and the rest of the rope, and come on down. I don't see nothin' here to tie to, so use as long a piece of rope as you got. We'll have to depend on it to reach another restin' place somewhere below, if there is one."

Sandoval came down the wall and reached the ledge without difficulty. The two of them stood peering into darkness so dense, the lantern's dim glow was barely able to penetrate it. For a long moment, neither man spoke.

"It's too far down," Sandoval said. "Pull it back up a ways, where maybe we can see somethin'."

"Hell," said Bowdre, "there's nothin' to see. That's why I let it down so far. From here, I ain't seen a damn thing we can rest a foot on that was near enough to show up in the lantern's light."

"It's goin' to be some risky," Sandoval said. "The next piece of rock offerin' us any kind of foothold may be a hundred feet down. Worse, there may not be another restin' place from here to the bottom."

"We ain't come more'n twenty-five feet," said Bowdre, "so we could still be close to four hundred feet from the bottom. But we got four hundred feet of rope yet, besides the piece you tied to the rock above us. I reckon we'd better tie the rest of what we got to that first piece, in case we don't find anything else strong enough to tie to. That'll give us more'n five hundred feet."

"By God, I don't like the looks of this," said Sandoval. "Suppose we hit the end of all that, and we *still* ain't at the bottom?"

"Then we're in one hell of a mess," Bowdre replied. "But I just don't believe it's that far to the bottom of this drop-off. Maybe we'll find us a ledge where we can rest. But we could just as well find nothin'—meanin' we got no choice but to hang on all the way to the bottom."

"If we have to," said Sandoval, "once we're down a ways, we can just drop into the river. It'll play hell with the lanterns, though."

"It might play hell with your carcass, too," Bowdre said. "Noisy as that stream is, it may not be more'n knee deep in places, and there may be some almighty big rocks near the banks."

"Talkin' won't get us down this bluff," said Sandoval, "and I reckon it's my turn to risk my neck. Wait till I get to a stoppin' place before you start down. I don't trust this rope with both of us on it."

Sandoval made his way down the rope as swiftly as he could, but the strain on his arms, back, and shoulders was almost unbearable. He soon reached the recessed ledge that had saved Arlo Wells, but try as he might, he was unable to gain the momentum to swing himself to it. Already his arms and hands were numb. There was nothing for him to do except continue down the rope, desperately

trying to reach the bottom of the drop-off before his
hands lost their grip. There was a roaring in his head and
cold sweat running into his eyes.

"Sandoval," Bowdre shouted, "are you makin' it all
right?"

But Sandoval was fighting for his life. He had a death
grip on the rope, despite having no feeling in his arms
and hands. Finally his tortured body could no longer endure the terrible strain. Icy fear swept over him and his
heart stopped as he felt his sweaty hands slipping, letting
go. Then he was falling. He hit on his feet, bending his
knees to absorb the impact. He fell face-down, skinning
his knees and elbows on sharp rocks. The lantern, fas-
tened to his belt and hanging to his rear, miraculously
was unbroken. Slowly he got to his hands and knees. His
right hand was caught in something slimy, and in the dim
light of the lantern he found it was human hair. Sandoval
let out a startled, involuntary squawk as he found himself
looking into the sightless eyes of a human skull from
which the scalp hadn't yet rotted away.

"For God's sake," Bowdre shouted, "what's goin' on
down there?"

"It's one hell of a drop," yelled Sandoval. "I lost my
grip and fell the last dozen feet or more. Skint hell out of
my arms and legs on the rocks, and then fell face-down
on some stinkin' dead hombre."

"From here on down," Bowdre shouted, "there's no
restin' place?"

"None you can reach," Sandoval shouted back.
"There's one other ledge, but it's cut back under an overhang. Ain't no way you can get to it, so don't waste any
time tryin'. Once you start, you got to skin down that
rope as fast as you can before your hands give out. My
hands played out, and so will yours. When they do, you'd
better not be too far from the bottom. The water's shallow, and there ain't a damn thing to break your fall but
these rocks."

Bowdre fared a little better than Sandoval, but not
much. His hands and arms soon gave out too, and he fell

the last few feet. He not only suffered skinned knees, hands, and elbows but managed to shatter the globe of his lantern.

"By God," Sandoval said, "there'd better be some way out of here besides back up that rope, or we'll be keepin' company with this dead varmint rottin' here in the shallows. The stink's enough to gag a buzzard."

"There has to be a way out," said Bowdre, "and tonight all I aim for us to do is find it. I twisted an ankle in that fall, and it's givin' me hell."

The two men set off down the river by the light of the single lantern. Bowdre carried the useless one, for it was still two-thirds full of oil. They kept their silence, and when they reached the waterfall, they worked their way down the slippery, mossed-over rock.

"Damn," Sandoval complained, "I'm sore as a beat dog. I feel like I been throwed and stomped twice in the same day."

"Same here," said Bowdre, "but we won't have to do that again."

They paused when they reached the point where, through some past volcanic upheaval, the underground river had been diverted.

"This cavern's gettin' smaller and smaller," Bowdre said. "I reckon we ain't gonna get out of here by follerin' the river. I'd bet a hoss this old dry riverbed is the way out."

"I wish I could believe that," said Sandoval. "Looks like a dead end to me."

"Look at that lantern's flame," Bowdre said. "We're gettin' some outside air from somewhere. It may not be much of a hole, but somewhere ahead of us, there's some kind of opening to the outside."

They reached the huge boulder that blocked what had once been an open passage, and by taking a sharp right turn, they were able to squeeze through the narrow aperture between the fallen boulder and the stone face of the mountain. Gratefully they stepped out into the cool darkness of the night.

"My God," said Sandoval in relief, "I never been so glad to see them stars and smell the sage. I feel like lopin' across the prairie and howlin' with the coyotes, just for the hell of it."

Cass Bowdre laughed. "Save it until we find the gold. I got to get back to camp and shuck off this boot, if my ankle ain't already swole too much to get it off."

Paiute, the old Indian, had waited in the darkness of the passage above the river until Bowdre and Sandoval were on their way down the wall. He was sorely tempted to cut the rope again, stranding them on that first ledge. But he restrained himself, for that would not accomplish what he had set out to do. These men must successfully reach the river and find their way out of the mountain. Only then would they bring Gary Davis into the cavern, where they expected him to reveal the location of the mine. Paiute smiled grimly in the darkness, for he knew that then the search for Hoss Logan's gold would come to a swift and startling conclusion.

Despite their resolve to continue the search for Hoss Logan's mine, Kelly and Kelsey Logan, Arlo Wells, and Dallas Holt lacked much of their former enthusiasm as they rode to the Superstitions yet again. They believed they had thoroughly searched the underground river, and they had found not a single clue to the location of the mine. Time after time, they had found Hoss's sign of three little oak pins driven into a crevice somewhere in the rock. The last such sign had been in the hidden passage Dallas had discovered partway down the bluff, on the way to the river. But for all their diligent searching, there hadn't been another sign, and it was Kelsey Logan who finally voiced what the rest of them were thinking.

"I'm not complaining," she said, "and not suggesting that we give up the search for the mine, but I just can't get excited about searching that river again. Somehow I don't believe that last sign Uncle Henry left was pointing us toward the mine. Why couldn't he have just been sending us to the river so that we could find a way in and out, without going up and down that drop-off?"

"But unless the mine's somewhere along the river," Kelly said, "why would we need a way in and out?"

"I think Kelsey's got something," Arlo replied. "We've been misinterpreting what Hoss is trying to tell us. Those three wooden pins led us to a crevice that brought us down to the river, and they must have been for that purpose alone. Hoss intended for us to follow the river, to find a way in and out. I'm thinkin' that's exactly what Hoss is tellin' us, that the mine is somewhere along the river, and that we most certainly *do* need a way in and out."

"Well, hell," said Dallas, "we're right back to where we started. I can agree Hoss is tryin' to point us toward the river, so we could follow it out. So if his purpose was to have us find a way in and out, then we can only conclude that the mine's somewhere along that damn river. But where?"

"I reckon we can also agree," Arlo said, "that when we finally reached that second ledge, where I almost knocked my brains out, all we wanted was to get to the bottom of that drop-off, to the river. Once you found that crevice at one end of that ledge, Dallas, and found those three oak pins Hoss had driven into that rock, neither of us thought of looking farther, that there might be other clues. We squeezed through that crevice, made our way down to the river, and that's where we've been ever since. We made the mistake of taking it for granted that the signs Hoss left was pointin' us directly toward the gold."

"That's exactly what we done," said Dallas, "and by God, we didn't bother seein' what was at the other end of that ledge."

"No," Arlo said, "and that's where we lost the trail. I think we'll find a sign from Hoss at the other end of that ledge and some kind of passage that will lead us to the mine."

"Oh, I can't wait to get there!" Kelsey cried.

"It wasn't easy, gettin' down that crevice from the ledge," said Dallas, "and I reckon it'll be just as hard, climbin' up it. It's a tight squeeze, and you got to just inch your way along sideways."

"I don't care," Kelsey said. "I just want to find the mine and put all this behind us. If you and Arlo could come down it, then I can climb up, and I'm going to."

"So am I," said Kelly.

"We're all in this together," Arlo said, "to the finish."

It was the middle of the night when Bowdre and Sandoval returned to their camp beneath the west rim. Bowdre told them what they had long waited to hear, and despite the lateness of the hour, nobody slept. Even Gary Davis showed some interest when Bowdre and Sandoval spoke of the underground river.

"River," Davis mumbled. "Gold under the river."

"What?" Carp shouted excitedly. "What did you say?"

Carp seized Davis by the front of his shirt, and again Davis became a virtual madman. On his knees, he lifted Carp like a rag doll and flung him against a stone wall. Dazed, Carp sat up, his hand on the butt of his revolver.

"Carp," said Bowdre coldly, "leave it be. If you pull iron, I'll kill you."

Gary Davis again became calm. He sat down and stared vacantly into the fire, speaking not a word.

"He knows," Sandoval said softly. "By God, he knows where the gold is."

"I think so," said Bowdre, "and I don't want him bothered before we get a chance to find out. You hear me, Zondo?"

"I hear you," Carp said sullenly.

"Wells and Holt will be back in there tomorrow," said Three-Fingered Joe.

"That won't matter to us," Bowdre said. "I think we got an edge on 'em, so we can afford to wait for them to leave. Tomorrow night, when they're done, we'll all go in and turn our dog loose."

* * *

Despite their haste, Arlo didn't get careless. He led them well north of their ultimate destination, and their horses and mules were picketed right where they had been left the day before.

"We'll take it slow," Arlo said, "just like we did yesterday, because we don't know they won't try to follow us again this morning. If they don't, I reckon that'll tell us they're exploring these passages under the mountain instead of trying to cash in on what they think we've learned. As far as we know, there's only one major passage they haven't been into, and that likely means they're only hours away from discovering that drop-off to the river."

"Let's just hope we're right about Hoss leavin' us a message at the other end of that ledge," Dallas said. "Another day or two of just wandering along that river, and we'll be face-to-face with this bunch, whoever they are."

Arlo and Dallas moved ahead, leaving Kelly and Kelsey far enough behind to remain out of harm's way if there was trouble. But there was no evidence of pursuit, and they went straight to the concealed entrance to the underground river.

"Dallas is right," Arlo said. "This is not a real passage that leads down from that ledge. It's no more than a split in one end of that stone drop-off, and I suspect it may be more difficult goin' up than it was comin' down. Kelsey, if you and Kelly would like to just wait . . ."

"No," said Kelly, "we *wouldn't* like to just wait. If that ledge offers enough of a hole for the two of you to go on, then we'll be going with you."

"Then this is how we're going to do it," Arlo said. "That crack in the stone is very narrow, and like Dallas said, you'll have to ease along sideways, taking it slow. I'll take one lantern and go first. Kelly, you and Kelsey will come next, and Dallas will follow you with the other lantern."

Arlo led them past the waterfall, and when they again neared the foot of the drop-off, the stench of rotting flesh became more oppressive than ever.

"My God!" exclaimed Kelly. "Be quick finding that split in the bluff, and let's get away from here."

Even though Arlo and Dallas knew the split existed, it wasn't easy to find, and when they did find it, the crevice seemed even more narrow and inaccessible than it had been when they crept down it before.

"I see what you mean," Kelsey said. "It is awful narrow, and it's knee deep in water."

"Considerably deeper than it was," said Dallas. "It wasn't more than a trickle when we first came this way."

"Yes," Arlo said, "and that bothers me. It could be bad news. The nearer we go to the head of this river, the higher the elevation. That's why this joker's so loud, because the water's runnin' downhill before it even reaches the falls. If there's passages somewhere along it, they could be flooded, which would account for this high runoff."

"Wonderful," said Kelly. "When we finally find the passage where the mine is, it could be full of water."

"It could very well be," Arlo said. "Or if it isn't, there may be a continual danger of it. This river is moving with one hell of a force, and it could break through. We'll just have to wait and see."

Arlo led the way, inching along the narrow cliff sideways, careful not to bump the lantern against solid rock. A few yards before they reached the low end of the narrow ledge, the water they were wading through played out. Finally they reached the ledge that ran across the face of the bluff, several hundred feet above the surging river.

"God," Kelsey said, "it must have been a nightmare coming down the face of this cliff with ropes."

"It did get a mite scary," said Arlo, "when I discovered that rock overhang wouldn't allow me to reach the ledge. I smashed my head against that rock up there, and I still don't know how I made it alive."

To their dismay, the opposite end of the ledge began to narrow as they progressed. Eventually they were inching along sideways, their backs to the rock wall, trying to keep their balance. But as they rounded the end of the bluff, there was a slight widening of the ledge, with yet another narrow, ragged crevice as uninviting as the one they had just endured.

"Tarnation," said Dallas, "that one looks even steeper than the one at the other end of the ledge, and from the angle of it, we'll be moving away from the river. It's time to see if Hoss left us a sign."

Arlo and Dallas began searching the ground beneath their feet and the stone wall to their backs. Finally Dallas found three wooden pegs driven into a crack in the rock about head-high.

"This may be it!" Arlo exclaimed. "We'll take it sideways, same formation as before. Dallas, you can lead this time, and I'll come last."

A dozen feet into the split, and the stone wall to their left vanished. One corner of the great stone bluff had peeled away, leaving them facing a steep, precarious ledge that led downward. They were assaulted by a rush of damp air that told them there was an open void before them. Somewhere below, well beyond the feeble glow of their lanterns, they heard the splashing of water.

"Dammit," said Dallas, "why in tarnation didn't we bring some rope? I'd feel better if we could lower a lantern and see what's down there. We could step off this ledge into ten feet of water."

"Not if we take it slow," Arlo said. "Don't step any farther than the lantern's light will reach. We can always backtrack if we have to."

But when disaster struck, it came swiftly and there was nothing they could do to prevent it. Something gave way under Kelly's boot, and with a terrified scream, she vanished into the blackness before them. Somewhere below there was a splash, and they knew she had fallen into water.

"Careful, Dallas!" Arlo shouted. "It won't help if you fall on top of her. We'll get down there as fast as we can."

"Careful be damned! Kelly, I'm coming. Can you hear me?" Dallas shouted.

But there was only silence and the horrifying realization that if Kelly Logan had been hurt in the fall, she might drown before they could reach her.

"Kelly, where are you?" Dallas cried desperately.

But he heard only the distant splashing of water and the thundering of his own heart.

Chapter 20

Dallas stepped down in water almost to his waist, with Kelsey right behind him.

"Kelsey," said Dallas, "take this lantern and hold it high."

Then Arlo reached Dallas with the second lantern, and by its added light, they found that they stood in what was most surely the backwater from the surging river that roared in the distance.

"There she is!" Arlo shouted.

Only Kelly's head was above water, and when Dallas discovered the reason, his heart sank. Beneath the surface fingers of stone protruded. If Kelly had fallen directly into them, her back or neck might be broken.

"My God," said Arlo, "if we move her, a broken rib could puncture a lung."

"Well, we sure as hell can't leave her here," Dallas said. "Arlo, take one of the lanterns and get back to the horses as fast as you can. Bring all our blankets from our bedrolls. This water's cold as melted snow, and if we don't move fast, she could die of exposure."

"You sure you can get her out of here on your own?" Arlo asked.

"I'll have to," Dallas replied, grimly determined. "There ain't room for two of us to move her back up that ledge. I'll have her out beside the river by the time you get back with the blankets. Kelsey can carry the lantern ahead of me."

They had all but forgotten Kelsey, and when Arlo

turned to her, tears streaked her cheeks, and in the pale glow of the lantern, she looked deathly white.

"Sorry," said Arlo, gathering her to him. "There's danger in moving her, but we have to do it."

"I know," she said, her voice breaking. "Go for the blankets. I trust Dallas to get her out of here."

Arlo made his way cautiously up the narrow shelf. Kelsey held the lantern high as Dallas lifted Kelly out of the water. Even in the poor light, he could see blood dripping from the back of her head. Kelsey crept well ahead of him with the light as Dallas moved sideways along the narrow ledge. He kept his back flat against the stone wall, careful not to jeopardize his balance. Slowly but surely, he reached the wider open ledge that overlooked the river.

"Have to rest a minute," Dallas panted.

While he rested, Kelsey took Kelly's wrist, feeling for a pulse.

"It's there," said Kelsey, "but it's kind of fluttery. Her hands feel like ice. Even if she's not hurt inside, I'm afraid for her, taking a fall into that cold water."

"So am I," Dallas said. "I'm hoping if we wrap her as warm as we can and get her back to the cabin, she'll be all right."

"You do care for her, don't you?" said Kelsey, her hand on his arm.

"More'n I ever cared for anything or anybody," he said simply. "Come on, let's get her down there by the river. Arlo ought to be there with those blankets soon."

Carrying Kelly in his arms, Dallas slowly worked his way down the narrow crevice, and when he reached the bottom, he carefully stretched Kelly out on a large flat stone. She tried to speak, but her teeth chattered so that she couldn't. Dallas knelt beside her, holding both her hands in his. Arlo returned with all eight of their blankets and quickly spread them out flat.

"Now let's get her onto them," said Arlo, "and wrap her tight."

"Not until we get her out of those wet clothes," Kelsey

said. "All right, sister, it's your turn to get all the attention, and the whiskey too."

Kelly had her eyes open, gritting her teeth against their chattering as they stripped her of her sodden clothes. Even in the poor light they could see the angry bruises on her arms, legs, and shoulders. When they had her rolled in blankets to her chin, Dallas took his belt and buckled it around her to hold the blankets in place. He then lifted her in his arms, and they began the long walk to the passage that would lead them out of the cavern.

"I brought the horses on in," Arlo said. "If that bunch is possumin' around in the brush, I reckon they'll find out what they're wantin' to know."

"Thanks," said Dallas. "Far as I'm concerned, Hoss Logan's mine just dropped back to second place. Kelly comes first."

"When you get tired," Arlo said, "I'll carry her."

"I won't get tired," said Dallas, "but I will need you to hand her up to me after I'm mounted."

When they eventually reached the cabin, Arlo took the swaddled form from Dallas while he dismounted. It wasn't quite noon. Arlo immediately got a fire going, and Kelsey readied a kettle of water. Dallas had laid Kelly on one of the bunks and was kneeling beside her. Her eyes were closed, and despite the thick wrapping of blankets, her teeth still chattered. Dallas got to his feet and turned to Arlo anxiously.

"Where's the whiskey?"

"It wasn't in the saddlebags," said Arlo. "Yours or mine. I reckon I'd better ride to Hays's store in Tortilla Flat and get some more. She's already having chills, and the fever's bound to come later."

"Make it as fast as you can," Dallas said. "She seems just as cold as when I hauled her out of the water."

Arlo rode out, and when the water began to boil, Kelsey took charge. She ripped an old sheet into large swatches and turned to Dallas.

"Unwrap her," said Kelsey. "We're going to bathe her

from head to toe in this hot water, and I'm going to clean that nasty gash on the back of her head."

Dallas and Kelsey applied the steaming compresses again and again, and slowly Kelly's body began to take on some warmth. Her teeth stopped chattering, and Dallas again wrapped her from head to toe in the blankets. By then, her eyes were open and he grinned reassuringly at her.

"How do you feel?" he asked.

"Like I was pitched off an ornery horse and he trampled me about six times," groaned Kelly. "Where's Arlo?"

"Gone to Tortilla Flat for some whiskey," Dallas said. "You've already had chills, and fever will follow."

"But I'm warm now," said Kelly.

"You're still going to get the whiskey," said Kelsey. "You have a nasty gash on the back of your head, and we'll have to use some of it to disinfect that, but you're going drink the rest. It's your turn to sweat and kick off the blankets."

"Sorry I took a fall," Kelly grimaced. "We were finally about to find Uncle Henry's gold and I spoiled it."

"Damn the gold," said Dallas. "You took a mean spill, and you could have broken your neck or your back on those rocks."

"But I didn't," Kelly said. "Tomorrow we're going back in there, before that other bunch gets ahead of us. After all I've been through, you think I'm going to let a few bruises and a whack on the head stop me?"

But by the time Arlo returned with the whiskey, Kelly was feverish, tossing fitfully and muttering in her sleep. Dallas and Kelsey forced half a quart of whiskey down her, and the three of them sat up with her until she finally began to sweat. Three times she kicked her way free of the blankets, until Dallas again secured them by buckling his belt around her.

"The two of you get some sleep," said Kelsey. "I'll watch her."

"That's not fair," Dallas said. "You need sleep too."

"I'll sleep tomorrow," said Kelsey. "We won't be going anywhere. Despite all that big talk, she'll be so sore by morning she won't be able to get up."

Sandoval had been watching from the rim when Arlo, Dallas, and Kelsey rode away, Dallas carrying the blanket-wrapped Kelly.

"Looks like one of them Logan women was hurt," he reported to the others. "I reckon they won't be back today."

"Then we'll do some lookin' on our own," said Bowdre. "It's about time we turned Davis loose and let him lead us to that gold, if he can."

"No," Davis shouted. Leaping to his feet, he again turned on Bowdre in a mad fury, shouting. "No, no, no!"

Sandoval again drew his revolver, prepared to buffalo Davis if he became violent. But Davis seemed to lose interest in Bowdre and lapsed into silence.

"You been coddlin' that loco varmint for nothing," Carp said. "Even if he knows where the gold is, he ain't gonna lead us to it."

"Leave him be," said Bowdre. "Today we'll search the river. Then if we still don't find anything, we'll take Davis with us, even if we have to hog-tie him."

Bowdre led the others down the ragged cleft in the side of the mountain, leaving Gary Davis apparently lost in a confused world of his own.

"It ain't far," Bowdre said, "but it's a hell of a place to find if you don't know what you're lookin' for."

Sandoval carried the lantern, lighting it once they entered the darkened passage that led to the underground river.

"Now that we're in here," said Three-Fingered Joe, "where do we start? That's what's botherin' me. Wells and Holt have already been in here for a while, and it seems like they ain't found nothing."

"Maybe they ain't," Bowdre admitted, "but we know they're in here for a reason. We ain't found but five passages under these mountains that wasn't dead ends, and the last one led to the drop-off above this river. That damn mine has to be in here somewhere along this river. I reckon Wells and Holt have come up with the same idea, and I think they're right."

Suddenly a stone shattered the lantern globe and the flame guttered out.

"Damn it," said Bowdre, "which of you kicked that rock?"

"Not me," Sandoval said.

The others were as quick to deny the foolish blunder that had left them completely in the dark.

"A day wasted," said Bowdre. "Now one of us will have to ride somewhere and buy replacement globes for our lanterns. That is, if we can find our way out of here without any light."

Slowly, carefully, they made their way back along the river, cursing the rocks on which they often slipped and fell. Behind them, in the darkness, Paiute chuckled silently to himself.

With the dawn, Kelly slept peacefully. The wound on the back of her head had been carefully cleansed with warm water, doused with whiskey, and then bandaged. When she awoke, she found Dallas sitting on a stool beside her bunk. He slid closer, taking her hands in his.

"How do you feel?" he asked.

"All right," she said, "but that may change when I try to move. Lord, I need to get up and run to the bushes."

"Oh, no, you don't," said Dallas. "There's a bucket on the floor, and that's as far as you're going. Arlo and Kelsey's outside. I'll join them for a few minutes, unless you need help. See if you're able to move."

"My God!" she cried, trying to rise. "I can't get up! I feel like my back's been broken, and my head weighs a ton. My arms and legs hurt like I've been beaten. Please, help me."

"You're stiff and sore from the fall," said Dallas, "and your head hurts because you're hungover from the whiskey."

Dallas helped her out of the blankets, and she gasped at the angry purple bruises on her arms, hips, and legs.

"Lord, I'm a mess," she said. "Who undressed me?"

"Kelsey and me," said Dallas. "You didn't kick off the blankets until Arlo got back with the whiskey. You've had some fever."

"How long have I slept?"

"Almost around the clock," Dallas said. "We poured some of the whiskey on that cut on the back of your head, and Kelsey made you drink most of what was left. You've been on one hell of a drunk."

"Kelsey gets the last laugh, then."

"She hasn't been laughing," said Dallas. "When I toted you out of that rocky backwater, Kelsey was scared half to death and so was I. You looked dead, and your pulse was really weak."

"I'm sorry I frightened all of you—and ruined our search for the gold."

"The hell with the gold!" Dallas exclaimed. "When we rode in yesterday, with me not knowin' how bad you was hurt, I'd have swapped all the gold in Arizona Territory—in the whole damn world—just to have you well."

"Thank you," she said sweetly. "Now would you wrap me up again? I don't feel very well."

Kelly was asleep again when Arlo and Kelsey returned.

"She needed to . . . to get up," Dallas said, his face coloring. "I had to help her, and then help her back to bed."

"That's what we expected you to do," said Kelsey, "so we gave you plenty of time. How is she feeling?"

"So sore she can't move," Dallas said, "and she has a hell of a hangover."

"I know exactly how that feels," said Kelsey. "Maybe she'll sleep it off."

"She's feeling guilty for having spoiled our search for the gold," Dallas said.

"No reason for that," Arlo replied. "Any one of us could have fallen and gotten just as stove up as she is. Thank God she didn't break any bones. The search can wait until she's on her feet."

"She needs chicken soup," said Kelsey.

"I can ride to Phoenix," Arlo said. "There's plenty of chickens in Mex town, if nowhere else."

For Arlo, it was a welcome diversion, something to do while Kelly recuperated. Besides, they needed other things—a new jug of whiskey, more coal oil. He rode into town with a list, and by the time he entered the general store, he had Sheriff Wheaton on his heels.

"I been needin' to talk to somebody about what's been goin' on in and near the Superstitions," said Wheaton.

He proceeded to tell Arlo of the killing of the five men associated with old Domingo Vasquez and of the disappearance of the horses.

"Old Vasquez is purely raisin' hell," Wheaton said. "He claims Yavapai and Sanchez, bein' part of the bunch, killed the other five and then made off with the seven horses. I'll grant they're a pair of shiftless coyotes, but I don't believe they'd murder five men so close to town just for the sake of seven horses. I'm stumped. Can you shed any light on this fool situation?"

"Maybe," said Arlo.

He then told Wheaton of Bowdre and his men being on foot, of the stampeding of the mules, and of meeting the vengeful owners of the mules.

"There were five mules left in place of the horses," Arlo said, "and I reckon the five men with Yavapai and Sanchez caught up to the mules. I'd say them Missouri mule drovers just killed the five hombres astraddle of their mules. That bunch from the Superstitions who actually took the horses only needed five, so two were turned loose with the mules. I'm bettin' Yavapai and Sanchez grabbed the two extra horses and lit out for parts unknown."

"It fits," said Wheaton. "Yavapai and Sanchez figured old Vasquez would have their necks stretched if he could. I'm near willin' to pay Vasquez for the horses myself. By God, Phoenix oughta celebrate. Yavapai and Sanchez have shucked out, not darin' to come back, and five of them border cutthroats have been shot dead."

Arlo quickly took advantage of Sheriff Wheaton's elation. He gathered his purchases and left before the sheriff got around to questioning him about the continuing search for Hoss Logan's gold.

This time, Three-Fingered Joe rode to Tortilla Flat, because it was nearer. When he returned, he had four extra globes and another gallon jug of coal oil for the lanterns. By then it was late afternoon, and a violent storm was building in the west. The sun had already set behind a bank of ominous gray clouds, and a rising wind out of the west had a chill bite to it. Bowdre had collected a pot of cold water, made pads from an old blanket, and after dipping them into the frigid water, he applied them to his still badly swollen ankle.

"If we're goin' back in that mountain tonight," said Carp, "let's get there ahead of the storm. In a while it's gonna rain like a longhorn bull waterin' a flat rock, and I ain't aimin' to walk no two miles in a downpour."

"Me neither," Os Ellerton threw in.

"I ain't much in a mood to take a hike in one boot," said Bowdre. "We got grub and a dry place to sleep. We'll ride out the storm where we are. I need some time to doctor this ankle."

Supper finished, they sat around the fire drinking coffee, listening to the thunder rumble and reverberate through the canyons. The very mountain seemed alive. Then, for no apparent reason, Gary Davis got up and walked to the split in the cavern that allowed access to the top of the mountain. Wind whipped in gusts of rain, fanning the fire's flames into a crazy dance. Lightning flashed continuously, and when it struck somewhere near the top of the mountain, it had a profound effect on Davis. With a scarcely human cry, he bolted out into the storm.

"Davis," Bowdre shouted, "don't go out there!"

"The damn fool!" yelled Sandoval. "He'll git fried to a cinder."

"I hope he does," Carp said sadistically. "I ain't never

seen a hombre hit by lightnin'. I'm goin' out far enough to see him burn."

"I'll go with you," said Ellerton. "That's a sight I'd admire to see."

"Hell, they're as stupid as Davis," said Sandoval when the pair had gone to the point where the passage opened to the mountaintop.

Carp and Ellerton went as far as they dared, pausing under an overhang. Lightning lit up the mountaintop like day, and they soon saw Davis. He stood with arms flung toward the violent heavens as though he welcomed—or dared—the lightning to strike. When it did, Davis screamed like a madman, but he didn't move. Unhurt, he stood there like some demented apparition, squalling like a panther.

"God," said Ellerton, "there ain't *nothin'* natural about this. I ain't wantin' to see no more." Turning away, he returned to the protection of the cavern.

"Well?" Sandoval inquired.

"Lightnin' struck all around him," said Ellerton, "and by God, he ain't been touched. I'm damn near ready to believe Davis is dead, and that somethin'—maybe the devil—has took over his body."

Three-Fingered Joe laughed uneasily, but Sandoval and Bowdre didn't. Even Zondo Carp, who had followed Ellerton back to camp, was awed.

"By God," Carp said, "I ain't never seen nothin' like it. He just stood there screechin' like a beaten whelp. It was like he was answerin' that storm, and it behaved just like it was hearin' him."

When Davis returned, drenched from the rain, he was eerily subdued. Without a word, he took his place at the fire. The rest of them stared at him in wonder, but he seemed not to notice or to care. They were all uneasy as the storm raged on, and they kept their hands near the butts of their revolvers. Suddenly, in the second passage that began behind the spring and continued to the foot of the mountain, there was a sound like a stone striking the wall.

"I hope the mountain ain't comin' down on our heads," said Carp, drawing his Colt. "I'll have a look."

He stepped into the passage carrying a lighted lantern. But he saw and heard nothing. Just as he was turning back, there was a tinkle of glass, and the lantern's flame guttered out. Carp made his way back in the dark.

. "Damn you, Carp," Bowdre said, "you've busted another lantern globe."

"By God," said Carp, "I ain't done nothin'. I didn't see or hear anything, and as I was comin' back, the damn globe just broke."

Before anybody could respond to his outburst, there was yet another noise in the passage, almost exactly like the first. Carp reached for the other lantern.

"Carp," said Bowdre, "leave that lantern be, and stay the hell out of that passage."

"I reckon you aim to set here all night," said Ellerton, "not knowin' who or what's out there."

"Hell, yes," Bowdre replied, "if it means gettin' a lantern globe busted ever' time Carp goes out there to nose around. Any of you that's wantin' to prowl around back yonder, light yourself a pine knot. We need them lanterns to search that underground river."

Gary Davis snored noisily, but try as they might, the rest of them were unable to sleep. Just when it seemed the troublesome noise in the tunnel had ceased, there would come again the sound of a solitary stone striking the passage wall and then clattering to the floor. Far into the night it continued, abating just long enough for them to drowse, then jerking them all awake. As they hunched there in silence, anticipating the sound, it became a kind of torture. The aggravation continued, and it was Carp who finally snapped under the strain. Angrily he got to his feet.

"By God," he said, "I'm takin' a light and goin' back there!"

He lit a long strip of pine, drew and cocked his Colt, and stepped into the dark passage behind the cascading

water. Time dragged on—ten minutes, twenty minutes—
and Carp failed to return.

"Somethin' must of happened to him," Bowdre worried.

Then, lending ominous credibility to Bowdre's words,
there came that devilish sound of a stone striking the passage wall and then clattering away to silence.

"I'm goin' to have a look," said Sandoval. "Anybody
got the guts to go with me?"

"I have," Ellerton said. "I've had about enough of
this."

Sandoval and Ellerton stepped into the passage, each
with his Colt cocked and ready, each with a lighted pine
torch. They had gone only a few yards when they found
Carp. He lay on his back, still clutching his unfired
weapon. Sandoval holstered his pistol, then knelt down
and felt for a pulse.

"He's alive," Sandoval said, "but out colder than a
dead trout."

"Hell, there's a lump over his right eye big as a horse
apple," said Ellerton. "I reckon somethin' or somebody
walloped him good."

"You carry the lights," Sandoval said, "and I'll get him
back to camp."

When they'd got Carp back, Sandoval stretched him
out before the fire, while Bowdre and Three-Fingered
Joe watched in silence.

"Maybe he fell and hit his head," said Three-
Fingered Joe.

"How the hell you figure that?" Sandoval demanded.
"We found him flat on his back, holdin' his pistol. He'd
have had to fall face-down and roll over on his back after
he was out cold."

"Somethin' or somebody slugged him," said Bowdre,
"and they done it facin' him. But how, without Carp
makin' some move to defend himself?"

His question was mocked by yet another stone striking
the passage wall, then falling away to silence.

"Maybe movin' into this damn camp wasn't such a

good idea," Three-Fingered Joe said. "I've about had my fill of these spooky mountains, gold or no gold."

"I've already said that," said Ellerton, "and I'm sayin' it again. I'm givin' it two more days. We get into the river cavern and find the gold, or we give it up and ride out."

"You gents have had your say," Bowdre snarled, "and now I'll have mine. I'm fed up with all your whining and bellyaching. Come first light, anybody that's of a mind to leave, just mount up and ride. Or for that matter, by God, you can leave right now."

"I'll stay," said Sandoval, "but when Carp comes to, let's take a vote. He might ride out too, and I like the idea of a two-way split of the gold."

Three-Fingered Joe and Os Ellerton cast black looks at Sandoval, as Bowdre laughed. At that point Carp sat up and looked groggily about.

"What'n hell happened to you?" Ellerton demanded.

"Somebody nearly bashed my brains out," Carp snarled. "You reckon I just growed this lump on my head to keep my hat from slippin' down over my eyes?"

"You was hit hard," said Bowdre, "but by what, and who done it?"

"I didn't see nothin' or nobody," Carp said. "Somethin' hit me, and I don't remember nothin' else."

"Os and Joe ain't satisfied," said Bowdre, "and they're threatenin' to ride out. What about you? Do you aim to saddle up and ride?"

"Hell, no," Carp said. "Not without a chance at the gold, and a shot at the sneakin', skunk-striped son of a bitch that near busted my skull."

Carp's bravado—especially after his recent experience—made his companions look small, and Bowdre glared triumphantly at Ellerton and Three-Fingered Joe.

"All right," Ellerton said, with poor grace, "I'll stay till the finish."

"Count me in, I reckon," said Three-Fingered Joe.

"Praise be," Bowdre said sarcastically. "We're one big happy family again. Tomorrow we'll search every crack and crevice along that river."

Chapter 21

The day following Kelly's fall, time hung heavy on everybody's hands. Kelly slept most of the day, and Dallas sat with her. Arlo and Kelsey spent most of their time outside, occasionally walking to Saguaro Lake.

"Kelly's my sister, and I shouldn't complain," Kelsey said, "but my God, this constant waiting, just doing nothing, is getting to me. I hope by tomorrow she'll be able to get up, so we can go look for the mine."

"Don't count on it," said Arlo. "In a way, I reckon she's worse off than you were when you were shot. You only hurt in one place, and she's likely hurtin' all over. She'll need about three days' rest before we continue our search."

"Two more days of waiting? Lord, what are we going to do with ourselves?"

Arlo laughed. "I had a suggestion, but that didn't appeal to you."

"I'm bored enough to reconsider," she said. "Let's walk back to the lake."

To Kelsey's and Arlo's immense relief, Kelly was awake by suppertime and insisting on getting up.

"This rawhide-strung bunk is doing more damage to my back than the fall," she said. "I have to get up."

She sat up groggily, and when impatience got the best of her, Dallas helped her to walk. With Arlo and Kelsey encouraging her, it looked like she was going to beat Arlo's prediction of three days.

* * *

The morning after the storm Bowdre and his companions filled both their lanterns with oil and returned to the underground river. Gary Davis, left in camp, showed no emotion when they departed.

"We should be able to search this whole damn river today and tonight," said Carp. "If we come up dry, you aim to bring Davis in tomorrow?"

"That's what I'm considerin'," Bowdre replied. "I'll bend a pistol barrel over his head and we'll tote him in feetfirst, if we have to."

"Then you'd better keep your pistol handy," said Carp, "because he'll go crazy when he wakes up and sees where he's at. I'm figurin' whatever happened to him must have took place somewhere along that river. That's why he goes wild just at the mention of it."

"We'll get out of his way and let him go as crazy as he likes," Bowdre said. "If he's seen the mine, and it's anywhere along this river, then I'm countin' on his recollection takin' over and sendin' him hell-bent-for-leather, right to the gold. All we got to do is foller him."

"Once he's led us to the gold," said Carp, "is they any reason why I can't just shoot the loco coyote?"

"Not far as I'm concerned," Bowdre replied.

Paiute waited on the ledge that dipped into the wall of the drop-off, and when he saw the distant bobbing lights of the lanterns, he made his way carefully along the narrow ledge from which Kelly had fallen. This day he would not hinder their search, and they would trudge the river from one end to the other, finding nothing. Only then, Paiute believed, would they bring the hated Gary Davis into the search. Tomorrow, then, Hoss Logan's revenge might be complete.

Bowdre and his crew followed the river to the end, where it sprang from a great gash in the rock.

"That's one side of it," Sandoval said, "and we ain't seen a thing that looked close to a passage to a mine. We ain't even seen a hole that a prairie dog could squeeze into, without suckin' in his gut."

"There's the other side," said Bowdre. "We might as well cross the river and see what's over there."

"I got me a hunch," Carp said. "I'm bettin' the other side of this damn river's just as bare as this side was."

"Well, just keep that hunch where it is," said Bowdre irritably. "Maybe we won't find nothin', but by God, we're gonna at least have a look."

And they did look, cursing as they slipped and stumbled over the slick, mossy rock.

"Careful," Bowdre cautioned. "The first clumsy son of a coyote that busts a lantern globe hoofs it back to camp for a replacement."

Slowly, they worked their way past the upthrusts of rock that began in the river and crowded outward against the very walls of the cavern. Once they were past the falls, the going became easier, but the chances of their discovering any crack or crevice diminished markedly.

"We ain't found a damn thing hikin' up and down this blasted river," said Carp, "and we ain't goin' to."

"Maybe not," Bowdre replied, "but we'll stay with it as long as we can. At least until we reach that old river-bed that leads us out of here."

"We still got time to go over it all a second time," said Sandoval. "Could be we overlooked somethin'."

"Go over it as many times as you want," Ellerton said. "I'll come in here one more time, and that's when we turn Davis loose."

"I reckon I'll have to agree with you," said Bowdre. "Davis has been there once. Maybe we can shock him into goin' there again."

"You aimin' to bring him in here today?" Three-Fingered Joe asked.

"No," said Bowdre. "We've been in here most of the day. I think we'll get a fresh start in the morning. I look to have a problem with Davis. After the day we just had, does anybody feel up to that?"

"Not me," Sandoval said, and for a change, nobody disagreed.

"Let's get out of here and back to camp, then," said Bowdre. "I'm ready for some grub and hot coffee."

It was considerably later than they thought, for the sun had already set. By the time they reached the treacherous trail up the mountain, the first stars had taken their places in a purpling sky. Entering their hidden camp, Sandoval lit one of the lanterns. But something was wrong.

"Davis," Bowdre shouted, "where are you?"

The only answer was an echo and then silence. Gary Davis was gone, and the contents of their packs lay scattered about.

Left alone, Gary Davis had lapsed into a kind of stupor for most of the day. When he awoke, it was as though from a nightmare. He screeched wildly, causing the horses to rear and nicker in terror.

"Logan," Davis shouted. "Jed Logan! Damn you, Jed Logan, I killed you once. Why won't you stay dead?"

Davis eyed the saddlebags belonging to Cass Bowdre and his men. Seizing one and ripping it open, he dumped its contents. In a fury, he emptied the rest of them in like fashion. The last one belonged to Bowdre, and its contents immediately interested Davis, for they included two gun rigs—belts, holsters, and Colts. One had belonged to Mose Fowler, the other to Pod Osteen. Davis checked each of the weapons, found them fully loaded, and shoved them under his belt. He removed all the cartridges from both belts and stuffed the shells into his pockets. He then left the cavern, making his way up the split to the top of the mountain. From there, he crossed to the east rim, fighting his way down the precipitous trail to the canyon where he had spent his first terrible night in the Superstitions. He waded the stream and entered the forbidding cavern where the woman he had taken from Jed Logan had died. He had taken her not because he wanted her, but solely because of his hatred for Logan. Now the woman was dead and Jed Logan was somehow still alive. But he would kill Logan again. And again, and again, and again, by God, until he stayed dead. But now he must rest. His head hurt and his vision dimmed, and he sank down against a stone wall and blacked out. Once more, the hated Jed Logan stalked through the shadows of his tortured mind.

"Wherever he is," said Bowdre, "he's well armed. He's got the pistols that belonged to Pod and Mose, and all the extra ammunition."

"I ain't sleepin' in here," Ellerton said. "That damn fool's likely to sneak in here and shoot us all."

"We'll have to keep watch," said Bowdre, "and come first light, we'll have to find him if we can. I still think he can lead us to the gold."

"I don't," Carp disagreed. "He took them guns and shells for a reason. When we find him, we'll have to kill him, or he'll kill us."

"When we find him," said Bowdre, "don't do nothin' foolish. Just hold your fire while I try to talk some sense into him."

"I reckon you're forgettin' somethin'," Sandoval said. "Wells and Holt will be comin' back. If Davis cuts down on them, they'll blow him to hell and gone. They don't need him."

"Then we'll have to find him first," replied Bowdre. "After we've had our grub, I'll take the first watch."

Although Kelly Logan had awakened at sundown the day after her fall and had insisted on getting up, her three companions didn't share her optimism.

"Kelly," Arlo said, "I think you're gettin' up a little too soon. You need at least one more day of rest."

"Maybe," said Kelly, "but I can't stand another day of just lying here doing nothing, while the rest of you are as restless as penned-up coyotes. Tomorrow we're going back along that ledge and find the gold. Once this is finished, there'll be plenty of time for all of us to rest."

Kelly was in some pain, but she refused to yield to it. She forced herself to get up and walk, to move about, to work the soreness out of her body. It was well past midnight before she again lay down to sleep.

Bowdre was making plans to search for Gary Davis, but he also needed to know if Arlo Wells and Dallas Holt would return. Soon as it was light enough to see, he sent Sandoval to the west rim. Growing weary of staring at the same greasewood and chaparral thickets, Sandoval climbed to the top of the mountain and crossed over to the east rim. He arrived just in time to see Gary Davis emerge from the cavern where he had spent the night. There would be no time for Sandoval to report this turn of events to Bowdre, for if he did so, he would risk losing Davis. He would just have to follow Davis and take his chances with Bowdre's wrath. As Davis followed the canyon where six men had died in the fight with Apaches, Sandoval skidded and slid down the hazardous trail in pursuit. Davis left the canyon, turning north along the foot of the mountain. Lest he be discovered, Sandoval kept his distance, but his quarry was oblivious to everything except whatever was foremost in his confused mind. Sandoval had trouble keeping up and eventually lost Davis in the thickets that cloaked the foot of the Superstitions. Fighting his way through the brush, Sandoval searched in vain. Where had the damn fool gone? Luckily, the ground was muddy from last night's rain, and Davis was making no effort to conceal his tracks.

"Well, by God," said Sandoval, under his breath, "he's gone into that passage where the river is."

Sandoval had seen enough. He hurried back to camp.

"Right where we want him!" Bowdre shouted exultantly when Sandoval broke the news. "This is workin' out perfect. Let's go! He's got somethin' on that crazy mind of his. What could it be, if not the gold?"

But the last thing Gary Davis had on his mind was gold. He stumbled on through the darkness where he had spent three terrifying days and nights with a ghostly presence that had robbed him of his sanity.

"Where are you, Jed Logan?" he bawled. "Damn you, I killed you once, and I'll kill you again!"

For Kelly's sake, Dallas and Arlo didn't arise as early as was their custom. While the girl was irked at them for making allowances for her, their concern was well founded. For all her grit and determination, Kelly still had trouble getting to her feet, and once there, she had trouble staying on them.

"Kelly," said Dallas, "you ain't ready for this, and you know it. Why don't you wait one more day?"

"Because I can't stand being laid up another day," Kelly replied. "Once I've been on my feet for a while, I'll do better."

Dallas helped Kelly to mount, and they moved slowly out.

"If that other bunch is watching for us," said Kelly, "they won't have any problem following."

"I doubt they'll be looking for us," Arlo said, "because we've never arrived this late before. Anyway, before we're done, I expect we'll be tangling with them over the gold. Finding the gold is one thing, holding it will be another."

"That's a blade that might cut two ways," said Dallas. "We could find it first and still end up in a gunfight over it."

"I know Uncle Henry wanted us to have the mine," Kelsey said, "but I can't believe he'd want any one of us dead because of it."

"He wouldn't," said Arlo, "and I believe he left us an ace in the hole that we probably won't recognize until the showdown comes. Remember also, Paiute's still around here somewhere."

"He may not be such an ace in the hole," Dallas said. "One look at that skull at sundown, and he lit out like his shirttail was afire."

"I've been thinkin' about that," said Arlo, "and I reckon he was supposed to leave us be. That was as good a time and as good an excuse as any."

"Even if he never does anything more," Kelly said, "he got us away from Gary Davis, and I'll always be grateful to him for that."

"What Arlo just said fits what Uncle Henry used to tell us," Kelsey said. "Do you remember, Kelly, when we begged him to bring us to the West? He said the frontier is hard on men, and harder on women. He said if we were ever to come out here, we'd have to prove ourselves worthy, or the land and its people would never accept us."

"I remember," said Kelly. "The gold was just a means of getting us here. Actually Uncle Henry wanted to see if we could survive being manhandled by hostile Indians, shot, dunked in freezing water, hung over on moonshine whiskey, and sleeping on solid rock or hard ground next to a pair of gun-slinging Arizona cowboys who aren't quite sure what the difference is between girls and boys."

Arlo and Dallas howled, slapping their thighs with their hats, until their horses threatened to bolt.

"If all this has been Uncle Henry's idea of a test—an education for us—then I don't regret it in the least," said Kelsey, "even if there is no gold."

"I don't regret it either," Kelly said, "but I'd have to think about it a while, before I'd start over and do it all again."

As they had done before, they picketed the horses and mules a considerable distance north of the hidden passage into the mountain. But as they drew near their entrance, they could see fresh depressions in the soft earth.

"Six sets of boots," said Dallas. "I reckon the showdown's gettin' almighty close. Do we go in?"

"We do," Arlo said, "but we don't light the lanterns. Not yet. We'll just have to take it slow in the dark. Once these hombres discover we're on their trail, they could cut down on us with lead. I'd like to find out what they're up to without them knowing we're here. Up to now there's been just five of them. Now there are tracks of six. Come on, let's tune up the fiddle and start the dance."

Once they reached the river they were able to see

distant twin dots of bobbing light ahead of them. There was shouting, but it was distorted by the echo, and they couldn't understand the words.

"My God," whispered Kelsey, "one of them sounds just like Gary Davis. Don't you think so, Kelly?"

"It does sound like him," Kelly admitted, "but I've never heard him screech like that. He sounds kind of wild."

"Let's ease in closer," said Arlo. "He's really raisin' hell about somethin', and I'd like to know what."

While Cass Bowdre and his companions could hear Davis well enough, his raving made absolutely no sense to them.

"He's lookin' for some hombre named Jed Logan," Sandoval said, "and that ain't the gent that found the mine."

"We'll just foller him and see where he goes," said Bowdre. "He's sure as hell headed somewhere."

Davis slipped and fell, and they could hear him cursing the rocks, the darkness, the river, and the very mountain. The four young people were soon near enough to understand his words.

"Jed Logan," Davis shouted, "I'm comin' after you. I killed you once, and by God, I'll keep on killin' you till you stay dead!"

"Dear God," Kelly whispered, "he's lost his mind. Daddy's been dead more than two years."

Suddenly there was the bark of a Colt and the hum of flattened lead as it ricocheted off stone.

"Get down!" Arlo hissed.

There were no more shots, but Davis continued his mad ranting. Finally, as he neared the falls, his shouting diminished. Then there was another voice, nearer.

"By God," shouted Zondo Carp, "he's in the water, headin' for the falls!"

"Cover them damn lanterns with your hats," Bowdre said, "and let's foller him. That's got to be where the gold is."

"Damn," Dallas said, "they've found it. Now what'll we do?"

"Go in right behind them," said Arlo. "What else can we do?"

"Ninguno," said a voice from the darkness behind them. *"Malo medicina."*

"Paiute!" gasped Dallas, amazed that the old Indian had suddenly appeared and that he was speaking.

"They've found the mine, Paiute!" Arlo explained. "We must follow!"

"Ninguno," said Paiute. "Come."

The four of them followed his silent shadow to the split in the rock—the narrow cleft that led up to the ledge—and to the treacherous trail beyond, where Kelly had fallen. Dallas raised a lantern globe.

"Ninguno," Paiute said. *"Ninguno."*

"Damn it, Paiute," said Arlo, "let us light a lantern. We can't get up there in the dark."

"Ninguno," Paiute repeated. "Come."

"He must have a reason," said Kelsey. "Let's try it his way."

Paiute saw the need to reassure them. He took Kelsey's left hand and placed it in Kelly's right hand. He then took Kelly's left hand in his own right hand, and started up the narrow cleft. Arlo and Dallas were left to follow as best they could. When they had reached the far end of the ledge that crossed the face of the drop-off, Paiute halted them.

"Lamp," said the old Indian. "Lamp *muy bueno.*"

"Thank God he ain't takin' us down that trail in the dark," Dallas said. "Another fall could finish Kelly, and maybe the rest of us."

Paiute led the way and Dallas followed. Behind Dallas came Kelly, Kelsey, and finally Arlo, with the second lantern. At the bottom of the precipitous path, Paiute stepped down into the water. The others followed him without mishap. As they progressed, the water became shallow, and at last they were out of it, on solid rock. Somewhere to their left they heard the muted roar of the falls. Paiute led them down a narrow corridor that seemed to parallel the river.

"He's taking us under the river!" said Kelsey.

There was a constant dripping of water from some-where overhead, and they heard the gurgle of a swift stream beneath their feet. They could also hear the muf-fled sound of gunfire, and as they drew nearer, they could see the faint glow of a lantern in the distance.

"*Ninguno,* lamp," said Paiute.

Understanding his gesture, Dallas and Arlo extin-guished the lanterns. In the inky darkness they could bet-ter see what was taking place ahead.

"Davis," Cass Bowdre shouted, "hold your fire. We're your friends."

But Davis, despite his muddled mind, saw through Bowdre's ploy and responded with more fire, the lead whanging off stone like angry hornets.

"Davis, you damn fool, listen to me!" shouted Bow-dre. "We're claimin' the gold that's here, and if we have to kill you, we will."

There was more fire from Davis, but from somewhere beyond his position, another voice answered Bowdre.

"You men shootin' at Davis, listen to me. I'm Henry Logan, and this is my claim. I only used it as a means of getting Davis out here, within my reach. He murdered Jed, my brother, so this is between Davis and me. The rest of you back off."

"Dear God!" Kelsey cried out, "it's Uncle Henry!"

"It sure as hell is," said Arlo, "and we can gun down those coyotes from here, if need be."

"*Ninguno,*" Paiute said. "*Ninguno.*"

"Mister," Bowdre shouted, "we don't know that you're Logan. Even if you are, you ain't registered a claim, so unless you can hold it, then it ain't yours."

"I didn't register it," Logan said, "because I didn't want it. True, there's gold here, but these passages under the river are a death trap. Every shovelful of ore taken out only brings the river that much closer. One day soon, the river will break through, and when it does, the gold will be buried beneath tons of earth and rock, and it will all be under thirty feet of water."

The sound of Henry Logan's voice brought more reckless firing by Gary Davis and, on the heels of it, a fresh outburst.

"Damn you, Jed Logan, where are you? I killed you once, and I aim to go on killin' you till you stay dead!"

"Logan, if that's who you are," Bowdre shouted, "we don't believe you, and we ain't backin' off."

"Then I'll make a deal with you that'll prove it's no bluff," said Logan. "All of you get out of my way until I settle with Davis. If I'm still alive, I'll walk away and you get the gold, with no argument from me. If Davis kills me, gun him down and you still get the gold."

"You'd better take that offer," Arlo shouted. "there's five of us behind you, family and friends of Henry Logan, and we'll cut you down."

"Hold your fire," answered Bowdre. "We're takin' Logan at his word, and we'll back off."

"Arlo," Henry Logan shouted, "all of you get out of here. This is my fight. I'll see you when it's done."

"We go," Paiute responded.

The old Indian drew them all back into the passage down which they had come, and from the darkness they watched Bowdre and his men take their lanterns and start back toward the falls.

"Oh, God," Kelly said, "we find Uncle Henry alive, and now we have to leave him in here with that crazy Gary Davis."

"Did your daddy and Hoss look anything alike?" Dallas asked.

"Yes," said Kelly, "especially as they got older. There was only a year's difference in their ages."

"Maybe that's the answer," Arlo said, as they crossed the face of the drop-off for the last time. "At some time in the Superstitions, Gary Davis must have come face-to-face with Hoss Logan. Now his mind is playing tricks on him. He thinks Jed Logan's haunting him."

"God, I hate this," cried Kelsey. "Suppose that devil Gary Davis kills Uncle Henry?"

"There's always that chance," Dallas said, "but I'm bettin' all my *pesos* on our old pard, Hoss Logan."

Once they were well beyond the falls and on their way out, Paiute paused. Sounding dim and far away, there were five quick shots from a Colt, followed by the single booming blast of a shotgun. Then, but for the sound of the river, there was only deathly silence. Kelly clung to Dallas and Kelsey to Arlo.

"We go," said Paiute. "Señor Logan come."

Chapter 22

Keeping to the stone wall of the passage beneath the river, Hoss Logan crept through the darkness, his shotgun cocked and ready. He was oblivious to everything except the pounding of his own heart in his ears. For two long years his hatred of Gary Davis had driven him, preparing him for this act of vengeance. But now that the time had come, his ultimate victory seemed empty, meaningless. He had subjected Davis to three days and nights of terror in the darkness of the Superstitions, and the man had literally gone mad, believing that the murdered Jed Logan was haunting him. Now there would be no reasoning with Davis. It was shoot or be shot, and Henry Logan wanted it finished.

"Davis," he shouted, "it's you and me. I'm comin' after you."

His challenge drew no fire, which surprised him. He had counted on Davis giving away his position. Now he must be more cautious, for while Davis might be insane, he was by no means careless. Logan's advantage was that a shotgun could lay down a swath of death that a Colt couldn't match, and in total darkness, aiming with a scattergun wasn't crucial. But the range was. Given a target, Davis could fire effectively with a Colt from a much greater distance. Logan found a stone and threw it as far as he could, but it drew no response. The passage was muddy from the constant dripping of water, and Logan's boot slipped. He didn't try to recover his balance, but threw himself facedown. Davis fired five times, the lead ripping the air in a fanned-out pattern above Logan's head. Steadying the shotgun, Logan fired once. He then rolled to the farthest side of the passage in case there should be return fire. But there was no sound except the constant dripping of water and the distant roar of the falls. For many long minutes, Henry Logan lay unmoving. Finally he got to his feet, keeping to the wall, and followed the passage until he reached the narrow upward path from which Kelly had fallen.

When Arlo, Dallas, Kelly, and Kelsey stepped out into daylight, there was no sign of Cass Bowdre and his men.

"I reckon we got nothin' to fear from them now," Dallas said. "I just wonder if Hoss is runnin' a bluff about the mine."

"No," Arlo replied. "There was water all through that passage, and dripping all around us. I believe the mine really is the death trap he said it was."

"I don't care about the mine," said Kelly. "Uncle Henry's alive, and I just want him out of there."

"Him come," Paiute said confidently.

"Damn it, Paiute, why ain't you ever talked before?" Dallas asked.

"*Habla bueno,*" Paiute said with a straight face. "*Mucho habla malo,* like squaw."

The old Indian grinned uncertainly at Kelly and Kelsey, but they laughed along with Arlo and Dallas. It soon became a grand and glorious reunion when Hoss Logan stepped into the sunlight, still carrying the shotgun. He tossed the gun to Paiute and gathered Kelly and Kelsey close in a bear hug. Arlo and Dallas held back, allowing the girls time with their uncle. When Hoss at last turned to his friends, he threw one arm around Arlo and the other around Dallas.

"Let's go home, boys," said Hoss. "Paiute and me will have to double with you on the horses, but it ain't that far. We got plenty to talk about."

"There's a big pot of boiled chicken left," Kelly said. "They made enough to feed me for a month. We can heat that up and celebrate."

"That pot of chicken will be almost enough for Paiute," Arlo joked, "but what about the rest of us?"

Cass Bowdre and his companions returned to their hidden camp below the mountain's rim. Sandoval, at their lookout point, reported the departure of Henry Logan, Paiute, and their four companions.

"Six of 'em," Sandoval said. "One of 'em is Logan's Indian. It must of been him that caused us so much trouble."

"Now we can go back and look for the gold," said Carp, "unless we're goin' to take it as gospel what that old varmint said about the river bustin' through and floodin' the mine."

"Well," Bowdre said, "it ain't so far, so first thing in the morning, we'll be in there with our lanterns."

"That was mighty damn easy," said Sandoval, "old Logan just walkin' away. I wasn't all that fond of Davis myself, but I can't imagine a gent usin' a gold claim to kill some no-account coyote he hates and then just walkin' away from the gold. Hell, I ain't believin' there *is* any gold, until I see and touch it."

"Me neither," Carp said. "That bunch is gone, and I'm ready to go back in there right now. To hell with waitin' for mornin'. Who's with me?"

They all were. Even Bowdre got the fever, so they filled their lanterns and returned to the cavern. There they immediately found what was left of Gary Davis.

"God," said Three-Fingered Joe, "there oughta be a law against shotgunnin' a man to pieces like this. Even a crazy coyote like Davis."

The farther they went, the more water dripped from above. When the passage suddenly widened, what they saw left them literally breathless. Above them, in the dim glow of their lanterns, thousands of tiny golden stars winked invitingly at them.

"Great God!" said Bowdre in awe. "The whole damn roof of this place is shot plumb full of gold!"

"And leaks," Sandoval said. "I believe old Logan was

telling the truth. Do we walk out, or go for the gold and risk bein' drowned like rats?"

"By God," said Carp, "I ain't walkin' away from this. Not after all we been through. What's this scaffold doin' here, and why's all this dirt piled up, if somebody ain't been workin' this claim?"

"I'll go with the majority," Bowdre said. "Do we risk workin' it, or do we walk away from it?"

"We work it!" they all shouted.

There was much talking to be done, and after supper, it was Hoss Logan who began the conversation. He spoke mostly to Kelly and Kelsey.

"Maybe it was wrong of me, using the gold to bring you girls west, but I couldn't do it any other way. At first I aimed to just lure Davis here, but I couldn't tell him directly about the mine, because he knew I hated him for what he had done to Jed, and he might have seen through my plan. So he had to learn about the gold through you girls. But I want you both to know I wasn't just using you. I hoped I could drag out the search for the gold until the two of you was eighteen. Your Ma was . . . well, you know what she was, and I wanted you away from her, regardless of what happened between me and Gary Davis. I worried some about you goin' into the Superstitions, but I counted on Arlo and Dallas lookin' after you."

"Most of the time," said Kelsey, "Arlo and Dallas were in more trouble than we were. They could have been killed trying to get to the bottom of that drop-off to reach the river. Arlo was hurt."

"Crack head," Paiute said. "Him don't fall."

"So it was *you* that hauled me in, you old coyote," said Arlo.

"I'd planned for Paiute or me to keep all of you in sight, and out of any real danger," Logan said, "but there were some things we had no control over that took us by surprise. Like the time, when Arlo and Kelsey were shot. I spent most of that night in the passage behind the spring, and I could hear Kelsey talking out of her head. I was there when her fever broke, and I knew she would recover. After Kelly's fall, I didn't know how badly she was hurt, so Paiute spent the night outside the cabin until he knew she had no broken bones."

"I'm glad to hear all that, Hoss," Dallas said, "but I'm real sorry we went through so much for a mine that none of us can claim. I feel like we went from poor to rich and then back to poor, all in the same day."

Hoss Logan laughed. "I wouldn't say that. From what I've seen, you got your brand on Kelly and both her ears notched. I'd say Arlo's done about the same with Kelsey."

"You sly old coyote," said Arlo, "don't try to tell us you didn't plan it that way, along with everything else. You plumb took advantage of two poor, ignorant Arizona cowboys, layin' more temptation on us than we could stand. Now our fiddle-footin' days are done, and we ain't got a damn thing ahead of us but thirty and grub, ridin' fence on somebody's ranch."

"He's right," Kelly said. "They're stuck with us, and now that we're not spending all our time searching for the mine, I expect Kelsey and me will soon be in all kinds of trouble."

"Kelly," said Dallas, his face rosy as an Arizona sunset, "I . . . you . . . we . . ."

"We slept beside them ever since Paiute rescued us from Gary Davis," Kelsey said.

"But that's *all* we done," said Arlo.

"Oh, not quite all," Kelsey said. "There was . . ."

"Whoa," said Hoss Logan. "Kelly, you and Kelsey are too old to spank, and this pair of cowboys happen to be my friends. They're the best pards an old man ever had, and I don't reckon they've done any more than they've been encouraged to do. Now, if the four of you want to stand before a preacher and let him read to you from the book, then you got my blessing. I already done picked out the weddin' present."

"God," said Dallas, "I hope it ain't another gold mine.

I'd as soon hire on somewhere, ridin' fence at thirty and found."

"Oh, I think you can do better than that," Hoss said, a twinkle in his eyes. "I'd kind of hoped you and Arlo might throw in with me—go pardners—in a horse and cattle ranch. We can settle on maybe a hundred thousand acres of Arizona land. That's more the life I'd planned for Kelly and Kelsey. But we won't stop at that. Someday, Phoenix will be a city. Maybe we'll start a freight line from here to Los Angeles. We might call it Logan Freight Lines, in memory of old Jed."

Arlo, Dallas, Kelly, and Kelsey just looked at him as though he had taken leave of his senses. At any moment they expected him to laugh, letting them know it was all a joke. But Henry Logan didn't laugh. Instead he turned to Paiute.

"I reckon it's time we told 'em, Paiute."

Logan said nothing more, waiting until Paiute returned to the cabin with a heavy iron bar. He used it to pry loose most of the boards in front of the fireplace. There, in the foundation, were many, many leather bags. Hoss tossed one of them to Arlo and another to Dallas. The bags were so heavy they had to be held with both hands.

"Open them," said Hoss.

The awestruck cowboys opened the bags and found the same gold-rich ore as the sample Paiute had first brought them—the very ore that had begun their search for the mine.

"I wasn't bluffing," Hoss said. "One day a volcanic tremor will hit that mountain, and all that passage beneath the river will be flooded and filled with tons of rock and dirt. It's a death trap now, but it ain't always been, and it didn't get like that on its own. I helped it some. This stash of ore you're lookin' at is worth near a million dollars. Now don't you reckon that'll buy us one hell of a spread, a right smart bunch of horses, mules, and cows, and just about anything else we got a hankerin' for?"

"God Almighty," Dallas said, "I reckon it will. I don't know what to say or do."

"Well, I know what to do and what to say," said Arlo. "What I aim to do, first thing in the morning, is find a preacher. What I aim to say is whatever he tells me to. Kelsey and me will have us a hotel room in town, tomorrow night."

"Kelly and me will be there too," Dallas shouted.

"Come on," said Arlo, "but you have to get your own room."

Hoss Logan and Paiute didn't understand why Kelly and Kelsey broke into fits of laughter, but it was contagious, and they joined in.

After breakfast it was time for some serious talk. There was the matter of all that gold, and Hoss Logan had a plan that appealed to Arlo and Dallas.

"I don't know of a town anywhere closer than Los Angeles with a bank strong enough to deposit the kind of wealth we're talkin' about," said Hoss, "so I think we'd better start Logan Freight Lines right now. I reckon this will conflict with your marryin' plans, but for the time being, I want all of you to stay out of Phoenix. Arlo, you and Dallas ride to the outlying towns, looking for a pair of suitable wagons and some teams of mules. Kelly, you and Kelsey can go along, if you want. Me and Paiute will set here on this gold till you get back. When you do, we'll load up and start out for Los Angeles. When we get our stake safely in the bank, we can buy some real freight wagons and first-class mule teams for the return trip. We'll need plenty of supplies, and we can load up in Los Angeles. After we get back, we can start lookin' for a suitable range for our spread. But I don't want word gettin' out that I'm still alive until we've got this gold stashed safe in a bank in Los Angeles. Any questions?"

"Yeah," said Dallas. "If you're serious about Logan Freight Lines, why can't we build us a freight terminal in Tortilla Flat, instead of Phoenix?"

"No reason we can't," Hoss replied. "You got some good reason for thinking of that, I reckon."

"I have," said Dallas. "Arlo and me owns that piece of ground where the saloon was, and I'm kind of partial to Tortilla Flat, because it's got a grand view of the Superstitions."

"I'm partial to it for the same reason," Kelly said, "and I reckon that could be said for us all."

"Well," said Arlo, "now that we've agreed on that, I reckon we'd better consider the possibility there won't be a mule for sale anywhere around here, and maybe no wagons. We may have to ride as far as Tucson, and with the silver mines there, we may still have a problem."

"I'll leave that to you and Dallas, then," Hoss replied. "I've got near a thousand set aside for just such a time as this, so you can pay more than the goin' price, if you have to."

"We'll have to buy at least two horses somewhere close by," said Arlo, "because we have only two horses and two mules. We can't ride as far as Tucson, leaving you and Paiute without mounts."

"Buy them, then," Hoss said. "Kelly and Kelsey can ride them and leave the mules for Paiute and me."

"Hoss on mountain," said Paiute, extending six fingers.

"But that would be stealing," Kelsey said.

"I reckon not," said Hoss. "He's thinkin' about what I told them hombres about the river comin' in, if they try to work that mine. If it does, they won't be needin' horses. I think, while all of you are away buying mules and wagons, Paiute and me will look in on that bunch."

"You don't know that they're working the mine," Kelly said. "Maybe they took your advice."

"I doubt it," said Hoss. "They had the fever, and I'd bet all the gold we're settin' on that they're in there right now, diggin' away at the same earth that's holdin' back the river."

Cass Bowdre and his excited companions worked like demons for three days and nights, feasting their greedy eyes on the growing pile of rich gold ore they dug from the passage over their heads.

"I'm gettin' a mite uneasy," said Bowdre. "Remember how the whole damn mountain shook yesterday? I keep thinking of what old Logan said, about all this comin' down on us. I'd feel better if we quit this place with what we got."

"Not me," Carp said greedily. "Maybe after another week."

They were two days into their second week when again a tremor shook the mountain. They paused, waiting for it to cease, and for a moment, it did. But when another tremor came, it was more intense.

"I'm gettin' out of here while I can," Bowdre shouted.

But time and their luck had run out. With a crash, the last restraining earth gave way, and the terrified men were buried beneath tons of stone, just as Hoss Logan had predicted. The river—which Dallas had named the Death's Head—rushed in and cut for itself a newer, deeper bed. The terrible act of nature took but a few seconds to bury Cass Bowdre and his companions forever deep within the Superstition Mountains, beneath the Skeleton Lode's gold, which would remain forever beyond the reach of men.

"A writer in the tradition of Louis L'Amour
and Zane Grey!"

—*Huntsville Times*

National Bestselling Author

RALPH COMPTON

THE KILLING SEASON
THE DAWN OF FURY
BULLET CREEK
DEADWOOD GULCH
A WOLF IN THE FOLD
TRAIL TO COTTONWOOD FALLS
BLUFF CITY
THE BLOODY TRAIL
SHADOW OF THE GUN
DEATH OF A BAD MAN
RIDE THE HARD TRAIL
BLOOD ON THE GALLOWS
BULLET FOR A BAD MAN
THE CONVICT TRAIL
RAWHIDE FLAT
OUTLAW'S RECKONING
THE BORDER EMPIRE
THE MAN FROM NOWHERE
SIXGUNS AND DOUBLE EAGLES
BOUNTY HUNTER
FATAL JUSTICE
STRYKER'S REVENGE
DEATH OF A HANGMAN
NORTH TO THE SALT FORK
DEATH RIDES A CHESTNUT MARE
RUSTED TIN
THE BURNING RANGE
WHISKEY RIVER
THE LAST MANHUNT
THE AMARILLO TRAIL

**Available wherever books are sold or at
penguin.com**

No other series packs this much heat!

THE TRAILSMAN

#325: SEMINOLE SHOWDOWN
#326: SILVER MOUNTAIN SLAUGHTER
#327: IDAHO GOLD FEVER
#328: TEXAS TRIGGERS
#329: BAYOU TRACKDOWN
#330: TUCSON TYRANT
#331: NORTHWOODS NIGHTMARE
#332: BEARTOOTH INCIDENT
#333: BLACK HILLS BADMAN
#334: COLORADO CLASH
#335: RIVERBOAT RAMPAGE
#336: UTAH OUTLAWS
#337: SILVER SHOWDOWN
#338: TEXAS TRACKDOWN
#339: RED RIVER RECKONING
#340: HANNIBAL RISING
#341: SIERRA SIX-GUNS
#342: ROCKY MOUNTAIN REVENGE
#343: TEXAS HELLIONS
#344: SIX-GUN GALLOWS
#345: SOUTH PASS SNAKE PIT
#346: ARKANSAS AMBUSH
#347: DAKOTA DEATH TRAP
#348: BACKWOODS BRAWL
#349: NEW MEXICO GUN-DOWN
#350: HIGH COUNTRY HORROR
#351: TERROR TOWN
352: TEXAS TANGLE
#353: BITTERROOT BULLETS
#354: NEVADA NIGHT RIDERS
#355: TEXAS GUNRUNNERS

Follow the trail of Penguin's Action Westerns at
penguin.com/actionwesterns